T0063117

Shadow-Wolf

THE LONELY TRAIL

Carolanne 'Caz' White

Order this book online at www.trafford.com
or email orders@trafford.com

Most Trafford titles are also available at major online book retailers.

Printed in the United States of America.

ISBN: 978-1-4907-1760-9 (sc)
ISBN: 978-1-4907-1762-3 (hc)
ISBN: 978-1-4907-1761-6 (e)

Library of Congress Control Number: 2013918949

Because of the dynamic nature of the Internet, any web addresses or links contained in
this book may have changed since publication and may no longer be valid. The views
expressed in this work are solely those of the author and do not necessarily reflect the
views of the publisher, and the publisher hereby disclaims any responsibility for them.

Any people depicted in stock imagery provided by Thinkstock are models,
and such images are being used for illustrative purposes only.
Certain stock imagery © Thinkstock.

Trafford rev. 11/11/2013

 www.trafford.com

North America & international
toll-free: 1 888 232 4444 (USA & Canada)
fax: 812 355 4082

ABOUT THE AUTHOR

Carolanne 'Caz' White was born in 1994 in Conisbrough. When she was growing up she had an interest in writing and creating stories, especially when her parents broke up in September 2004. On her way to school she thought of the idea of a secret high-tech navy blue helicopter named "Shadow-Wolf" and with it most of the characters using her alter-ego Kiba White as the main character.

TABLE OF CONTENTS

CHAPTER ONE

Taking Chances

Kiba struggled with the paperwork in the Brad's Air Service office. Paperwork never had been one of her strong points, and she didn't find answering the phone all that exciting either, but she still couldn't fly, and she had to do something.

She doubted she was supposed to hear it, but from just outside the door Mr. Brad was grumbling about needing more help but obviously Kiba couldn't fly. That only left him, Adam and Chezia.

'Where's Chez?' she asked taking a break from the ever-growing mountain threatening to cause an avalanche on her.

'Her and Kenty took some mission from Jason,' Mr. Brad answered, 'It's supposed to be really important.'

'Oh.' While she didn't miss being shot at, the missions were a break to the usual routine, and she did miss her boy. She couldn't even fly the Jet Ranger though; she definitely wasn't in any condition to be flying combat. Being shot, she decided, was still more appealing than the misery she'd been living through lately. She was making good progress, but it just wasn't anywhere near where she'd like it to be.

★   ★   ★

Chezia piloted Shadow-Wolf just beyond the hills and landed there. The mission should be easy-find out where these big shot arms dealers kept their goods, report to Rhino-Gate, and then see what they wanted to do about stopping them. Actually, it was more of an undercover mission than a Shadow-Wolf mission. He probably only be needed if their plan was found out and someone had to go after the bad guys.

'We'll scout out the area and meet back here in two hours.' Chezia explained

'Agreed.'

They set their watches to match exactly then set off their separate ways. Chezia set off at a fast clip through the woods, intending to come in undercover of the bushes and trees. Her army fatigues made blending in easier, but she had to make sure she didn't leave a trail, and she had to be absolutely silent the entire time.

Simon would take a more direct route but, amazingly enough, less guarded. Earlier attempts had tried to come in through the seemingly less defendable hidden end Chezia was on. Here, they figured they would be seen too easily and killed before they got close enough to do any damage.

Chezia gathered what information she could without getting herself caught. From what she gathered, she guessed they were hidden in an underground bunker, pretty heavily guarded. Hopefully, she would confirm her assumption with some news from Simon when they were to meet in now only twenty minutes.

Simon started his jaunt back to Shadow-Wolf. A quick glance at his watch told him he would have to hurry to get back in time, but it would be well worth it from the information he'd just gathered. Just before he reached cover of the woods, he was spotted by one of the guards.

Two shots rang out, the second catching him in the arm. He clutched it tightly with his other hand trying to slow the bleeding while running toward Shadow-Wolf. The guard followed him, now with his own platoon. They were gaining on him.

Please let Chezia be there already and not walk straight into a trap, he thought, but there was no chance of turning back now. It was Shadow-Wolf or nothing.

Chezia had heard the gunshots and ran into the safety of the bullet-proof cockpit. Running thermal scans, she saw someone coming towards her at a full out run followed by a large group. 'Bless Simon's made some new friends, too bad we don't have enough room for them,' She giggled humourlessly. She went ahead and started up the engines while Simon was still en-route so that they could take off as soon as he was there.

'Come on, Kenty' she said aloud, 'They're gaining on you.'

Finally, Simon made it just before the guards caught him. He threw himself inside and slid the hatch behind him. 'Let's get out of here!'

Chezia, who was already in the pilot's seat, took off immediately, disappearing out of sight. They landed in a clearing about fifteen minutes away. Chezia found the first aid kit and joined Simon outside.

Simon poured some antiseptic on the wound as Chezia fought with the gauze. 'I did find out a little bit about the weapons,' Simon told her. 'They're being stored underground now, but they are planning on moving them by tomorrow. That would probably be the easiest time to stop them.'

Chezia agreed. 'I think I'm going to need some back up though, and you're not it.'

'I'll live,' Simon retorted.

'You'll live, but the sooner they get that bullet out of you the better, and you're not going to be able to fly like that.'

'What do you suggest?' Simon asked, 'If you notice, we didn't bring anyone else.'

'I'll radio Jason. He can get you a spot in the Rhino-Gate clinic to get your arm taken care of, and he can have some back up waiting for me there.'

Simon gave in; like it or not, he didn't need to be fighting right now and that long run had taken a lot out of him. Right now a comfy bed and a lot of sleep sounded good. Chezia pulled open the door and reached to the communications panel to connect a call to Jason.

'Rhino one,' Jason answered from his grey Rhino-Gate Jet Ranger. 'I read you.'

'I need to drop off Simon at one of the clinics up here and get some backup.'

'How bad is it?'

'He's been shot. It's not life threatening, but he shouldn't be here with me.'

Jason confirmed the request. 'I'll take care of it.'

★   ★   ★

Adam walked in carrying dinner. Mr. Brad set it out while he went to tell Kiba it was here. He opened the office door and slipped into a chair across from her. Behind the recently dyed spring green hair he could see she looked tired and frustrated, yet she continued to steadily plug away at the paperwork.

Finally she looked up, tired blue eyes meeting his brown ones. 'Adam, can we talk for a minute?'

'Yeah, sure. What is it?'

'I've given it a lot of thought, but I'm not where I want to be-'

'Kiba, you're making good progress,' he interrupted.

'Maybe, but it's not good enough. You deserve better.'

'I said I would stick with you,' Adam argued.

'I know what you said, but listen to what I'm saying. You can do better. I can't take care of you or Domanick Graham right now and you know it, maybe it would be better if you found someone else.'

'Found someone else?' he didn't know whether he was more upset about the stupid idea or hurt. 'I don't need to find someone else.'

'I can make sure you're well provided for,' she continued, 'it's not that I don't love you, I just want what's best for you and that's not me.'

'Well maybe I don't want what's best for us then. I want you.'

'Adam! It's been five years, it won't work. You don't need me' He sat stunned in his chair as she started to walk out. 'I'm sorry, Ad.'

She went to sit in the back. She knew she had hurt him; she'd hurt herself. She didn't want to send him away anymore than he wanted to leave, but she had to do the right thing, and he would be better off without her.

Adam sat alone in the silence of the office until Mr. Brad came in after hearing the yelling. 'Is everything ok in here?' he asked.

'Not really,' he admitted, but he wasn't ready to expand on any further details about their fight.

Mr. Brad thought maybe he could get something more out of Kiba, unlikely but possible, so he went to ask her what had happened.

Towards the front of the hangar, the grey jeep pulled up. Coming around the corner quickly, Jason almost ran into Adam.

'Hi Adam,' he greeted, 'is Wolf able to fly yet or Michael around?'

'Kiba, no; Mr. B, I don't know where he went, but he's got a charter flight in fifteen minutes. Why do you ask?'

'Mission work,' he answered quickly.

'I thought Chezia and Simon were on a mission for you.'

'They were, Chezia still is, Simon was injured and unable to finish the mission,' Jason explained. 'White needs backup.'

'I could go,' he volunteered.

Jason knew he was capable and he shouldn't be in much danger, but Kiba would kill him if she found out. 'I don't think Wolf would like that very much,' he disregarded the idea. 'I can send in one of my agents if I have to, I just thought if part of the crew was available I wouldn't have to involve anyone else, and they would already be familiar with Shadow-Wolf.'

'Kiba shouldn't mind too much.'

Jason knew that couldn't be the case. Kiba wasn't always excited about having him involved before the whole family thing came into play. 'I highly disagree.'

'It doesn't matter; I can make my own decisions, and she just told me to leave anyway.'

Jason's mouth dropped open. They couldn't be talking about the same Kiba White. She was protective, loyal and she loved him. There was no way she'd just tell him to leave, especially when they had Domanick.

He might have laughed at his expression had it not been for his sour mood. 'She said I deserved someone that could take care of me-something she couldn't do.'

'I'm still not sure it's a good idea.'

'I can do it. She can't fly and Mr. B's busy. Your agents won't know the controls; I'll do it.'

Jason finally conceded. He was right he could do it. 'Alright,' he agreed. He'd probably regret it later though. 'Get in. we've got to get you ready to go.'

Adam readied himself to go. 'Ok,' he told Jason, 'I'm ready.'

He had Alex drive them to the Rhino-Gate clinic where Simon had been dropped off and Chezia was waiting.

Chezia sat playing cards in Shadow-Wolf on the roof off to the side, in case life flight needed to land on the helipad. Adam soon came up to join her. Before she'd even seen who it was, she'd packed up the cards and started the engines, the rotors circling slowly gaining speed with every rotation.

'Let's go,' Adam said climbing into the engineer's seat in the back.

'Adam?' she blinked in confusion. Why is he here?

'Yeah, I'm ready to go.'

'You, uh, weren't exactly who I was expecting,' she stammered, still trying to figure out why he was here. 'Kub doesn't know does she?'

'No. But it doesn't matter,' he retorted. 'I'm here and I know it; you know it. Now let's go.'

Chezia complied, slowly lifting off the hospital roof, let's just get this finished, she thought and I had better get him back without as much a single scratch, or Kub will have my head. They flew across the sky to the hideout where the armament was being hidden. 'The plan is to stop them when they're en-route, but you don't leave this helicopter until we get back without a good reason,' she told him firmly. 'I'd like to stay in one piece, and if you don't, Kub will make sure I don't either.'

★   ★   ★

Mr. Brad's group for the charter flight came in just as he finished the preparations. 'All ready to go?' he asked.

'Ready,' each confirmed as they climbed into the waiting Jet Ranger.

'Alright. We should arrive in Blackpool about in about thirty minutes.'

'Have fun Mr. B' Kiba smiled as she watched the Brad's Air Service helicopter rose up and disappeared into the sky. She was alone in the hangar. She looked at the clock, still half an hour before her or Adam needed to leave to go pick up Dante. She sighed and slumped back into her chair. She hoped she was doing the right thing sending Adam away; she didn't want to, but it was for the best she decided. She couldn't care for him, and Domanick deserved an able mother, able to do things she couldn't, maybe never would be able to do again. She dozed off thinking of what could have been.

A low rumble of thunder sounded in the distance, wind rushed in the open window scattering papers across the floor. Kiba woke; a glance at the clock told her it was time to go get Dante.

'Adam,' she called, walking over to shut the window. No answer. 'Ad, can you go get Dan?' The doctors had recently given her the ok to drive again, but she'd feel better letting him especially now that the roads were wet and slippery and she had a mess to clean up.

Adam didn't appear or give any answer. She looked for any sign of him. None. Next, she looked outside for the jeep; maybe he'd left while she was still asleep, the black, white and red jeep still sat outside, now collecting rain drops from the slight drizzle. She didn't have any more time to hunt for him; she'd just have to go herself and clean up the mess later. She grabbed the keys and ran outside. Ducking into the 4x4, she put the keys into the ignition and started it up. She drove along the wet roads until she reached Dante's school. Dante was waiting under the overhang to stay out of most of the rain when she pulled up. The thirteen year old climbed in and sat beside her.

'Hey,' Dante said surprised to see Kiba picking him up.

'Woof, Woof' She greeted. 'Got any ideas where Adam might be?'

'No,' he shook his head, sending bead of water flying off his black hair. 'Why?'

'Chez's on a mission, Mr. B's on a charter, and I can't find Adam.'

'Oh. I haven't seen him since he dropped me off at the hangar yesterday after school.'

They arrived back at the hangar. 'Will you help me clean up this mess?' she asked pointing to the mess of papers strewn across the floor. They picked up the papers and reorganized them neatly. Still no sign of Adam. 'It's been an hour and half and he's still nowhere to be seen,' she said to him, worry starting to mount up. What had happened to him?

Finally she decided to call Jason, the last person she knew to ask. She dialled the number to Rhino-Gate

Jaime picked up. She'd hoped to get at least Alex, but he'd have to do.

'It's Wolf; I need to talk to Jason.'

'He's not here right now,' Jaime answered.

'Where is he?'

'Alex was driving him to a Rhino-Gate clinic two hours away.'

She hung up the phone in disgust. Chez and Simon are on a mission. Mr. B a charter and Adam can't be found. Wait. Jason's going to a Rhino-Gate clinic, realization finally hit her, why? He obviously wasn't hurt if he was going two hours away. Maybe something had happened to Chezia or Simon. 'Come on, Dan. We're going on a trip.' They both climbed into the 4x4, heading for the clinic.

Two hours later, they finally arrived. She walked, limping slightly, to the nurse at the front desk. 'Is there anyone here by the name of Chezia White?' she asked. She silently turned to check the computer. Looking up, she shook her head in response to her questioning eyes. 'How about Simon Kenty?'

Again, keys clacked away as she typed in the name. 'Yes, he arrived about four hours ago. Room 216.'

'Thank you.'

Practically dragging Dante behind her, she lengthened her stride, quickly covering the distance to the elevator. She pressed the up button and tapped her foot impatiently waiting on the elevator. The doors finally slid open slowly. Walking inside, she pressed the button for the third floor. The elevator ascended two stories then the doors slid open. Kiba slipped out and made her way to room 216. Dante, almost running to keep up, followed.

She arrived at the room and walked in, her limp now more obvious from exhaustion. Simon was sitting up on the bed, almost as if he was expecting her. 'Hey, long time no see. Last time I heard you were dead.'

'I guess news doesn't travel that fast with you then. I've been alive again for five years'

'Don't want to grace us with your presence?' he asked. 'Chezia and I could have used another solider out there.' Sadness again showed in her eyes, causing Simon to wonder what he had said wrong.

'I won't be flying any time soon.'

'Oh.'

The burns had healed with minimal scaring; leaving no visible signs of the numbness and struggles she still had to face in her everyday life. 'The doctors don't think I'll be flying again, but I think eventually I should be able to at least fly the Jet Ranger again; Shadow-Wolf missions are pretty much out of the question though, no combat flying.'

Jason couldn't help overhearing the conversation. As soon as it was over though, he turned to leave before Kiba noticed his attendance. But it didn't work.

'Jason, do you know where Adam is?' she asked bluntly.

'Why?' Jason asked his own question to avoid Kiba's.

'Do you or not?' Kiba's exhausted blue eyes looking straight into his own.

He doubted there was any point in lying. Kiba could probably look right through him. She had the amazing ability to get past the agent's mask that stopped so many. Maybe she learned it when learning to mask her own emotion so well. 'I have a good idea,' he said hesitantly.

'Where?' Kiba demanded.

'With your sister.'

'You sent him with Chez?' she shouted incredulously, 'I can't believe you would do something like that!'

'It was his idea,' Jason tried to excuse himself.

'You knew he shouldn't be out there,' Kiba retorted. 'What if something happens . . . I'm not capable of looking after Dom without him'

'I know, but I needed someone who could handle Shadow-Wolf, and he was the only one available. He said that he could make his own decisions and you'd just told him to leave anyway,' Jason returned.

Exasperated at the lack of knowledge she was getting, Kiba demanded the exact location of the armament base they were seeking. Jason, not seeing much choice in the matter, told her all the information he knew. Kiba absorbed the information intently.

'You take care of Dan; I'm going after them.' She stated as she started to walk away,

'Wolf, they've got it under control, just let them finish.'

'Not a chance,' she replied determinately, 'You sent Adam out there.' Jason tried to stop her; all Kiba had was the jeep, and he'd most likely just be in the way, 'I told you, I'm going. Bye Jason.'

She trucked out to the jeep leaving Dante with Jason and Alex. Keying the ignition, she raced out the car park toward the hideout via Jason's directions. Long since having left the main road, she covered a bumpy, dirt road, that and a grey sky the only thing visible for miles.

Camped out, Shadow-Wolf's navy blue metallic skin contrasted against the grass. The jeep pulled up next to it. Chezia came around from the other side, lugging a portable missile launcher with her. 'I need to use the jeep,' she said abruptly. Not waiting for any comment, she hauled it into the back of the jeep and climbed in. 'You and Adam work out your problems here; I'll take care of the arms dealers.'

Kiba looked at her sister confusedly. 'What problems?' She didn't know how Chezia would know about their fight

'I think you can figure it out. Now I have some business to tend to. The communications all seem to work alright, but we had a few troubles on the way out here. If you can get him running ok, go ahead home; if not, I'll come back once I take care of the mission.' Chezia left with the jeep, leaving Kiba, Adam and Shadow-Wolf alone. Kiba walked around the nose, pulling open the door and sat inside.

'I don't know why, but we had a little trouble coming in on the way over here,' Adam told her, avoiding the topic he knew Chezia had left them to discuss.

'Do you know what the problem is?'

'It's something to do with the engines. Engine two keeps stalling.' After a careful examination, she thought she'd figured out the problem.

'So what do we do?'

'We can't fix him out here, so we'll have to limp home on one engine and if he starts to overheat, we'll have to stop and give him a chance to cool down for a while,' she answered.

'Alright, let's get going then.' They started the trip off in silence until Adam finally broke it. 'You decided you could finally drive again just so you could pick me up and take me home again?' he questioned, still angry that after all this he still wasn't finishing the mission.

'I could drive before,' she said defensively. 'I just thought I was looking out for your best interest.'

'Yeah, sure, just like you were looking out for my best interest when you decided to send me away.'

'Actually, I was. I told you I could make sure you were well provided for. Financially, is no problem, I just physically can't take care of you or Domanick.'

'You're getting there, and it would be ok; sure, it'll be hard, but you're always up for a challenge. I'm not totally incapable, if you haven't noticed, I can do things for myself. It's not like I'm expecting you to do everything.'

'I can't do what I would need to be able to though, I can't even protect you. Look at this; I've always thought of Shadow-Wolf as, Y'know, kind of mine, and I can't even fly him.'

She looked around the cockpit silently. It was nice to be back in here, but it wouldn't last. No more combat missions, which meant no more Shadow-Wolf for her. She knew the controls well enough, but it still seemed so strange to be in the back. Her life had been turned upside down—a new fiancé, a kid, not being able to fly, along with other struggles. Things weren't really going that well either; she was sending her chance at a family away because she couldn't take care of them; she knew they deserved better than she could provide, but it didn't make the decision any easier. She just couldn't do what she used to be able to, and there was no way to get around it.

★   ★   ★

Jason waited as the final papers were signed and Simon was released from the hospital. Alex would take them back to Rhino-Gate headquarters, but that was still two hours away, and he'd already had a long day—a day that wasn't even over yet. Maybe he could catch a little shut eye on the trip home.

★   ★   ★

Elevation 20,000 feet, Engine two stalled, Engine one slightly overheating,

Kiba tried to work on the telepathic connection she'd previously had with Shadow-Wolf before her accident five years ago. It was a special link between them, something no one else had gotten the chance to experience; it had been gradually getting stronger with use, but after not using it at all for so long it hardly seemed to exist anymore. The only thing she could get were some simple reading that were right in front of her and she could open her eyes and see them long before she could mentally picture them.

'Adam, the engines are starting to get a little hot, you might want to glide him down for a little while,' she felt the aircraft descend but realised they were dropping too fast. 'Adam?'

★   ★   ★

Jason had dozed off when his napping time was interrupted by a call to his mobile. Pulling it out of his inside pocket he read the Caller ID—Wolf. He knew it must have been something important for her to ring his mobile instead of using the radio, so he answered it.

While taking charge of piloting Shadow-Wolf. Uncharacteristic worry evident in her own voice, she focused her attention in the call with Jason. 'Where's the nearest hospital?' she asked after giving their location.

'The closest Rhino-gate clinic' he tried to think of the one closest to them.

'I don't care if it's Rhino-Gate or not! I just need a hospital now! I'm at ten thousand feet; struggling with flying Shadow-Wolf and Adam's passed out!'

'The nearest one is a Rhino-Gate hospital, and it's just off the main road on a dirt track, you drove the jeep down it. You should see a large house, it's actually an undercover hospital, but it's got some of the best doctors there are.'

'I'll keep you posted,' she ended the call abruptly.

Now in the co-pilot's seat beside Adam, she had complete control. It felt weird to be flying again, despite the years of practice she'd had; she had been told she would never fly again, and here she was, flying. On the other hand, she didn't have much choice. An alarm went off in the back, warning them that the engines were overheating.

Come on, Shadow, just a little farther. We gotta keep going.

The incessant beeping didn't stop, it only grew louder.

Restart engine two.

Nothing.

Fear started to creep up again. What if she couldn't do it? Adam and her own life depended on her doing exactly what she had been told she couldn't do, would never be able to do again, for the last five years. She pushed the fear into the back of her mind; there was no time to worry about the mess this could turn into; she had to do, there weren't any other options. She reached over to manually restart the second engine. It wouldn't restart

'Damn it, Shadow, you gotta help me out here! Restart the second engine.' Gradually it helped take the load off the first engine.

Engine two restarted. Stall imminent.

Please don't stall, she mentally pleaded.

At long last, the hospital came into view. 'Hold on this could be a little bumpy. I haven't done it in awhile' She started the descent into the field. Jason had already arranged to have a team of medical personnel waiting when she landed. They unloaded Adam, and took him inside. She sat, still in shock from the sudden events, alone in the cockpit. She ached from the sudden action, physically, emotionally and mentally, added to the tiredness of before.

★　　★　　★

Chezia pulled the co-pilot side door open. 'Kub, you ok?'

She blinked a couple times and shook the fog out of her head. 'Huh? Oh, yeah. Fine.'

'Do you have any clue how long you've been out here?'

'I don't know, a little while,' she answered, still trying to sort out the fuzz in her head.

'Try a long while,' Chezia replied. 'Why don't you come with me, I think someone would like to see you.'

'Adam, is everything ok?'

'Why don't you ask him yourself? He's been asking for you.'

'He has?'

Her questioning tone had Chezia wondering what had really happened between them; she said it as if he'd never wanted to see her again. 'Why wouldn't he?'

'He was pretty upset with me, and with good reasoning too,' Kiba answered sheepishly. Stepping into the quiet hospital room, she saw the brown eyed pilot she had come to know and love so well. She wondered how in the world she was ever going to live without him.

'About time you showed up,' he teased. 'I thought I was going to have to send out a search party.'

She looked at her sister then at him. 'You didn't think I would drop you off then run'

'Never even crossed my mind. Why would someone who cared enough for me that she was willing to send me away and deprive herself of joy, just to care for us and give us what she thought was best—just drop me off and run? In fact, I couldn't think of a better person to take care of us.' She still didn't seem entirely convinced. 'I don't think you can do it, Kiba White, I know you can't.' he said with certainty. 'And to hell what all the doctors think. You were told you'd never fly again, and you did; you flew at mach one just to make sure everything turned out ok.'

'That fast? It seems like an eternally, and you're sure everything is alright?'

He could sense the tension in her voice. 'I'm positive. I'll have a headache in the morning, but nothing to worry about from what the doctors say.'

CHAPTER TWO

Back in the game

Mr. Brad grumbled as he worked on the Jet Ranger. It was just normal routine maintenance, but the stubborn helicopter wasn't being very helpful.

Thinking over the last five years, he realized just how much had changed. Chezia had been rescued and returned to the UK, even if Kiba and he hadn't been able to rescue her themselves. Chezia understood. It wasn't like they didn't try, and being half dead, probably more than half dead, in the hospital was a valid excuse. Things with Adam and Kiba had also progressed well. Their relationship had been further along than anyone else had imagined, and now they had their adopted baby boy. Actually, that's where they were now, at the cottage with that cute little munchkin. Tomorrow, Kiba had promised she would get back to work at the hangar, but he could understand Kiba hesitancy in leaving her son. Life hadn't treated her very well in the past, and she always got worried every time things started going too well. Mr. Brad would dare say he'd had his fair share of problems lately. Kiba had mostly recovered from her last mission. In the end, they had all thought she was dead for three months before she showed up on his doorstep. Even then, she hadn't been flying again until recently. She had been forced to take over in Shadow-Wolf, while he was acting up, nonetheless, and Adam had passed out and unable to fly. Now she was flying the Jet Ranger again and obviously could pilot Shadow-Wolf, although maybe not in combat. Her injuries, as severe as they were, had been healing rather well, all things considered; her limp was mostly gone except for when she was tired, and the burns had healed with minimal scarring. Even the numbness that had plagued her from nerve damage due to the second and third degree burns was almost completely gone.

Mr. Brad climbed down the ladder and let out a long sigh. He needed a holiday. Shadow-Wolf was having some engine trouble, and he still needed to stick around the hangar. Kiba was flying again, but that didn't mean she was ready to do the stunts, and Adam was taking some time off to spend with Domanick Graham.

★   ★   ★

Kiba laid back on the settee with her year old son on her lap.

Domanick Graham looked up at her with irresistible round eyes the same distinctive shade of blue as Kiba's. He took a firm grasp on Kiba's finger and refused to let go.

'Hey you,' she smiled fondly, 'I see you finally decided to wake up.' The little baby gurgled happily in response. She still worried a little about the slight lack of feeling in her hands and arms, afraid she would drop him that was already so precious to her, but Adam had insisted she would be fine, and to enjoy the time while he was still small.

Kiba shifted her weight slightly and stood up. Carefully, she set Domanick down into his playpen while she went to warm a bottle.

★   ★   ★

The next morning, Mr. Brad stretched, trying to ease the tension in his sore back. Spending hours leaning over helicopters from the top of the ladder hadn't made his back feel great and today was going to be no better. After work at the hangar, they planned to work on Shadow-Wolf so, if anything, he'd probably hurt worse by the end of the day.

Chezia walked into the hangar soon followed by her twin sister.

'Mr. B,' Kiba said bluntly noticing the stiffness in his movements, 'You look like hell.'

'Gee thanks, you sure know how to make a guy feel better,' he tried to shrug it off, but he knew Kiba was right.

Chezia wasn't much more tactful. 'You should go home and get some rest or better yet go on holiday.'

Mr. Brad looked back at her. 'I can't; I'm needed here.'

'Mr. B, we'll be alright for awhile,' Kiba disagreed. 'Chez can fly the stunts, and I can fly again. Mike's coming all next week, and the schedule's not that full. You could use the time off'

Together, they finally convinced Mr. Brad. He decided to take a week off and go visit Australia. 'You're sure everything will be alright?' Mr. Brad asked. 'Oh wait. I never got a chance to take a look at the Devil.'

'Mr. B,' Kiba assured, 'It'll be fine. Now go have some fun.'

Mr. Brad stayed at the hangar insisting he should finish whatever work he could before he left. At half past three, Kiba took the driver's seat as Mr. Brad climbed into the passenger side to take him home to pack. Fifteen minutes later he returned to the 4x4 with his bags and they set off back to Robin Hood Airport.

★   ★   ★

Chezia was already waiting upon her sister's return. 'You wanna go ahead and take a look at Shadow-Wolf?'

'Yeah. It would be nice if he didn't stall every time we got off the ground.' She grabbed the keys to her motorbike and threw Mr. Brad's to her sister.

'Umm . . . Kub'

'Oh yeah that's right' she said in an sarcastic voice 'You can't ride one of these since you don't have a licence' putting the keys back she got the 4x4 keys 'You think you can drive this? You've only had your driving licence for three years now'

'Shut up' was all she got in return as her sister climbing into the 4x4 followed by Kiba and she drove off to the canopy.

Kiba finished the call to Jason. Turning her attention back to Chezia, she said, 'Jason said that he would have the necessary part for us by tomorrow afternoon.'

'Ok. We can take care of it right after business at the hanger.'

'Sounds good.'

Chezia dropped Kiba off back at the hangar then drove to her own home. Kiba took the Jet Ranger back up to the cottage. It was late by the time the cottage came into view, and darkness had long since set in. Adam was standing outside to greet her when she landed. She greeted him with a hug. 'Everything ok here?'

He nodded in response. 'How about you? How was your day?' Adam asked. 'From what I can tell from the looks of you, it was tiring.'

'Yeah,' she agreed, 'We kind of sent Mr. B off; he needed a holiday, so right now he's on his way to somewhere in Queensland for the week.'

'Australia? You want me to come in and help with Mr. B being out?' he offered.

'Nah, it's ok. Chez and I can handle it.'

'Just tell me if you change your mind.'

'Oh, before I forget, don't wait dinner on me tomorrow; I'll probably be late again.'

'Why? Is everything alright?'

'Chez and I were gonna work on my boy a bit. You remember the engine stalling problem.'

'How could I forget?' He asked rubbing his head, he didn't like the idea of dining alone again, and he'd probably be asleep long before she even got back if she was going to work on the Devil all night, but it didn't look like he had much choice.

'One more thing, I know you're already doing a lot, but would you mind watching Dante for Chez too?'

'No problem,' he answered. In truth he wouldn't mind the extra company.

★   ★   ★

After business at Brad's Air Service, they took the 4x4 over to Rhino-Gate to pick up the parts then out to the canopy. The busy roads transformed into a remarkably warm quiet land.

'I'm glad I don't have to spend many nights out here'

'At least it's not as bad as those jungles in Burma'

Burma? What did that have to do with anything? Chezia thought she'd gotten the short end of the stick being stuck in that hellhole for eight years, but now her nightmare was over; it seemed her sister's would never end, even now that everything was going well. 'Kub, Burma was years ago. What does it have to do with anything?'

'Nothing,' she refocused on the task at hand. 'I was just thinking.'

★   ★   ★

Chezia rolled over and fell out of the bed. They'd been late coming back from the canopy, and she didn't even consciously remember climbing into bed, but here she was.

She moaned, looking up at the clock. It was already half-past eight and she needed to get to the hangar. Summoning the little bit of energy she had gathered from the few hours of sleep, she shuffled into the bathroom for a nice hot shower then threw on her favourite tank top and matching pink shorts. Afterwards, she grabbed a bottle of water. At least it was something for breakfast.

Jason greeted her as soon as she pulled into the car park. What could he want this early?

'I have a mission for you,' he said without introduction.

'Why does that not surprise me?'

Jason ignored the remark and continued, 'A Burmese prison camp with ten, maybe more, prisoners has been located near the border.'

'So you want me to break them out,' she supplied. 'Sounds easy enough, which means there's a catch. What is it?' She definitely could identify with the prisoners and would do what she could to help, but there was something more; she just knew it.

'No real catch. I'll have a pickup ready a mile out. Break them out, leave them at the pickup, and come back home; I'll take care of the rest.'

If possible, she didn't want to close the business, but she wanted to help the prisoners. It would be short handed, but Kiba and Mike could handle it for a few days if it came down to it. Kiba would understand.

'Alright, I'll do it. Contact Simon and have him wait for me at the usual spot.'

Jason nodded and returned to his spotlessly grey helicopter. Alex piloting, he watched as Jason connected a call on the radio while settling into his seat.

Chezia walked back to the side door and went to unlock it. It was already unlocked. She carefully peered inside. Everything seemed to be in order; Kiba walked out of the office carrying a newspaper and coffee. 'Kub. When did you come in? I never heard the Jet Ranger.'

'Same time Jason was leaving . . . what are you wearing?' she asked at her sister's choice of clothes

'Normal clothes Kub, No tartan trousers and leather jackets for me'

'Dad was right . . . You are a pretty pink princess' Kiba stated as she threw the empty foam cup in the bin

'At least I'm not a green haired freak with more tattoos than friends' Chezia smiled slightly as she walked into the office.

'At least I'm not a green haired freak with more tattoos than friends' Kiba imitated in a harsh whisper, 'I have friends'

'Name one'

'Jason'

'He's more of a boss than a friend Kub'

'I can be friends with the boss . . . What did he want anyway?'

'He wants me and Simon to go to Burma and rescue some prisoners'

'Oh, does this mean I'm on my own?' Kiba asked, still disappointed she couldn't fly Shadow-Wolf like before.

'I guess so,' she could sympathize with Kiba, but nothing she could do would change the facts.

'I'll take care of things here. Just try to come back in one piece.'

'I'll try,' she promised and turned to leave.

★   ★   ★

The day dragged on, but eventually it drew to a close. Kiba climbed out of the helicopter and walked inside. 'Dante's going to be staying with us for a couple days. Chez went on a mission for Jason,' she answered Dante's unspoken question when Chezia didn't follow her in.

Adam could sense the sadness in her mood, although totally hidden in her actions.

'How have things been around here?'

'Oh, you know, the usual,' Adam answered. He liked the cottage, but he hadn't left it in two weeks and was starting to need a change of scenery. 'With Chezia gone too, you'll need some help at the hangar won't you?'

'Nah. Mike and I can handle it. Besides, it's only for a couple days.'

'Oh, ok. If you change your mind just tell me.' Actually that wasn't the answer he'd been wanting at all.

★   ★   ★

After picking Simon up, Chezia flew toward Burma.

'Where's the punk twin this time?' Simon asked.

'She's out of the Shadow-Wolf missions, can't do the combat flying after her last mission,' Chezia replied.

'Oh yeah, she told me about that when she went looking for Adam.'

Chezia looked over at the man, 'and now I know who it was that told her where we were.'

'Not me,' Simon denied it. 'Jason told her. I guess that means Adam flew home then,' he reasoned. 'It must be hard not being able to fly this baby anymore.'

'I said she couldn't fly combat,' Chezia corrected. 'Coming back was interesting to say the least. Adam was flying back, at first, but then . . .'

★   ★   ★

Time was running out. She had just enough time to shoot two bullets before she was caught, if she hurried. Too many were coming to kill them all; four were already on Chezia, and only two bullets to be fired.

'Kub!' Chezia yelled, 'Do it. I can't go through that hellhole, not again.'

'Do it . . . It's not fair on her' Looking beside her, she saw the black spiky haired make-believe friend.

'Jimmy?'

'Do it . . . It's too late to save her'

Her fingers tightened on the two pistols with a white knuckle grip. Jimmy was right it wasn't fair, but no one deserved to go through that pain and torture, especially after they'd already done it once. Considering how tightly she held onto the two handguns, one would think she was fighting against the whole world for it, yet no one was on her, not yet anyway. They were gaining, only seconds remaining before she would have no chance to change anything, to end her sister's misery, or to kill two of their seemingly ever growing number of enemies. About to squeeze the triggers, to end her sister's life as she was pleaded to do, time seemed to stop.

'Do it Kub!' Chezia pleaded helplessly. 'Just do it!'

The pistols fell to the ground as she was pulled away. 'I'm sorry, Chez, I just can't do it,' she whispered, 'but I'll get you out again, I don't know how, but I will; I swear I will, no matter what it costs!'

The muscular soldiers dragged Chezia back into the deep shadows of the jungle. Her breathing came in harsh short gasps. Kiba looked at Jimmy, he too slowly disappeared and she was alone.

★   ★   ★

'Kiba,' Adam shook her gently, 'Kiba, wake up.'

She opened eyes, still half asleep. 'Jimmy'

'It's Adam.' He stroked her green hair lightly, 'Everything's going to be alright.'

She suddenly remembered what had happened. Focusing on her real surroundings, she let go of the awful nightmare. She got up to fix herself a drink. Adam followed.

'Nightmare?'

'Yeah.'

He knew when she didn't offer any further explanations like that he wasn't likely to learn any more no matter how hard he pushed, so he let it go. 'You wanna get back to bed? I know you have to get an early start, but we could still fit in another hour or two of sleep.'

She shook her head. 'You go ahead. I wouldn't be able to sleep anyway.'

★   ★   ★

When Adam woke again, it was just after half six. He planned on insisting on helping out at the hangar, especially since she was more likely to be tired, but he soon found that she had already left.

Dante awoke to the pleasant aroma of eggs and bacon being cooked in the kitchen. He stumbled in and took a seat at the table. 'Morning Ad, Smells good.'

'Here you go,' he said putting a plate of food down in front of him. Soon he sat down to join him, trying to finish breakfast before Domanick woke up.

★   ★   ★

'Ok, we can land in this clearing here,' Simon suggested, 'come in under the cover of the trees all the way to the fence.'

'We can drop in from this tree here,' Chezia added, making a visual mark on their sketch of the prison camps grounds. 'All we have to do then is take out the guards here and here, rescue the prisoners, and get out.'

'Sounds good,' Simon gave his approval. 'We should start this afternoon, before it gets too dark since we don't know the area.'

Chezia landed in the clearing a mile away from the camp. After informing Jason's extraction team of their location and estimated return time, they set off; and carefully picked their way through the tangle of trees, vines, and overgrown bushes. Upon their arrival nearer the site, each made an extra effort to stay out of sight.

Chezia was the first to cross the shallow river only fifty yards from the fenced parameter. She cautiously climbed a tree that hung over the barbed wire topped eight foot fence. She dropped down and hit the ground with an almost silent thump. The noise wasn't much, but it was enough to wake the two guard dogs.

Damn, she mentally cursed. They hadn't seen the dogs earlier. 'Simon,' she said barely above a whisper, 'Don't come . . .' it was too late. Simon landed on the dirt ground beside her.

'What'd you say?'

'We've got dogs,' Chezia answered bluntly.

Simon knocked out the oblivious guard who happened to be nearing them. 'Let's get these guys and get outta here then. No time to party tonight.'

The door to the prisoner's quarters was directly in front of a window in the guard's barracks. 'Any other way to get in?' Chezia asked.

'None that I can see,' Simon answered. 'There is a window, but it's barred.' The keys to the door were hung just out of reach of the prisoners in the concrete block comprised prison. Chezia grabbed the key and thrust it into the old fashioned lock. After tugging on it for a minute, the prison door swung open with a loud creak.

'Follow me,' Simon instructed. Chezia took up the rear.

The guard dog noticed the sudden activity and decided to take a closer look. The Doberman gave a low growl followed up by a vicious snarl.

The Shadow Wolf crew and the captives both tried to ignore the threats and continue focusing on getting out, but the dog blocked their path.

'On the count of three, get through those gates and run straight through past the river until you reach the Huey waiting to take you all home,' Simon ordered, 'don't stop not matter what happens. One, two, three!' With a sharp kick, he temporarily removed the dog from their path as Chezia shot the lock.

The gunshot alerted the two off duty guards as well as the one conscious on duty one. With guns drawn, they charged after the fleeing prisoners.

The dog bit at Simon savagely, tearing a piece of flesh off, but they continued on. Chezia and the last prisoners were just escaping when the guards caught up.

'Go on!' Chezia yelled above the chaotic noise of soldiers and escapees, as they pulled her and two others back.

At the Huey, two camouflage clothed pilots waited next to the olive drab coloured Huey for their passengers. Simon finally led them in, making sure each made it to the Huey before takeoff, then found his own way back to Shadow-Wolf. He took advantage of the first aid kit in the back before starting his flight back home.

★   ★   ★

Kiba let out a long sigh. Her sister got all the fun now; she just wasn't a combat pilot anymore, and she had to face the fact. She wouldn't be needed for Shadow-Wolf missions unless she could fly like before, and putting other people's lives at stake just wasn't worth trying to beat the odds, and she already knew she wasn't as good as before without jeopardizing anyone's life. Things were different. She had a family, a reason to care. Not too long ago, her only goal in life had been to find her father's killer, but more had come to life. Adam, Dante, Domanick and finally Chezia were added to her family.

'Everyone gets their fifteen minutes of fame . . . I guess mine are over.' She whispered as she stepped outside and readied the Jet Ranger for takeoff. She was off to Rhino-Gate to officially resign from her position as head pilot for Shadow-Wolf. Jason would, undoubtedly, be surprised; no one had every informed him of the full extent of

Kiba's injuries, but she wouldn't be flying anymore missions, and Jason deserved to know.

★   ★   ★

Jason walked down the hallway towards his office. He greeted Jamie and reached for the door.

'Sir,' Jamie addressed him, 'There's someone here to see you.'

He wasn't expecting anyone this morning, at least not this early. 'Who?'

'Kiba White, sir,' he replied without missing a beat.

'Bring us some coffee and send her in, please.'

'Yes, sir,' he answered efficiently.

Jason sat down in his grey leather chair as Alex leaned on the edge of the desk just as Kiba came in. Emotionless, she walked across the spacious office, stopping to look at the expensive piece of computer hardware, All it needed was Jason, Alex or her own hand to be scanned and a hidden compartment would slide open and relieve the cell rods used only for Shadow-Wolf. She continued towards Jason's desk, sitting on the corner her arms crossed and choice to mask all emotions, the only visible signs of unrest.

'Wolf,' Jason greeted, 'What brings you here this morning?'

'I've come to resign my position from Shadow-Wolf.'

Jason and Alex's jaws dropped. 'You're what?' they said simultaneously

Jamie came in bringing their coffees. He paused momentarily. 'Sorry if I'm interrupting anything, but I'm supposed to inform you of the return of your extraction team and eight captives.'

'And Shadow-Wolf,' Jason supplied the seemingly obvious.

'Actually,' Jamie reported, 'There have been no signs of Shadow-Wolf.' A howl cutting through the air before reaching the helipad outside changed his message. 'Until now.'

Only a minute later, the brown haired Marine came through the doors, still clothed in a blue Shadow-Wolf flight suit. 'Jason, I need more fuel rods and some backup.'

Jason took a moment to work through the latest requests. 'Backup for what?'

'I'm going back,' Simons answered immediately.

'Why?' Kiba asked joining the conversation. Under normal circumstances Burma wouldn't be her first choice to go back to, but maybe she personally had just enough during her years of duty.

'Chezia,' he answered. 'Two of the prisoners and her are still over there. We had a little trouble getting out.'

Chezia in a Burmese prison camp. It was like replaying the previous years of her life. Her dream came suddenly back to her; she couldn't let it come to that. Before she hadn't been able to rescue her sister because she was in the hospital, now her excuse was she'd lost the skill necessary in combat flying, but someone had to go with Simon, and Chezia was not going to stay in that prison camp any longer than necessary.

She made a visible change as her guarded expression became more readable but with nothing but determination. She looked as if not even a speeding truck running over her would stop her.

'I'll go,' she volunteered, using the biometric scanner she grabbed two fuel rods.

Jason looked at the younger pilot questioningly. A minute ago she was quitting, now she was jumping back into the game head first.

Without a second thought, Kiba left Jason's office and ran with Simon out to Shadow-Wolf. Within minutes, she was also changed into the blue uniform, stored in the back of the navy blue helicopter.

Simon was first inside Shadow-Wolf, automatically taking his seat as co-pilot/weapon's engineer. Obviously Kiba was serious about bringing Chezia back and he wasn't going to stand in the way. Kiba took her place as pilot and started off for South East Asia.

Simon tried to make conversation. 'How've thing been going? I heard you weren't flying combat anymore and you'd settled down with a family.'

'That was the plan.'

'Why?'

'I was told after the incident, I would never fly again, and it probably would've been true without Adam. He helped me through it, believed in me when I didn't believe in myself, but combat still wasn't really in the cards.'

'What changed your mind?' Simon asked.

'Chez. And I never said I was doing the combat part anyway.'

'You know, for sisters that are so close, you two don't seem to be doing many missions together lately, except to bail each other out.'

'I guess that's the way it's always been. Even back in Burma she was dragging me out of trouble; after she was shot down and captured, I took it upon myself to do the same for her.'

Simon looked back at her. 'Back in Burma you say? Weren't you a little young to have served in Burma as long as you supposedly did?'

'I went early,' Kiba explained.

'Oh. I missed all the action because my parents wouldn't sign off to let me go early.'

Kiba almost grinned. 'Mine wouldn't either.'

Simon gave a look of confusion. 'What do you mean yours wouldn't either?'

'My mum left when I was fifteen and dad was always out working for Jason; Chez tried to lie about the age, but she got caught. Finally she made it out there though, and I forged my papers.'

'Sneaky,' Simon commented. 'I didn't have that opportunity and my folks made me finish collage first.' He let his gaze fall to the screen in front of him–still another hour of travel. He went to question Kiba further, but no such luck. 'Why won't you tell me anything else?' he pushed.

'I've done more explaining in the last few minutes than I've done in years, you should be happy with that and leave me alone.'

'You always this friendly when you're in a good mood?'

Kiba sent him an icy glare. 'Woof, Woof'

They spent the rest of the trip in silence. Simon was the first to break it. 'The clearing's a mile out, right in the middle of all those trees. Kiba landed with a slight thump in almost the exact same spot Shadow-Wolf had landed before. Simon handed her the sketch of the previous attempt's ground plans.

Kiba piloted Shadow-Wolf past the prison camp at a low altitude then came back around.

'What was that for?' Simon asked.

'To let them know we're here.'

Simon didn't understand. 'Obviously, you and I think a little differently. Last time we focused on not letting them know we were here.'

'That worked real well for you too, didn't it?'

'Hey, everything should have turned out fine.'

'Yeah,' Kiba allowed, 'it should have, but you all had a mile long hike, and you didn't know what kind of condition the prisoners were in; they could have very likely been in bad enough condition that they wouldn't have made it anyway. Back to letting them know we're here, it's not to let the guards know, although they'll know too, it's to let Chezia know. She'll recognize the sound and be ready when we land.' After making a big loop, Kiba asked for matrix scans.

'They're all against the right wall in the first building,' Simon reported.

'Bring up a missile.'

Choosing the red cell rod Simon slotted it in the compartment, 'Ready.'

With a single shot, she took out a big chunk of the wall. 'Lasers.'

'They're ready.'

Kiba laid down a line of fire, warning off any brave soldiers, as she landed. Chezia and the two prisoners climbed into the back.

'Let's get out of here.'

★   ★   ★

Adam radioed in earlier and gotten no response which worried him. He tried again several times later but still no answer. In the end, he took Dante and Domanick in the Jet Ranger left at the cottage down to Brad's Air Service. The phone rang and Jason was on the other end.

'I just thought I'd warn you that Wolf won't be back until at least three or four tomorrow morning.' Jason told him.

'Why?'

'Her and Simon set off a few hours ago for Burma to rescue Chezia and two other captives from Chezia and Simon's raid.' Jason finished explaining all the details.

'She told me her mission days were over,' Adam returned.

'That's what she was at my office this morning, to officially resign, but our meeting was interrupted by Simon's return, without Chezia. The two of them left to finish resolving things.'

Adam hung up the phone and turned back to the kids. Why does everybody go out of town without telling me and leave me to babysit? He questioned himself.

★　★　★

4:30AM

Shadow-Wolf landed on Rhino-Gate's helipad to drop off the ex-POW's. Surprisingly, Kiba turned around and came face to face with Jason.

'Geez Jason . . . What you trying to do? Give me a heart attack or something'

'Wolf,' Jason warned, 'you need to watch out for Adam and Michael and anyone else you plan on keeping around.'

'What do you mean?'

'Six Burmese Vets have been reported missing since yesterday. I've been up here all night working on the case, but the only thing they seem to have in common is Burma, in your unit specifically.'

'The Coyotes are dead Jason'

'Not with the records I have . . . Apparently they weren't in the camp when the fire broke out . . . They were lookalikes'

'But the only unit that would use lookalikes to trick the enemy were . . .'

'The Reptile unit' Jason finished.

'My team were either taken prisoner or they abandoned me for Major Cobra . . . Either way they're after me'

★　★　★

Kiba and Chezia returned to the cottage.

Adam greeted both with a hug. 'You, Chezia, don't disappear like that, and you, Kiba White, don't run off to some foreign country without some explanations. I was worried sick about both of you and didn't have a clue where to find you until Jason called telling me to keep the kids safe and lay low and that only made me more worried. So, anyone want to explain what happened?'

'The coyote unit is alive and have gone missing since yesterday and no one knows why or where,' Kiba explained, 'but Jason thinks it has something to do with me.'

★   ★   ★

'What do you mean stay in Australia?' Mr. Brad questioned.

'Things have been a little off here, and it would be best if you weren't over here since they're going after people I know,' Kiba explained.

'If people are after you, it sounds like you like all the more reason to come back. To give you some backup,' Mr. Brad argued.

'Mr. B, stay. We can handle it. I just want to make sure everything is back to normal before you come back.'

'So you've got whoever was after you handled?' he queried.

'Yeah,' she lied. 'Everything should go back to normal now. I just wanted to make sure we've solved everything.'

'Alright,' Mr. Brad relented, 'but I am coming home at the end of the week.'

Kiba hung up the phone. Honestly, she couldn't blame Mr. Brad for being worried. In his place, she probably wouldn't have given them the week; nevertheless, they had a problem to solve and only a little time to do it in.

★   ★   ★

It was late and dark, but even on silent nights the cottage wasn't this quiet. Kiba took the desert eagles from beneath her pillow and put them into their holsters after buckling them onto her upper legs, using her bare lower legs and feet she crept silently down the fire pole. A dark shadow danced across the far wall from the outside tree casting shadows through the window. No, it was somebody inside.

Carrying a bundle, the long haired man slipped out into the cool night. Kiba followed.

The object, no person, she soon realized, was loaded into a dark coloured helicopter perched on the jetty next to the Jet Ranger. If it was a person, that size had to be Dante. He, whoever he was, wasn't going to steal her brother.

Kiba slipped up behind the swarthy man, about to bring a heavy fist down on him, when the man swerved out of the way. Turning back, he took a quick kick at her knees, sending Kiba sprawling on the ground. She rolled out of the way to avoid the knife slicing through the air coming to meet her. She had just made it to her feet when the blade came for her again; she kicked, getting her leg cut in the process, but knocking the knife out of her attacker's hands. Abandoning the knife, he clutched at Kiba's throat.

'You've aged well Wolf!'

'Hawk . . .' She struggled to relieve herself of the man's hold, but to no avail. Darkness threatened to overcome her, but she fought it with every inch of strength in her body. In a last ditch effort, she suddenly dropped all her weight to the ground, knocking the man off balance.

Chezia awoke and stepped outside onto the front porch. She could have swore she heard something, but it was too dark to see clearly. A splash in the water confirmed her suspicions.

She ran over to see what it was. On the way over to the water, she noticed a bloody knife and only a few steps away her sister's guns. What was going on? From the edge of the jetty, she could see a steady stream of bubbles. Not about to jump in without knowing what was down there, she searched for more clues. She walked across the jetty almost running into the black helicopter parked there. What was it doing here?

Back at the water's edge she heard another noise. The bubbles had ceased. Was that a good thing? The water remained still for agonizingly long minutes. Finally, more bubbles then Kiba come into view gasping for breath. 'Chez, help me out,' she called.

Chezia hauled her twin sister up out of the water. Kiba obviously had been in a struggle. A blood stain covered her leg where the knife had cut through her skin, and she tightly held onto her wrist as she shook wet green hair out of her eyes.

'Get Dan,' she panted. 'He's in the back of the chopper.' Kiba told her then started towards her guns picking them up she limped back to the cottage. Only a moment after she had come in, Chezia walked through the door carrying Dante and set him down on the settee.

'Is the other guy dead?'

'Yeah. Hawk drowned, and he almost took me with him.'

'Hawk? As in Lieutenant Hawk from CU?' Chezia asked as she turned a worried gaze down at Dante.

'Yeah . . . he'll be ok,' Kiba assured her. 'He was tranquillised so he'd be quiet.' Chezia turned back to Kiba again. 'Thanks, I don't know what I'd do without you sometimes.'

'It's nothing. You always used to pull me out of trouble, this time it was my turn.' Chezia saw how badly her sister was limping, much more than the usual tired limp she'd acquired in the last five years she caught notice of the source of the problem. Her sister's right lower leg had a knife cut dragging down the side of it, and from the sight of the blood seeping out, she had no doubt that was a pretty deep cut. 'Kub, let's get you cleaned up while we wait for Dante to come round'

'It's not that bad. It just looks worse because it's wet.'

'Lake water—that's not really going to make it any better.'

'I'm fine,' Kiba insisted.

'Fine. You stay here, and I'll bring the first aid kit to you.'

Chezia returned a few minutes later with a warm wet rag and the first aid kit. Within ten minutes, she'd clean and bandaged Kiba's leg and taken a look at her wrist, which proved to be only badly bruised.

Dante was just starting to come to when they finished. Chezia handed him a cup of water which he gulped down greedily. 'Is everything ok?' he asked.

'Yeah,' both White sisters answered in unison.

'Then you might want to put Dom back to bed then. He's underneath it'

'Why is he under the bed?' Kiba asked, and unmistakable mark of confusion filled her face.

'I hear someone in the cottage, and I could tell it wasn't one of you guys so I hid him under the bed, but before I could hide they dragged me off.'

Smart kid, Kiba caught herself thinking not for the first time. 'I'll put Domanick back to bed then we can all go back to sleep.'

★   ★   ★

Kiba was up early the next morning, unable to sleep after the previous night's events. She limped down the stairs to the kitchen and began fixing some toast. Adam was the next one awake. Stealing a glance at the other bed beside him, he noticed Kiba's absence. Pulling on a robe, he trudged wearily down the stairs from the bedrooms. He appreciatively smelled the delectable aromas from the breakfast being fixed. Coffee was among these.

Coffee, he thought blissfully, a cup of coffee sounded like heaven right now.

'You're up early,' he commented. 'Even for you.'

'Couldn't sleep.'

He painfully noticed the limp in her every step. For her limp to be that bad, she must be exhausted not to mention in a lot of pain. He watched as she started to set the table, carefully avoiding caring anything heavy in her left hand.

'You want some help?' he offered.

'Nah, I'm almost done,' she replied as she handed him a cup of the strong brew he was craving.

He took it gratefully, but couldn't help but notice something was different. Her movements were rigid and stiff, like a different kind of pain than usual though. 'You ok?'

'Yeah, sure. Why wouldn't I be?'

He shook his head. 'What happened? I know you weren't all gimped up like that last night.'

'It's nothing,' she insisted.

He thought about just letting it slide this time, but when he walked towards the counter, he caught sight of the first aid kit.

'If it's nothing what's that for?' he queried as he pointed at it.

Should've put that away last night, she mentally scolded herself. 'Chez insisted. I promise it's not that bad though.'

'What happened?' he repeated his earlier question, his firm tone told that he wouldn't leave until he got an answer.

'We had a break in last night; I tried to stop Hawk without shooting him and waking everyone else up, but you're the only one who didn't get woken up.'

Chezia started stirring in the other room.

The others were getting up and this conversation could wait until later, but the look in his eyes told her she wasn't going to get out without a very thorough explanation.

★   ★   ★

An hour and a half later, all of them were up and ready to go. They all loaded into the Jet Ranger and set off for Rhino-Gate.

Jason was waiting for them when they entered his office. 'All I have is an educated guess,' he admitted. 'The Coyote unit are trying to get revenge on you. For betraying them for a group of kids, but have been reported back in Burma, but our reports show all of them having fled the country.'

'They're after me because I was doing my job?'

'It sure looks that way. Right now there's not much we can do without some evidence though.'

'Do you have any idea who's left?' Kiba asked.

'Originally there were nine, take you and your sister out and also Lion and Viper. That leaves five. But Fox was killed in a plane hijacking a year ago, so four.'

'I think you can safely make it three.'

'Why?' Jason question the last remark. Last time he checked five minus one was still four.

'We had an attempt at the cottage last night,' she answered as she limped to the chair across from him. 'If you want the body, I suggest you start looking near the jetty.'

'The jetty? Why the jetty?'

'Because I didn't feel up to pulling Hawk out after he almost drown me, but the body will wash away so your search is getting harder by the minute.'

Jason now fully understood why Kiba was even more determined than ever to get these guys. They tried to take Chezia away from her again and attacked the one place that was usually a safe haven for them.

'Just try to stay out of dangers way, I'll let you know as soon as I find something out.'

★   ★   ★

Mr. Brad shifted nervously in his seat. Something in his gut told him that back home things weren't going as well as Kiba had let on, but he had said he would give them another week. He looked at the calendar anxiously. Normally, he would enjoy the extra holiday time, but not with these problems back home in England. Maybe he had made the wrong decision to stay. The calendar told him he still had two more days before returning, but if time didn't start passing a little more quickly, he would be found on the next flight back to the UK.

★   ★   ★

'Brad's Air Service,' the recording picked up, 'we're out right now, but leave a message and we'll get back to you.'

Jason slammed the phone down on the receiver. Where the hell were they? No answer at the cottage or the hangar, not even the radios in either of the Jet Rangers. There was only one other place he could think of. He dismissed the idea as abruptly as it had come. Any of them could be qualified as stubborn, but not stupid. Oh why did it matter anymore? He'd already tried every other logical place.

Chezia reached for the buttons to connect the radio transmission.

An answer, he thought hopefully. That was more than he had been able to get all day. 'Wolf?'

'Well, one of them,' Chezia answered.

'What happened to keeping a low profile?' Jason interrogated.

'Sorry,' Chezia apologized, 'none of us thought playing pontoon in a willow tree in the middle of Nottingham was particularly high profile.'

They were still in the canopy-that actually surprised him.

'We thought we would make sure Shadow-Wolf was ready for battle whenever he is needed.'

Jason changed the subject back to his original purpose. Where they were and why wasn't all that important right now. 'The earlier information has been checked out and confirmed, and we think that we have located the area where the others are being held.'

'Ok,' Chezia answered impatiently. 'Where?'

'Tyneham in Dorset that village is a ghost town. If you'll hold on a minute I'll have Alex send all the information to Shadow-Wolf's on board computer system.'

'Now you're talking. We'll get out there and see what we can find.'

Shadow-Wolf was pulled out into the clearance and ascended above the tall trees that was his home and shot through the sky. Shadow-Wolf ate up the distance effortlessly.

'We're approaching the target,' Adam reported.

The thermal scan locked onto the village.

'Kiba, there are seven heat sources in the church and an aircraft approaching. It's a cobra, and it's armed with Sidewinders.'

'Ironic that my unit left me for Cobra and now they're flying one' Kiba stated.

'Let's get the people in the church first if possible.'

Adam studied the screen in front of him momentarily. 'The cobra is still pretty far out, if we hurry'

Kiba landed in a field just outside the village. Chezia was the first out. Running up dirt road the only sounds that could be heard were the birds chirping and the heavy footsteps. A single well placed kick caved in the fragile wooden door.

'Come on,' she called.

Kiba noticed a forest about four hundred feet away. 'Get to that forest now.'

'We can't,' one of them answered.

'Why not?' Then Kiba realised they were all kids apart from two who looked to be in their late teens.

'They said we would only have a chance to survive if we followed orders exactly.'

'If we get caught trying to leave, death will be the only thing we have to look forward to,' another joined. 'I saw what they did to the guy who tried to escape.'

'If you stay you'll eventually get the same treatment,' Chezia retorted. 'We'll cover you, now get moving.'

Adam radioed the girls from Shadow-Wolf. 'They're only two miles out and closing.' Kiba radioed back a quick alright and carried on persuading the kids to run.

'I've been a prisoner of war long enough to know, if I were you I'd take this opportunity and get out,' Chezia advised then loped back toward Shadow-Wolf.

'If you don't want to run the risk of being hit by flying shrapnel, which I personally don't find fun, you best get out of here,' Kiba added pointing towards the trees.

'You're a coyote' one of the teenagers spat upon seeing the Coyote unit tattoo, 'She's one of them'

'No . . . I'm a good one'

'The only good ones are White Wolf and Wolf-Cub and they died years ago'

'Yet they still managers to save kids like you from getting killed . . .'

'You're lying!'

'No child gets left behind' was all Kiba said in return as she passed them her radio and went to follow her sister.

'Why did you say that?' Chezia asked when her sister caught up.

'Getting them to trust me it was my motto' Kiba smiled.

One by one, the kids left the church and made their way down the dirt road. Machine gun fire shot the stone houses just in front of them. 'I wouldn't do that if I were you,' a rough voice called out. 'Now nice and slowly, I want you all to march yourselves back inside or you'll end up like your friend.'

'You'd do that anyway,' one of the kids shot back.

'I don't know where this sudden braver came from, but I don't like it,' the British man snarled, 'now get back inside.'

'No child gets left behind,' one of the older ones added before slamming a kick into their British captor, causing him and the gun to fall and land on the dirt.

'White Wolf!' He shouted as he picked up the gun, more gun fire had the kids and Chezia all ducking, but they continued on.

'Chez!' Kiba shouted running back to her sister who now lay dazed on the ground.

Chezia brought herself back to reality. 'I'll be alright,' she assured her worried sister, 'it's just a graze.'

Nevertheless, Kiba made sure Chezia made it back to the safety of Shadow-Wolf without acquiring anymore injuries. She pulled Chezia inside as the Cobra let loose a missile. Adam yanked the door closed just before it impacted with the ground, a little too close for comfort.

'Come on, Kiba, we've got to get off the ground or we'll be toast, make that burnt toast.'

'I can't do it,' she had allowed fear to enter her mind. 'Maybe one time, but not anymore.' As much as she hated to admit it, this wasn't her game anymore.

'Kiba,' Adam pleaded, 'please. I'm not trained for combat flying and Chezia's hurt. You have to.'

She shook her head in defeat. 'I can't-not anymore.'

Chezia took a hand off her wounded arm and wiped the blood off. 'Wish me luck.' We're going to need it, she silently added. Clutching the collective in one hand and the cyclic in the other, she took Shadow-Wolf up.

Shakily, the sleek navy blue helicopter rose up, narrowly escaping the missiles that came hurtling toward them. Adam looked up to the front of the cockpit; he hoped Chezia could do it even though she didn't look like she could; all their lives depended on it. More gun fire chattered along the metallic body until it reached its target. With the tail rotor out, a controlled crash was all you could typically hope for, but in Shadow-Wolf, if necessary, you could temporarily avoid the problem by using the jet engines. Chezia wasn't in any condition to be flying though, much less with the jet engines, that is, if she could hang onto consciousness that long. There weren't any more options.

'Come on White Wolf . . . Or have you grown out of your fur!' Bear mocked over the radio,

Kiba took a firm grip on the stick in front of her. 'Woof, Woof' she called.

Adam let out a sigh of relief as he put in the green cell rod. 'About time you got your head in the game.'

'Yeah, I know,' she mumbled. Uncertainly tried to sneak back into her mind, but she ruthlessly pushed it aside. If they were to have any chance she had to get back into the game.

They raced forward, out of range of the Cobra. Pulling up into a slow loop, they ended up behind the other helicopter. 'Load a heat-seeker.'

Adam efficiently the rocket pods slid out and loaded the missile. Before Kiba had a chance to fire the Cobra went down lighting the darken sky.

'Good job Kiba, I knew you could do it,' Adam smiled.

'I didn't do anything . . .' reaching for the radio to answer the incoming call,

'You own me one Wolf' a man stated as he finished the transmission with a high pitch squawking sound.

'Who was that?' Dante asked, talking for the first time their entire trip

'Captain Eagle' She smiled as she allowed the building tension in her shoulders to lower. That hadn't been too hard, and the doctor's prognosis had included the Jet Ranger which she was now flying on a daily basis. Maybe there was still hope. 'You kids alright down there?' Kiba radio as she came to a hover.

'We are now Major Wolf' one of the teenagers radioed back

'What's your name kid?'

'Smith . . . Tony Smith'

'Alright Tony, Stay where you are, a grey chopper will be here shortly to take you all back home'

'Thanks . . . Will we meet again?'

'You keep that radio and whenever you're in trouble, you call. I'll be there'

'Thanks again Wolf'

Kiba ended the transmission and turned to her sister. 'Let's get Chez to a doctor.' She knew she wouldn't be excited about the idea, but the wound needed to be cleaned anyway, and if it was as minor as she claimed they should be able to get out without too much problem.

★   ★   ★

Chezia groggily lifted her head from the pillows. She opened her eyes, only to snap them shut again. Bright florescent lights and neutral coloured walls were not what she wanted to see right now. She opened them more slowly, allowing them to adjust to the light. Kiba's blue eyes peered back down at her.

'I thought you'd never wake up. I know they had you pretty well drugged for how minor you were injured, but geez.'

Chezia looked around the room. 'Where's Adam?' she asked expecting him to be lurking around somewhere

'He stayed for a while, but when it started getting late he decided he should go and take Dan and Domanick home.'

'What time is it anyway?'

'Almost midnight'

She'd been asleep for three or four hours she estimated. 'So you got whatever your problem was solved?'

'Yeah.'

'Good. Next time don't do that though; I don't think you can understand how much effort it took to hold on as long as I did, and once we actually started pulling a few G's I was out like a light.'

Kiba gave an apologetic half smile. 'Sorry about that. I know I'm normally not like that. I honestly don't know what was going on inside my head.'

Chezia shrugged. 'We all have times of self doubt; you just need to work on the time of yours better.'

'Yeah,' she promised, 'I'll work on that.'

CHAPTER THREE

Wedding Plans

Kiba sat out on the jetty with her new white acoustic guitar, playing as the sun slowly sank beneath the horizon, leaving only a few rays of light behind. Inside, Adam and his mother were finalizing wedding plans. They seemed to be enjoying it between fights, and by staying out of it, she didn't have to listen to the individuals who had invaded her cottage squabbled about what colour the flowers should be. Adam's mother wanted red and white for a traditional wedding while Adam wanted black and red for a Punk Rock theme.

Chezia walked out to join her on the jetty. 'Sounds pretty good,' she commented, 'A lot better than when we were kids at Mr. B's. It was about the only thing other than flying you'd stick with, but it sounded as bad as . . . Oh never mind. It just wasn't good.'

'Thanks, I think.'

'So you wanna come for a drink with Mr. B and me tonight? It doesn't sound like they'll be done anytime soon. Honestly, I didn't know planning a wedding could be so complicated, but I think that if there is the wrong amount of dew on the grass they'd freak. Maybe they're taking it a little too far.'

'I'm not taking part in the extraneous details, but if I was, it would be held in an abandoned warehouse with a Punk theme but I'm not so I guess it couldn't hurt.'

Kiba had just set her guitar inside when the black, white and red Brad's Air Service Jet Ranger came over the forest. It slowed only as it reached the jetty. A moment later, it landed heavily on the wooden jetty. Mr. Brad climbed out and walked toward the cottage where Kiba and Chezia were already waiting.

'You in a hurry or something, Mr. B?'

'I was just trying to make up some lost time since I was late. Now are you guys ready?'

'Yeah, we're ready.'

'Let's go then.'

The Jet Ranger rose up off the jetty and back into the ever darkening sky.

'So where are we going?' Kiba asked casually.

'It's a surprise,' Mr. Brad answered with a chuckle.

★   ★   ★

'Thanks for all the help,' Adam said as she collected the bits of paper, with final details and preparations to be taken care of, to be put away.

'Let me get those,' his mother admonished. 'I'm sure you could find something more interesting to do and as a husband and eventually dad you'll get plenty of time to pick up after others. You've only got a week until you're married; enjoy them.'

'Mum, you make it sound like being married is terrible,' Adam complained.

'Well, I can't honestly say that I don't think you could've chosen a better girl, but at least you picked a nice cottage to rent for the wedding, and I have to admit, the view is stunning.'

'What do you mean rent a cottage?' Adam asked confusedly. He hadn't remembered renting any cottages, but with all that had happened in the last few days, he could've bought a boat and have it sitting right outside his window and he would've noticed.

'Here. I think you said it's on the Loch Of Toftingall. Are you sure all your guests can get in though? I know you said that you wanted a very small wedding, but helicopters are the only way to get in, don't you find that a little too obscure?'

'Mum, I said small and I meant really small, and this cottage isn't rented. It's Kiba's.'

'Really small—that is such a pity.' Adam's last sentence started to sink in, or at least he thought it did. 'She has her own cottage out here? That's really nice; you can come out on the weekends and-'

Adam interrupted. 'Mum, it's not a weekend thing. We live here and every morning fly into town to work.'

'She lives out here?! No. You are not going to live in the forests with a . . . I don't know what she is . . . A green haired banjo playing loony.'

'It's a guitar and I find it relaxing, and so does Domanick Graham.' Oops, he thought. Maybe now wasn't a good time to introduce his son. He tried to move the conversation on. 'It's a guitar and I am going to live out here, just like I have for the last five years.'

His mother looked back at him, stunned. 'I think you need to take some time to think this out. Last time I heard from you, you were shot doing something for this stranger and now you're living with her in the middle of nowhere—Wait. You said Domanick Graham finds the guitar music relaxing too. Who is he?'

Adam's cheeks flushed. He knew eventually the truth would have to come out, but they didn't get along well and he kind of avoided talking to her unnecessarily very often. 'Kiba's not a stranger. I love her and yes we, all three of us, are going to live here whether you like it or not. Domanick is a gift, he's . . . '—memories came flooding back

★   ★   ★

Mr. Brad climbed out of Shadow-Wolf, a look of sadness and despair heavily cloaked his face. Why he didn't know, but the mission had been successful, that's what mattered right? Soon his ideas of what mattered where changed when he heard Mr. Brad talking to Dante.

'I'm sorry kiddo, Kib's gone and she's not coming back'

★　　★　　★

'I thought he was Kiba's last gift, but he is more than that. He's our son.'

His mother's confused look immediately told him that he needed to explain better, although, Kiba almost dying during a mission he couldn't give many details about wasn't going to make her feel any safer about having Kiba as his wife.

'Five years ago Kiba was on a job, but when Mr. B came back without her we all got kind of worried. Mr. B said that she'd been killed, and that's what we all thought for the next three months. During that time, I found out that we could adopt a kid. At my birthday dinner, I planned to announce the news as Kiba's last gift, but she was still alive, standing on the doorstep'

'This incident that had you all thinking she was dead, did she get seriously injured in it?' his mother questioned with a hint of added worry. She had already noticed the limp and what if this woman had acquired some injury that would impair her ability to take care of her new grandson?

'Yeah,' Adam answered slowly. 'She couldn't even fly again, but we worked though it together.'

'So, Domanick Graham does it have a special meaning or something?' his mother inquired about her new grandson.

'It does,' Adam answered happily. 'I have to give her credit for trying, but, she made me so mad. How could she think I'd leave her just like that?'

'Want to explain?' she asked, still trying to make sense of the random statements.

'She got out of the hospital twelve weeks later, but she still had a really bad limp and the second and third degree burns had left very little feeling in her hands and arms. She finally told me that I should find someone else, that she loved me but couldn't take care of us as well as we deserved. In the end, she had to work past her fears because I wasn't about to leave her, and when I asked her what she wanted to name the baby, she said Domanick Graham after her old brother Vergil Domanick and her dad Graham'

His mother nodded in acknowledgement. She didn't know much about this Kiba White her son was insistent on marrying, especially her line of business, which worried her greatly, but at least she was responsible and tried to do what she thought was best even if it wasn't to her benefit.

★   ★   ★

Adam sat in the office by the phone, hoping desperately for it to ring. Business had been slow and seemed to drag on eternally. Mr. Brad walked into the room, obviously in a good mood.

'I'll see you guys later. I got me a charter to Whitehaven.'

He'd never seen him so excited about taking a charter, maybe that reflected on just how poor business was.

'You and Kib can take care of locking up right? Cause I don't know exactly when I'll be back. It's been a while since I've flown out there.'

'Fine, go have your fun and leave us to do all the work,' he teased.

Finally, it was time to close up. He trucked off to find Kiba. A few minutes later, he found her dozing in a chair just outside the roll door.

'Hey, Kiba', she called.

No answer.

He tried to gently shake her awake.

Still nothing.

'Man, she must be tired,' he turned to finish closing up before attempting to wake her again, the edge of his shirt brushing her lightly as he did so.

She jerked wide awake.

'Now you wake up,' he rolled his eyes. 'I could take off in a jet right next to you and you would sleep through it, but if I dropped a feather you'd wake up.'

'Sorry. I'm not that bad though. It's just how it is; usually when someone is sneaking around is when there's a problem. If they draw attention to themselves you'd never suspect them.'

'Like hiding in plain sight,' he agreed. 'I know, but you have to agree you take it to a new extreme, and it is kind of strange. Anyways, it's time to go if you want to help me close up.'

After picking up Domanick, Kiba and Adam flew back to the cottage.

★　　★　　★

Chezia unlocked the side door to the hangar so they could all come in. The three of them spread out quickly finishing the necessary things to get ready for business, that is, if they had any today.

By one o'clock, there still hadn't been a single customer or phone call.

'When's Mr. B supposed to be back?' Kiba asked.

Adam shrugged, but he had to admit, it did worry him that they hadn't heard from him.

'He should be back by now,' Chezia answered.

'He did say he might stay awhile though,' Adam rejoined.

'True. It's probably nothing.' She could only hope that was really the case.

Ringing from the phone on the other side of the hangar interrupted their conversation.

All three ran for it but longer strides eating up the distance, Adam was the first to reach it.

'Brad's Air Service,' he answered. 'Uh-huh, ok. Hold on just a minute please.' Adam turned to the two who waited expectantly. 'It's some movie company. He said they've dealt with us before.'

'Ok, what do they need?' Chezia asked.

'That's the problem, they'd prefer someone they've dealt with, but since they're behind schedule, any of us that can do it will work. The stunt isn't an easy one though. They need us to take off, follow a train, go through a bridge, show off a little fancy stuff before being supposedly shot, and taking a plunge towards the ground.'

'Not easy, but doable,' Chezia commented.

'The bad news is,' Adam continued, 'that after this death defying drop you only have thirty, maybe forty feet to pull out.'

Kiba seemed to be working out the figures in her head.

'That's practically suicide!' Chezia exclaimed.

'He said he'd pay double because of the short notice and the danger involved.'

'I'll do it,' Kiba finally answered.

'I know we could use the business, but I think we should sit out on this one; it's just too dangerous,' Adam decided.

'I second that,' Chezia agreed.

'I'll do it,' Kiba repeated with even more determination. 'I've worked with him before, we need the business, and I can do it.'

Adam looked back at his soon-to-be wife with concern. She'd done the daily stuff and a couple of charters, but no stunt flying since her accident, and this one wouldn't be a good beginning stunt, he thought worriedly. 'You sure? I mean, there will be other jobs and-'

She cut him off. 'I said I'll do it.'

'Kiba, the money won't do us any good if we have to pay for Mike to come in to cover for you because you're in the hospital.' She hadn't even wanted to take on a cobra in their last mission and that was usually a piece of cake for her. This was a different kind of challenge, but certainly not any easier.

'I am doing it,' she stated firmly, 'and there's not much you can do to stop me.'

'Kiba look how much danger is involved in this stunt'

'My middle name is Danger' She finished turning on her heels and stormed off. What was their problem? No one ever questioned her flying ability, why start now? She focused on the helicopter resting in front of her. If she was gonna pull this off, she'd need her bird in top condition.

★   ★   ★

Mr. Brad checked out of his hotel room and hauled his overnighter into the back of the Jet Ranger. A severe thunderstorm had hindered him from being able to fly back the night before, as well as, ruin just about any chance he had at getting a clear connection back to Adam and the girls.

Fortunately, the weather seemed to have cleared up enough for an overcast but enjoyable flight.

The rotors turned slowly as he counted off the seconds until he could lift off. Finally, they had gathered enough speed and he took off.

★　　★　　★

Kiba stood in front of Brad's Air Service's second Jet Ranger. It wasn't the same distinctive black, white and red hues, but it was essentially the same helicopter.

'Mr. B's not back yet?' Kiba questioned nervously.

'No,' Chezia answered. 'I even tried radioing him, but I didn't get anything.'

'If he's not back by the time I come back, I think we need to start a search. I heard Cumbria got hit by some bad weather last night. Maybe he had to sit it out and that's what delayed him,' she said more to encourage herself than actually believing it.

'Kiba, are you really sure you want to do this stunt? If you miss, you could get really hurt or even killed . . . I want to be encouraging, I really do, and I'd love to have you flying stunts again, but I don't want to lose you.'

'Adam, I can do this. The business needs it, and so do I. I need to know for sure that I can do it.'

'Even if it kills you?' he stated.

'Yeah, But I'm not planning on killing myself'

He nodded understandingly. There wasn't anything he could do to stop her, and he knew it. Not letting her fly would just kill her just as quickly, not to mention put her through more misery. 'Be careful,'

She turned to leave. 'I promise I'll be careful.'

Rubbing a dirty hand across his cheeks, 'Come on, Chezia, let's go find Mr. B.'

★   ★   ★

Mr. Brad fiddled with the radio some more. They'd all be worried about him and he knew it, but there wasn't anything he could do about it with the radio out.

A loud rumble of thunder brought his attention back to the sky. If he was lucky, he'd be able to out fly most of the rain, he decided and continued on, increasing his speed. The thunder only seemed to get closer and flashes of light lit up the grey heavens as the rain came pelting down. He had no choice. He had to set down and wait it out.

★   ★   ★

The director looked out at the ominous black clouds forming in the distance. He picked up his portable radio and gave Kiba the signal. 'Ok, White, we can fit in one run through now then we'll see how the storm looks.'

'Roger.'

After rising almost effortlessly she slung the helicopter up into the sky then followed the train through the tunnel.

'Go ahead and dive!' the director instructed. The immediate response was almost a completely vertical nosedive to the ground. The ground rushed up to meet her, closer and closer. She needed to pull out, but it was just a little farther.

The wind started to pick up, adding an additional unwanted challenge to the difficult stunt. She struggled to maintain on course. It had to be perfect or she'd mess up the stunt and end up dead, or at least seriously injured. Neither option was good, especially the previous.

'You're beyond the hill,' the director's voice sounded over the radio, 'pull up now.'

Now fighting wind, as well as velocity and gravity, she fought the collective and the cyclic, trying to pull out in the very few feet allotted. Gravity pulled her down, trying to flatten her like a pancake, A mere five feet separated her from the ground by the time she had regained full control of her helicopter and had it righted. She landed heavily on the grass still wet with morning dew.

'How was that?' Kiba asked over the radio. She hoped it would be good enough so that she wouldn't have to do it again, but at least she knew she could. If she could do that, the other stuff should be a piece of cake.

'Very good,' the director praised. That was a new one; maybe he had learned his lesson last time when Kiba had come in close scaring him half to death because she was annoyed at the director critiquing her flying no matter how many times she did it right. 'I think that should work, but if not I'll give you a call, after all, I want the best.'

Soon Kiba was paid and heading back to the hangar. Maybe it hadn't been the smartest thing to do, but she had survived unscathed, and she knew for sure that she could do the stunt flying again.

Upon entering the hangar, she called for Mr. Brad. No answer. Next she tried Chezia and Adam. Still nothing. 'I guess they went ahead with the search.' That hurt her feelings, she wanted her surrogate father back as soon as possible, especially with the wedding scheduled in two days and a storm moving in.

There were about 100 miles between Doncaster and Whitehaven and Mr. Brad could be in any one of them, perfectly fine waiting on a storm to blow over or injured from a crash. He needed to be found and fast. The incoming storm wasn't going to leave much time for looking though. Grabbing the keys she climbing onto her bike, she raced off, determined to find Mr. Brad.

The gusty wind was turning into a steady gale by the time Kiba reached the canopy. She connected a call to Jason.

'Jason, I need a search-'

'Team looking for Michael somewhere between Doncaster and Whitehaven,' Jason supplied the rest. 'I know. Adam already called while you were out supposedly trying to kill yourself and yes we are already doing all we can, but if the weather keeps acting up there won't be much we can do'

'Alright thanks Jas,'

'Oh, and White,' Alex entered the conversation, 'please, remember to be careful. Even Shadow-Wolf's isn't invincible.'

'Yeah, I know.' She ended the call and pulled him out from under the canopy, before starting the engines. Impatiently waiting on the rotors to gain momentum, she started her search.

★　　★　　★

'Where could he be?' Chezia asked aloud, not expecting an answer. If Adam knew where he was they'd have already found him.

He looked up from the map he was holding and shook his head dejectedly. 'We've covered just about every foot of land between here and Cumbria.'

'I know, I know, but he's got to be out here somewhere, and the wedding's supposed to be two days from now.'

'Special alert from Robin Hood Tower,' the radio voice said, 'We are closing all commercial lanes at Robin Hood Airport due to severe weather conditions and high winds. There will be no more commercial flights until further notice, and all private businesses are advised to do the same.'

'Damn,' Chezia muttered, 'just what we need.' The weather was getting worse quickly and she knew it would only be a few minutes until she would be forced down, so she started back for the hangar.

Back at the hangar, there was no sign of Kiba. 'She should be back by now,' Adam said worryingly. 'Why isn't she here?'

'Adam,' Chezia said holding up a white envelope marked Brad's Air Service 'This has the money from the job in it, so she's been here. Maybe she went out looking for Mr. B,'

'The 4x4 is here though, and the Jet Ranger can't get through that storm.'

'That doesn't mean she wouldn't try on her bike,' Chezia quickly stated, but Kiba wasn't stupid. She may not have enough sense to come in immediately, but she'd wait it out somewhere. One thing was for sure, she wasn't going anywhere on her motorbike in a storm like that.

Another hour passed and they still hadn't heard from Kiba. Where was she? The phone rang only once before Chezia and Adam lunged for it. Jason was on the other end.

'Oh don't sound so excited to hear from me,' he teased when he heard the disappointment in Chezia's voice when she found it wasn't Kiba.

'Sorry,' she apologized. 'We were still hoping to hear from Mr. B and now Kub's gone missing.'

'She's not back?' alarm was evident in his voice.

'No, do you know where she is?' Chezia asked hopefully.

'Hopefully on the ground. She probably got forced down by the storm. Hold on a second and I'll have Alex radio her.'

Alex reached for the radio. 'Shadow-Wolf, do you read?'

'I read you, Alex,' came the short reply.

'Where are you?'

'At a hundred and fifty feet above Kendal'

'Kendal! That's the worst part of the storm and you're flying!' Alex fumed. 'Set down immediately.'

The loud crash of thunder couldn't be heard outside the soundproof cockpit, but Alex could hear the array of beeping and alarms going off inside the helicopter. 'Sorry, Alex, I'm a little busy right now. I'll get back to you later,'

'White,' Alex began, but it was too late. Kiba was already gone. He caught himself cursing mid-word. 'Actually, God help her. She's gonna need all the help she can get to survive a storm like that much less rescue Michael.'

Jason explained the situation to Chezia.

'She's near Kendal? Is she alright?'

'She's fine. Let's hope she can stay that way,' he silently added.

'Then why do I get the feeling you aren't telling me the whole truth?'

Why did she have to be so good? Most people would simply be glad she was alive; no she had the same eerie sixth sense her sister had. 'She's a hundred and fifty feet off the ground, fighting the storm and still looking for Michael.'

'So help me, Kub, if you don't kill yourself I might be tempted to do it myself," Chezia ranted on about the foolishness. 'Ok, Thanks Jason,' She hung up the receiver.

'So?' Adam queried.

'She's above Kendal'
'Above? As in flying?'
'Yeah.'

★   ★   ★

Fighting to hold the stick steady, she scanned from the horizon to directly underneath her. Finally, among the trees, she caught a glimpse of something red and white. She brought Shadow-Wolf in a slow circle to take a closer look. Now only thirty feet up, she stared at the muddy figure. It was the Brad's Air Service helicopter. She quickly set down in the squishy mud.

Sliding out, she crossed the mucky earth to search the helicopter. It was dirty and a few small branches had blown onto it, but no damage; that was a good sign. But there was still no sign of Mr. Brad though. The rain continued pouring down, causing the already saturated ground to hold inches of water.

'Mr. B,' she yelled out.

Her only answer was more rain and a bright streak of lightening nearby, followed by another wave of rolling thunder. She shouted again, but still no reply. About a hundred yards away, a den was visible on the mountain side.

Making her way to it, Kiba attempted to climb the slippery muddy grass. Moving too fast she slipped and slid back down the eight feet she'd just climbed up, cursing in frustration, she wiped away most of the mud then began to climb again. Finally she reached the ledge. A dark, damp den greeted her unwelcomingly, but she heard a soft crackling noise deep inside. Cautiously, she crept in.

★   ★   ★

Adam tried to radio his fiancée. 'Kiba, come in. It's Ad,'
Only silence answered him.

'Kiba where are you?' First Mr. Brad and now Kiba were missing and they didn't have much of a clue where they might be. How was he going to explain this one to his mother? She already wasn't very fond of Kiba, now she disappeared two nights before her own wedding.

Again the phone rang. This time it was Adam who picked it up. 'Alright, we'll be right over.'

'Come on, Chezia. Let's locked up and go back to your place. Dante said Domanick started crying for awhile and he can't get him to stop no matter what he does.

★   ★   ★

'What's wrong?' Adam asked.

'I don't know,' Dante answered. 'I was just watching him like I was supposed to and everything was going well until about twenty minutes ago when he woke up crying and hasn't stopped since.'

Adam picked up the crying baby. 'Hey, Daddy's got you; its ok,' he said in a soothing voice. The crying didn't stop, but it did lessen slightly.

'You stay here with him, I'll see about fixing him a bottle, maybe he's just hungry,' Chezia suggested since the storm was still too strong now to even attempt flying back to the cottage.

★   ★   ★

The dank den was actually much larger than its external appearance suggested, but in this case that wasn't necessarily a good thing. She rounded another dark corner cautiously. The last thing she needed was to trip over an adder, or to find bats or a fox in this den. A cool breeze blew through and the crackling noise was much louder here. A campfire, she thought hopefully. A campfire meant someone was here, maybe she'd find Mr. Brad here after all. Hopeful, she continued onward.

★   ★   ★

Where they were, the storm finally died down enough for Adam to be able to fly back with Domanick to the cottage. His mother was at his side the moment he stepped out.

'I was worried you'd gotten stuck in the storm. See, a cottage only accessible by helicopter isn't such a great idea.'

'Mum, I'm fine,' he said absently, his worry concentrated on Mr. Brad and Kiba. They weren't going to have the wedding without Mr. Brad, and they certainly couldn't have it without Kiba either. 'I think the wedding's going to have to wait,' he muttered.

His mother gave a shocked look. 'No, it can't! We've worked so hard on it, unless,' she paused, 'of course, you're having second thoughts about Kiba,' her eyes narrowed shrewdly.

'No, that's not it,' Adam answered defiantly. 'Mr. B never came back after his charter, and Kiba has gone missing now as well.'

'So she's waiting out the storm out in who knows where and can't get back in time,' his mother supplied snottily.

'That's better than the alternative!' Adam shot back angrily. 'I don't think that's the case though; last I heard from her, she was fighting the storm above Kendal.' His mother could be so irritating sometimes, he thought in frustration. She wasn't even sympathetic, all she was worried about was the wedding she'd work on, and figured Kiba was just too irresponsible to get herself back home in time for her own wedding.

★   ★   ★

Beside the fire, lay an older man resting on the cool ground.

'Michael!' she'd never been so glad to say that one single word.

Mr. Brad woke and rolled over, his green-blue eyes looking up just long enough to see Kiba standing in the den. Hurriedly, he scrambled to his feet and engulfed the young woman in a bear hug. 'Kib, my girl! How'd you find me? I thought I might be safer in here with the wind blowing things around like that but it isn't exactly where I'd first think to look.' He grinned looking at the sight of her in the dim light. 'At least, I guess this means the storm finally blew over. I'd have radioed you, but it went out.'

'I'm just glad I found you, but you sure didn't pick an easy spot to get to once the grass gets wet . . . Come on, Mr. B. Let's go home; we have a wedding to get to.' The storm hadn't slacked up much while they were gone. Together, they skidded down the grass as they trudged down through the mud toward Shadow-Wolf. 'You won't be able to get anywhere in the Jet Ranger, so we'll take my boy and pick up the other helicopter after this place has dried up a little.'

'You actually flew through the storm? Even with the Devil, you're crazy.'

'Maybe, but it's still not a nice thing to say.'

Mr. Brad laughed heartily, 'alright, let's go. It doesn't look like anything would stop you today.'

★   ★   ★

By the time they reached the canopy, the weather had subsided enough for them to ride back to the hanger then up to the cottage.

Adam stared out the window from the bedroom. He loved his mother, he really did, but sometimes she just made him crazy, and having Mr. Brad and Kiba missing hadn't helped matters in the least.

A sound in the distance tickled his hearing. It was a helicopter-a Jet Ranger. Maybe Kiba was back!

He ran down the stairs and out to the jetty where he waited for her to finish landing.

Kiba slid out from the pilot's seat, exhaustion evident.

He ran up to her and slipped his arms around her, pulling her into a tight hug. 'I was so worried about you. I tried to radio you, but didn't get any answer, and I was afraid something had happened to you.'

'I'll be alright. A couple hours sleep, a shower and a change of clothes and I'll be good as new.'

'Same here,' Mr. Brad joined.

'Mr. B! She found you. We were getting worried.'

'Well, I have to admit, it's nice to be found,' he chuckled as he hugged him.

Kiba slipped her colourful tattooed left arm around Adam's waist and wrapped her black and grey right arm around Mr. Brad's and the three of them walked back up to the cottage.

★   ★   ★

The following night,

Adam started mixing the ingredients for a vegetarian dinner—perfect for Kiba. His mother came in. 'You know, I could make a delicious meat sauce for that,' she offered,

'It's nice of you to offer, but no thanks,' Adam declined politely.

'It would really make it though,' his mother insisted, 'I won't get in your way, but I know it would just finish it, make it truly perfect.'

'Kiba won't eat it,' he said abruptly.

'What do you mean she won't eat it? It would make it.'

'Can't we just go with the recipe and have the marinara sauce?'

'It's just so much better with a little meat.'

'Mum, she won't eat anything to do with meat, she's vegetarian'

She rolled her eyes dramatically. 'Adam Blake Davids, I just can't see for the life of me why you can't pick a normal lass that eats normal food instead of one of these new-age health nuts.'

Adam ignored his mother's ranting and continued on with the marinara sauce.

At dinner the conversation started off friendly enough. Passing Kiba her plate, Adam's mother questioned Kiba. 'So what exactly do you do?'

The question caught her off guard. 'My job? I fly for Mr. B's business, Brad's Air Service, charters and stunts, Y'know that kind of thing,' she recovered quickly.

'How exactly did you and Adam manage to get shot in a flying stunt? And do you think it's really a good idea trying to raise a kid, not knowing if you'll both make it home every night? And don't get me started on those pathetic tattoos that cover your entire arms, I mean why is one arm coloured, and the other just black and white that's a stupid idea'

Kiba fought to keep her temper under control, but it doesn't last for long. 'You don't know anything about me, so don't start judging me for what I do!' She stormed off out of the cottage.

'What'd you do that for?' Adam question angrily. 'No wonder you don't like her. You don't want to.'

Dante, who had asked to be excused to stay with Domanick who was still fussy, came tearing down the stairs. 'Adam, come quick! There's something wrong with Dom!'

In a sudden panic he charged up the stairs after him.

Domanick, laying in the crib, fussed hysterically. Adam reached over to lay a hand on his forehead to see if he had a fever as his mother walked into the room. He suddenly bowed up and went into a seizure. Adam, going into full fledged panic, yelled for Kiba.

Kiba, hearing the shouting coming from inside, took the stairs two at a time up to the upper deck. She lunged into the room to see Adam's mother trying to calm him and the baby seizing in the crib. She yelled for Dante to grab her jacket as she hustled Adam, now holding the baby, into the helicopter outside. By now the infant had gone limp.

As soon as Adam, Domanick, and his mother were in the back she started up the rotors. Dante came scurrying into the co-pilot seat and they took off for the nearby hospital. On the way, she tried to get a hold of Mr. Brad or Chezia, but no such luck. She hoped to call Jason to see if he could track them down.

At the hospital, Domanick was immediately rushed in, leaving Kiba, Adam, and the others only to wait and worry. Kiba's concern was evident for Adam and her son. Adam's mother started to think maybe she had been a little too hard on her.

Jason and Alex soon arrived with Mr. Brad and Chezia in tow. Mr. Brad tried to comfort the worried Kiba and Adam while Chezia waited with Dante. Time passed slowly, still baring no news.

Adam caught his mother saying something about cancelling the wedding plans for the following day. 'How can you be thinking about the wedding when your grandson could be dying in there for all you know!' he launched at her.

Kiba looked more than a little stricken herself at his words. Mr. Brad just patted her gently on the back, not knowing what else he could do.

Alex silently slipped down the hallway to find a doctor and see what news he could find out. After a few minutes, he returned with the news. 'The doctors think they've stabilized his condition and that he'd picked up some infection. The seizure was just caused by the high fever.'

All of them heaved an enormous sigh of relief. After things started to settled, Adam's mother said that she guessed she needed to call everybody and tell them the wedding was off for now. This time Adam looked down sadly, but saw no other option but to agree. 'No' Kiba said firmly. 'This just goes to show how much he needs his family. We could go ahead with the wedding plans, just do it at the hospital.'

Shaking her head, Adam's mother started listing off reasons why it couldn't be done.

Adam who had started to look hopeful again, seemed crushed.

'Jason?' Kiba inquired, looking at the spy, 'Can you make it happen?'

He ran his hand over his black and red spiky hair as he pondered it for a minute. He sent a brief glance at Alex. He nodded slightly, his eyes twinkling. Jason grinned and agreed. 'We'll make it happen.'

★   ★   ★

Kiba and Adam spent the night at the hospital with Domanick while the others went home to get some sleep and get ready—the reception was to be held at Mr. Brad's house, Adam's mother would bring his suit, and Chezia would bring her twin sister the punk outfit Kiba had worked on.

The wedding began without any problems in Domanick's room, Adam in his black suit, and Kiba in her tartan trousers, striped T-shirt and her sleeveless denim jacket, looking joyful holding Domanick. The hospital preformed the ceremony and congratulations were offered all around just as the doctor came in to check on Domanick.

Nodding his approval, the doctor gave his prognosis. 'He should be out of danger now. We'll just keep him another day as a precaution.'

As the others started to leave to go back to Mr. Brad's house, Kiba told them to go and enjoy themselves. She put an arm around Adam, rubbing a finger softly over the sleeping baby's cheek.

Adam's mother pulled her aside, telling her that she needed to talk to her.

'I'm sorry,' she began, 'You sure wouldn't have been my first choice as a wife for my son, and I'm still not happy about the getting shot part, but now I realize how much you care for him and your son and that they are pretty lucky to have you. He couldn't have picked a better girl.' Looking back at her son, she noticed Adam's bittersweet happiness. He was ecstatic to know Domanick was going to be ok, but he was going to miss his own wedding reception. 'Go,' she decided on impulse. 'I'll stay with Dominick'

'Who?'

'Dominick Graham'

'No . . . It's Domanick, with an A not an I'

'Alright, I'll watch him now go on, even if it's only for a little while. I'll call you if anything goes wrong.'

She finally nodded, meeting her eyes and gave her a shy half smile.

Placing a gentle hand on Adam's arm, she whispered something in his ear. He turned to look at the sleeping baby and his mother who promptly shooed them out with a grin.

Adam placed an arm around Kiba and led her out.

Adam's mother sat down in the chair beside her new grandson, stroking his soft, blonde, baby hair 'Domanick Graham . . . nice ring to it' then started to hum a lullaby.

CHAPTER FOUR

Heir of the Wolf

Danica walked into the bedroom of her flat just outside Asheville, North Carolina. The small flat suited her needs, but the peaceful countryside where her husband had lived had much more of her needed room. It didn't matter though, she'd never found his will and the animals he had, had to be sold to pay off previous debts he had. The massive debts made her curious though, just what had her husband been up to in his life? All she knew was that he worked for the same agency she did in the UK, England exactly.

She pulled open the desk drawer; it was filled with paperwork that were utterly meaningless to her. It had a few sketches of a helicopter but all the rest was in code. The papers had sat here in this drawer since she found them in her husband's office after he died. To her they were useless and ineffective but somehow, they looked important, not something to be taken lightly and definitely not thrown away.

A quick glance at her silver plated watch told her that she had better hurry if she wasn't going to be late for work. She slid into an overcoat, grabbed her shoulder bag, and scurried out the front door, locking it behind her. Leaving the steps up from her flat, she walked just down the street to a library; she started her duties-arranging books and dusting the bookcases.

A familiar looking man entered the shop. He looked absolutely exhausted, tired lines causing him to look older than he actually was, but she knew who it was, even if she hadn't seen him in six years.

'Danielle,' he began in a hushed tone.

'Danica, please,' she reminded. Her husband had always favoured his twin daughters, they seemed so special to him, until he decided he'd had enough of the government games and had disappeared without a trace. After his daughters went to war she had used a stranger version of her name, as first in an attempt to please her husband, but later she found it fit her better.

'Danica,' he amended. 'When is your next break? I need to talk to you.'

She looked down at her watch. 'In thirty minutes. I'll meet you across the street at the coffee shop.'

He agreed, turning to leave.

Reaching for her dust rag, she thought about the man that had mysteriously come, Jack. Why? She wondered. Her business with the government had ended almost thirteen years ago, and while they'd gotten along alright, she and Jack had never been very close. So why did he show up now?

Thirty minutes later, she appeared, as promised, at the doorway of the coffee shop. Gingerly sitting down in a chair across from Jack, she asked the question that had been plaguing her mind for the last half hour.

'So?' she queried. 'I know, being an ex-government agent myself, you didn't come for just coffee and talk so what is it?'

He stifled a laugh. Ex-government agent—it was true. She had been one, and a very good one at that, but it seemed strange that a fifty two year old like her had been a fierce government agent. 'Your husband's papers, I think I finally got a lead on them.'

Her husband's papers? This guy was more persistent than she could have ever imagined. She would have told him it wasn't a big deal and that he didn't need to worry about them if she had known he was still looking, but with all the time and effort he had invested she might as well listen.

'It was the helicopter project your husband worked on in England, known as Blue Demon.'

'Blue Demon,' it sounded familiar. She chewed on the word for a long minute. 'Got anything else?'

'It was supposedly destroyed not long after your husband's death, but I've seen it since then.'

The new information captured her imagination. In all truth, it was hard leaving the action of government spy work, but she had decided it would be easier before she had a lifetime of memories.

'Danica, I told you about all I can, but if you want to know much more . . . There is one way.'

It had killed her husband and driven her parents away, but it drew her in so easily. The whole library thing wasn't going to work long-term and she knew it. She'd had several jobs since her husband's death but nothing else had held her attention that long. At long last she answered. 'I want to know. I'll do it.'

★   ★   ★

Entering the conference room the next morning, Danica was dressed in a smart business suit. Nothing like making a nice impression before begging for your job back, she thought half-humouredly.

Not much begging was necessary though. Ashley Barnes, the deputy head of Group-Rhino, greeted her sincerely. 'It's nice to have you back Danica.'

★   ★   ★

Domanick's crying had Adam rushing over to his side. After the scare he'd given them not long ago, he would admit that he was jumpy, hardly leaving his side.

Dante came in with a beaker. 'Ad, it's ok. He hasn't eaten, he's hungry.'

Subsiding, he set him on his lap and took the beaker. Dante was right. Domanick guzzled the juice greedily. 'Slow down,' he warmed, 'or you'll get-' He hiccupped. 'So much for the warning.'

A sudden shiver travelled down Dante's spine as he carried the finished beaker back to the kitchen. It wasn't cold in here so why the shiver? It was nothing he told himself, but he couldn't help but wonder if that was really the case.

★   ★   ★

Danica's fingers slid across the white paper. Hidden amongst the pages and pages of mysterious sketches and code, she laid eyes on the neatly printed will of her husband.

Silently, she skimmed through it. At the end was a strange message. The will left her the woodland, and the necessary information to access a trust fund with vast amounts of money in it. It was more than enough to pay back his owned debts. The only thing left for her to wonder was how he had died and what the strange message said. Glowering in frustration, she struggled to decipher the strange words. After nearly an hour of struggles to translate, she decided it was Spanish. Why Spanish? Suddenly she remembered—it was the one language her husband had insisted on the family learning, maybe this was why, but after years of not using it, she struggled with the message.

'Special gift . . . supersonic helicopter . . . Blue Demon . . . British . . . find in Yorkshire . . . made deal with Rhino.' She figured out most of the message. This special helicopter-Blue Demon—was supposed to be held by Jason Black at Rhino-Gate, just waiting for her. Fifteen years had passed since the will had been written and anything could have happened though, besides, what would she do with a helicopter anyway? Even if she moved to his cottage in the woods, she couldn't think of any reason for needing one. Something tickled her about it though. It had been described as special, supersonic, and her husband called it Blue Demon; she had a feeling this wasn't just some ordinary bird.

The next morning, she used her newly renewed status to check up on some of the details about this Blue Demon. For a top spy in a highly knowledgeable secret intelligence, the information was remarkably difficult to come by, which meant there wasn't much information to have or, more likely, somebody was being very careful to cover their tracks.

Finally, something came up. Shadow-Wolf, as it was called, had been used to get revenge on the co-pilot Wayne by Wolf. Who had previously been the best until she dropped out because of an argument with Jack White. Evidently, the rumour of Shadow-Wolf being destroyed was just that—a rumour. It had since then been used by Wolf for missions before her death five years ago.

She punched in the computer for information on Wolf. The information came up on the screen. White Wolf—Burmese Veteran, POW for two months, honourable discharge, secret operative for eight years, and pilot on Shadow-Wolf, living blood relations? Wolf-Cub.

Next, she tried Wolf-Cub. Her information appeared a moment later.

Wolf Cub—MIA since Burma, thirteen years ago.

She skimmed the rest, nothing of any interest to her. Any doubt she might have had was now gone. Without a shadow of a doubt, she knew Blue Demon, or Shadow-Wolf, must be a very special helicopter to have such little recorded information and such high security clearances. She knew so little about it, yet longing for it surged through her blood, like it truly belonged to her. She would get it.

★   ★   ★

Flying high above the mountains in North West Scotland, she then piloted Shadow-Wolf higher and higher into the sky.

'What are you doing Kib? I'm tired and it's not like we had a good ride from Canada.'

Kiba allowed a sly grin to spread across her face beneath the cover of her green hair. 'Put in the green cell rod and Hold on, we're going up,' Once the rod was secured in the compartment she hit the button just beneath her thumb sending them racing up into the heavens.

Mr. Brad chanced a look at the altimeter—they were already closing in on seventy five thousand feet. 'What's the point in this?' It wasn't a comfortable ride up here and it would only get worse as they rose farther into the thinning air.

'I just want to be the first person to fly a helicopter into outer space,' Kiba replied wryly.

Topping out at eighty five thousand, she began their descent. She allowed them to practically free fall for a good distance before even trying to regain control. Not like it would have done them any good anyway in such thin air.

Mr. Brad muttered. 'That was some ride.'

'Yeah,' Kiba agreed, enjoying Mr. Brad's expression.

'I heard you're just about out to get yourself killed lately,' Mr. Brad said referring to the almost impossible stunt she'd done and the vicious storm she had fought for eight hours straight, 'but if you gotta do it, don't take me down with ya.'

'I'm not actually planning to get myself killed,' she said defensively. 'Both of those were with good reasoning.'

'Let's just get home,' Mr. Brad said figuring he'd deal with the arguments another time.

★ ★ ★

'So? How'd it go?' Adam inquired.

'Pretty well,' Kiba answered. 'How about here?'

He remembered her anxiety about leaving them this morning. 'Everything is alright here,' he reassured her. Ever since Domanick's seizure the night before their wedding, they'd both been afraid to leave him, but this morning he sensed there was something more.

'You're positive?'

'One hundred percent,' he confirmed. 'I can't say I got much done though,' he added with a small laugh.

Taking her black acoustic guitar into the living room, she played while Adam fixed dinner. The relaxing music lulled Domanick right to sleep.

The night was dark and still, a quiet calm washed over the overcast skies, yet it wasn't peaceful to Kiba. A blanket of cold sweat covered her body and she rolled restlessly from side to side.

Adam, woken from the words she was crying out in her sleep, turned a sympathetic eye towards her. He wished that somehow he could rid her of the awful images that she witnessed in those terrible dreams, but he couldn't. He got out of bed and walked over to hers. 'Kiba,' he said soothingly, 'it's alright.'

She seemed to calm down momentarily before returning to the restlessness of before.

'Kiba,' he aborted the idea of trying to lull her back to sleep after a couple attempts, 'wake up,' he shook her gently but she probably couldn't even notice the difference between that and her own shaking. From the neighbouring room he could hear Domanick's cries. Great. Now he's upset too. He moved to endeavour waking his wife once more.

Waking, she reached for him, just him very presence comforting her. Desperately, she clung to him like if she let go she'd never get to be with him again. He stayed, offering what comfort he could. Finally, she loosened her grip on him, coming back to reality. 'Not getting much sleep, huh?'

'No,' he admitted, 'but I'll be ok as long as you're alright.'

'I'm fine.' Now she too heard the crying coming from the next room as Adam started to get up to tend to the toddler. 'I'll take care of him, you go back to bed.'

'I can get him.'

She shook her head. 'You look tired, go back to sleep. You know I won't be able to sleep anyway.'

Sighing, he agreed and shuffled back to the other bed and slipped under the covers. 'If you're sure.' And with that, he fell back asleep.

She made her way into Domanick's room. 'You not sleeping well either?' she asked the little kid. Cradling the young child, she took him downstairs to find something to calm him. She made sure he stayed with her the whole time though, if anything, she knew how consoling it was to have someone there after waking up from a nightmare. She stilled worried about Domanick's random fussy spurts, but oddly enough, lately they had coincided with moments of her own uncomfort.

★ ★ ★

At Brad's Air Service, Mr. Brad peered over the side of the playpen where the two year old played happily. 'I don't see anything wrong. He looks fit as a fiddle to me.'

'That's what worries us the most. One minute he's fine the next he's crying, then he'll be fine again.'

Chezia interrupted their conversation as she re-entered the hangar after dropping off some film. 'I think I brought back some company,' she warned, 'in the form of a grey 4x4 and a matching Rhino-Gate agent to go with it.'

Jason stepped from the jeep not a second after it had stopped. 'Wolf,' he addressed briefly, 'I thought I'd warn you that the files on Shadow-Wolf have been accessed quite often lately, and that probably means trouble for you.'

She shrugged it off. 'Others have tried. So my boy and I could be in trouble, thanks Jas, but I know that much every day I wake up.'

'I know it's not much,' Jason admitted, 'but I'll keep you updated. Just be careful because whoever it is must be pretty serious to be checking up on it that often.'

'I'll keep an eye out, but the location isn't in any of those files, and I can't think of a much safer place for him right now.'

Jason couldn't say he disagreed. Some place like Rhino-Gate headquarters would be the first place to start looking for a piece of top secret hardware.

★ ★ ★

'Not dead?' Danica repeated, 'But the computer said she died five year ago. They even had a memorial service for her how can this Wolf not be dead? She was hit by a damn missile!'

'We don't know that she isn't dead,' Ashley amended, 'but we don't know for sure that she is dead either. There has only been limited activity that Shadow-Wolf could have possibly been involved in lately, and there haven't been any identifications that are totally positive, but there is some speculation that she's not truly dead.'

'She was hit by a missile!' she was outraged that Ashley could think anyone could live through that. It simply wasn't possible. 'Why wouldn't it kill her?'

'Let me tell you a little about Wolf,' Ashley suggested, 'maybe that would give you a better understanding.'

'Ok, I'm listening.' She doubted anything he would have anything new, but how could it hurt to listen?

'I've dealt with her a little, so I'll tell you what I know. First off, she has an amazing ability for surviving. She's lost nearly everyone else, but she always manages to get away, not always unscathed, but she's lived through what would kill normal people. No one's managed to kill her yet, and many have tried. The time you'd probably be most interested in was when she came back on leave.'

'If you say so. I would think something more recent would be more useful, personally.'

'The last mission we know of was a stopping a major drug run from entering the UK, but that's where she had the whole missile incident.'

'That she couldn't have lived through,' Danica muttered.

'She did at least survive long enough to be taken to the hospital, and she was there for a while, but her records are very unclear as to whether she was released or not and her latest condition. There was an uprising with some grudge holding Burmese only a few months ago. Her sister, Wolf-Cub got grazed and we think Wolf was there too.'

'What kind of injures were received? If she did somehow survive, I know she would have gotten hurt.'

'Like I said, the records aren't very clear, but they said a concussion, second and third degree burns, and she was hit by some shrapnel. She had a bad limp and pretty much no feeling in either of her hands and arms. None of the doctors had any hope of her ever flying again, but it wouldn't be the first time she'd proved them wrong.'

'What about combat flying?'

'Out of the question, especially with something as complicated as Shadow-Wolf.'

'But she could still be weapons engineer or something.'

'It's possible, but unlikely. Just about anyone could do it more accurately and probably faster with the numbness.' The clock ticked closer to three o'clock. 'I have a meeting to get to, but now you know a little more.'

'One more thing.'

'Yes?' Ashley turned back around.

'You said I'd be interested in when she came back on leave, why?'

'She is the one who killed your husband-mostly out of revenge.'

Anger boiled up inside her. The will left Blue Demon to her. She was going to get it back, and this Wolf-woman would pay dearly

★   ★   ★

Mr. Brad drove the jeep out to the canopy. 'Tell me one more time why you want to stay out here. You said yourself that there isn't a much safer place and all you're going to do is get a sore back.'

'I just think it's a good idea. Something has felt wrong all day.' Kiba replied from the side of him.

She rarely did something without a good reason, and Kiba's sixth sense had saved them before, so they didn't tend to doubt it.

'Mr. B, hurry.' Kiba's concern for her boy's safety suddenly increased. Someone was out there, she just knew it.

'I'm hurrying already,' Mr. Brad replied grumpily as he pushed harder on the accelerator.

Upon entering the large willow tree, the two climbed out Mr. Brad noticed the eerie blue glow inside the cockpit. 'Funny, I was almost positive we turned everything off.' He walked toward the sleek navy blue helicopter. 'Kib, we shut down the computers didn't we?' No answer. 'Kib?'

Kiba had an absent faraway look about her.

'You ok, Kiddo?'

★   ★   ★

Adam trudged across the landing wearily. Domanick was crying again, but for the life of him, he couldn't understand why. He'd been fed, changed, bathed, and seemed perfectly fine when he had put him to bed.

'It's ok' he soothed. 'It's alright.' Maybe he should have stayed at the canopy and let Kiba take care of Domanick; they seemed to get along perfectly.

He wondered how things were going at the canopy. Thinking about radioing them, he decided against it. It was too late.

Adam took Domanick down into the living room. He picked up Kiba's white guitar and began to play something that always seemed to get him to sleep, but nothing Domanick just kept on crying. He had always had Kiba's propensity to get up early, but lately it was like he didn't sleep at night either. After putting the guitar back, he took him back upstairs. 'Back to bed, Dom.' Lowering him into the crib, he kissed him goodnight and stroked his blonde streaked, baby hair until he went to sleep. Tiredly, he went back to the master bedroom. Slipping under the covers, drifting back off to sleep.

★   ★   ★

'Kib?' Mr. Brad repeated.

Kiba blinked a few times before answering. 'Fine. I'm fine.'

'Did we leave the computer on when we were here yesterday?'

'No.'

'You sure? Cause they're on now.'

'I know we didn't,' she answered definitely.

Mr. Brad's voice quieted to a whisper. 'You think someone was . . . or is here?'

Thermal scans indicate life human life form two hundred yards out.

'Mr. B, there's someone out there. Two hundred away.'

At night in the middle of Sherwood Forest was like an eternity away without the proper equipment, but to be out there whoever it was probably had a good reason for being there. Why else would anyone be out there at two in the morning?

They both slipped into the darkness. Time passed slowly, minutes ticking away like hours. By morning nothing had happened.

'You think it's alright?' Mr. Brad asked.

Any life scans? Kiba mentally questioned.

Running scans . . . No life forms.

'We're ok.'

They stepped from the shadows, rolling the tension out of their shoulders.

'I'm getting too old for this,' Mr. Brad muttered.

Kiba couldn't say she didn't feel the same way. A night in a cold forest with only the grassy floor as a bed wasn't going to be nice to anyone's body.

Finally convinced the danger had passed, Kiba went back to the jeep.

'I'll stay here,' Mr. Brad volunteered,

'You sure? I mean I could–'

'I'm sure' He nodded, and with that Kiba drove back to the hangar. Adam was just unbuckling Domanick from his seat on the Jet Ranger. Chezia and Dante were already inside.

'Everything go alright?' Adam asked.

'For the most part' Kiba answered. 'We almost had a visitor, but they chickened out two hundred yards away. How about you? Did Domanick behave?'

'He was kind of fussy in the middle of the night, but nothing major.'

'I'm gonna go and pick up dinner,' Chezia announced, 'and I think Dan wants to come with me.'

'Alright, see you two later.'

Kiba studied the schedule on the wall.

'I'll take the charter at two,' Adam said.

She looked at him in surprise. 'I thought I was going to take that one.'

He shrugged. 'Ok, I want to take that one. I need some time out.'

She could understand. In the air it was just so free, and he had done a lot of babysitting lately. 'Alright.'

★　　★　　★

Kiba was working on the paperwork in the Brad's Air Service office when Domanick started crying again. 'What now?' she murmured, abandoning the unbalanced bank work. She couldn't ignore the tearful blue eyes that pleaded for her to come, but she wasn't getting anything done, and the random on and off crying was starting to get to her. 'What is it?' she asked cradling the crying baby in her arms. Then the phone rang. 'Brad's-'

She was cut off. 'I know who you are and where you work,' her voice was as solid as stone. How could she be on the phone with the woman that had killed her husband when all she wanted to do was slit her throat? she questioned herself. 'If you want to see your sister, brother, husband, or father again, I suggest you get back to Nottingham in two hours.'

'Where?'

'I think you would know the place well, you did stay there last night. Remember, come within an hour or all of your family will be delivered back to you piece by piece.' Then the phone went dead.

She shifted the crying baby. He always seemed to cry right before something bad happened, nonetheless she had to go. She couldn't let the family she'd spent so many years piecing together be taken away from her like that, but sure wasn't going to take Domanick into this. With any luck, they didn't know about him yet, and she would like to keep it that way.

She took out her mobile and dialled Jason's office.

Alex picked up. 'Hello White'

'I need you to watch Domanick. There's a problem at the canopy.'

'Do you want Hit-Rhino?'

'No,' she answered immediately, 'all that would do is get them killed for sure. All I need you to do is take care of Domanick and make sure nothing happens to him.'

★　　★　　★

The Jet Ranger dropped down onto the grassy clearance near the canopy, and she climbed out.

'Wolf!' Danica greeted coldly.

She stared back at the woman in front of her. She didn't know her, she'd remember if she did, but something about her looked familiar. Wavy blonde hair cascaded across her shoulder as she jerked her head in the direction of the willow tree.

'Stand over there,' her American accent was evident.

'Now, Wolf . . . Michael, Chezia, Adam, Dante or the helicopter? You have five choices, but you only get to keep one.'

Blonde hair, American accent, how did it fit together? 'You couldn't get Shadow-Wolf out of here even if I did let you have him.'

'Don't be so sure.'

'It's not a normal chopper,' she warned.

'You don't think I know that? My husband trained me to fly Blue Demon!'

'Blue Demon—that's what dad called—Mum!'

'I'm surprised it took you this long to figure it out'

'But you left, you don't deserve Shadow, he's mine dad made sure of that'

'Will you be quiet! Now, if you don't mind getting back to business, who will you let live? Michael who raised you like a daughter, Chezia your long lost sister, Dante your brother, or Adam your husband? Unless of course, you wish to let them all die, but keep Shadow-Wolf, as you call it, for yourself.'

Silence filled the air. She couldn't choose just one of them, and she couldn't risk Shadow-Wolf getting into the wrong hands. What was she to do?

She only saw Danica as an enemy. If that was the case, the odds were in her favour, but what if she had backup?

Shadow, are there any other threats detected?

Threats detected–eight. Orders?

'Damn,' She inaudible muttered. Eight would be a lot to take out; she definitely came prepared. Stay on standby and wait for orders.

Confirmed

'So, Wolf, who will it be?' Danica asked impatiently.

She took a bold step forward.

'No farther,' she warned

She stopped. 'Can I have a moment? I'll regret not saving any one of these people for the rest of my life.'

'One minute,' she gave, 'If you haven't made a decision by then, they'll all die.'

She sure didn't give her any extra time to think. Shadow, alert Jason and . . . she thought better of the idea. Jason would send in Hit-Rhino and they'd all be killed for sure. Don't alert Jason.

Cancel alert, he confirmed.

Contact Simon Kenty, tell him we're in trouble, but not to tell Jason

Confirmed. Sending message.

She estimated having about twenty seconds before she had to make the decision that could very well be fatal to part of her family. She stalled, taking all the time she dare, hoping Simon could get there sooner than she knew was humanly possible. Her time was up and she knew it; she would just have to take her chances.

'I'll take Chez.'

'Fine. Take your sister,' she said shoving Chezia toward her. 'It won't do you any good anyway.'

Shadow-Wolf, lock hatches, she mentally commanded.

Hatch locked.

Now without the correct finger prints she couldn't even get inside Shadow-Wolf that at least was a step in the right direction.

'Chez,' she whispered, hopefully unnoticed by Danica, 'We gotta take her, but there are eight more hidden.'

'How'd you know?' Chezia asked. She didn't see anyone else.

'Later.' Together, they stepped forward toward Danica. She didn't wait for them to take the first swing. Instead, she struck out at them viciously and signalled for her backup to take over. Sisters standing back to back, they fought the incoming onslaught.

Mr. Brad and Adam quickly rid each other of the ropes that bound them and joined the fight. Dante started to scramble behind a tree when he noticed the burly man heading for Adam. He jumped onto the man's back and pounded against him. He threw Dante off to the ground and continued after Adam.

Mr. Brad took a hard swing at him, leaving him unconscious on the ground. Two more came. One took Mr. Brad by surprise while the other came for Adam.

Kiba choked out the one going after Chezia then took on another. Chezia covered her sister's back and took out the last attacker. Kiba turned around to see the others. Adam picked himself up off the ground, and Chezia helped Mr. Brad up. She knelt down beside Dante to make sure he was alright.

'He's just knocked out. Actually, he's starting to come around,' she reported breathing a sigh of relief.

The sound of an incoming 4x4 was quickly drowned out by the howl of Shadow-Wolf's engines as he started up outside the canopy.

'Shadow!' Dante cried out, coming to full realization. The Devil was taking off and not a single one of his crew members were inside.

Simon looked past Kiba, Chezia, Mr. Brad, Adam and Dante. 'But if you're here, who's in Shadow-Wolf?'

'We just got him stolen right out from under our noses,' Adam said in self disgust.

★   ★   ★

Alex carried the child back into the living room of the cottage. He'd decided the cottage would be just as easy to babysit at as the hangar, if not more comfortable, but he couldn't help wonder what Kiba's problem at the canopy was. Maybe they should go check it out anyway.

★   ★   ★

Shadow, Kiba tried reaching him unsuccessfully. Shadow listen to me, Shadow-Wolf . . . Don't take orders from your current pilot. She's only out to hurt you and us. Come back, shut down, whatever you can do.

Error. Cannot take separate orders at once.

It made sense, if Graham had been training her for this like she said, she would have been put in the computer system. She just had to figure out some way to get her boy back. Override pilot, She tried.

Can't override.

'Mr. B, get Jason. Have him activate a tracking signal on Shadow-Wolf so we can find him.'

★ ★ ★

'White,' Alex radioed the Jet Ranger. 'White, come in.'

'I'm here.'

'How do you get this kid of yours to be quiet? He was fine until ten minutes ago. Does he have your bad luck with dreams or something?'

'I sure hope not.'

Adam found himself hoping the same thing, but he was beginning to wonder. Every time Kiba had been having a rough time or a nightmare lately, he'd also found Domanick crying.

'Just do what you can for now. You might be babysitting for a while. Our problem just got kind of out of hand.'

'How out of hand?'

'You don't really want to know,' Chezia said, joining the conversation.

'How, out, of hand?' he repeated.

'If you really want to know, Shadow just got stolen by Danica.'

'Graham's wife? Shadow-Wolf is in the hands of that—'

'Idiotic, psychopathic maniac' she interrupted. 'Could you tell Jason to activate the tracking device on Shadow-Wolf and send a clean-up crew to the canopy?'

'I'll get right on it,' he guaranteed.

★ ★ ★

Danica and her remaining two men climbed out. Ashley was waiting as they stepped off the helipad. 'So how accurate was my information on Wolf?'

'Almost accurate, but she wasn't near as hard to get rid of as I expected.'

'So you killed her? I never thought I'd live to see the day she died.'

'I don't know for sure she's dead,' she admitted, 'But I do know it won't be a problem.'

'If she isn't dead she'll come back for it,' Ashley warned.

'I know, and I'll be waiting for her.'

★   ★   ★

'It looks like Shadow-Wolf did make a trip to Cardiff, but only stayed a day. After that the physical homing beacon was removed. Our records show that Danica took him to North Carolina next, but'

'But what?'

'We have coordinates for the day she arrived, afterwards, the computer tracking device was disabled,' Jason informed him. 'So we don't know for sure that Shadow-Wolf is still there.'

'She knows I'm not dead.'

'So what? Why does that matter? She got what she came for and now she's making a run for it.'

'Danica knows a lot about me, my family, and what my priorities are. She knows I'll come after Shadow-Wolf. All this is just to slow us down so she has a chance to prepare the trap.' Kiba stated as if they were well known facts.

'You don't know that. Maybe she just wanted Shadow-Wolf, a lot of people would be happy with just that.'

'She wants to get even.' Whether right or wrong, she would want to get revenge on anyone who killed her family. Maybe that was why she'd been so determined fighting the storm when looking for Mr. Brad. She wasn't willing to lose another father.

'So what do we do?' Jason said, already thinking through all the possibilities.

'We go in and take him back.'

'If what you said is true, you'd be walking straight into a trap.'

'It wouldn't be the first time.'

'Wolf, there has to be some other way.'

'Just get Chez and me a flight to North Carolina.'

Jason turned to Alex, who started arranging the flight. 'Fine, we'll pick you up from Brad's Air Service in an hour.'

'Alright, bye.'

★   ★   ★

'I can go,' Adam argued. 'I've been doing a lot of sitting out on the sidelines lately and I want to go.'

'You could if it were anything but Danica . . .' her voice trailed off. 'Dad was smart, but mum is prepared. She's not going to let it sit out somewhere, and I'm not going to risk losing you.'

'But this time is different.'

'Maybe, but I don't want it to end the same way.'

'You aren't willing to risk me, but you're taking the sister you spent nine years looking for with you?'

'She wouldn't say no.'

'What's the difference? I'm not saying no either.'

'I can physically force you to stay,' she said seriously. If it were possible, she'd go alone, but she couldn't do it all by herself, and Chezia wasn't backing down. 'Besides, one of us has to stay around for Domanick.'

'Don't say it like that.'

'I'm sorry, Ad. I didn't mean it like that, but we do have to take that into consideration.'

'I know,' he said softly. 'Just promise me you'll be careful. I like having you around and Dom deserves to have a first-class mum.'

'We had that conversation before we adopted him'

'Yeah, and I still think you're the best one for the job, so you better stick around.'

'You know me, I'm always careful.'

'Sure. That's why when you first admitted your feelings you were in the hospital.'

'You were too,' she returned playfully.

He grinned bashfully. 'At least I didn't end up with an infection.'

'I didn't have any control over that one.'

'The doctors seemed to think that if you had stayed in your room and rested like you were supposed to; you probably wouldn't have caught it.'

'Maybe, but then we wouldn't be where we are today and that would be a shame.'

'More than a shame.'

She stroked the sleeping baby's hair then hugged Adam. 'Take care of yourselves. I'll see you when I get back.'

★   ★   ★

The plane took off the runway and into the air. Kiba and Chezia had separate seats for security reasons and because of the last minute arrangements. Chezia was wishing she had gotten to sit next to someone like her sister. Quiet and reserved sounded good right now. Instead, she was stuck next to a noisy business man that wouldn't stop talking to his co-worker who couldn't stop talking either. Thirteen hours was going to be a long time.

Kiba was awoken by some sudden turbulence. The stewardess was obviously panicked as she tried to get everyone calmly back to their seats. Kiba looked down at her watch. It sure hadn't been anywhere near thirteen hours, taking the stewardess aside, she asked what was wrong.

'Please just remain in your seat. Everything is going to be alright.' The stewardess panicked

They were losing altitude, now below ten thousand feet. 'Listen lady, there's something wrong. What is it?'

'Everything is fine; we're just experiencing some turbulence.'

'We're too low, and you're not a good liar.'

'We are flying low because-' the stewardess began

'We're below eight thousand feet. I'm a pilot and I'm not stupid; I can tell you we shouldn't be this low and something is wrong.

She looked slightly less afraid, like a sudden realization hit her that hadn't during her panic. 'You fly?' she asked

'Helicopters mostly, but planes too, among other things.'

'Do you think you could finish the flight? Someone tried to hijack the plane,' she said in a hushed tone. 'We have stopped them and have they contained, but neither our pilot nor our co-pilot can finish the flight.'

'I'll do it.' She was glad she had at least gotten a few hours sleep, but what choice did she have?

She led her to the cockpit at the front. It was a typical Boeing 737 she should be able to fly it without too much problem.

Chezia too noticed the low altitude of the plane and began a search for a stewardess to ask what was up or in this case down.

'This is your captain speaking, we've had a few minor problems, but things are under control. If I could please have your cooperation, I need everyone to take your seats and fasten your seat belts until the seatbelt light goes off. We will now resume normal course.'

Chezia listened to the message, but couldn't help wondering. She stole a quick glance at her sister's seat. No, she thought, That's ridiculous.

Once the plane finally came to a stop on the runway and the stairs were lowered, people filed out. Chezia waited for her sister and waited, and waited. 'Where are you Kub? How do you lose a lass when you're on the same plane?'

At last, Kiba, accompanied by a blonde haired stewardess exited the plane. 'Thanks again,' she said.

'No problem.' She turned to leave and joined her sister.

'Who's the woman?' Chezia asked.

'Just the stewardess. I think her name was Kim or something like that.'

'Since when were you the social one? Last I checked, most people still classify you as the silent brooding hermit who lives in a cottage in the middle of nowhere.'

'I wouldn't push it if I were you. I'm tired and she were just thanking me for flying the last nine hours.'

'Flying why?'

'Attempted hijacking. Now let's find someplace to crash I'm shattered.'

★   ★   ★

'This is Christopher Hanson reporting live from the International Airport in North Carolina where only an hour ago, this Boeing 737 was expertly landed by one of its passengers who reportedly had to fly more than half of the trip alone after an attempted hijacking. The hijackers are being held for trial. The impromptu pilot remains anonymous. Will have a full report tonight at six.'

Jason clicked the TV off. 'Alex!' he yelled.

'Yes'

'Find out what plane that was and have a full report-before six.'

'Aye, aye captain' He immediately handed him a file containing all the information he could find. He knew there was a good reason why he had hired him as his senior aid; times like this reminded him exactly of that reason. 'It was White's plane.'

'Thank goodness it landed alright,' Jason sighed in relief.

'We have good reason to believe she was the one who landed it,' he continued.

That would explain the anonymous pilot. Most people would be glad to have their name plastered on every front page and a main topic on television, but Kiba wasn't that way. And she needed to remain low profile if she was going to recover Shadow-Wolf.

★   ★   ★

Chezia locked the door. 'Are we still planning on going in tomorrow or waiting a day? You do look exhausted.'

'Tomorrow. The less time we spend here the better. If we're late Adam will be worried, and I really don't want to have to explain the hijacking to him if possible.'

She understood well enough. She was sure Dante would want them back too, and Jason would want them back in British territory. A knock on the door interrupted her thoughts

'Delivery.'

'We didn't order room service did we?' Chezia asked her sister.

'No.'

'Sorry, we didn't order anything,' she called through the closed door.

'This room 258?'

Chezia pulled the door open to reveal a man dressed in a long trench coat and a hat pulled low to avoid the rain. 'This is 258, but we didn't order anything.'

The man pulled the trench coat and hat off. 'Not even a Simon Kenty?'

'Simon! What are you doing here?'

Simon came in and made himself at home. 'Oh, I was just vacationing around and I thought I'd come visit the heroic pilot that landed here about two hours ago.'

'Sure.'

'Ok, you caught me. Jason's a bit upset after the loss of Shadow-Wolf and he sent me after you two.'

'Sorry, Kenty, but we've already got everything planned, even who gets what bed,' Chezia said.

'I see. I come in just a little late, and all I get is cold water for a shower and I have to sleep on the floor. Can I feel the love? You bet.' He took a blanket off each bed and two pillows. 'I guess I'll just have to sleep on the floor.' He made himself a pad on the floor that was probably more comfortable than the old mattresses anyway and settled in. 'See ya in the morning.'

★   ★   ★

Early the following morning

Kiba crept quietly along the neatly trimmed grass to the large downtown building. Peering inside, she could see suit clad people bustling in different directions even this early in the morning. About twenty of them filtered out of the rhythm into a conference room lined with expensive computers from what she could see before the door closed. It sure looked a lot like Rhino-Gate headquarters on the inside. Once back to safety of the trees, she radioed back to Chezia and Simon.

'I'm pretty sure this is the building alright, but still no signs of Shadow. How about you guys?'

Simon answered first. 'No sign of him here either.'

'Same here.'

'You guys stay where you are,' she said suddenly seeing a large metal building-a hangar. 'I think I might have found it.' She left their previously scheduled plan in search of the Devil.

Arriving at the metal building, she tried to look in the window, but it was a little too high. Climbing onto a nearby crate, she struggled to see through the small window. A faint blue glow illuminated the hangar just enough for her to see the sleek navy blue helicopter she was seeking. Quickly retreating, she told of her findings to the other two.

★　★　★

'My plan is almost complete,' Danica said all too happily.

'You're sure it will work?' Jack asked sceptically. 'Because if it doesn't, you'll let her and that pretty bird get away.'

'It will work. I'm the rightful heir of Shadow-Wolf, and I will get him. Not even my daughter can stop me.'

'I'll make sure everything is in order then,' Jack excused himself briefly to tend to the details.

'You better not let her get away,' Ashley stated firmly. 'I'd enjoy taking her out personally. Wayne had something special in mind for her from the beginning and I'd like to complete that plan.'

'No. She killed my husband, and she's going to die for it my way. She didn't even deserve to live this long.'

'Can't we do this some other way?' Jack inquired upon re-entering the room. 'You'll kill her, but we'll lose Shadow-Wolf in the process.'

'It deserves to die along with her. It has served her all too well. I have blueprints for another in my desk if that's really what you want, you could make a better one, but I'm personally taking this one and its pilot out permanently.'

One of the assistants walked by. 'Not trying to intrude or anything, but I know one thing that would be more painful to White and her loved ones than even her death.'

'What?'

'Not being able to fly. It's a daily part of her life, her job, and that doesn't even touch combat flying. It would kill her family to see her suffering and not being able to do a thing about it.'

Danica thought about it for a long minute. She wanted her dead, like she'd killed her husband, but not being able to fly sure had its possibilities. 'It's a really good idea, and I like it, but no. She's proved the doctors wrong too many times; she must be killed.'

★   ★   ★

Creeping carefully around, Simon picked the lock and pushed the door open. Kiba took a wary step in both guns drawn, followed by her sister and Simon.

Lets go Shadow

The cockpit came to life with a hum of computers and the rotors started to whirl lazily. Obviously they forgot to take the purple cell rod out, as they started walking toward Shadow-Wolf, gunfire rang out. The first shot ricocheted of the metallic side, but soon moved closer to the crew. Each diving for cover, machine gun fire covered the air between them and the guards.

'Cover me!' Kiba called back as she made a mad dash for Shadow-Wolf. With the lasers she could easily take out the guards, otherwise they weren't going to be able to fight the guards very well.

'Kub no!' but it was too late, she was already running for it.

One of the guards received a radio call. 'Get out of there,' the voice yelled angrily on the other end. 'In thirty seconds that building won't even exist anymore. I told you to stand down.' The guards obeyed, retreating behind another curtain of gunfire.

As the guards left, Chezia and Simon hustled into Shadow-Wolf to join Kib. 'We gotta get out of here. This place is gonna blow in less than a minute.'

'Give me a hellfire'

Chezia placed the red cell rod into the holder and pressed the button 'Loaded.' Soon the door was no longer a problem and they started out. The rotors whirled dangerously close to the walls. One mistake and they'd all be done for with only fifteen seconds left. Taking off they cleared the hangar just before it burst into flames.

'Simon, take over,' Kib said tiredly relinquishing the controls. Chezia overheard the conversation and wondered what was up. Rarely did Kiba willingly hand over her position as pilot; so what was wrong?

'Kub you ok?'

★ ★ ★

Adam shifted the crying infant to the other side of his lap to answer the phone. 'Shh, daddy's got to answer the phone.' Kiba had said something about his crying not being as random as it seemed, maybe he'd ask her about that again when she came back.

'Brad's Air Service,' he answered.

'Is this Mr. Davids?'

'Yes it is,' he answered after a slight hesitation. 'Who is this?'

'This is Doctor Jackson from John Hopkins Bayview Medical Centre in Baltimore, Maryland. I was calling to inform you that your wife was dropped off here a little over two hours ago.'

'Kiba is she ok?' worry seeped through his voice. 'Where exactly are you? I'll catch the next flight out.'

'Currently she is still unconscious. The two friends that dropped her off said that they'd take care of your transportation and not to worry about that.'

'Thank you doctor. I'll be there as soon as possible.'

He gathered Domanick and his nappy bag before calling Mr. Brad.

'Yeah,' Mr. Brad answered sleepily, like he'd just been woken from a very restful nap.

'Kiba's in the hospital. Simon and Chezia said they'd arrange for our transportation and I'm thinking Shadow-Wolf should be showing up within half an hour.'

'Is she ok?'

'I don't know, but I sure hope so.' He could hope so all day, but that wouldn't help what he actually thought. Chezia and Simon weren't much fonder of hospitals than Kiba was and they weren't likely to have left her at one for something minor, much less she actually let them leave her there.

'I'll be at the hangar in five minutes.'

Shadow-Wolf landed by the hangar door and Chezia climbed out. 'Come on.'

Adam, carrying Domanick, and Mr. Brad clambered into the back. Soon they were back in the air on their way to Baltimore.

'So what happened?' Adam asked. 'And wouldn't it have made sense to take her to one of the hospitals there if she is as hurt as it sounds like she is?' Because it obviously wasn't a non issue if she couldn't be hauled all the way back to England.

'Recovering Shadow-Wolf was, to say the least, interesting. She got hit in the machine gun fire from the guards, but she was alright long enough to get us out of there and into the air where Simon took over,' Chezia explained. 'She said it wasn't as bad as it looked, but she was tired from the flight over and the adrenalin rush from Shadow-Wolf's rescue. We were on our way home and I thought she was just sleeping until an alarm in the back started going off, and was soon identified.'

'Yeah, because it told you exactly what was wrong,' Simon interrupted. 'The alarm specifically said weak and erratic vital signs for pilot. We were over the middle of Maryland and Baltimore was the closest we had.'

★   ★   ★

Shadow-Wolf landed on the hospital helipad abruptly. Chezia was tired and had other things to worry about; perfectly smooth landings were not one of them.

'Hey, if she wakes up, tell Sleeping Beauty I'll be in to see her in a little while,' Simon said to the others. 'I'll hide the Devil and contact Jason. We're gonna have to do something about not reporting a gunshot wound, but we didn't really have much time to find a Rhino-Gate clinic.'

'Thanks Simon,' all three said appreciatively.

A doctor met them in the hallway. 'You're Mr. Davids, right? And you're . . .'

'Chezia,' she supplied, 'Kub's sister. And this little guy here is Domanick.'

'I'm Dr. Jackson, White's primary physician.'

'What's the news?' Chezia asked plainly.

'Break it easily as possible or straight out?'

'Straight out.'

'It's touch and go. The wound sure isn't anything minor and she's lost a lot of blood. She also is already showing signs of an infection with a high fever. The antibiotics haven't done anything yet, so all we can do is hope and pray.'

'Can I see her?' Adam asked.

'Sure. She's just down the hallway—room 196.'

Adam stepped into the small room cramped with a variety of medical instruments; his stomach clenched even tighter. She didn't look good at all; he couldn't even imagine the excruciating pain she must be going through.

A red stained bandage covered her midsection and restraints had to be used to prevent her from pulling out the IV during her violent shivering and jerking movements despite the heavy blanket of sweat that poured off her body.

He collapsed into the chair beside the bed and sobbed desperately. Domanick wriggled free from under his arm on the bed. 'No, Dom.' he admonished gently. 'Mummy can't play right now.' He moved to pick him up and remove him from the bed, but he took a firm hold on his mother's leg and refused to let go. He could have easily removed him, but allowed him to stay. He wasn't hurting anything and he knew that he wanted to be with Kiba, It was like Domanick fully understood the seriousness of the situation, sitting still on the bed without uttering a noise.

'Kiba, we need you. Don't you dare leave us.' His brown eyes filled with tears. He couldn't lose her; she meant so much to him. He didn't think he could bear to live without her. Almost five and half years ago, he had lived without her for three months thinking her to be dead, but it had been hell and he had been a total wreck all three months. Kiba had risked her life before, but right now Domanick was the only part of her he had left. She'd been in some pretty bad shapes before, but never before could he so strongly sense that she was dying and there wasn't a thing in the world he could do to help her.

★　　★　　★

Nothingness was such bliss. Free, careless, but she was drawn back to consciousness. Annoying beeping and excruciating pain halted her from allowing herself to be pulled any farther. It was just too much. She permitted herself to fall back into the dreamy subconscious state she'd previously been in. Where she had just started to go was full of pain and suffering, if one thing was for sure she didn't want to go back.

★　　★　　★

'Adam,' Simon pried softly. 'You want to go get some coffee?'

He opened a bleary eye. It was early morning and he had spent another restless night with Kiba in the hospital. 'I should stay.'

'Chezia will keep watch. She's more the morning type, and she's got Domanick all ready too. Come on. We'll just be a few minutes.' He finally coerced him into going.

'Just for a few minutes.'

Just a cup of coffee soon turned into a trip to their hotel for a shower and full breakfast, lately he hadn't been eating but at least Simon could get him to eat occasionally.

★　　★　　★

Pain, pain, too much pain. Why did so much pain almost appeal to her? She didn't like it, yet something more . . . Voices, so familiar, faded in and out of the background. She was cold and clammy, but covered in sweat. What was the problem here? Something was definitely very wrong.

'About the same,' Dr. Jackson reported. 'She'll come around or she won't. I'm afraid it's just a matter of time.' It was the same report she had been giving for two weeks now.

She started to drift off again until something touched her. Small and delicate . . . fingers. Little fingers wrapped tightly around her index finger and held on tight.

'Mummy.'

Mummy. Domanick-he needed her, she couldn't give up yet. Adam, Chezia, Mr. Brad, Dante too. All of them, they needed her.

'Come on, Dom' Chezia called, reaching for the young child. 'Let daddy have some time alone.'

She felt the grip being pulled away, but it tightened again. 'Mummy'

Summoning every ounce of strength she had, she came back to consciousness. There was pain every second of it, dreary nothingness sounded really good right now, but she fought to hang on. Lifting her eyelids like they were hundred pound weights, but she eventually succeeded.

'Kiba!' brown eyes looked intently down at her. Then she was attacked by a wave of hugs. Painful as it was, it was the very best thing she could imagine, and somehow she knew everything was going to be alright.

CHAPTER FIVE

Fight for your life

'When can I go home?'

'Kiba, be patient. Not too long ago we thought we'd lost you; you can't just march out of here like nothing happened.'

She had recently been transferred to DRI, and that had only intensified her requests to go home. 'That was a week ago. I'll be fine; I just want to get out of here.'

'I'll ask the doctor for an estimated schedule,' Adam promised. 'You stay until they give you the all clear though because you won't rest a day. I know you; you'll go straight back to work trying to pretend none of this ever happened.' He got up to find a doctor. 'I'll be right back so don't try anything.'

After he left, she let out a pain filled groan she'd been holding in. He didn't know half the pain she was in and it was best that way. If he did, he'd probably be asking the doctors to let her stay longer and give her even more pain medications. She was hazy enough; anything else would totally knock her out.

'Her muscles have atrophied some from non-use, and she's still on a lot of medications. If she heals exceptionally quickly, another week and a half.'

Adam came back in to give her the news.

'No. I can't take much more of this place.'

'I know you want to go home, but he's right. Another week and a half won't kill you.'

'It might.'

'Oh don't be like that you'll be fine.'

★ ★ ★

The next week, the doctor came in for his daily morning examination. 'Your progress is amazing. If everything continues to be good, you can go home in two days.'

She breathed a sigh of relief. She'd been afraid that they'd somehow figure out the misery she was going through and make her stay longer. Two more days was plenty. 'Thank you.'

'Now, once you go home, you'll still need plenty of rest, a healthy diet, and you'll need to relax and take it easy.'

She nodded in agreement, but Adam could almost hear her thinking, Yeah sure, whatever I do what I want when I want and I don't care what you think.

But two more days and she could go home.

★ ★ ★

'I said if everything continued to go well she could go home,' Dr. Thomas said, 'but I'd like to keep her for observation a while longer.'

'Why?' Adam asked. 'Is something wrong?'

'That's what I'd like to find out,' The older man replied. 'We were planning to release her today, but last night her stress levels were far above normal last night. I wasn't sure if you'd like to tell her or if you'd prefer me to.'

'I'll tell her, but she's not going to like it.'

'I understand. We'll try to get her out as soon as possible, but those readings being so high could point out an underlying problem.'

'Alright,' Adam replied. Kiba wasn't going to like this one bit. 'I do want what's best for her.'

'Can we leave now?' she asked impatiently the second Adam had set foot back inside the room. She had already wasted way too much time here.

'They want to keep you for observation,' he told her frankly. It wouldn't matter how he broke the news she wouldn't like it any better.

'No observation. I just want to get the hell out of this place.'

'Your stress levels were abnormally high last night. All they want to do is make sure everything is alright. So help me Kiba, you make this so much more difficult than it needs to be; just let them help you!'

'I don't need any help,' she argued.

'Maybe not, but you are going to get it. It shouldn't be too much longer; you'll be fine.'

★   ★   ★

Mr. Brad came up to visit her later that evening.

'Mr. B, can't you persuade them to let me go?' Kiba pleaded. 'Nobody will listen to me.'

'What are they keeping you for? Last I heard you were being released tonight.'

'The doctor decided my stress level was a little high,' she answered grumpily.

'That's all? Ok, I'll see what I can do.'

Mr. Brad left the room and walked down the tiled hallway to the nurses' station. 'When he's free, can I speak to Dr. Thomas?'

'No problem,' the cheerful blonde answered. 'In fact, he's coming down the hall now.'

'Is there something I can help you with?' the doctor asked cordially.

'My friend is here, Kiba White,' Mr. Brad began.

'Ah yes, Ms. White. She's a mighty determined lass.'

'She wants to know why her stress levels being a little off are such a big deal. As you are undoubtedly already aware, she wants to go home. She has been here two weeks and four weeks at the hospital in Maryland before that.'

'Normally stress levels being slightly off isn't really a problem, but Ms White is a little different. She was very seriously injured, and we just want to make sure everything is on the mend before we let her go and that she gets the best possible treatment if there are any underlying problems. Besides that, her stress levels weren't a little high, they were extremely high. We can't figure out any logical reasoning for her to suddenly be worked up about. If you saw her charts you'd know exactly what I mean; She was perfectly fine, then they drastically rose higher and higher, only to drop back down to almost normal range again,' he explained. 'All I ask for is a little patience and some more time.'

'Thank you, doctor,' Mr. Brad said politely before returning to Kiba with the answer.

'So?' she queried before Mr. Brad had even fully made it into the small room. 'Can I go home?'

'No. He said they weren't a little high they were through the roof.' He walked over to the bed and looked up at the clock—almost eight o'clock—visiting hours would be over in five minutes. 'Listen Kib, I know you don't want to be here, and I don't blame you, but it doesn't look like you have much choice. I'll let your sister know how you're doing and come by tomorrow.'

'Don't bother,' she grouched and rolled over uncomfortably.

★   ★   ★

She pulled out the IV and grabbed the few belongings she had there. Kiba crept carefully into the hallway and toward the elevator. Pain throbbed throughout her body, but she'd just have to get used to it and take a few basic pain killers; there wasn't enough time to grab anything on the way out. Just outside the hospital she called for a taxi.

'Where to?' the driver asked as soon as Kiba climbed in.

She gave the address to Chezia's flat.

'You sure lass? You don't look so good.'

'Just get me there.'

The driver obeyed, trying to make the best possible time for once instead of letting the meter run. If something happened to the woman in the back he didn't want to be held accountable.

Arriving at the flat complex, Kiba paid the driver and wearily stumbled toward her sister's unit.

'Just a minute,' Chezia yelled upon hearing the knock at the door. 'Alright, thanks Mr. B, bye.' He hung up the phone and went for the door, puzzled at who it could be this late. The only one usually around by now was Simon Kenty, but he was out of town doing something for the Marines.

'Who is it?'

A muffled answer from the other side sounded a lot like Kiba, but she was still in the hospital.

'Who?' she asked even as she pulled the heavy door open.

'Kib,' the exhausted woman answered again. Chezia helped her to the settee, but before she could form a question her sister made her request. 'I need a ride to the cottage. I-I'd do it myself but the medicine' she said woozily. 'Will you fly me to the cottage?'

'What are you even doing here? Mr. B just told me you were still in the hospital,' Chezia blurted out.

'And I told him not to bother telling you. I wasn't going to stay there any longer; they had been going to let me go today anyway.'

'What about the stress levels?' Chezia asked worryingly. 'They were trying to help you.'

'I'm fine,' Kiba assured her. 'That's the least of my problems.'

'You always are,' Chezia retorted. 'It may not be anything big now, but it can turn into something serious.'

'Then I've been screwed since I was ten. It was a nightmare, that's all.'

It made sense. A nightmare would increase brainwaves and stress levels, and Kiba's could be pretty gruesome at times. 'So you decided to just take off?'

'Pretty much,' Kiba replied matter of factly. 'Nobody would listen to me. Now, are you going to fly me to the cottage or do I have to fly myself?'

'I'm not sure you'd make it right now,' Chezia said noticing the exhausted figure threatening to collapse right before her. 'You look pretty tired and I don't even know half the stuff they've got you on.'

'That's my problem not yours!' she snapped.

'Alright, alright, I'll take you, but can it wait until morning? You can crash here tonight; it looks like you're about to do that anyway.'

'Fine,' she subsided, 'but we go first thing in the morning.'

'You want the bed?' Chezia offered. She couldn't in good conscience let her sister, who was obviously in pain; take the uncomfortable settee without at least offering the bed.

'I'll sleep here,' she answered, grimacing as she dropped down into a laying position.

'Suit yourself.' And with that, Chezia went back to bed.

★   ★   ★

Bacon sizzled in the pan before it was added to two of the plates. Chezia finished the coffee and poured it into the mugs.

Kiba pushed away the covers her sister had provided her and groaned in pain as she struggled into a sitting position. She carefully padded barefoot into the kitchen where Chezia and Dante were setting out breakfast.

'So much for first thing in the morning,' Chezia teased. 'I've never seen you sleep so late in my life.'

'What time is it?'

'Just past nine.'

'Nine? We gotta leave now or Adam will be at the hospital and he's going to be mad when he finds out I'm not there.'

'Relax. Five minutes to eat breakfast won't kill you. Here,' she said handing her two tablets, 'You're going to need them and a lot more.'

Kiba gratefully swallowed them without question. She may be somewhat better, but she wasn't ready to be off all the pain medicines.

Next she took a seat and began eating the plate of toast. It tasted so much better than the hospital food. 'Thanks–for everything.'

'What are sisters for? Now let's get you to the cottage.'

★　　★　　★

Adam buckled Domanick into his seat and started up the Jet Ranger. Another one came over the treetops. It was the other Brad's Air Service helicopter. He shut off his helicopter and waited for the second one to land.

'Kiba?' he asked questioningly. 'What are you doing here?'

'What does it look like?'

'I know, but you're supposed to be at the hospital.' His anger returned. 'I know you don't like the places, but you have to stop being so stupid about your healthcare.'

'It wasn't anything to be worried about,' she said calmly.

'Nothing to be worried about! It was too, and you are going straight back to that–'

'It was a dream,' she interrupted.

'A what?'

'The reason the readings were so high is because last night I had a nightmare.'

'That's all? You're sure?'

'Yeah, that's all.'

'I'm sorry,' he apologized, 'but you don't always listen to common sense when your health is concerned, and I figured you were just being stubborn.'

'I know. I'm just glad to be home.'

'Chezia, when you fly back up, will you tell Mr. B I'm taking the day off to look after Kiba? She looks like she needs it.'

She shook her head persistently until a nauseating wave of sickness hit her. 'Go to work. I'll be fine.'

He looked at her sceptically. 'Sure you will, just like you look fine, and you probably feel fine too.'

'I feel like I got hit by a truck,' she admitted, 'Actually, that might have been less painful, and I probably don't look much better, but I don't need you standing over me all day either. I'll stay here and be a good girl' She held up her left fist 'I promise'.

'You win this time, but remember, you promised.'

As promised, she took a warm shower, had a small lunch, and even took a nap, all without even thinking of leaving. What she'd told Adam about not getting far was far more truth than he needed to know.

Jason walked in the front door and came upon Kiba sleeping on the settee. Maybe she's more sick than she admitted, Jason thought grimly, and what she had said didn't sound very good, but she had been know to downplay her injuries before, and being able to walk in on her was a very, very rare event. Making himself at home, Jason poured himself a glass of wine and went to admire the six different guitars, picking up the priceless White 1956 Gibson Les Paul Junior, he began to play a simple tune.

Kiba woke up and rolled painfully to her other side, no more running into the line of fire without a good reason, she told herself, Opening her eyes, she saw Jason. She slowly sat up, immediately regretting doing so. 'Put Fang back,' Kiba demanded rubbing her head 'He means more to me than you do.'

'It's only a guitar Wolf' Jason replied putting the guitar back.

'It's not just a guitar Jason; it's Vergil's guitar, you still owe dad a black 1973 Fender Stratocaster guitar which you smashed up . . . Now you've got five seconds to tell me what you're doing here'

'I just thought I'd check up on you after you disappeared from the hospital last night. I wanted to make sure you were alright.'

'I'll live.'

'You sure? Honestly, you don't look very good, and I didn't get any angry glares when I came in.'

He got one now. 'I said, I was fine.'

Jason still looked sceptical.

'Look, if you have something to say. Say it; otherwise you can go ahead and leave. You've done your good deed and now you can go tell everyone how bad I look.'

'Alex went on a date last night, but swore he'd be on time this morning. On time was five hours ago and he's still not back.'

'Who was he on a date with?' Kiba asked drearily.

'You know Ashley Barnes right? The deputy head of Group-Rhino well, he went on a date with his sister'

'You shouldn't date the sibling of someone who owns a gun, it's like an unwritten rule . . . But then again we're talking about Alex here so Ashley's shot him'

'This is serious, I think you need some medical attention, and I'll get a hold of the others to look for Alex.'

'No medical attention.'

'Wolf, go look at yourself, you need it.'

'No. I promised Adam I would be fine and I would stay here. I intend to do both of those.'

Jason shook his head. 'Fine, but you aren't going to be there flying Shadow-Wolf. You're not in near enough good condition to fly so don't get any ideas, and please Wolf, take care of yourself.'

'Thanks for your concern, but I'll be alright.'

Jason climbed back into his waiting Rhino-Gate helicopter, and Joshua took off.

Alone again, Kiba let out a moan of pain; she couldn't understand why she wasn't healing as fast as she usually did. If anything, she felt worse. Maybe it was being off all the painkillers at one time, yeah that was it. She trudged off into the kitchen to look for some medicine; there had to be something useful in there somewhere.

★   ★   ★

'Alex's gone missing?' Adam asked. Alex knew too many secrets and too much about Shadow-Wolf to just go missing, and he had promised he'd be back on time; something was definitely wrong.

'He said he'd be at work before eight, and he never showed up,' Jason explained.

'You don't have any clues as to where he might be?' Adam asked.

'He had a date last night at Piccolino in Sheffield. That's the last thing I heard from him'

'Alright. We can go check there, but without something else there isn't much chance of finding him.'

★   ★   ★

Chezia dressed up in a pink evening gown with strapped gold coloured heels. She was just finishing her hair when Adam returned to the hangar, dressed in a becoming dark suit.

'Ready?'

'Almost,' she answered.

They planned to dine at the same restaurant Alex and his date had the previous night, hoping to dig for some clues without being too conspicuous. Kiba wasn't well enough to go, or even babysit for that matter, so Mr. Brad volunteered to watch Dante and Domanick while Chezia and Adam went out.

It wasn't long before they were handed two menus. They ordered from the list of exquisite entrees.

'It will be just a few minutes,' the waiter informed them as he picked up the menus.

As soon as he was gone, Chezia queried, 'Where do you suggest we start?'

'Don't worry,' Adam answered, 'I have a plan.'

After dinner that night, they both climbed into the Brad's Air Service jeep. Arriving back at the hangar, Chezia offered to fly Adam back to the cottage.

'Thanks, but I should be alright.'

'I can fly you there and bring the chopper back,' she said, 'since we flew in together this morning there's still one at the cottage.'

'Ok then.'

Together they picked up the kids and flew toward the cottage. Darkness had settled over the area long ago, and the only visible light was a single light in the kitchen. 'Maybe she already went to bed.' He lifted Domanick from his seat. 'Thanks for the ride,' he said as he headed in.

Chezia waited on the jetty for Adam and Domanick to reach the cottage, and then began to restart the helicopter, waiting for the long rotors to gain speed when she heard a terrified yell just beyond the door.

★　　★　　★

Chezia quickly flung open the door, not even thinking to shut off the helicopter. She rushed inside to hear what the matter was.

Adam knelt down to see if Kiba was still alive. She was breathing, just barely and had a faint pulse. 'Help me get her to the chopper. We got to get her to a hospital now!'

'The closest one to us now is the one in Wick'

Every critical second dragged on endlessly. The miles to the hospital had to be multiplying. Shallow breaths became even less frequent, she was slipping away. Her body temperature had already dropped well below normal.

'Hang on,' Chezia silently prayed. Everything would turn out ok; it had to.

After a tormenting long time, the hospital finally came into view, just a little farther.

'Chezia we're losing her!' Adam cried out urgently from the back.

'We're almost there,' she answered, desperately hoping they wouldn't be just seconds too late.

★　　★　　★

At midnight the phone rang continuously. Muttering all the way, Mr. Brad rolled to the edge of the bed and shuffled tiredly down the stairs. Who was crazy enough to call at this hour?

Panic stricken, Adam was on the other end. 'Mr. B,' he began trying to get his message out before worry overtook him again.

'What is it?'

'I'm here . . . At the hospital . . . in Wick'

'You're where?'

'With Kiba. Come please, there's something wrong, really wrong.'

'Ok, I'll be there as soon as I can.'

'Please hurry.'

He returned to Chezia, Dante and Domanick in the waiting room. 'I called Jason,' she told him, 'he's going to pick Mr. B up at the hanger and fetch him up too.'

'Thanks. Any news?' he asked weakly.

'None.'

He blinked back a few tears, but more fell. 'Please let her be ok.'

They sat in silence for the next hour and half, each wanting to hear some good news, but only if it was good.

'You have any idea what is wrong with her?' Chezia asked.

'No, she didn't feel too great this morning, but that was because of being shot. She never said anything about being sick and . . . I just don't know.'

Mr. Brad came in, jacket half fasten and his dark blue beanie hat on his head rather than spiking his hair. 'Is she alright?'

'I don't know,' both of them answered. That wasn't a good sign. Not even a single encouraging word.

Jason entered the room. Even Mr. Dull looked a little rumpled; maybe midnight hospital runs weren't their best thing.

At long last, one of the doctor immerged from the emergency room, but it didn't look like he had much good news. They all tried to brace themselves for the worst, but they knew what the worst was, and if she wasn't there yet she wasn't far away.

The doctor could sense the tension, but that only made his news harder. 'Well, she's not dead. Unfortunately, she's not much better. We have her on the ventilator and are regularly checking her vitals, all of which are extremely low. As far as what's wrong with her, she appeared to have been shot. Someone's removed two bullets, but didn't do a second check, somehow they missed one. This isn't your typical light machine gun fire. They are filled with slow acting poison. By removing the first two and them being slow release, it appears nobody didn't see the results until now. Currently I have her on just about ever painkiller and antibiotic we have, but nothing has helped yet. In thirty years of practice I've never seen anything like this.'

She wasn't dead, that was good; she was dying and there wasn't a thing they could do about it, that was bad, very, very bad.

'How long?' Adam asked.

'I'm sorry, but a week and a half if she's lucky. Without an antidote, it's like fighting blindfolded; you don't know where your enemies are and how to defeat them.'

'What about with an antidote?' Chezia inquired.

'If she fights and the antidote is strong and given soon, she might make it, but the probability of survival is still only about ten percent,' the doctor answered. 'I'm sorry, I really am. If there's anything I can explain or help you with just let me know.'

'Can we see her?'

'The poison is only spread throughout the body by the blood, so you can see her, but only one at a time.' The doctor led them down the hall in the ICU to a little window they could see her from. 'If you want to go in just tell one of the nurses over there.'

'Chezia, you go first,' Adam told her. 'Kiba would want to see you.'

She politely declined and turned to leave.

Mr. Brad gaped. She couldn't just leave. Her sister that had risked her life countless times for her was dying here, and she planned to just walk out. Mr. Brad didn't care how much she disliked these places or whatever her problem was. She needed to stay. Mr. Brad started down the hall after her, but she was gone. Long gone

'What was that about?' Jason questioned upon Mr. Brad's return.

'She left. She just turned tail and left,' he said frustrated. 'How can she do that?'

Jason gave a puzzled expression. 'I don't know, Michael. I've always considered those two closer than Wolf and I, but even I can't turn a cold shoulder on this one, and I sure as hell know Wolf wouldn't do that if it were Chezia in there. She might not be useful to the rest of the world. But she would spend every last moment she had with her sister.'

★   ★   ★

Simon gathered his bags and started out the door. On his way back to the airport he'd had a nice nap, but it would be nice to get back home. He signalled for a taxi, nothing. He tried again. Instead of a taxi, a different kind of car pulled up. Shrugging, he threw his bags into the back and hopped inside Chezia's car.

'Thanks for the pickup buddy, but I wasn't expecting a pickup. Aren't you supposed to be working? Oh wait; it's two in the morning. Aren't you supposed to be sleeping?'

'I'm not the only one missing out on a restful night, but if you'll fly I can catch up on our way to America.' She continued focusing on the road. Now onto the main road, they headed for the motorway.

'I like to travel as much as anybody and America's alright, but we just left the airport and you can't drive to America. Cars and miles of water don't mix well.'

'We're flying—in Shadow-Wolf.'

'Oh. That's better than the airport anyway, no baggage checks. What're we going for?'

'Not pleasure. By the way, don't get shot, even a graze could kill you.'

'I wasn't planning on getting shot, but I don't think a graze would literally kill me.'

'It could if this doesn't go well.'

'What'd you mean?'

'Kub got out of the hospital yesterday; she's back in today.'

'Why?' Simon queried.

'Those bullets are filled with slow acting poison.'

'Not cool. She's gonna be alright though, right?' he asked, his voice full of serious concern.

'I hope so; that's why we're going to America. We have to find a cure.'

'That bad?'

'The doctor gave her maybe a week,' Chezia answered gravely.

'Let's get going then; the clock is ticking.'

Chezia pulled into the entrance of the willow tree. Before long, both of them had changed into their flight suits and done a thorough pre-flight check. Pulling him out from his cover each climbing in, and started up the clearance.

★   ★   ★

The nurse rushed out of Kiba's room. 'Dr. Rogers, Dr. Rogers! We need you in the ICU!'

'Who?'

'White, Kiba White.'

Joining the hustle, he came in.

'We're losing her!'

★   ★   ★

Adam walked numbly out of the room.

'How is she?' Mr. Brad asked, somehow missing the flurry down the hallway.

'Worse.'

What could they do to get her back? They had to do something. Adam was already a wreck, and wouldn't be much better. Even Jason had had better days. Kiba had battled some pretty fierce things, had close calls with death more times than anyone wanted to count, but at least the doctors had been able to try something. Now, it was a matter of how long she hangs on, and there wasn't anything in the world for her to hang onto . . . this time.

★   ★   ★

'America's coming up,' Simon reported. 'Let's go in now. We can't afford to wait.'

'I'll go in,' Chezia volunteered, 'you can stay and provide a diversion.' A beep from the communications panel warned them of the incoming transmission. 'It's Donavon.'

'Hi Jacob,' Simon greeted, 'we're currently a little busy.'

He ignored them. 'How fast can you get to America?'

'Pretty fast.'

'Alex's being held captive there by someone named Danica . . . Who wants to make an exchange.'

'What exchange?'

'Shadow-Wolf for Alex and an antidote, she said you'd know what she meant.'

'I do. Where do we make the exchange?' Simon asked.

'By the status of Liberty. Simon, you can't let her have Shadow-Wolf, but you've got to get Alex back; I don't know anything about the antidote.'

'It's for White'

'I just heard from Jason. White's probably only got a few hours; she's going down hill fast. The doctors are doing all they can just to keep her alive and she's definitely not doing any better.'

'Sounds like we had better get a move on then.'

'By the time you get there; it'll probably be too late already,' Jacob told him. 'She won't be able to hang on long enough for you to get there and back.'

'We're already in America. Got to go, Jacob.'

Somehow, they had to save Alex, get rid of Danica, find the antidote, and get back with it before Kiba was dead, and right now it didn't look like that gave them very long.

★ ★ ★

It didn't matter anymore. She was beyond pain, beyond everything. It didn't matter whether she fought or gave in; she was here, wherever here was. A sudden jolt brought her back to semi consciousness. Even it was painful. She could feel herself slipping away again and with it all the pain, another jolt. More pain. Why did they want to bring all this pain back to her? She wanted to let it go. She finally knew she was dying. There it was, they wanted her back, but there was nothing left, no power, no life, no willpower. She'd finally gotten too far over her head; she just couldn't handle the pain anymore. Adam, Domanick, they were there; they wanted her back, needed her, but she had nothing left to give. She'd already given it all she had.

'I'm sorry,' she whispered, and the slow beeping for the heart monitor turned into one long mournful siren.

'Bring her back!' the doctor ordered and started giving directions, trying to keep her alive, but there are some things only God can do.

★ ★ ★

Shadow-Wolf landed near the statue of Liberty and Simon climbed out. 'You win Danica. Give me the antidote and Alex and you can have Shadow-Wolf.'

Alex struggled in her men's grasp.

'Why Simon? You know you can't get back in time to save Kiba White. Call now; I'm sure you'll find she's already dead.'

'Just give them to me, and it won't matter to you anymore. I told you, you win, but I still want Alex and I doubt you're going to sweeten the deal any.'

'Have it your way, but don't worry about your friend. I took the liberty of calling my friend at the hospital, and he said Kiba White died just a couple minutes ago.'

Simon pretended that didn't hurt him. 'I'm sorry to hear that. White was a good pilot, but at least now I can have the pilot's seat full time.'

'Forget so soon? You gave Shadow-Wolf to me. Personally, if I were you I'd stay in America. Your country is going to be experiencing heavy missile fire.' She tossed her head defiantly and hoisted herself into the pilot's seat. 'Have your antidote and your boy. I'm the new chief pilot of Shadow-Wolf.' She sat down in the seat and closed the hatch door.

Like a wolf waking from his slumber, Shadow-Wolf growled and came to life, but not without question.

Chief pilot—Danica White. Error. Does not match. Chief pilot Kiba White

Orders?

Nothing.

Orders? It was like a young child without parents, no one to turn to. The programming told her to use a secondary pilot if the primary wasn't available. But which one? There were several secondary's that wanted different things. Chief pilot, Kiba White?

★   ★   ★

'Mummy!' Domanick wailed.

Adam tried to hush him. 'Shh, no mummy. You have to be quiet.' He continued fussing. He took him outside. How could he explain to a child only two that his mother was probably already dead? He couldn't understand it all himself. 'Dom, mummy's gone and she isn't coming back.'

'Mummy,' he insisted then remained quiet. Finally he took him back inside.

'What was that about?' Jason queried.

'He wants to see Kiba. Can you make it happen?'

'Adam, what difference did it make? She's gone. I could hear the heart monitor myself.'

'I know,' Adam answered, 'but I need to see her one last time.'

Domanick sat on the bed next to the lifeless, dull body.

She'd spent too much time here; Adam reflected sadly, this wasn't what she would have wanted. He knew she would have preferred to die just about any place other than a hospital, and yet, It was too late for that now.

★　★　★

Opening bright blue eyes, Kiba found herself on the floor, sitting up she looked around. She wasn't in the hospital bed anymore; she wasn't even in a hospital so where was she? Limbo maybe, just a plain white scenery nothing but herself as company, turning around as if she was expecting someone to be there but no one was there…

Crossing her legs and resting her head in her right hand as the other relaxed over her legs she waited, and waited hoping she wasn't alone; out of the blue she heard a voice, a voice so familiar yet distant.

'Hi Red' the sixteen year old greeted as he sat down beside her.

'Vergil?'

'Last time I checked I was…How've you been?'

What do you tell a lad who's been dead for nineteen years? 'I've been good…Where am I? Limbo or something?'

'Yeah, they say when you die you come here for a while, you either meet an angel or your hero and they tell you whether you're ready to go to Heaven'

'I can't go yet Fang, I haven't found dad's killer yet…'

He gave a slight smile, 'I know you haven't, this is why I've been trying to help you out'

'Help me out?'

'Yeah...Ever noticed how you always get yourself into life threatening situations and survive, how you've cheated death more times than anyone can count...I've been there Kib, been protecting you'

'For how long?' she asked

'Remember that road accident you were in on your motorbike when you were helping that woman out with her baby that was left at the hanger?'

'Zaria's baby, when I climbed out from under the truck...that was at least five or six years ago'

'And the time you and Adam were in the hospital after Nathan double crossed you in Germany, and when you were stopping that drug run and everyone thought you were dead'

'So you've always been there...Tell me something Vergil, Shadow-Wolf when you were helping dad, could you-'

'The only thing I did was pick the colour, everything else was you and Dad'

'This may sound crazy but I can communicate with him, Is that-'

'Best bet is to ask dad...' he smiled.

'Dad's dead...Has been for twelve years...Even if he was still alive wouldn't he have shown up by now?'

'Follow me I need to show you something before you go back' Vergil stated as he stood up and Kiba climbed to her feet. She followed him until they came to a six foot brick wall.

'I don't get it' Kiba said rolled up her right sleeve.

'This is your wall Red, to see your future you've got to climb it'

'I don't want to see my future...It's just going to be pain and suffering, like it's always been'

'You wouldn't know unless you climb it...Look at it as an obstacle in life, you can either run away from it or you can learn from it' he said as he cupped his hands together.

'I'm twenty-nine Vergil, there's no way you can hold my weight...'

'Trust me.' Not knowing what else to do she put her foot in her brother's palms as he lifted her up, grasping onto the wall she pulled herself up about to give her brother a hand up until she saw what her future really looked like.

'It's not good is it?' Vergil asked as he too climbed the wall, finding his sister sat with her knees close to her chest, her head resting on her folded arms. 'Kib...Kib?'

'I didn't expect it to be like this...' she whispered as she looked out onto the sea of souls.-lifeless souls all walking in the same direction as if they were off to war.

'Nobody does Kib, they expect something less-'

'So it's true what that Burmese leader said then... About the path I walk on has no end, no matter how far I go, or how many corpses I crawl over. The killing will never end!'

'You kill because you're protecting people-' he stopped mid-sentence as he pointed to something running in the opposite direction. 'Is that?'

'Vamp...someone else I made up' Kiba explained as she looked up

'What happened to Jimmy?'

'He died...' was all she said as she put her legs down dangling them over the wall, Vergil did the same. 'Vamp looks like me, talks like me, acts like me-'

'She's a reflection of who you think you are' Kiba looked at her brother 'Kib, you feel dead inside because of all the killing you've done, and all the pain you've been through, that's why you're make-believe friend is a vampire because they're already deceased'

She looked back at Vamp again, she had the power to disappear then reappear again in a different location weather near or far. 'What is she doing?'

'Saving someone, People do that when a loved one is in danger, they bypass everything just to help them...Much like you Kib'

'So what happens now Fang?' she asked changing the subject as she looked at him again, 'I mean you've shown me my future and you're my guardian angel, do I go back or go to Heaven?'

'Your time's not up yet, taking you to Heaven now would break your promise you made to dad, anyway you have a son who is calling you' he swiped his hand back and fourth as if he was washing a window and shown her what was happening below them.

'Mummy woof' Domanick cried, gripping his mother's hand tighter,

'He's a miniature you, He needs someone to be there for him, to help him when he's in trouble...he needs you to be his hero Kib'

'Mummy woof' Domanick cried again,

'But I'm not a hero Vergil'

'Don't make the same mistake I did Red...Domanick is your son, and you will do anything to protect him, you are Kiba Danger White and you are a hero, a very good one... Now go, before it's too late' he stated as he jumped off the wall and walked towards a seventeen year old boy. 'I'll look after Matthew for you...Oh and remember what dad says–'

'Don't do anything stupid Nimrod...How can I forget?' she smiled as she too jumped of the wall

★   ★   ★

'Mummy woof.'

'No, mummy can't play dogs today,' Adam gave the slightest half smile. At least he still had Domanick.

'Mummy woof.'

'Do you woof like a dog?' he played, Kiba would want him to, or at least prefer that to him crying over her

He looked frustrated. 'Mummy woof'

'Mummy's wolf,' Kiba struggled. Every force in earth seemed to be against her,

He gave her a wide smile. 'Woof.'

Was something wrong with Shadow-Wolf? Maybe, that was where Chezia had gone; she tried to find some antidote. She knew her sister had tried, it was comforting to know she hadn't just left.

Orders?

'Chez . . .'

Chez, scanning . . . Closest file reference to Chez, Chezia White.

★   ★   ★

Orders?

What was that? Random words appearing in her head, now that was odd.

Orders? Shadow-Wolf repeated.

'Duh, it's Shadow,' she scolded herself. Kiba had said something about him talking to her. 'How could I be so stupid?'

Danica whirled around to see Chezia in the back. 'I should've known you'd come along.'

Open right door, she commanded.

Hatch open.

The right door flew open with a powerful whoosh, and the second Danica made the mistake of turning around to see what it was, Chezia ended their problems with her mother.

Simon and Alex took advantage of the situation and climbed in.

'What took you so long?' Alex asked.

'Let's just say we had a few mishaps.'

'Where's White?'

'Hospital. Hopefully still alive.'

★   ★   ★

'Chez?' Adam repeated. 'Oh, she went after the antidote.' He received no answer. 'Kiba, you still with me?' he whispered. He saw a slight twitch. 'Hang on, Kiba,' he pleaded desperately. 'She's got to be on her way back by now. Just hang on.'

'Adam . . . Can't'

'You can, I'd like to keep you around for a while, so hold on.' he cried, tears streaming down his cheeks.

'V-Vamp . . . Dad . . . P-Promise' she said incoherently.

He took her hand in his and smiled not knowing how to reply to the random words she just said, Domanick followed suit, taking a surprisingly strong grip on his mummy's hand. 'We've got you, but you have to hold on.'

The warmth felt good against her clammy pale skin, something ought to feel good, she thought sourly. 'Dy-ing . . .' her hoarse whisper trailed off.

'No, not dying. Don't you dare,' he commanded frantically. 'Living Kiba, you have to keep on living.'

Don't let the pain change who you really are Wolf, always find something to hang on to Captain Eagle's words trailed into her head. Her life did have meaning again, but only if she kept on living. 'T-ten percent.'

'Forget it, all of it. You never listen to the doctors anyway,' Adam said. He didn't think now was the best time to start. 'Just hang in there a little longer.'

★　　★　　★

Above, Shadow-Wolf landed on the roof. Simon and Chezia climbed out, hitting the ground, running and not the least bit concerned about changing out of their Shadow-Wolf uniforms.

They barged in, ignoring the array of signs that cluttered the floor with various medical information and warnings. Chezia slammed through the heavy door into Kiba's room, skidding across the tile floor as she did so. Steady hands took her sister's arm, quickly administering a syringe full of the medication and praying it would be enough as she did so. 'Hang on sis,' she whispered huskily.

'Have any idea how long it takes to affect anything?' Simon asked.

Chezia shook her head. 'Hopefully soon.' It looked like Kiba was fighting for every breath she took and she was getting too tired to fight much more. It would kill her to be this close to saving her sister and fail by being just a little too late.

Feeling like the rope in a tug of war game, Kiba had to choose a side. So easily she could just slip away, be with her dad and Vergil and never have another pain, but her family wanted her; she would have to fight and it sure wasn't an easy fight to live, but she could imagine the grief that would plague them all if she didn't make it, all the memories she'd never get a chance to have. Dante growing up,

Domanick starting school and Chezia had only been in the UK six years. She was even starting to get along pretty well with Simon. If she could hold on long enough for the medicine to start taking effect, with the support of her family and friends, maybe, just maybe she could live through this too. After all, wouldn't want to disappoint anyone who might be following her record for proving the doctors wrong.

Alert, pilot door still opened.

Starting in surprise, Chezia realized they'd been in such a hurry they hadn't properly secured Shadow-Wolf. In frustration, she started to leave the room, afraid to leave her sister, unsure whether she'd still be alive by the time she came back, yet knowing she couldn't leave Shadow-Wolf unsecure.

Lock up . . . secure systems . . . and override all Danica files, Kiba commanded weakly.

Secured, files overridden. System Standby.

Barely daring to hope, Chezia glanced to her sister, who gave her a weak smile as her vitals started a slow upward climb and her heart rate steadied.

'Don't bother getting up,' her sister murmured, her voice the barest of whispers. Her breathing eased, the weight on her chest subsiding somewhat.

Maybe, just maybe, she thought, she could find the strength to keep fighting. Her weak grasp tightened, just slightly on Domanick's hand. She certainly had enough reasons.

'Here we go again with the don't bother stuff,' Mr. Brad rolled his eyes, 'and I ain't bothering, because it didn't do me any good last time.'

Adam looked confused, 'What'd I miss?'

'Nothing,' Mr. Brad and Chezia both answered, looking at Kiba.

Hanging onto his mother's hand, Domanick giggled happily. It was like even he knew what was going on and Adam didn't, but no one would tell him.

'Oh well, I'll figure it out eventually.' As long as Kiba was okay, he really didn't care if he ever figured it out.

'Let's just hope not under the same circumstances though,' Chezia remarked, wiping suddenly moist eyes, watching her sister's vitals improve out of the corner of her eye.

'Yeah,' Kiba agreed softly. 'I could skip ever having to go through that again.'

Adam still looked puzzled. Shaking his head, he gave up. Whatever it was could wait; he'd had plenty of excitement in the last couple days.

CHAPTER SIX

Midnight Murderers

Kiba sat alone in the dark hangar. Only a single light above was on. 'Why did I volunteer for this?' she asked aloud. She knew why though; Mr. Brad had been grumbling about the amount of paperwork there was to be done and filed for taxes. Having been in the hospital for seven weeks and under Adam's orders resting and recuperating at the cottage for another week, she hadn't been at the hangar to help with much of anything lately. She felt that she owed Mr. Brad for the tireless hours he spent at the hospital with her that was why she was sitting here all alone in the evening, but only sitting. She had done every possible other thing before coming in here, and she still wasn't getting anything done. True, taxes and paperwork weren't her strongpoint, but she'd done absolutely nothing.

A thought occurred to her. Half nine wasn't too late, and she needed to talk to somebody. Picking up the phone, she dialled his number.

'Hello?' a tired sounding answered.

'Hi Jason' she greeted.

'Wolf what's wrong?'

'Nothing I just want to talk . . .'

'Don't you have some paperwork to be doing? Michael already rang and said you volunteered to do it, and don't say you've finished it all because why else would you be calling me at half past nine at night?'

'Y'know I–'

'Good Night Wolf' he finished as the line went dead

She hung up the receiver harder than necessary. That hadn't gone well. She looked at the enormous pile in front of her then back down at her watch. She had better get started if she was ever going to get home.

★　　★　　★

Adam tucked Domanick into a bed and made himself a cup of coffee. Sitting on the hearth, he grabbed his book and flipped to his page. Kiba had been putting off that work all day, but he planned to wait up for her, if she ever came home. She had promised she would do some of the paperwork, and being honest to a fault, she would, but she'd never said anything about doing it quickly.

He had started to doze, long since having finishing his coffee, when Kiba slipped in the door silently. She had started up the stairs when she saw her husband leaned against the stone fireplace, and went back down to gently wake him.

'You're gonna be sore if you sleep there.'

He blinked a few times. 'Yeah,' he said stretching his cramping muscles, 'I think you're right.'

She silently padded up the stairs followed by Adam.

★　　★　　★

Chezia stepped into the bathroom to take a shower; towels littered the ground. Afterwards, she went to fix breakfast, only to find every single dish was dirty. She let out a long breath. Somebody was going to have to start doing a couple chores around here. Dante appeared in the doorway looking for breakfast.

'You do the dishes, and I'll fix breakfast after I take care of the towels.'

Dante mumbled an ok. He didn't want to do the dishes, but this early he didn't want to do anything, and obviously the dishes weren't going to clean themselves. He'd sure hoped, but they still sat in the sink just as dirty as when he had left them. He grabbed the soap and sponge and set to work.

Twenty minutes later there was a noticeable difference in the flat. It wasn't clean, but it sure was a lot better. What would be ideal, would be to have someone to stay home and take care of the house, but Chezia had work and Dante had school so things would just stay the same.

★   ★   ★

At the hangar, Mr. Brad was surprised to find all the paperwork in order and everyone else already there.

He reached for the ringing phone, the first call of the day. 'Brad's Air Service,' he greeted. Only a few minutes later, he was adding work to their schedule. He answered the phone once more on his way out. 'Kib, there's some lad on the phone, and you best not keep him waiting; he sounds upset.'

She rolled her eyes in disgust. Why did they want her? She wasn't exactly known for her tactfulness, so why did all the problem customers want to speak to her? Interrupting her conversation, she walked back inside the hangar to pick up the phone.

'Hello?'

'It's Private Viper,' the tearful voice sobbed on the other end.

'James, are you alright?'

He didn't answer her question, but instead proceeded with his own. 'Do you still work for that special agency?'

No answer.

'Come on Kie, we all knew you worked for Rhino-Gate.'

'Why?' she asked without actually answering his question.

'Because I was hoping maybe you knew some of the higher ups.' Emotion flooded into his voice again. 'My wife Debbie, she's dead.'

Debbie was dead? Why would anyone want her dead? The only reasonable explanation was some accident like a car wreck, something like that, but that wouldn't involve Rhino-Gate though.

'She was killed in her office last night,' he sniffed, 'All the police think it was suicide, and the only fingerprints are hers, but she wouldn't kill herself. She seemed perfectly fine yesterday; I got worried when she wasn't home on time, but you know how traffic is sometimes. Then this . . .' his voice trailed off.

'I'll see what I can do,' she promised.

'Thanks Kie, I don't know what I'd do without you sometimes.'

'Talk to you later.' She hung up the phone as Mr. Brad re-entered.

'So? Any business?'

'Yeah, but I'm thinking more the Devil kind of business.'

★　★　★

Jason sat down in his plush, grey office chair and spun around to watch the activity outside. It felt good to have nothing to do, yet. But if he had nothing to do now, most likely he'd have lots to do later.

Alex entered the office bringing coffee and a message. He thanked him for the warm brew. 'White is on the phone, said she needs to speak with you.'

'Thank you,' he said appreciatively before picking up the phone in his office.

'Good morning Wolf,' Jason greeted.

'For some.'

What was her problem? Wasn't it still kind of early for that kind of sarcasm? 'What do you need?'

'A black 1973 fender stratocaster guitar, remember . . . But more importantly an investigation on a murder.'

Somebody was dead, the question was, who? Even Kiba White, master of covering all emotions common to man, wouldn't be that put together if it were someone in her family.

'James Ward—Private Viper from Burma. His wife Debbie is dead. The police think suicide, but he wants a second opinion. I've come to the best, expecting the best.'

He could vaguely remember her mentioning James Ward before, and he could look it up in their computer files, but they didn't just go around giving second opinions. 'I'd like to help, but we can't send in a team just because he doesn't want to think his wife killed herself.'

'I understand that, but at least get me onto the scene then. He doesn't have any reason to think she was even considering suicide, and judging by the little I saw last time I saw them, which admittedly was a while ago, I wouldn't think any differently.'

Jason looked over his empty desk and thought briefly. 'Alright, I'll see what I can do.'

Kiba hung up the phone in satisfaction. Jason could do just about anything if he put his mind to it.

★ ★ ★

'But being married to an accountant isn't exactly Friday night in Yangon with Chezia White,' he said with a slight laugh, but there was something more to it. Regret?

'At least you're happy.'

He gave a half smile and kind of shrugged. 'We had it all, her and me. But my one night of stupidity with Private Sasha Burns from the Reptile unit, didn't I blow it.' He let out a short sigh. 'An argument with Captain Wolf-Cub, the lass you always dreamed of . . . Then a one night stand with Private Mamba because we had a fight and too much booze, and bingo, our future's down the line.'

'You were apart of Reptile unit James, you knew Mamba longer than Chez'

'Kie, why in the hell are you bringing her back into my life?' he demanded, a single tear glistening in his eye.

'James she's not dead.'

'Kie . . . don't torture yourself after all these years,'

There was no doubt about it; he wished things had been different. He wasn't unhappy with his life; he was content enough with it, and she certainly hadn't helped by bringing back memories from Burma, but he definitely had his regrets.

She should tell James about Chezia but now wasn't the right time; it would just have to wait.

★   ★   ★

Dante waited outside for someone to pick him up from school. At last, Mr. Brad's black and red motorbike pulled up. Climbing onto the back, he pulled on the helmet, 'oh hi Kibby.' He greeted

'Chez is out flying, Adam already took the 4x4 and my motorbike is getting fixed,' she explained.

'What happened to it?.'

'To much racing round and blown my engine' She smiled as they rode in silence back to the hangar. 'I've just got a few things to do' she said as she pulled in stopping at the side of the helicopter and taking off her helmet, 'Mike!' she called out to the other side of the hanger where he was working,

'Kipper!' he shouted back

'Will Dante be alright here with you until somebody gets back?'

'Sure. I see why not' and with that, Dante scrambled off to find something to do.

'Thanks' the phone rang several times before Jason himself answered it. 'Have you gotten anything yet?' Kiba queried.

'I can meet you at the Accounting offices in thirty minutes, and we can take a look.'

'Alright,' she said, about to hang up.

'Wait. Is anyone else coming? You know, for security passes.'

She looked about the hangar. 'No, just me.' Mike and Dante didn't need to be in any way involved and no one else was around.

Climbing back on to her bike she did a 180 degrees skid then raced out the hanger Arriving at the office, she putted off her helmet and leaned on the motorbike, waiting for Jason to show up. Eventually, they were both ready to walk up the stairs to the crime scene.

After checking in with the on duty police officer, they ducked under the blue and white tape into the office previously belonging to Debbie. How did she get involved with this? Jason wondered to himself. Dealing with people that were alive was plenty of work for him; homicides were definitely not the routine work. He wouldn't even be here except under Kiba's requests. It sounded like it was important, but at first glance suicide seemed like the only reasonable explanation.

A cold lifeless body still lay on the floor, a spattering of blood marked the left side of her chest where the single bullet had gone through, but otherwise she was completely uninjured. The murder weapon laid zip locked on the desk.

Kiba took a careful look at the woman then the desert eagle. 'Have they ran an autopsy yet?'

'No we haven't,' the officer answered. 'We were going to earlier this morning until Jason here asked for a quick look at the victim. We thought it'd be easiest if everything was in its original position. Except the weapon, of course, has already been moved.'

After they had begun the autopsy, Kiba came back in to question them and the results so far.

'We haven't pulled the bullet, but it looks to be lodged right about here,' he explained showing his sketch.

'Something's not right here. Either that isn't the murder weapon or somebody else shot her. Most likely someone else.'

He turned back to the pilot. 'Like I said before we haven't finished the autopsy, but I'm more than willing to hear your opinions.'

'First off, if I were going to kill myself, a bullet to the head would be a lot more likely than the chest. Secondly, with that gun, the bullet would have gone all the way through. It needs to be a lower velocity gun or a longer distance.'

'The fingerprints,' he reminded her.

'Could have been staged'

'What about this then?' he said as he shown her Debbie's left forearm, She had a replica of the Coyote unit tattoo.

'Other reason why someone would kill her . . . You said yourself there wasn't any record of her ever owning a gun of any kind didn't you?'

'Yes, but people who are willing to kill themselves don't always do everything perfectly legal,' he retorted, angry that she might just prove him wrong. Who was this woman anyway? She didn't even look like she was with the police, just some green haired lass off the streets. Who was she to waltz right in wearing a leather jacket held together with safety pins, and tell them that they were all wrong? They hadn't even come up with an official report yet, still in the stages of guessing until they finished running all the tests, and she immediately thought she could pinpoint exactly what happened. She probably hadn't much experience with this kind of thing anyway. The only likely way of her knowing much of anything about this was if she'd served in Burma, but she looked a little young for most of that action. 'Your points are possible, Ms. White but where then is the murderer, and how do you find him? Why would they even want to kill an accountant? It wasn't like they had messed with any of the money or books as far as he knew. I'm sorry, but until there is evidence for your hunches,' he stressed, 'We will continue with the theory of suicide. I've got the fingerprints and the gun, what more evidence do I need?'

'I've been around guns enough to know that something isn't right here. Whether you honestly don't believe it, or you just don't want to doesn't matter to me. Do whatever you want. It wasn't suicide, and I am going to prove it.'

'Just how do you plan to do that?' he challenged.

'I have my ways.' She said as she shown him her own coyote unit tattoo.

Jason escorted Kiba out of the building before she started telling her ways. As they stepped down the last couple of stairs, Jason began in a conversational tone saying, 'You really think that was planned?' He hadn't really been able to do much observation for himself to know his thoughts.

'Yeah. I've been shot with one of those before; it's goes all the way through unless you're pretty far away or it lodges against the bone. Neither was the case there. Honestly, do you think she could have shot herself in the chest that neatly and precisely? I personally don't; I'm not even sure I could. One bullet to the head though, and you can say goodbye. Whoever the murderer was had a reason for killing her-'

'The coyote unit tattoo, do you think someone's after the unit again?'

'They're only me, Chez, Viper and Eagle left, if Eagle wanted me dead he would have killed me there and then down south . . . Unless it's someone who's getting back at James'

'Who and why then?'

'I don't know, but I intend to find out, and I'm going to need your help doing it.'

Jason saw the determination glitter in Kiba's eyes. Whoever this mysterious murderer was, he'd better look out because all hell was likely to break loose if Kiba White got a hold of him. 'Who is this James that you are so set on helping?'

Kiba looked up in surprise that quickly subsided; Jason was most likely wanting a personal story not whatever the computer he had undoubtedly already checked had said. 'A good friend and an even better one of Chez's.'

Jason asked for more.

'All the way back in Burma. It was a long time ago, and this morning I got a call from him with the news.'

'How did he think you were going to help?'

'He knows I work for Rhino-Gate, or at least that I did.' Having enough of the questions, she climbed onto the motorbike. 'If you'll excuse me, I have a murderer to find.' She excused herself, throwing on the helmet and speeding off down the road.

★   ★   ★

James saw Kiba coming long before she got there. Ok, maybe he'd been waiting on her, but nonetheless, he greeted her just as she was about to knock on the door

'Was I right?' he asked.

'They still working on getting enough proof to say it wasn't suicidal, but I'm almost positive she was killed by someone else.'

'Glad to know I'm not the only one who thinks that.'

'I want to find whoever did it, but it'll take some time and some help.'

'I'll do anything you need me to,' he volunteered, 'and of course you've got all those Rhino-Gate guys,' he added, soon realizing she probably wouldn't need him to do anything. He did wish there was something to do though. Lately there just hadn't been much of anything to do.

'I know, but there is someone else—Chez.'

He hastily blinked back a tear that threatened to roll down his cheek. He'd just lost Debbie, why'd she have to pick now to bring up her obsession of finding Chezia, the other woman he'd loved and lost.

'She's been MIA since Burma for thirteen years Kie.'

'She's alive,' Kiba insisted.

'I know you think she is alive, but whether she is or not, she's not going to be able to help in this.' He was already beginning to regret asking her for help.

'She lived at my cottage until about five years ago. Actually somebody at Rhino-Gate found her, and I tried to go save her before the jeep or helicopter explosion that almost killed Mr. B and me, but she's back in the UK, and she has a flat not too far from here. I know I should have told you sooner, but–'

'You aren't making any sense. Even if you did find her five years ago, that would have been nine years, and how is she back if you were in the hospital?'

'Jason, my friend at Rhino-Gate, located her. Mr. B and I went to go save her, but there was a bomb in the jeep. A guy named Simon Kenty and Adam went to save her. Her and our brother lived with me at the cottage until five years ago when I went on a mission that left everybody thinking I was dead. Chez got a flat because she couldn't handle living at the cottage, while Dante and Adam stayed. It wasn't until three months later that things changed. Adam found out that we could adopt a kid, and was just about to tell everybody when I showed up. We got engaged and I found out about the kid the same night. Even after twelve weeks in the hospital, I was told I'd never fly again. Adam promised me we'd work through it, and I was getting better, but not fast enough. We worked through our issues though and got married about five months ago, and Chezia stayed at her flat in town.'

He stared in disbelief. So much had changed; he didn't think he'd ever heard her say that much at once, nor that she'd overcome her fear of being jinxed long enough to have a family of her own, and Chezia was actually living back in England again, not MIA anymore. Shocked and surprised, but overjoyed, he didn't fight the overwhelming urge to hug her. 'I'm happy for you, Kie. And yes you certainly may bring your sister in to help, on one condition I get to see her first.'

'It's a deal.'

★ ★ ★

James sat behind Kiba on the motorbike. 'When'd you get this?'

'It'd borrowed; I've got my own but its getting fixed, too much racing round on it' she smiled.

Arriving back at the hangar, Kiba led him in as the motorbike pulled up. 'Coming in now is my husband Adam and our son Domanick. Mr. B and Chez should be back pretty soon, so just make yourself at home in the meantime.'

Ten minutes later, the Jet Ranger landed and Chezia slid out from the right side. James ran to greet her with a hug like it had been a long summer that he had missed her and not seen her instead of nearly fourteen years. 'Chezia White, it's really you.' She had changed some and had scares that she hadn't back then, but it was definitely the same Chezia White he loved.

Her surprised look only grew when she realized who it was. 'James! I haven't seen you in an eternity.' She returned the hug.

'You and I have some catching up to do when Kie finishes with you.'

'When Kub is finished with me?'

Seriousness returned. 'My wife,' he started.

Her heart plummeted at the words. So much could change in so long, but she couldn't help thinking of him as her Private Viper back in Burma.

'Debbie's dead. The police think it was suicide, but I disagree, and your sister agrees with me. She said that you would find the killer.'

She nodded solemnly. 'We had better get started then.' Chezia rejoined her sister inside the hangar. 'We're looking for killers now?'

'Yeah,' Kiba answered simply.

'So what's he look like, all that stuff?'

'I have no idea; I've never even seen the man.'

'Then how are we supposed to find him?' Chezia asked. 'We have about as much chance finding him as we do finding hot coco in the arctic.'

'I've got a plan, don't worry.'

Chezia shook her head in disbelief. 'You better sis, because I'm not going door to door asking for murderers.'

'You been hanging out with Simon again?'

'Yeah, why?'

'You're starting to sound like him.'

Chezia shot her a glare, but Kiba could have done so much better. 'Whatever. Let's go find this Mr. Murderer.'

'First we have to find Mr. Dull.'

Jason sat at his desk awaiting the arrival of the duo who planned to foil a murder case, but for the life of him, he couldn't figure out what they were planning. How do you find a guy that had gone to such extreme measures not to be found? Even if he wasn't as professional as he wanted them to think like Kiba had suggested, he was still pretty good.

★ ★ ★

'Who was the lad?' Mr. Brad asked Adam after James had left. 'Obviously they knew each other, but you should have seen the look on that girl's face when he said my wife.'

'I didn't get the full autobiography, but I think they knew each other from Burma.' He shook his head. 'Sorry, but now you know about as much as I do. His wife was killed and the girls are going to try finding out who killed her.'

'Great. Kiba's going after another killer, she doesn't even know; that's just wonderful.'

★   ★   ★

'No,' Jason stated firmly. 'You're not going in there asking to get yourself shot.'

'We're trying it either way, but I'd be helpful if you were behind us.'

'It's just too risky,' Jason argued.

'Been through worse,' Chezia rejoined.

'Listen, it's an accounting office and they'll need accountants.'

'If they hire someone it happens to be one of us then we can have the inside edge.' Kiba explained 'Whoever it was that killed Debbie will most likely come back unless they just didn't like her, but I heard she didn't have much of a social life, so why would anyone dislike her?'

'Fine,' he conceded. Kiba was right. It was risky, but they were less likely to get themselves shot than some innocent individual who thought they were getting a safe job.

★   ★   ★

The next morning Chezia applied for a job at the accounting office. After filling out her application, she turned it in.

'Thank you,' the receptionist said. 'You should get a call within a week.'

With much persuasion, Simon also filled out the necessary paperwork to apply.

'You did use your alternative name right?' Kiba asked her sister once they got outside.

'Miss Anne yeah I used it, Miss Abby'

'You guys used fake names' Simon whispered in disbelief

'We have to Simon, Can't have our real names on job applications forms' Chezia stated

'Why? And why use them names?'

Kiba and Chezia shown him their coyote unit tattoos, 'That is why we can't use our real names . . . So we used the name that we were going to be called . . . I was going to be called Caitlin Abby while Chez was going to be called Jessica Anne'

'What happened?' Simon asked hiding the smirk that was threatening to cross his face. He couldn't imagine these two exceptional girls having normal names.

'Our parents joined Rhino-Gate' Chezia supplied

'Yeah, and now our names for Kiba Danger and Chezia Princess . . . You say anything about my middle name Simon and I will kill you or better yet let you take this job after all they wouldn't keep you long once they learn you can't add.'

'Then why did you apply? You're not very good at math either, and wouldn't want you as soon as they realise you have green hair'

'What's the colour of my hair got to do with me getting a job!?'

'People expect smart looking not green haired pilots with tattoos covering their arms'

'Do you wanna take this outside?' Kiba argued

'We are outside!' Simon shouted back

'Now, now ladies,' Chezia started, standing between them 'They can find themselves a real accountant once this is over. We just have to have options. It'd be my luck that they'll pick me. I have the ability, but I'd probably go crazy sitting in an oversized office chair at a desk all day.'

★　★　★

A week later

The phone rang and Kiba was the first to reach it.

'Caitlin Abby?'

'Yeah, that's me.'

'You had applied for a job at the Accounting office; I was just calling to inform you that you go the job.'

'Thank you. When do I start?'

'Monday morning at nine.'

'Alright, I'll see you then.' She hung up the phone.

'So?' Chezia asked.

'I got the job.' She was already beginning to hate her own plan.

★   ★   ★

Monday morning came all too fast. Kiba came down the stairs from the bedroom dressed in a bespoke grey suit.

'You look nice.' Adam admired.

'I look like Rhino-Gate, and you need to learn to lie better,' she retorted grumpily.

'I'm not lying. You really do look good.' He smiled before he walked to the other side of the room to finish setting the table;

'I still think you're lying. I can't see why I have to get all dressed up to go to work anyway.'

'Because you're not going to be crawling around under helicopters getting your hands all dirty.'

'I prefer crawling around getting my hands dirty than being all clean and smart.'

'Oh, you'll be fine.'

'Sure, that's what you said before I had to spend another week and a half in the hospital, and I came pretty close to losing all sanity then.'

He handed over the cup of coffee. 'You're doing this because you want to help a good friend, not just because you grumpy old husband made you.'

'You're not old, not even grumpy, most of the time,' she added with a smile.

He ignored her latest statement, knowing he'd set himself up on that one and continued. 'Maybe you won't even have to be there long.'

'Why do I even have to wear jacket? It covers up my tattoos'

'Because you're an accountant and they look smart . . . You can take your jacket off while you eat something. You'll have to leave soon.'

She took off her jacket, rolled her sleeves up and sat down. Maybe he was right. Maybe she wouldn't have to stay long at all.

Domanick ran into the room and sat beside his mum, he smiled as he rolled his own sleeves up on his pyjamas

Kiba chocked on her coffee at the sight of his arms. They were covered from his wrist to his elbow in felt-tip pen ink. 'Geez Domanick' Kiba chuckled. 'You got attacked by your pens?'

'Wanna be like mummy!' he giggled

★   ★   ★

Chezia came out from under the Jet Ranger upon hearing her sister's arrival. 'How was it?'

'How was it? How was it? I had nothing to do all day but add and subtract. Can't we switch or something? Hey,' she said noting how late it was, 'what are you doing here anyway? The hangar should have been closed an hour and a half ago.'

'It did, and everyone went home but me. I've been up here trying to finish so that you can fly home tonight.'

'You about done?'

'Yeah, give me ten minutes and she'll be right as rain.'

'I could help,' Kiba offered.

'In that fancy garb? I don't think so, and by the time you get changed into your overalls I'll be finished.'

'If you're sure.' She still eyed the overalls as if figuring whether she could be dressed in time to do anything useful.

Chezia had never seen her sister this eager for work around the hangar. 'I'm almost done now, so go ahead and get your stuff together.'

'I'm ready as soon as you are.'

★   ★   ★

The next week went pretty much the same way. 'I can't handle all this paperwork all day long.' She slammed the cup down with such incredible force it was a miracle that it didn't shatter into a million tiny pieces. 'I don't care how good or bad of an idea this was, I can't do it any longer.'

'Kiba,' Adam soothed, 'Just give it a little more time.' In all reality, he wouldn't mind her coming back to the usual business at

Brad's Air Service; they could use the help, and she hadn't been in a good mood ever since she had started the job, but he also knew how important it was to her that she helped James.

'Tell you what, finish what you can, but bring whatever you can't reasonably finish home and I'll help.'

She declined. 'No. It wouldn't be fair. I came up with this idea; I need to do it myself.'

'I insist. We all knew this was going to be tough from the beginning, but that's what family's for, to help you when things aren't easy.'

'Alright thanks. You're a lifesaver, and I'm sorry you've had to listen to my ranting.'

'That's another thing families do.'

'Only cause they have to,' she remarked dryly.

'I love you all the same; we all do.'

★   ★   ★

Kiba made her way to her office like she belonged, but she knew she didn't. Nevertheless, she was here, and she had a job to do. She just hoped it was almost over. Having been working there for nearly a month and a half was more than plenty accounting for one lifetime.

'Miss Abby,' her assistant Daniel announced, 'There are two parties waiting for you.'

'Go ahead and send the first one in please,' she answered in a professional businesslike tone.

'Yes, miss'

It was nice having someone to answer the phone for you, but occasionally she had to come up with some excuse just to get up out of her chair, and with him offering to do everything but the accounting work, the one thing she wanted him to do, it wasn't always easy.

An elderly couple came in and took their seats.

★   ★   ★

Chezia drove up to the hangar late that morning. 'Sorry I'm late. What fun did I miss?'

'Just picking out jobs for the day. Everything's been taken but one, so you get to be the lucky one to work on the Spitfire,' Adam answered.

Joy. She was going to have to learn to get to work on time.

★   ★   ★

Waiting patiently on the elderly couple to leave, Kiba jotted down a few notes for her to work out later.

The next customer wasted no time coming in. 'Where's the lady who used at have this office?'

'She isn't here anymore. Is there something I can help you with?' she asked hiding the growing impatience. Something about this guy just didn't add up.

'Are you the new regular round here or just here short-term?'

Inconspicuously, he studied her carefully as she answered. 'I'm the new regular until somebody decides differently, but that doesn't matter; what's your business?'

'I come to make you a deal. Me and my boys got some money. We'd like you to put it in a special account. We'll pay you twice the normal rate for it plus an added bonus, but a few rules are gonna have to slide.'

'Which rules?' Kiba asked noncommittally. She couldn't seem too eager, but this was most likely the guy she was looking for.

'This needs to be a very private account, only me and you know about it. Secondly, I also need it to be insured higher than the usual hundred though,' he continued.

'I can't do that. Even if I wanted to, I don't have enough power to secure anything above the normal limit.'

'Then personally secure it. With what I'm paying ya, ya ought to be able to do at least that much.'

'It sounds like a very interesting deal, but I'm afraid I can't take up your most generous offer, Maybe once my title is a little more firmly established, Mr . . . What did you say you're name was?'

'I didn't say what my name was, and I don't intend to. I personally thing you should reconsider. I'm talking about six digit payloads.'

'Thank you sir, but I think I'll pass at this time,' Kiba rose determinately. 'If that is all, may I escort you out? I have other clients waiting, and I can't accept your most generous offer at this time.'

'Goody-goodies these days. I can escort myself out, but you don't need to be going nowhere.'

'I swear I won't tell a soul about our little discussion.'

'That's very kind of you Miss Abby, but I'd like to make absolutely certain it stays that way.' Not even a second later, he pulled a gun from beneath his overcoat and shot one, precise, deadly bullet.

It was just what Kiba had been expecting, but was it enough to save her life? Despite him appearing right handed, he shot left handed. Normally she would have ducked the other way, but she realized seconds too late. All she could do was hope for the best.

Not a single sound was heard other than the dull thud as Kiba hit the floor. The criminal looked across the desk. She wasn't breathing. Smugly laughing to himself, he wiped the room for fingerprints.

'Don't take another step,' the security officer ordered. 'Drop your weapon and put your hands above your head.'

★　　★　　★

Chezia wiped the forming beads of sweat off her forehead with a greasy hand. Already regretting doing so, she looked around in search of a clean rag. None was in sight. She walked back inside the hangar to clean up. Inside, Mr. Brad flipped lazily through the channels on the TV. Chezia pulled a bottle of water from the fridge and set it on the counter.

'Get me a beer will ya,' Mr. Brad requested.

Chezia responded with a bottle. Just as she was turning around, something caught her eye. 'Hey Mr. B, go back a minute.'

Mr. B flipped the channel back one. 'Oh, I see. Channel 4 has a pretty new reporter,' he teased.

'Shh.'

'Don't you shush me,' Mr. Brad warned sternly.

Chezia held up a hand, signaling him to be quiet. Mr. Brad looked up at the screen Chezia was staring at so intently.

The mid-aged reporter repeated his message. 'Police have arrested Mr. Peter Burns this afternoon for murdering Miss. Caitlin Abby at the accounting office in Doncaster. Is this crime in any way related to the killing six weeks ago?'

Adam caught only the tail end if the report, but it was enough to send a steady stream of tears rolling down his face. Mr. Brad moved toward him, tear drops dripping down his cheeks, but an angry fire burned in Mr. Brad's eyes that threatened whoever this murderer was. 'He better hope the police sentence him to death, or I'll take care of it personally,' he ground out.

James came in from where he had been waiting outside he took a glace at the headlines at the bottom of the screen. 'Who's Caitlin Abby? And what happened to Kie?'

'Caitlin Abby is Kub's undercover name'

Kiba White was dead and it was all his fault. Chezia moved toward him to offer what little comfort she could.

It felt good to be in each other's arms once more. He hugged her tighter, tears running onto the shoulder of the pink overalls she was wearing. He'd never been as close to Kiba as he had Chezia, but he still loved her and didn't want her dead any more so. Chezia tried to be comforting, but knew she wasn't doing a good job. She had just lost her one and only sister. As kids they'd been inseparable. Even as adults, they had maintained the close bond, but now that Kiba was gone, it was like half of her was missing too. James pried himself away from Chezia; it was harder for him to pull away, realizing how much he still loved her, but she wouldn't ever be able to return the love, especially since he was the reason her sister was killed.

'I'm so sorry,' he apologized, wiping the tears from his eyes. 'It's all my fault.' He shook his head silently. 'God knows how sorry I am. I should've never come . . .' he hurried away from the hangar without another word or backwards glance, but Chezia barely even registered him leaving.

★   ★   ★

The phone rang the next morning; Adam picked it up on the second ring. 'Brad's Air Service.' he wretchedly.

On the other end, Jason frowned. Why was he so melancholy today? In all honesty, he hadn't even expected to get an answer at the hangar at all. 'What's wrong?' he questioned sympathetically.

'What do you think?' he flared irritably.

He truly didn't know. 'I don't know. I was just surprised to actually get you at the hangar; I had figured you would be here.'

'Stop playing games Jason. What is it you want? Shadow-Wolf?' Now that Kiba was dead he didn't have any more use for him. Leave it to Jason to turn his back on even the largest disasters and be all business. Why would he be there anyway? What good would being at Rhino-Gate do?

'Don't worry about it though. I'll be by there in forty-five minutes tops.' He hung up the phone, still confused. It was probably nothing he told himself, although he knew there had to be more than that. He shrugged it off and went back to his previous task.

★   ★   ★

Adam tried to bury himself in paperwork, but soon realized most of it was still caught up from when Kiba had worked on it before her short lived accounting career. He wandered aimlessly about the hangar for the next twenty minutes.

Jason's Rhino-Gate 4x4 pulled up, immaculately grey as always. Jason lighted from the jeep doorway, and before he could as much as say a word, a green haired pilot hoisted herself out from the other side.

Adam's eyes grew wide at seeing the sight of his dearly missed wife. 'Thank God you're alive!' he threw himself to her and wrapped his arms tightly around her. 'You're back,' he said as if still trying to convince himself this was really happening. 'If this is a dream then I don't ever want to wake up.'

'Good thing it's not a dream.'

Adam quickly withdrew himself. 'Are you hurt?' What a stupid question to ask, he told himself. Of course she'd been hurt; yesterday she was pronounce dead on the TV, she just came from the hospital. Why would he think she wasn't hurt? Her arm was all bandaged up—maybe he shouldn't have hugged her so hard.

'Not very badly,' she assured him.

★   ★   ★

Everyone gathered around the table at the cottage for dinner. Adam carried out a big dish of food and set it in the middle of the table.

'What is it?'

'Vegetarian Shepherd's pie,' he answered, 'and I'll be the first to admit it tastes delicious. My compliments to the chef.'

'Why thank you,' Kiba appeared from the kitchen. 'Now let's get started. I haven't eaten all day.'

Conversation drifted lifelessly from one topic to the next until finally Mr. Brad asked the question they all were wondering. 'What exactly happened? We all thought you were dead.'

'That's what the news reporter said, and with the perfection of that last kill it didn't ever cross my mind to think differently,' Alex put in.

'I probably would have ended up just like Debbie if I hadn't known exactly what happened to her. This guy came in, right from the beginning I could tell he didn't add up. When I didn't take his most generous offer, he pulled the gun. If I had noticed he was left handed a little sooner, I might have gotten out of being shot all together, but that probably would have cost me my life.'

'How?' Chezia asked. Normally not getting shot was preferred.

'I tried to duck, but the bullet caught me in the shoulder anyway. It hurt like hell, but I was able to act dead long enough for him to think I actually was and press the emergency button of the bottom of the desk.'

'So that's how the police caught the criminal. I guess we just missed the part about you being alive.'

'I had security call Jason when the button was pushed, and he arranged for my short stay at the Rhino-Gate clinic,' she finished explaining. 'What worried me the most was that you all typically make such a big deal over everything, but not a single one of you showed up this time.'

'Believe me, we would have if we had known,' Chezia told her. 'But then again Caitlin Abby doesn't have any family'

'Glad to know I'm not forgotten.'

'Never forgotten,' Adam joined.

'This calls for a toast,' Jason said, holding up his glass of wine. 'To Wolf, to life, and to a job well done.'

★ ★ ★

Kiba looked over the newspaper automatically, not really paying attention to what she was reading until a short article under the main story caught her attention.

It read: Mysterious murder case solved. The murderer, Peter Burns, charged with murder for Debbie Ward and Caitlin Abby, will be held for trial a week from tomorrow. The Accounting office will be closed until further notice checking security and procedure safety.

'A paragraph. For how much news coverage that one got I figured it would be more than a small paragraph under the main story,' Kiba said aloud. It was probably better that way. She didn't want people finding out she was Caitlin Abby and asking her about it, and the less people she had following her, the better safety for Shadow-Wolf. 'It doesn't look like it was Devil business after all, but maybe that's not all bad. We haven't gotten a chance to spend much time at the canopy since that incident where Chez and Simon rescued Alex and got my antidote.'

'Talking to yourself again? Mr. Brad asked. 'Or you talking to Jim-Vamp?'

'Yeah, a bit of both I guess.' She slumped back into the folding chair in the outer portion of the hangar just inside the roll door.

'Y'know, you could stop being so antisocial and come into the office with everyone else,' Mr. Brad offered.

'That's ok. I've been enjoying it out here.'

'You sure you're alright?'

'I'm fine,' Kiba assured him, 'I swear I am. I just haven't liked the idea of stepping back into an office lately. So much paperwork and getting shot sure didn't help.'

'I understand, but remember you're welcome to come join us anytime.'

'Ok.'

The hangar was closed but not locked up yet, but everyone planned to leave pretty soon with that early stunt job in the morning. Kiba skimmed the headlines for anything else of interest. Nothing, she set the paper down and gazed out at the slightly darkening blue sky. If they left soon, her, Adam and Domanick should be able to get back to the cottage just before sunset. Maybe they'd sit out and watch it. Her temporary accounting job hadn't left her much time for those kinds of pleasures, and she wondered how some people could do a job like that their whole lives.

'Same as some people wonder how I get up at five some mornings just to be ready for a seven o'clock stunt,' she thought to herself.

★   ★   ★

Kiba drew the plectrum across the strings one last time to end the song. Domanick toddled across the front porch over towards her, smiling broadly.

'You like that?'

He giggled and placed a hand on the white guitar, leaving a sticky handprint.

She looked at the handprint 'Domanick Graham' she stopped herself, 'You know what, I quite like that . . .'

'Mo!'

'More?'

'Mo!' he agreed.

Smiling softly as she did so, Kiba resumed playing the white acoustic guitar. Domanick dropped down to sit on the ground and stare up in wonder as his mother played the beautiful instrument.

Finishing the piece, Kiba gathered the guitar and started back inside, 'Come on,' she called.

Domanick put the leaf he had started studying down and tottered back inside.

Adam set dinner on the table inside and began dishing out servings for each of them. 'It's good to have you back at Brad's Air Service,' he commented idly.

'It's good to be back, but it's even better to actually get to spend some time up here enjoying it.' It'd start getting cold soon, and she was glad she hadn't missed all the calm warm autumn breezes.

'Well, I'm sure glad you're back in a better mood. You were awfully hard to put up with when you had all that work to do.'

'Sorry,' she said.

'It looks like things can at least go back to normal for a little while, and this time you didn't even have to get Shadow-Wolf involved.'

'True. I was pretty sure it was going turn out differently.' Especially when that shot caught me in the shoulder, she mentally added. All too well, she remembered the pain that coursed through her entire body. It was all she could do to keep from getting caught, and then she had to think clearly enough to get help before she passed out. Enough of that, she told herself, it was time to enjoy time with the family.

★   ★   ★

'Brad's Air Service,' Mr. Brad answered the phone.

'Hi Michael its Jason, Wolf just left and should be on her way to the hanger, when she gets there keep an eye on her'

'What's she been getting into lately?'

'The murderer that she got arrested is loose. He had a few accomplices that broke him out last night.'

Kiba casually ambled across the almost deserted hangar with a new black 1973 fender stratocaster guitar.

'I found her,' Mr. Brad told Jason.

'Keep her in your sight and when the others get back you might want to do the same with them. Hit-Rhino is already after this guy along with most of South Yorkshire police, but no one has even sighted him yet. Every airport, bus station, and train station is on the look out, but if he's got friends in high places, who knows where he could be by now.'

'You think maybe we ought to bring the Devil into the search? He is pretty good at finding people.'

'If we haven't found him by tonight, but right now it's too risky with most the town on lookout as it is.'

'Keep us updated.' Mr. Brad slammed down the phone in frustration. This guy kills an accountant, wounds Kiba, and the police don't even keep tight enough tabs on him to keep him from running away the first night!

'Yikes don't break the phone' Kiba jumped as she put the guitar in the office.

'What's with the guitar? And there's something under that tarp for you'

'Jason gave it me to replace the one he smashed' she asked coolly as she pulled off the green tarp, recovering the newly painted navy blue and white motorbike. 'About time' she smiled as she sat on it and started it up, the engine howled just like Shadow-Wolf.

'They fitted in a bigger engine'

'Nice, So who was on the phone?' Kiba asked climbing off the bike and headed into the office for her leather jacket and helmet.

'Jason, your friend from the accounting place could be coming to visit you.'

'He's loose?'

'Yeah.'

'I risked my neck, got shot, and they can't even hang onto the guy?' she stormed out the office and mounted back on the bike and revved the engine.

'Kib wait!'

'I'm tired of waiting.'

'Kib listen. Jason thinks he's coming after you.'

'If you see him then tell him I'll be waiting.' She pulled on her helmet. Mr. Brad tried to sweet-talk her out of riding off but Kiba raced off out the hanger and down the road.

'Wait!' Mr. Brad yelled after her, but it didn't make any difference.

The motorbike sped around the corner towards the town centre.

Mr. Brad let out a long sigh of frustration and walked back into the office. After scribbling down a quick note to Chezia and Adam, he started up his own motorbike and started toward the canopy. He was sure that was where Kiba was headed, and she probably shouldn't be flying after just getting shot the day before.

Kiba pulled up into the willow tree, pausing briefly to gaze at the beauty. 'Hey Shadow, looks like we've got another little mission if you're up to it.' She started a thorough pre-flight check since no one had done one after the latest incident. It looked like everything was alright, no damage. She went to pick up the navy blue flight suit and change into it.

'Hope you're not planning on going alone,' Mr. Brad's voice cut through the cool darkness.

'This is my problem.'

'Well I'm making it my problem too,' Mr. Brad stated finally. 'You just got shot; you don't need to be flying.'

'It was a graze, and not even a bad one. I'm fine and I am flying,' Kiba said defiantly. 'Not you or anyone else is going to stop me.'

'Then I'm at least going with you.'

★   ★   ★

Chezia landed the helicopter smoothly onto the black tarmac outside the hangar, and her and Adam climbed out. 'Mr. B, we're back.'

Only silence greeted them.

'Mr. B?'

'Look at this,' Adam said as he picked up a scrap of paper with a message scrawled almost illegibly across it. 'Says he took his motorbike to go after Kiba.'

'So where'd Kub go?'

'The note didn't say.' He rifled around on the desk for anything that might give them a better clue as to where the others might be. 'Check this out,' he held a newspaper. 'This says that the murder is being held for trial next week, but whoever was reading didn't seem too happy.'

Chezia picked up the phone and dialled the number to Jason's office at Rhino-Gate.

'Chezia?'

'Yeah.'

'Is your sister there?'

'No. that's what I was about to ask you. Mr. B left a note saying he took the motorbike after her, but didn't say where he was going.'

'Damn,' Jason cursed in frustration.

'Care to fill me in?'

'The murderer your sister helped catch broke out of jail last night and I have a strong suspicion he's coming for Wolf. I told Michael to keep her in sight, so the first think she does is run off.'

'Where is she going?'

'I don't know anything for sure, but my best guess is that she plans to find Peter Burns, the murderer, and take care of things personally.'

'The canopy. She's going to get Shadow-Wolf, thanks Jason got to go.' Chezia dropped the receiver back on the hook and grabbed Adam by the arm, 'come on, we have to go.'

'Where?' Adam asked as he was dragged to the Jet Ranger.

'To the canopy' Maybe they could join them before Kiba got herself more seriously injured, and they could be at least some help.

★   ★   ★

Shadow-Wolf cleared the clearance of the canopy and screamed off through the sky, offering a howl. 'He's ready to go today,' Mr. Brad declared from the back. He hadn't gone along on the last couple missions and had missed it; it definitely felt good to soar through the air with the Devil.

'Yeah, and whoever this murderer is better be too, because I'm going in guns a blazing.'

'Five miles out there's a plane landing. It could be the one.'

Searching the area below, Kiba quickly recognized him as the client she'd had; a string of fire from the lasers sent him reeling backwards.

'Easy there,' Mr. Brad warned. 'Don't get too carried away keeping him honest.'

'There isn't any keeping him honest now; it's too late for that.'

'Kib . . .'

'Yeah, I know.' She punched the buttons, connecting a channel to Jason. 'We've got your man. This time I suggest you keeping a hold of him.'

'Give me your coordinates and I'll be there as soon as possible.'

In the seconds it took her to reach over to the communications board to disconnect the call, Peter Burns had made it to a Huey and had anxiously awaited the seconds until he could lift off. 'Get back out here and into the open now,' Kiba commanded over the loudspeaker.

Instead of obeying, the Huey lifted off into the air and started south.

'Let's dance,' Mr. Brad chuckled.

As abruptly as it had started south, the Huey turned fully around and fired a sidewinder.

Kiba evaded the missile easily and was about to let off her own when two more came hurtling towards her. Burns knew he couldn't out fly Shadow-Wolf, his only chance was if he could out shoot him, and he was going to make the most of his firepower.

'Two more.'

'Radar seeking or infrared?'

'Heat seekers,' Mr. Brad replied. 'Deploying flare.'

'Wait.' Kiba allowed the missiles to lock onto her as target. 'Give me the jet engines, Mr. B.'

'Jet engines.' Mr. Brad confirmed after slotting in the green cell rod

Shadow-Wolf zipped through the air just under mach two, lower and lower to the ground. Finally one missile didn't make it over the last hilltop and collided violently with the earth below.

'Still one and it's right on our tail,' Mr. Brad warned.

'Good.'

The missile was gaining on them, closer and closer.

'Kib do something!' Mr. Brad urged.

She continued to allow the missile to chance after her.

'Missile impact in 5 . . . 4 . . . 3 . . . 2 . . .' Mr. Brad clenched his eyes closed deathly tight and prayed that by some miracle the missile wouldn't hit them, '. . . 1.'

Shadow-Wolf dropped stomach lurching straight down and the heat seeker crashed into the Huey directly ahead of it. The aftershock shook the entire helicopter as Shadow-Wolf persisted on the daredevil course straight down. At last they pulled out and hovered neatly just above the green landscape, the burning Huey visible in the distance.

'That was one hell of a ride,' Mr. Brad commented, as he opened his eyes.

'Yeah,' Kiba said with a loud sigh, 'I guess my problems with him are over.'

'I guess it was Devil business after all.' Mr. Brad looked up at her. They sure couldn't have done it without him. 'Debbie killed at half nine at night and the murderer getting killed not too far from the same time only it's a month and a half later.'

'Let's go home, Kib.'

'Yeah, and get some sleep. I've had enough midnight murderers'. She said yawning tiredly.

CHAPTER SEVEN

Till Death do us part

James slumped back down onto the settee. He needed to do something. The house looked like a tornado went through it, and every day it grew worse, if that was possible, but he didn't feel like it. In all actuality, he hadn't done much of anything the last few days. Derek had snacks whenever he got hungry and ate whatever he wanted, typically leaving empty wrappers or dirty dished throughout the house. He ate occasionally if he happened to be shuffling through the kitchen. His reason for this sudden sluggish, depressive state was still had not happened all too long ago. About two months ago his wife had been murdered. Cursory investigations said suicide, but he couldn't believe it. In his desperation, he went to see a woman he knew would do anything she could to help, Kiba White. At first she mentioned her MIA sister Chezia, and he was worried that he'd made a mistake in asking her. Sure, he and Chezia had been close, really close, but he couldn't honestly hold out the devout hope she was still alive; she would have been in a Burmese prison for almost thirteen years! He soon found however while she had been over there a long time, not quite that long. After spending nine years searching,

Kiba finally found her sister; he was happy for her, although a little ashamed that he had given up hope on the women of his dreams. Things between him and Chezia would never be the same again though, they couldn't be. Kiba was dead and it was all his fault. She was killed by the same one that had killed Debbie. Chezia could never forgive him; she owned her life to her sister, but she wouldn't even be able to start repaying her because Kiba was dead. What could you do to help a dead person?

James thought about flipping through the TV channels, but decided against it. There probably wasn't anything to lift his mood. He trudged into the kitchen and pulled a half eaten carton of ice cream out of the freezer and a spoon from the drawer. The doorbell rang just as he plopped back down on the settee. He ignored it; whoever it was would come back if it was important. Derek ran to the door.

'Derek wait,' he called after him, but he didn't even hesitate at flinging the door open to the stranger.

Chezia looked at the brown haired, blue eyed, five year old boy who stared wide eyed back up at her. 'Does James Ward live here?' she asked tentatively, hoping she had gotten the right house.

The little boy ran off into the back parts of the house. Did that mean yes or no? Chezia wondered. Her question was quickly answered when he came to the door.

'Chezia,' he said uncomfortably. 'I, uh . . .' What was he supposed to say? Look, I'm really sorry about your sister?

'I just wanted to make sure you were alright. I tried to call, but didn't get any answer.'

'I'm fine'

She looked at him her eyes narrowed slighty

'Ok, I'm not fine but how can I be? It's all my fault. I shouldn't have even brought her into this mess. Debbie was bad enough, does it really matter if she killed herself or someone else did? She's just as dead, and now . . . and now Kie . . .'

Chezia wrapped comporting arms around him. 'James, it's alright,' she soothed.

'It's not alright; it's all my fault!' he wailed.

Chezia continued talking to him, but to no avail.

Her warmth, it was comforting, she was comforting, but it wouldn't work, and he knew it which made him cry all the more. 'I'm sorry. I just wish there was something I could do,' he sniffed, rigidly pulling away from what his heart wanted most–somebody to love, to love him, not just anyone—Chezia.

She settled onto the corner of the settee. There wasn't any use in trying to calm him; it wouldn't work, so she just sat there, offering the silent comfort and compassion. Eventually, all his energy was spent and he fell asleep.

Once convinced he was truly asleep, Chezia carefully scooted off the settee. Then she made her way into the kitchen and began looking for something to eat. Finally she settled for tomato soup and cheese on toast. Still trying to be quiet not to wake James, she hunted for a clean pot. None was to be found. Her flat was by no means clean, but this . . . this was disastrous. In the living room alone she found a carton of melting ice cream, a bag of open crisps and empty dinner plates, and half of an uneaten pizza. While he was asleep she might as well pick up a little; it sure couldn't hurt.

As she picked up and threw the rubbish away, she realized most of this had been in the last few weeks. Hardly any dust was around, and all the carpets were freshly hovered except for the area next to the settee and the coffee table. 'At least he doesn't normally live like this,' she said consoling herself.

An hour later, James opened two tired green eyes. A questioning glance confirmed it; someone was in his kitchen, but who? Chezia would have no reason for sticking around. He doubted, however, that they, whoever it was, weren't any threat since they were cooking in his kitchen. It was Chezia. He seated himself at the little dining table in the nearby room.

'Smells good,' he commented. Probably anything warm would though; he hadn't had a proper meal in over five weeks.

'Hope it tastes as good as it smells then,' she said as he carried in a bowl. 'What do you want to drink?'

He looked longingly at the creamy tomato soup and the steamy cheese on toast. 'Anything is good.'

She poured him a cup of coffee.

'Thanks,' he said gratefully between mouthfuls. 'For the food and the cleaning. I'm grateful, but you didn't have to do anything.'

'No problem,' she said, shrugging off the thank you. It was still only one o'clock. 'If you want, I fly you to dinner. That is, if you don't mind vegetarian.'

He gave her a puzzled look. 'How long have you been vegetarian? And why fly?' Somehow Chezia White just didn't look like the vegetarian type, and she'd think she got enough flying during the day, not to mention the fact most restaurants didn't have enough room for landing many helicopters.

'I'm not, but I have a feeling that's what Kub will want, and if you don't fly you have to get there by horseback or walking and that's a tough way to get to dinner, not to mention time consuming.'

Kiba would want, he mentally corrected, if she were alive. It would do him good to get out of the house for a while though. 'Yeah, I'd like to go. What time should I be ready?'

'I'll pick you up at five,' Chezia offered.

'Ok. I'll be ready.' And anxiously awaiting you.

★   ★   ★

Dressed in a green top and dark blue jeans, James finished pulling on a red jumper. He grabbed his bag and answered the door. Chezia stood at the door, her hair still damp, indicating her recent shower.

'You look nice,' he commented approvingly.

'This? Nah. You though, you look very nice.'

He self consciously looked down at his outfit. 'Is it really ok? I didn't know exactly what you had in mind for dinner.'

'It's perfect. Ready to go?'

'Just one minute.' He called Derek. 'I have to drop him off next door then I'll be ready.'

James dropped Derek off with the neighbour and climbed into the front seat of the Jet Ranger next to Chezia. Soon they were off.

'So, what's for dinner?' he asked casually.

'I still don't know,' Chezia smiled wryly. 'Vegetarian.'

A distressed look crossed his face, and she thought he was going to start crying all over again. What was wrong with vegetarian? He said it was alright, but every time she said it, he got this guilty, grief stricken look.

'Is that still ok? If you want we could go somewhere else. I just thought you might like to see everyone again.'

Everyone but Kie he thought miserably. Maybe going to dinner wasn't such a great idea after all 'Where,' he hesitated, 'where did you say we were going?'

Chezia thought for a moment. 'I don't think I never did tell you; we're going up to Kub's cottage for dinner.'

Kiba's cottage he felt another guilty blow. Dinner had been a really bad idea, but how could Chezia act as if nothing in the world was wrong? He knew how close they'd been. Why did she not seem to mind her sister was dead?

'Chezia,' he tried to collect himself; he wanted to tell her how much he still loved her, maybe one day . . . No she couldn't love him–not anymore, especially after what happened to her sister because of him, although she didn't really seem to care. Was it really not that big of a deal to her? He shook the idea out of his head. Maybe she was just acting strong for him; she didn't want him to feel guilty. But if she didn't like him, at least as a friend, though why was she taking him to dinner?

'Yeah, James,' she answered.

'Do you remember back in Yangon?'

★　★　★

'Do you love me Wolf-Cub?'

'Of course I do Viper'

He smiled. 'So are we going to get married and have lots of kids?'

'Yep. Lots of kids.' Their lips met for a brief kiss, not caring who was around watching them.

'Guys' Kiba stated as she walked past with Fox, 'Let's go'

Ignoring her sister she carried on 'Lots of very beautiful kids . . .' Chezia's voice faded out just as she had faded out of his life for the last thirteen years.

★　　★　　★

'Yeah, I remember. Those were good times. You know, in between the battles,' she added.

'Yeah,' he agreed.

'Why? You still want to take me up on that offer?'

He laughed half heartedly, giving no actual answer. He couldn't tell if she was joking or serious. Of course he did; his love for Chezia White had never truly disappeared even after all these years he realized, but she had to be kidding after what happened to Kiba because of him, although her insensitivity about that still puzzled him. Even if she was serious, which she couldn't be, she wanted kids with him, not Debbie's kid. Now he felt guilty again. Not only was Debbie dead, and yes he had loved her, but it was now that he truly realized where his heart was.

'Just to warn you though, I'm a packaged deal.'

'A packaged deal?' he repeated questioningly. 'What do you mean?'

'Family. You know Mr. B, Adam, Kub, Domanick, and the other catch, the one that would affect you the most, is Dante.'

'Dante?' she reiterated. Kiba didn't have any children other than Domanick. Dante—he tried to place the name; sure he had heard her use it sometime.

'He's my brother, but more of a son' Chezia replied.

'Oh.'

'I figured I ought to let you know up front,' she explained.

'Well, I guess we could be closer to lots of kids than I thought, but to let you know up front, the kid you saw at my house, if you didn't already guess, is mine and Debbie's.'

Chezia turned the helicopter around and went back the direction they'd just come.

Well, this is it. He had been right; she wanted her children not Debbie's. He sighed. Derek was his and he wasn't about to leave him even if that meant no Chezia White.

The journey was silent. Now she'd be late for dinner, he had just ruined all chances with Chezia, and Kiba was still dead. Staying out of all of their lives would have been so much better, and saved him a lot of unnecessary grief. Nothing could be changed now, but if he had it to do all over again . . . His thoughts drifted, thinking about life might have been without Chezia at all, with Chezia, if Chezia hadn't been MIA all those years, and if Debbie hadn't gotten killed, mentally picturing the differences in his life.

They were almost back to his house. He gathered his jacket and prepared to get out when they landed.

'What is your neighbour's name?' she inquired.

What difference did it make? 'Mrs. Clark, why?'

She gave no explanation, only landed off to the side. 'I really wish you had told me he was your son a long time ago.'

James carried a bemused expression. Wasn't he supposed to be the one getting out? This was it; goodbye Chezia White. Why then was he still seated in the Jet Ranger as she climbed out and dashed across the garden?

She returned a minute later with an excited six year old in tow.

'Daddy, Daddy! This nice lady is going to take us in a helicopter'

He glanced at her, perplexed.

'He deserves to meet everyone,' Chezia explained, 'but I really should have guessed that he was yours.' She shook her head to herself, silently scolding herself for being so ignorant.

James smiled. Maybe, just maybe, there was hope after all.

★　　★　　★

An hour and half later, they landed on the jetty. James looked out at the picturesque cottage with fading rays of sunlight leaving only a shiny glint on the waters, further adding to the majesty of the area. 'It's beautiful-the cottage, forest, lake, music. Wait, where's the music coming from?'

'The porch,' Chezia replied while helping the child out of his seat in the back.

He looked toward the cottage, and sure enough, a beautiful black acoustic guitar was being expertly played by Kiba. He ran up the steps and threw his arms around her, interrupting her playing.

She saw who it was and hugged them in return.

'Sorry for messing you up, but it's just . . . I thought you were dead. The bank thing and the reporter . . .' He saw the slightly pained look in her eyes as she slipped her arms back down to her sides. 'I didn't hurt you did I? Oh, I'm so sorry,' his words came out all jumbled.

'I'm alright,' she assured him, 'just a little sore. I'm glad to see you again and I really am alright. I thought Chez was supposed to have already told you and brought you up-to-date on everything since we couldn't get a hold of you on the phone.'

Now he felt guilty about not answering the phone during his depressive state. At least she was alright. Relief and joy flooded through her. Nobody would ever be able to understand it, and that was fine. All of them were safe and sound, that was what mattered.

'Go ahead on in. Adam's been looking forward to seeing you.'

He agreed, having enough babbling like an idiot, and went inside.

'Do you go out looking for kids or do they just find you?' she asked her sister.

'They find me. But it's not as bad as you in Burma, I think every kid there was looking for you.' Chezia walked up the porch steps. 'This is Derek'

She kneeled down to Derek level, 'It's nice to meet you Derek, I'm Kib.'

'Kib,' he repeated.

'Now come on, let's see if we can find something to eat around here.'

Kiba followed them in as James came back to the front door. 'Dinner's on, but I can't find Adam around here anywhere, or any signs of any little boys other than Derek.'

Kiba hurried into the kitchen to make sure dinner was ok. 'I forgot. He said something about having to leave, and he'd be back.'

'Where'd he go?' Chezia inquired.

'The hangar. He was just dropping me off then going back for Dante, Mr. B and Domanick.'

'Because I was off with the other chopper,' Chezia reasoned. 'If I'd known, I could have picked them up on the way here and saved him the extra trip.'

'You wouldn't have all fit; besides, he dropped me off early, before the hangar was even closed.'

'How come?'

Kiba shook her head in disgust. 'I was busy today, and he was afraid I would hurt my arm worse somehow.' She tilted her head toward the sky. 'They're coming in now, and Dante's flying.'

James stared, amazed. 'How can you tell?'

She shrugged. 'I heard them coming, and somehow Dan just flies differently.' They landed and the rest of the group climbed out, and introductions were made.

★　★　★

James looked down at his watch; it was half ten already. Stifling a yawn, he got up from his seat to look for Derek. Adam followed him across the room.

'If you're looking for Derek, he's playing in Dom's bedroom.' Adam smiled as he led the way upstairs.

James thanked while summoning Derek to join him. 'I really do appreciate all of this. It was nice getting to see everybody, dinner was excellent, and I had a great time; and by the looks of it, he did too.'

Kiba smiled. 'Anytime, it was good having you.'

On the trip back the exhausted boy immediately fell asleep. 'I wish you would've told me Kie was alive earlier, but I had such a good time. How can I ever repay you?'

'Repay me?' she repeated as a question. She had thought she had told him about Kiba being alive though. Maybe she had forgotten after her unexpected greeting and the long minutes of sobbing before he'd fallen asleep . . . She guess she did forget to tell him, she finally figured. She wished she had realized that earlier and told him. It would have made both their lives easier and saved him a lot of heartache.

'You know, coming to check up on me, fixing lunch, cleaning my house, inviting me to dinner . . . Wow, you did even more than I thought. There must be something I can do.'

'Nah, you needed a boost and I just happened to be the one to give it; it really wasn't a big deal.'

Not really a big deal-so none of this had been because she still loved him. He was just in need, and she was helpful. He should've seen it coming; just because he still loved her, didn't necessarily mean she felt the same way.

'Anything. I owe you,' he tried. Even if it was out of sympathy instead of love, she still deserved something.

'Anything?' she asked mischievously. 'Ok, how about dinner Friday night?'

'Sounds good to me. What do you like?'

'Anything but hospital food. For all I care, jam sandwiches.'

'I think I can do a little better than that,' he laughed.

'Fine by me. I'll see if Kub can babysit Dante and Derek'

'Friday it is.' She dropped him off at his door, 'say seven?'

'Perfect. I'll see you Friday.'

She gave him a gentle hug and went back to the Jet Ranger.

She returned a moment later carrying Derek. 'Forget something? Just show me where his room is and I'll leave him there.'

He led her up the stairs to a cosy blue walled boy's room, and watched as Chezia gingerly set his child down, tucking the blankets around him.

'Looks like you're an old pro.'

'I don't think so. When Dante first came to live with me I was totally clueless; I'd never really taken care of kids all that much, at least Dan was eight by then. I just wished I hadn't missed so many years out of his life.'

'Things like this, they make you think. I mean, I loved Debbie, but I don't think that's where my heart was, and she was perfectly fine that morning. I never would have thought about her getting killed. You have to consider yourself blessed for everyday you get. I didn't want it to happen by any means, but I guess I have to make the most of it. I also plan to make the most of my time with Derek . . . Kids, they grow up so fast.'

'They do,' Chezia agreed. 'Well, I guess I ought to be going now that it's almost midnight.'

'Goodnight.'

She turned to leave. 'See you Friday.'

'Yeah, Friday.' He could hardly wait.

★　★　★

Friday morning James bustled around the house making sure everything was perfect for when Chezia arrived that evening. For dinner, he planned chicken with roasted carrots, rice, and a bottle of wine for them to share. He had the table set and everything ready to be cooked by half two. He flopped back into a plush arm chair to relax. He flipped through the channels on TV, trying to find something decent to watch. Finally deciding on an old movie rerun. Not realizing how tired he was, he dozed off during the movie.

The chiming of the grandfather clock on the opposite wall woke him and had him hurriedly rushing to get a shower then dressing in nice jeans and a jumper Debbie had bought for him. He took the jumper off only seconds after putting it on, he just couldn't do it. Shrugging into a black and white striped shirt instead. Next, the food was put on, and he readied Derek to go.

The doorbell rang at seven sharp. The door flew open. A second look told him it wasn't even who he was expecting at all.

'Kie you here for Derek?'

'Actually Chez isn't here by any chance is she?' Kiba asked hopefully.

'Not yet, why?'

'I haven't seen her since dinner at the cottage Wednesday night. Evidently, Jason had some-' she caught herself before she said too much. 'Had something for her to do, but she should have already been back. I've called the flat already and every place I can think of, but no luck.'

'She's supposed to show up around half seven, so if you want to wait around feel free,' he offered, hoping this wouldn't obstruct with his dinner plans, but whatever her sister wanted her for was probably more important. 'No, that's alright, but if she does show up, give me a call at the hanger'

'No problem.'

Kiba had just climbed into the Jet Ranger when she decided to try reaching Shadow-Wolf again.

'Wolf to Shadow, do you read?'

Only silence.

'Shadow-Wolf, come in.'

Still nothing.

Where could they be?

She radioed Jason again. 'Where were Chez and Simon headed?'

Jason knew her exact intentions. 'Wolf, if I tell you, you'll go after them. Believe me, I want to, but if they're just running behind schedule going in after them could ruin everything.'

'What if they aren't just running late?' Kiba growled. 'What if they're hurt?'

'Just give it some more time,' Jason tried to calm her. 'If we haven't heard from them in four hours, I'll send Hit-Rhino in after them.'

'That's not good enough, Jason.'

'It's going to have to be,' he ended the transmission. Loosing his temper with Kiba wouldn't help anything, but going in all reckless and riled up wouldn't either.

Kiba swung by the hangar and Dante jumped in; she took off again before anyone had a chance to stop her. 'Fly towards Rhino-Gate and fly high,' Kiba directed Dante.

Dante obeyed without question although he did wonder why.

Kiba focused on trying to reach Shadow-Wolf. Come on Demon, where are you?

The answer she received wasn't much help, like mental static. Where could they be? For all she knew, they could be directly below her, twenty thousand feet above them, or on the other side of the ocean. There wasn't any logical way to even begin looking for them. They were almost to Rhino-Gate when she thought she was actually starting to get somewhere.

'Keep going,' she told Dante.

'Where?'

'Nowhere. Just keep flying in this direction.'

He kept on flying.

Kiba reached over to try the radio again. 'Wolf to Shadow, do you copy?'

This time she got static.

'Where are you and is everything alright?'

More static, but she understood the words down and out. Down as in on the ground, low altitude, or systems are down? What about out?

'You're really choppy. Will you repeat?'

'. . . Down . . . Chez . . . out . . .' was all she caught.

'Dante, fly a little lower and be on the lookout for Shadow-Wolf anywhere.'

'Alright'

She mentally tried reaching Shadow-Wolf again. Shadow, are you there?

More mental static, which was extremely painful and way too loud, but how do you turn down something that's only in your head? Finally she started to get something, but the message was all garbled. She wasn't in the mood to play word scramble, but, not having many options, she did her best.

Irritation was starting to get the better of her. Where were they and what was wrong? Something had to be. She considered trying to contact Jason again, but decided against it; he probably wouldn't be much help and radioing him would jeopardize the frail link she was beginning to establish with Shadow-Wolf.

Still not having much luck in reaching them. She tried yet again with the radio.

'Wolf' the radio crackled. The message was choppy, but mostly understandable. 'Jason . . . mission successful, systems failure . . . need help.'

'Where are you?' Kiba asked, hoping the connection wasn't lost yet.

No answer.

'Where?' Kiba repeated.

Simon started giving coordinates to their location, but the message was full of static to understand them clearly.

'One more time.'

'Down . . . near forest . . .' Simon said. The radio crackled again and the connection was lost. No matter what she tried she couldn't re-establish it.

Retaking control of the helicopter, Kiba director the Jet Ranger toward Sherwood Forest. Wishing she had the scanners and equipment available in Shadow-Wolf, They began their search for the Devil, Simon and Chezia.

★　　★　　★

James stared up at the clock and watched as the minutes slowly ticked by. It was now nearing half nine. Dinner was stone cold, but he was more worried about Chezia. She was missing and obviously Kiba was worried. She said Jason, who is—if he remembered correctly her friend at Rhino-Gate, had something for her to do, but didn't expound on any further details.

James picked up the phone and dialled the number Kiba had left him. Adam answered.

'Has there been any update?' James queried.

Adam shook his head then realizing James couldn't see him, 'No. Kiba came by about two hours ago, picked up Dante, and left. I'm beginning to get worried about them too.'

'Thanks. Please just tell me if you find out anything.'

'Will do'

★　　★　　★

Jason picked up the phone, having sent Alex home around eight.

'What's going on and where is everybody?' Mr. Brad interrogated.

'Chezia and Simon were on a mission for me,' Jason explained, 'but we lost radio contact with them and have been unsuccessful in locating them. If Wolf has gone missing too, she is no doubt looking for them.'

'I want to learn something new,' Mr. Brad grumbled. 'See if you can find out something.' He hung up the phone no better informed than before the call. Mr. Brad wandered around his house wishing there was something he could do and hoping everything was alright.

★   ★   ★

Adam scrounged up a little something to eat and fed Domanick. Afterwards, he tucked him in with the blanket he'd brought in his playpen. 'I guess we're sleeping here tonight.' With Chezia and Simon taking the Jet Ranger to the canopy, and Kiba taking the second one to look for them, he had no way of getting back to the cottage. He laid on one of the settees and settled on it, trying to fall asleep. Sleep evaded him, only worry crossed his mind. What if something had happened during the Shadow-Wolf mission? What about Kiba and Dante? He desperately tried to rid himself of those thoughts and sleep, but some good news sure would have helped.

Domanick rolled around restlessly. He couldn't sleep well either, he thought dryly. Hopefully morning would dawn with good news- and soon.

★   ★   ★

'Any sign of them?' Kiba asked her young co-pilot. Concern was building up more each minute. Sherwood Forest was a big area and it would be easy to miss them, and time could be crucial depending on if either of them was injured.

'No,' Dante replied as bravely as he could. The way he understood it, he was supposed to spend the evening with Simon, Derek and Domanick at Simon's house. Lots of movies and pizza were anticipated, not a night above the cold forest looking for his sister, Simon and Shadow-Wolf.

'We'll find them,' Kiba promised him, hoping they'd both be in one piece when she did find them. 'It's too dark,' she muttered under her breath. Some extra light would be really helpful right about now. 'This is hopeless,' she finally admitted. 'They could be right underneath us and we'd never see them.' She carefully landed in the darkness below. 'I guess we'll have to wait until morning to continue the search,' hoping it wouldn't be too late, but it wouldn't do them any good to mope around in the pitch-black midnight that engulfed the forest.

'Wait!' Dante said suddenly. He peered ahead into the dark night. Nothing, then a blueish glow, then nothing again. It could be Shadow-Wolf's computers, but why would they be going on and off like that? Simon had said something about a systems failure; maybe that was the systems trying to reboot themselves unsuccessfully.

A new glimmer of hope, fighting back the hopeless defeat that had almost triumphed.

'Good job Dan. Let's go find them.'

They gathered two torches, jackets, and prepared themselves to go searching through the cold desolate land.

'Should we bring the first aid kit?' Dante asked. 'In case one of them if hurt.'

Kiba shook her head. 'It's a good idea, but it'd be more to carry and Shadow-Wolf has a good first aid kit on board, better than this one actually.'

Once they had gathered everything, they slipped into their jackets, took the torches and began the hunt on foot.

★ ★ ★

Simon sat in the quiet cockpit; not even the usual hum of the computers was there. It was so lifeless, almost dead. Scanning the darkness, he looked for something to console himself, to prove things were starting to turn up and everything would be alright.

He looked at Chezia, still in the pilot's seat where she'd been for quite some time. 'I sure hope she's ok,' Simon said aloud, his own voice the only noise to interrupt the deafening silence. He was afraid to move Chezia in fear of her having some neck injury he would only worsen, but the still woman with a bloody gash on the left side of her forehead wasn't what he would call comforting. 'Head wounds always bleed a lot,' he told himself over and over again. 'It's probably only something minor.' He still worried though. He shifted his sore arm uncomfortably. All there was left to do was to wait and pray that everything would work out. He looked at Chezia once more; praying, lots and lots of praying.

★　　★　　★

Somewhere in Sherwood forest . . .

Kiba travelled across the seemingly endless growing stretch of darkness, Dante trailing along behind her. The earlier glow hadn't even blinked anytime recently, but she didn't dare deviate from their course. It was like walking around blindfolded, if she didn't keep on track she might never find her way to Shadow-Wolf.

Dante came up beside her. 'Do you think we passed it already?'

'No. It was pretty far away,' she replied, not allowing any of her growing doubt to seep into her voice.

'Oh, ok.'

She admired Dante's ability to trust her fully and wished she could do the same.

They continued trekking along alone in the endless forest. In the darkness the distance seemed even farther than it actually was, and even Kiba was beginning to doubt her navigation. Maybe that hadn't been Shadow-Wolf at all, or maybe they had just wanted to see it so badly they thought they had . . . She tried to push the doubt aside, but it kept creeping back up. They could be fifty yards away and never see him. She had been so eager to find him and his crew that she hadn't even thought of the consequences if the mysterious light stopped blinking or if they got turned around.

'You got the time Dan?'

Dante glanced down at his watch, but in the darkness he couldn't read it. Shining the torch on it, he made out the time.

They had already been walking for a good while. As much as she hated to admit it, they should head back to the Jet Ranger and wait until morning; that would have been the more logical, safer, and easier thing to do in the first place. She let out a long breath, half smiling to herself; some things she couldn't learn to do the easy way.

She reluctantly turned to start back, her torch catching something as she did so. She turned back to see what it was, but the torch went out.

Brilliant, she thought, I was too stupid to bring extra batteries. What good is a light if you can't use it?

Secondary battery—affirmative. Lights on.

Simon was suddenly awoken by an abrupt flood of light inside and around the cockpit.

Kiba spun around, squinting at the blindingly bright search lights through the trees. Shadow-Wolf! She ran over ducking under low branches, Dante only a few steps behind her.

Simon, trying to ignore the pain in his left arm, slid the door opened and ran out to meet Kiba and Dante.

The greeting was brief and Kiba was relieved to find Simon had not been seriously injured.

'It's pretty sore,' he admitted, 'I'll even bet it'll be four nice shades of purple, but I don't think it's broken.'

Kiba's relief didn't last long when Simon continued though.

'I don't know how bad your sister is hurt. She's been unconscious since we landed, crashed, skidded, whatever you call it. She hit her head pretty good and I'm sure she'll have a killer headache when she wakes up, but I don't know when that'll be.'

'How long have you been out here?' Kiba asked,

'A few hours, my best guess.'

'What happened?' Dante interrupted with his own question, unable to keep quiet any longer.

'After our mission was completed, we started heading back to the canopy. It didn't take us long to figure out the radio was dead, but that could wait until we got back. It spread like some kind of disease though and soon every electronic was fried.'

'Why didn't you switch to manual override then?'

'Tried. Nothing worked; it was like trying to fly a model with no wiring. It can't be done. With what Chezia tried we should have been doing back flips or at least landing alright, but as you can see, that didn't go too well. It's seemed dead pretty much since we got here. I tried to fix the radio, but it wasn't cooperating too well either,' Simon explained. 'I figured I could call you guys and let you know what was going on or call for help, but I didn't keep it working long enough to do either very well.'

'I guess our first priority should be to get medical help,' Kiba decided, 'then I'll figure out some way to get the Devil back to the canopy at least.'

'I'll do whatever you need me to,' Simon volunteered. 'I'm tired of making decisions though. It's nerve racking to have everything depending on you.'

'Gee, thanks for the encouragement,' Kiba remarked. 'Go ahead and try the radio one more time.'

'Whatever you say, Major,' Simon said with a mock salute then went back around and tried the radio again. 'It looks like we have power again, but still no electronics,' he reported.

'Do we have enough power to get him back in the air?'

'I don't know, but if we do you'll still have to do it all manually.'

'That's doable. Let's try getting him back into the air.'

Simon took the engineer's seat and Dante sat in the seat next to him. Kiba took the pilot still leery of moving Chezia too much. 'You sure this is a good idea with Chezia . . .' Simon asked

'Nope,' Kiba admitted, 'but even if we were able to for medical help, they'd have to use life flight anyway. This is my choice of life flight, much faster anyway.'

Kiba tried to restart the engine. Nothing, she tried again,

She could almost hear her dad saying if you keep doing the same thing you'll only end up with the same results.

'That's all he's got.'

'Alright,' Kiba said, releasing a sigh of frustration. 'Hold on I got an idea?' leaning over she pulled out the keyboard underneath the monitor from the co-pilot's side and began typing in some code.

'What are you doing?' Simon asked

'Trying to fix Shadow what does it look like?'

'How you going to fix him?'

'I type in this code and I can check Shadow-Wolf for any viruses that might have gotten into the system'

'I have a bad feeling about this' Simon called out.

'About what? It's only a check up but with a chopper'

With the code now in the computer system Kiba waiting for it to respond with a problem, once found she started to fix it, 'Alright, here goes' she smiled as she pushed the keyboard back underneath the monitor.

After a long hesitation, the rotors began to slowly circle until they gained enough momentum for lift off.

'You got him into the air!' Simon sated obviously over excitedly. 'Now let's see if we can get somewhere.'

'We can tell the doctors she hit her head in a controlled crash. They don't need to know it was a top secret helicopter she crashed instead of a normal one.' Looking at the console in front of her she searched for a hospital.

Simon casted her a questioning glance. 'True, but I would call that crash anything but controlled,'

'DRI is the closest one in this database, anyway, Dan, me and you will have to update it when we get back' she stated as they started off.

'Alright'

'Jet engines,' Kiba called out.

'No can do,' Simon answered. 'I don't think Chezia needs to be pulling the G's.'

No reply.

'Look on the bright side, Shadow-Wolf is faster than the Jet Ranger would be.'

'Yeah, I know,' Kiba allowed. 'I just want to do all I can to help her, and it's seeming like that is getting to be less and less.'

★ ★ ★

At last, they landed on top of the hospital.

'You go stay with your sister. I'll guard the Devil.'

Kiba nodded. 'Thanks.'

'What are buddies for?' Simon grinned. It didn't matter how much he'd have liked to be in there to support Chezia; she needed Kiba more and somebody had to stay with the Devil.

★ ★ ★

James stirred restlessly. The phone rang across the room, and he picked it up even before the second ring. 'Hello,' he answered. It had to be something important to be calling him at eleven PM.

'It's Kie,' the voice on the other end said.

'Where are you? Is everything alright?'

'I'm at DRI'

James tried not to leap to conclusions but it was difficult. 'Are you ok?'

'Physically just tired. Mentally exhausted and worried. Dan and I found Chez and Simon; I'm still waiting on some news though.'

'DRI you said? I'll be right there.' He hung up the phone before she had the chance to say another word.

Kiba next called Mr. Brad's house

A tired, slightly grumpy man picked up, obviously not liking having his sleep interrupted.

'It's Kib' she began again.

'Kib! What are you doing calling me in the middle of the night? Just cause you don't sleep doesn't mean the rest the world doesn't either.'

'I just wanted to hear your voice that's all'

'Ring me when you need something' Mr. Brad stated even as he put the phone down, less than five seconds later it rang again, picking it up with more force than necessary he almost threw it across the room, 'What!'

'I just thought I'd tell you we found Chez and Simon. She's at DRI if you want to come by.'

'The hospital! Why didn't you say so? I'll be there as soon as I can.'

'Mr. B,' she addressed before he could hang up.

'Yeah, kiddo?'

'It's not nice cutting people off like that and would you stop by the hangar and radio Adam; he'll be wondering where I am.'

'No problem,' Mr. Brad answered. 'I'll see you soon, kid.'

★   ★   ★

Adam awoke from the light sleep he finally drifted into after hours or worrying. Somebody was trying to get in. Instinctively, he reached for the weapon but the intruder was in before he got a chance to get Domanick.

The door slowly opened to the office and Adam took a shot

'Holy cr—Adam?' Mr. Brad questioned as he flicked the lights on

'Mr. B, What are you doing here?'

A puzzled look crossed his face. 'I could ask you the same thing.'

'I was sleeping here,' he explained. 'Chezia and Simon had to get to the canopy as fast as possible so they took a Jet Ranger, and Kiba disappeared with the other one.'

'You could've stayed over at my place,' Mr. Brad offered.

'Didn't even think of it until well after you had left. So, do you visit the hangar this time every morning or is today special?'

'I came to tell you Kib's up at the hospital–'

Panic washed over him before he even finished the sentence. 'What's wrong?' Awful ideas flashed before his eyes. There could've been a crash, she could be a little scratched and bruised or what if it was worse? What about Chezia and Simon? Something terrible might have happened.

Mr. Brad interrupted Adams self induced nightmare with only semi calming words. 'Kib is fine.' He took the weapon from him 'Her and Dan found the others but there isn't any news on their condition yet.' He finished as he locked up the top drawer.

'Let's get up there then,' he said even as he finished grabbing Domanick.

★　　★　　★

Kiba paced the floor anxiously awaiting some kind of news on her sister's condition. Simon appeared from the elevator area.

'Still nothing,' Kiba reported, already making for the elevators. Someone had to stay with Shadow-Wolf.

'It'll be ok,' Simon assured her. 'Dante's up there and I'll go back in just a little while, but if I'm here anyway, I guess it can't hurt to get one of the doctors to take a quick look at my arm. That kid's pretty good Y'know. When did you teach him all that stuff?'

'What stuff?'

'All the electronics and all. When I left he was working on fixing the radio and he seemed to have more of a clue than I did. I'm no professional mechanic, but I don't think I'm that bad either.'

Kiba shook her head, totally dumbfounded. 'I've been teaching him a few things but I haven't taught him how to wire it all up unless Chez has been teaching him.'

Simon shrugged, then immediately stopped. 'Oww, I guess maybe that isn't such a bright idea. Anyway, I was just curious, but it's no big deal. Don't worry I'll be back up there before you know it.'

Kiba went back to pacing. This waiting and not knowing was tough on even the most patient people, and she didn't consider herself all that patient. Time passed at a snails pace, if that, every second like a minute, every minute like an hour. So tired of waiting that she felt like pounding her own head on the wall until she was unconscious just so she didn't have to go through this unbearable wait, she marched down the hall, demanding to know something, anything, what they were doing, trying, or thinking.

'Let's see,' the young nurse said aloud while typing information in on the keyboard. 'Simon Kenty . . . He was released after a quick check with the doctor and an x-ray, severely bruised, but otherwise ok.'

'And Chez White?' Kiba asked impatiently.

More clicking of keys; she had to be the world's slowest typer. 'She is currently under thorough examination.'

'What else?' she interrogated.

'That's all it says,' the young brunette answered.

'That's not good enough,' she muttered as she stalked down the neutral coloured hallways in search of a doctor that would hopefully give her more information. Finding one, she asked about her sister's condition.

The doctor, much more helpful than the nurse, said, 'She's got a nasty bruise on her forehead, but no neck or spinal injuries were obvious. Her assigned general physician, Doctor Miles, plans to get a CT scan and an MRI as soon as possible. She will be treated as though she has head trauma and possible neck and spinal injuries until we can confirm she doesn't though; so don't be too alarmed if you see her and she doesn't look too good with a neck brace and backboard. Off the record, I haven't seen her much after she first arrived, but I think maybe a concussion and some bruises, nothing life threatening.'

'What about her being unconscious for so long?' Kiba asked inquisitively.

'That did add some worry as far as I'm concerned, but if she hit her head pretty hard, unconsciousness is to be expected.

'Thank you,' Kiba said, genuinely grateful. She made her way back to the waiting room to wait more definite, hopefully equally as good news and company.

James showed up first, highly distressed about Chezia's condition. 'What happened to them in the first place?'

'Systems failure, controlled crash in a very dark place,' Kiba replied without missing a beat. 'The doctor I talked to seemed to think she'll be alright though.'

A doctor and two nurses escorted one of the gurneys down the hallway. It was Chezia.

Kiba tried to explain what the doctor had told her about it probably looking worse than it was, but she wasn't getting though to him. She caught the sharp looks from a passing by nurse who looked like she really didn't enjoy the nightshift and the young brunette unsubtly urging James to be quiet and that there were patients sleeping while she carried on.

'James,' she whispered, 'James.'

He ignored her and kept on whimpering. 'It's too much. Debbie and now Chezia too,' he fussed.

'She's going to be fine, James'

He continued on.

Taking him by the collar, she led him out of the waiting room and down the hall back to the elevators. She took a firm grip on him. 'James, listen to me,' she said authoritatively.

He looked at her with large, teary, green eyes like a guilty child.

She didn't fall for the puppy dog look. 'If you want to be any help to Chez you're going to have to get a hold of yourself.'

'But . . .' he sniffed, 'but-oh you saw her. How is she supposed to be alright after that?!' he demanded, growing irritated at her detached lack of sympathy.

She was glad he hadn't been there for the bomb incident that had almost killed her and Mr. Brad or when the Burmese had used the twins as target practice. They wouldn't have been able to keep him quiet until they were safely home, and both times they had spent a good about of time at the hospital.

'The doctor said it wouldn't be as bad as it looked; that extra stuff is just precautionary. Now get a hold of yourself, or I'll take you home until you can.'

Walking back to the waiting room, they were greeted by Mr. Brad, Adam, Domanick and some good news.

'The doctor just came by,' Mr. Brad reported, 'Chezia has just regained consciousness. She doesn't have any injuries to her spine, neck, or skull. Her only problems other than the minor cuts and bruises that were expected are a concussion and mild amnesia.'

'Amnesia?' she questioned worriedly.

'Doctor Miles said it's only temporary most likely, and she remembers up until yesterday night anyway.'

They all looked relieved. 'Let's go see her,' Simon said as he reappeared with Dante. 'And don't worry; we took the Devil home.'

Chezia sat up against the three pillows piled up behind her and watched as everyone came in, the only sign of injury to any of them was Simon's bruised arm.

'So I'm the only one that gets hurt? That doesn't seem hardly fair; I don't even remember it.'

'You're the lucky one then,' said Simon, 'it wasn't exactly one of your better landings.'

'Is the Devil alright?'

'We'll have a little work to do, but he's fixable,' Kiba replied. 'You're ok, that's what matters most.'

'Simon and Dan took him back, but I guess I need to leave pretty soon and pick up that Jet Ranger. It might make somebody curious if they happened to be in the area.'

'We took care of that too,' Simon told her. 'Dante flew in one Jet Ranger and I took the other from the canopy.'

Adam returned from talking to the doctor. 'Dr. Miles says he needs to run a few more tests, but since everything appears to be good, you can go home in a day or two.'

'Good. I was hoping this wasn't going to be another lengthy hospital stay.'

★　★　★

James stayed behind after the others had left. 'You're really ok?' he asked as if making sure this wasn't some trick his mind was playing on him, making him think his troublesome times were finally over.

'I'm really ok, but if you do recall, you still owe me dinner.'

He smiled. 'I'm not the one having problems remembering. it's stone cold on the kitchen counter; maybe I should just start over.'

'Sounds good enough to me,' Chezia agreed, 'What time should I be over?'

'I love you Chezia White' He laughed then stopped realizing he'd actually said that aloud.

'I love you too, James Ward.' She reached past the arrangement of medical equipment to draw him into a tight, loving hug.

CHAPTER EIGHT

Gone fishing

Simon strolled casually into the Brad's Air Service hangar, but only seeing Mr. Brad 'Where is everybody? It looks like everybody disappeared and left you all the work.'

'Adam and Domanick are in the back. Chezia is honeymooning with-'

'She what?!' Simon interrupted abruptly. 'I didn't even know she was getting married!'

'She's not really,' Kiba assured him as she joined them. 'She's just having dinner over there. Mr. B, here, is just so sure they'll be getting married any time now.'

'I thought you and Adam would get together and that worked out,' Mr. Brad pointed out. 'Just glad I didn't bet on how long it would take you,' he mumbled

'I didn't say she would or wouldn't get back together with James, but I wouldn't expect anything immediately. His wife did just get killed not too long ago, and that takes a long time to get over.'

And you know the loss all too well, Mr. Brad silently added. 'So what brings you here?' Mr. Brad asked Simon, bringing things back to business before they got too personal.

'I just wanted to see how Chezia was doing and offer any extra help you might need in repairing Shadow-Wolf.'

'We already requested new parts, but it'll be tomorrow morning before they show up. I guess just come by tomorrow.'

'When do you want me?' Simon inquired.

'Oh, say about four AM,' Kiba suggested.

Simon grew wide eyed. 'You mean PM, right?'

'I meant in the morning.'

'That's a little early don't you think? I'm not exactly a morning person.'

'She's kidding,' Mr. Brad laughed, 'or else she better be; otherwise she's going to be the only one there.'

Kiba allowed a wry grin to spread across her face. 'Even I'm not that bad. I wouldn't be there until about eight, but it does take me an hour and half to get there from the cottage.'

'Better, but how about something later in the afternoon,' Simon tried.

'We can all meet at the canopy by about noon,' Mr. Brad compromised.

★   ★   ★

The next morning dawned crisp and cool, a light mist rising from the lake. Adam poured himself a cup of coffee and sat out on the front porch to watch the morning sunrise. Domanick didn't seemed to have their early morning routine. Surprisingly enough, he'd even bet Kiba up this morning. He sat alone, gathering the thin quilt around himself to ward off the chilly morning breeze. 'It sure is cold for September,' he mused.

Quiet footsteps from inside warned him Kiba was now awake, but they seemed to drag a little this morning, she was still tired.

She came out to join him, not even having bothered pulling on her jacket or pouring herself a warm cup of tea.

'Cold?' he asked.

She shook her head, farther messing her green hair.

'It's late for you,' he remarked. 'Missed the sunrise.'

'Yeah,' she replied groggily. 'I don't know why I am so tired today,' she said, stifling a yawn.

He offered over his cup. 'Have some. You look like you could use it.'

She took the cup appreciatively, taking long warm sips. 'Thanks,' she mumbled.

Adam left the quilt around her shoulders despite her proclaiming not to be cold, and went inside to work on fixing breakfast. He started with Domanick's when he heard him stirring upstairs. After finishing his breakfast and getting the rest started, he climbed the stairs to get him.

After getting Domanick started on his breakfast, Adam slipped back outside to tell Kiba that her breakfast was almost finished, but he found her dozing against the railing.

'Kiba,' he said, waking her gently, 'your breakfast is ready.'

She blinked sleepily several times then nodded. 'I'll be right in.'

At this rate, he figured he'd be out there waking her again in about five minutes, but, true to her word, she managed to gather herself and stumble inside for breakfast.

She slowly ate her way through the pancakes, hardly avoiding falling asleep face first in them.

'You should radio the hangar and tell Mr. B you won't be in today,' Adam suggested.

'No. I have to go to work. Gonna work on the Devil,' she murmured, catching herself before she nodded off again.

'Not like that you're not,' Adam stated firmly.

'Have to,' she returned defiantly.

'At least stay and sleep until then,' Adam tried to persuade her, 'then we can both be happy.'

'Fine,' she gave in, too tired to argue any farther.

He was pleased that she was being reasonable, but that also worried him. She gave in too easily She must be extremely tired or coming down with something.

Taking Domanick with him, Adam reluctantly started out the door.

'I don't see why you can't leave Dom here,' Kiba complained. 'It would leave you free to do more at the hangar, and he wouldn't be that hard for me to watch.'

'Because he isn't that hard for me to watch either, and you're supposed to be sleeping. I'll have Mr. B pick you up on his way out to the canopy,' he stated matter of factly.

'It's the opposite direction. I should just come up to the hangar with you now and save him the extra trip.'

'You're sleeping,' he reminded her, secretly glad to see some of her stubbornness returning. 'I'll see you later,' He walked out the front door with Domanick in tow

'I'll see you later' she repeated in a sour tone of voice

★   ★   ★

Mr. Brad landed the helicopter on the jetty outside the cottage like he had countless other times, expecting to see Kiba come out.

Nothing.

She must have heard him coming, she always did, and she knew Mr. Brad was coming because he had radioed to tell her that he was on his way only ten minutes ago.

Mr. Brad hefted himself out of the Jet Ranger and walked inside; Kiba was asleep on the settee. Mr. Brad considered leaving, letting Kiba sleep, but she would, no doubt, be grumpy about that later if he did.

'Kib, wake up.'

Kiba lifted two heavy eyelids, her baby blue eyes still appearing cloudy and tired. Realizing what time it was, she moved from her position on the settee, pulling on the jumper and denim jacket she had retrieved after Mr. Brad's radio but never managed to put on, and silently started toward the Jet Ranger. Mr. Brad quickly caught up to Kiba who was moving at half her normal pace.

'You ok, kiddo?' he asked, voice full of concern. 'You aren't moving too fast and you've had plenty of time to sleep.'

'I'm fine.'

Mr. Brad made sure he reached the helicopter first so that he would be pilot. Kiba didn't need to be flying when it looked like walking was more than she could handle. Kiba slid into the co-pilot's seat with a moan and they started off.

Mr. Brad didn't push the issue any further, but was beginning to hope they didn't make enough progress to take the Devil out today because she would, undoubtedly, want to claim her usual position as pilot instead of someone else just because she was a little tired.

Nearly an hour and half after starting, they reached the canopy where Simon was waiting. Simon ignored Mr. Brad's subtle gestures saying, 'I thought I was the one not being a morning person. You look like you just crawled out of bed buddy.'

In return he received an impetuous glare. 'Shut up,' she growled, 'even I get that way once in a while.'

Simon didn't back down. 'So you are human, I was beginning to wonder. Go home and get some rest. You need it.'

'I'm fine.'

Mr. Brad agreed with Simon on this one, but figured it would be best not to take sides. 'Let's just get to work then we can all go home and get some sleep.'

He succeeded in interrupting the argument long enough to get everyone working.

'Like I said before, everything was fine during the mission. On the way back though, everything just quit working and we fell like a rock.'

'Ok, so there has to be some reason everything quit working at once,' Mr. Brad reasoned.

'Somehow, Whitey was able to put in some code and we got back, but isn't there some warning before a battery just dies?'

'There should be-'

'It was jammed, short circuited kinda thing,' Kiba explained, reappearing from the opposite side of the beautiful navy blue helicopter badly in need of some attention and a detail job. 'Somehow the wire were short circuited, causing all the electronics to go down, including the computer functions that let you switch to manual override. By putting in an emergency code, we were able to run off the secondary battery, some things straightened themselves out, but you can't run everything off the second, that's why we couldn't get enough power for the jet engines.'

'How do you know that?' Simon asked suspiciously. For someone as exhausted as she was, she sure figured that out pretty quickly and without much problem.

'Don't ask.'

'Then I'm asking', Mr. Brad joined.

'I just do, ok? Now trust my judgment or figure the same thing out on your own,' she snarled.

'How do we fix it then, if you've figured this all out?'

'Replace the battery and re-circuit all the electronics,' Kiba answered easily. 'Some of the electronics might work, but I wouldn't bet on it, so might as well redo them all. None of this, of course, includes any of the physical damage caused when he hit either.'

'Of course. Everything has to be complicated.'

'I'll start work on the physical end if you two want to start on the rewiring.'

What was this? Simon asked himself. Kiba White-she can tell you what is wrong and how to fix it, but when it comes time to get to work she finds a different task to work on. It would be more physically demanding anyway. Why couldn't she just admit she wasn't at her best today and take the less physically straining job?

'Aren't you the one that's supposed to know all this computer stuff?' Simon questioned.

'It's a master in Applied Physics. I prefer the more physical side of things,' she stated simply before returning to inspecting the armour plated skin.

'You got to be kidding me,' Simon muttered under his breath. 'She shows off this wonderful computer knowledge then goes on like she doesn't have the slightest clue of anything even slightly computer related.'

'It's true,' Mr. Brad quietly agreed. 'Don't ask me where all that information came from, but she always does the more physical jobs, combat flying while I do the computers, that kind of thing. I do the computers, imagine that, but that's how it always has been.'

'If she supposedly doesn't do all the computer stuff, how did she figure out what the problem was and how to fix it so fast?'

Mr. Brad thought for a moment. 'Y'know, once she did say something about that. I don't know exactly how, but sometimes she knows things only the Devil should know.'

Simon shrugged. 'I guess it doesn't really matter all that much. She's going to work herself into the ground, and we have a lot of resetting and recruiting to do.'

Mr. Brad let his gaze slide over to Kiba briefly, hoping Simon was wrong about her working herself into the ground, but by the looks of it, she was already well on that track.

'Yeah, we had better get a move on because if by some miracle she doesn't collapse from exhaustion, at that rate, she'll be done long before us.'

Simon agreed except for the by some miracle part. Right now Kiba could use a nap, physically she might be less tired and maybe she'd also be less grumpy. Shrugging it off, he set to work.

★   ★   ★

Adam went about his work methodically, only stopping once in a while to worry about Kiba. Why was she so tired? Normally, it wouldn't be a big deal, but she wasn't just a little tired, she was exhausted even after a full night's sleep, and she had even had calm restful nights lately, not those dreadful nightmares. Laughing to himself, he finished zipping the red overalls. He was being stupid; why did it matter if she was a little more tired than usual? Just a nice day of rest and relaxation and she would be good as new. Chiding himself for worrying about something so trivial, he set to work on the Jet Ranger.

Chezia cuddled the irresistible little child once again. She should be working, but Domanick was her only nephew and he was growing up so fast. She set the little boy down and watched as he crawled a few yards then, leaning against the side of the desk, stood up and tottered forward a few steps before tumbling ungracefully into a giggling heap. Finally she put Domanick back into his play pen; concrete floors and wooden desks weren't very forgiving, even to collapsing giggling balls of fun like him. Sighing wistfully, she returned to the work she should've been doing instead of playing with Domanick.

★　　★　　★

Simon glanced past the mess of tangled wires inside the cockpit at Kiba who was working at an exhausting pace in spite of her weariness even before she started.

Mr. Brad wiped a hand across his sweaty forehead. 'Anyone else want a cold beer?' he asked, mostly trying to distract Kiba at least for a few minutes. She hadn't even stopped for lunch, instead insisting on working straight through it.

Simon obliged.

'Kib, how about you?' Mr. Brad offered.

'Nah, I'm—I'm almost finished' she panted.

The day was that odd temperature—too cold to go without a jacket, but too warm to wear it. Simon and Mr. Brad had both opted to shed the jacket, but Kiba had gone a step further. Her sweat drenched jacket, jumper and shirt lying in a heap near the nose of the helicopter, her hair, damp as if she'd just gone swimming, clung to her neck and black sleeveless t-shirt.

'Take a break kiddo,' Mr. Brad advised in an authoritative, fatherly tone. 'Even if you weren't tired to begin with you will be now. Just watching you makes me tired.'

She hesitated momentarily, but quickly returned to herself appointed duty as if she stopped she wouldn't be able to start again. That was it. She didn't want to quit because she would lose the momentum and wouldn't be able to complete her task.

'Just a short break, have a beer,' Mr. Brad said.

'In a minute,' Kiba replied tersely. 'I'm almost done.'

Mr. Brad let it go, she did say she would quit in a minute

'You're making good progress,' Simon commented, 'how long do you think until he's airworthy again?'

Kiba disappeared from sight momentarily then returned and grabbed the bottle Mr. Brad had left out for her. 'How long do you think? I'm done.'

Had to give her credit, she finished the job efficiently even if she was exhausted. 'Uh, probably not for a while,' Simon answered. 'I guess we just aren't as good as you.'

Kiba gave a weak half-hearted grin.

Mr. Brad chided in, 'it shouldn't take long. If we work hard, we can have it finished in forty five minutes or so.' The glass bottle clinked as he set it back down. 'I guess we had better get working.'

Simon joined him.

Seven o'clock came and went. Now nearing eight, Simon and Mr. Brad climbed out, letting out contented sighs.

'All done?' Kiba asked finally reappearing, this time donning a navy blue Shadow-Wolf flight suit.

'Yeah,' Simon said hesitantly, still not relishing the idea of letting Kiba fly, especially now that she had been working for six hours straight. He yawned. 'It's been a long day; I guess we ought to be heading home now.'

Evidently Kiba didn't get the hint, or more likely, she chose to ignore it. 'We've got one more thing to do—take him out and make sure everything works like it's supposed to.' She zipped up her flight suit and started to pull Shadow-Wolf out.

Simon and Mr. Brad cast concerned glances at one another. 'Well, I guess we better get changed and ready to go,' Simon said. 'If one thing's for sure, it's that she doesn't need to be flying alone.'

As Kiba prepared for takeoff, Simon's nerves grew even more ill at ease. He positioned himself so that he could take over at the slightest hint of Kiba starting to doze off. God only knew what she was planning to do, but this was for sure, Kiba liked to test things to their limit, and if they happened to be doing mach one at low altitude when she started snoozing, about a second to react would be the best case scenario.

'All systems in the green,' Mr. Brad reported from behind the engineer's console.

'Then what are we waiting for?' She eased the collective back with easy practiced effort. If flying was like a second nature to her, then flying the devil was her first. They cleared the clearance and set off, flying high above Nottingham into the sunset.

'What are you doing?!' Simon couldn't contain himself any longer. 'Just a little while ago you had us up high, now we're fifty feet off the ground and pushing past mach one.' This couldn't be safe during the day when you could see much less so now that it was getting dark.

Kiba had to be fully awake to perform the precise movement necessary to keep them from coming to a terrible fate with the suburban terrain just below.

At this speed and altitude, they'd all be dead before he even realized they were slipping. 'Would you mind slowing down some, rising up a little, or better yet both'

Kiba sighed 'Mr. B, put in the blue cell rod, It's been a while since we last used it'

Mr. Brad slotted in the cell rod as the bullet-proof windows slowly turned navy blue

'Moonlight vision' Kiba explained 'it multiplies the available moonlight by a thousand times.'

'So you can see what you're doing even at night,' Simon supplied his version of the rest. 'Fine, it's all nice and cool, but can we still slow down a little'

She pulled up some, eased up on the foot peddle, and let Shadow-Wolf glide around into a wide left turn sending them back toward the canopy. 'Your turn,' she said, relinquishing the controls over to Simon.

'I thought you'd never ask,' he said reaching for the collective and cyclic as he realized too late they were headed straight for the top of an electricity pylon.

Kiba's tired eyes snapped opened and the jet engines reengaged even as she pulled back on the stick, skirting the top with less than a foot to spare.

Mr. Brad didn't say a word, only trying to recapture the breath that had escaped him. Finally he spoke; interrupting the tentative silence that had fell over all the occupants. Simon, having taken the controls, for once seemed at a loss for words.

'I . . . you . . . we . . . I don't know,' he spoke disjointedly, shaking his head. 'I don't have any clue how we survived that without any damage or the big crash and explosion I wasn't looking forward to, but I'm just glad we're alive,' he managed, even his own voice was comforting after that close call.

Mr. Brad finally caught his breath, but didn't voice his opinion on the near incident. 'I think we should all get home,' he said non-partially.

Simon risked a glance at Kiba beside him and shook his head in disgust. 'I know she was tired, but how can anyone sleep after something like that? I can hardly breathe.'

'I don't know,' Mr. Brad agreed. 'Just get us back in one piece and I'll take her home.'

★   ★   ★

Adam stirred the pan absently, still thinking about the previous night. Mr. Brad had dropped Kiba off by half eleven, and she was out for the night. He had invited Mr. Brad to come and spend the night since he was so tired which he gladly accepted, but that was nothing compared to Kiba. Mr. Brad had draped her arms around his neck as he put her onto his back and then managed to stumble inside, laying her on the settee instead of taking her upstairs.

★   ★   ★

The next morning Mr. Brad emerged from the downstairs bedroom and strolled into the kitchen 'Smells good,' he complimented Adam's cooking.

'Thanks, but it's nothing special—just bacon, eggs and toast.'

'How about a cuppa to go with that?' Kiba asked after she unclipped her quiver and leaned her bow against the window frame.

'Sure. When'd you go out? I never even heard you get up.' She was a little more lively this morning, but the tiredness was still there.

'A little while ago.' She set to work cleaning the cups that were in the sink.

'Here, let me do that,' he obliged.

She obliged.

He frowned; she was simply being pushed around too easily. It wasn't Kiba-like. 'Are you coming down with something? You still seem kind of tired.'

'I'll be fine,' she grumbled.

Still doesn't want any medical care, Adam observed. As much as he hated to admit it, that was a good sign; whenever she willingly gave into actually seeing a doctor something was usually really wrong. It didn't keep him from worrying though.

He started to say something about staying home again, but she quickly dismissed the idea. 'I stayed yesterday; I'm fine, and I am going to work today.'

Still stubborn as always. Maybe he was just making this up to be more than it really was after all, yes, she'd been exceptionally tired yesterday and she obviously didn't take it easy at the canopy, but it was only natural to be tired after a day like that, and she did seem better than yesterday.

'Alright, but promise me you'll take it easy, ok?'

'What are you so worried about anyway?' she asked.

'Probably nothing,' he admitted, 'you've just been dragging a little the last few days and I want to be sure you're alright.'

'You worry too much,' she admonished. 'I'll be ok, don't worry about it anymore.'

Other than a brief argument over who would fly the helicopter to the hangar, the rest of the morning went well.

Chezia walked about the hangar in search of her sister. Mr. Brad had left to get dinner and Adam was busy with Domanick so she planned to ask Kiba who was scheduled to take a charter in forty five minutes—if only she could find her.

Eventually she gave up and walked back toward the other end of the hangar where Adam had been, figuring she'd just have to interrupt him since she couldn't find Kiba anywhere. As she opened the door, she almost collided with Kiba who was carrying an eight foot ladder.

'There you are. I've been looking all over for you.'

'Here I am,' Kiba said as she leaned the ladder against the wall. 'What do you need?'

'Who is supposed to take the charter in forty five minutes? I just wanted to know and everyone else was busy so I thought I would ask you.'

'Forty five minutes? Time flies and I should be.' She hastily left the room to clean up before her charter.

Chezia shook her head. While it wasn't a direct answer. That did answer her question.

She went back to the main area to see if Adam needed any help.

Re-entering, she overheard the couple arguing there.

'I'll be fine. I've been scheduled to take this flight for two weeks and I plan to do it.' She was more convinced to prove her point than actually wanting the charter, but some time away would be good, give her a chance to clear her head.

'Kiba, please,' Adam pleaded. 'I know I'm probably being stupid here, but let someone else take it, just to make me happy if nothing else. You said you'd take it easy, and I don't think a long flight is such a great idea if you might be catching something and you're not taking it easy either.'

'I never agreed to that this morning,' she told him bluntly, 'and I am flying this. It's only an hour's flight anyway.'

'An hour there, an hour back, then another hour and half to the cottage after the work you've already put in. I just don't think it's a good idea.'

'I'm sorry you don't think it's a good idea, but I intend to do it anyway.' Without another word, she turned on her heels and left to move the Jet Ranger outside.

'Why does she have to be so damn stubborn?' he fumed as he stormed past Chezia.

'What was that all about?' she questioned. Ok, maybe she should have asked a little more tactfully, but she had asked, the damage was done.

'Your sister is being too stupid to do something for her own good.'

'How so?' An hour charter flight wasn't all that abnormal or challenging and it wasn't even as if she'd any problems lately, had she? Missing a day at work and you miss out on so much some days.

'Yesterday she woke up late and she was exhausted. I tried to persuade her to stay at the cottage and rest, but she insisted she had to help work on Shadow-Wolf; in the end we compromised—she stayed home half a day and Mr. B picked her up from the cottage.'

'Uh-huh.'

'This morning she was still tired, understandably, she had a long day yesterday, but you know her. She refuses to rest even one full day.'

'So you're worried about her,' Chezia surmised. 'Hey, I know she isn't doing what you would consider logical, but she wouldn't put the passengers at risk if she thought it was really that big of a deal. It'll be alright; you'll see. Just help her through tomorrow then she'll have the whole weekend to relax. I'll even try my best to make sure the man in grey doesn't interrupt her weekend.'

'Thanks, Chezia. You're right, that's all I can do, and I guess that'll just have to be enough.'

★　　★　　★

Kiba's bare feet hit the wooden floor and with it came an overdose of reality. She was sicker than a dog. Her stomach churned at just the thought of breakfast, but if she didn't have any Adam would be more concerned than ever. She silently contemplated which was worse, losing her breakfast or fighting with Adam all day. Neither appealed at all. Thankfully, he wasn't up at the moment; he'd immediately be able to tell just how terrible she felt. She didn't even have some excuse to blame it on. Slowly, she made her way to the bathroom, brushed her teeth and turned to leave, not yet up for a even a quick shower; definitely not quick. If slow movements were this bad, she didn't even want to think about moving quickly. After pulling on her red and black jumper, she slowly made her way down the fire pole. Adam was nowhere to be seen, and Domanick hadn't been in his bedroom, so where could they be?

Shuffling over to the kettle, she made herself a cup of tea and set herself upon the task of finishing the entire cup.

With each mouthful it was like two more appeared—a never ending cup of tea. Most mornings something like this would be a pleasant surprise, but this morning was the exception. Still pondering where her husband and son were, she poured the remaining half finished tea down the sink. It was simply too much.

'Good to know it's September again,' she said aloud, her voice merely a harsh whisper. 'Maybe they went for a walk.' Adam had recently started going for occasional morning walks, and if Domanick had been stirring he might have very well taken him with him. Honestly, a leisurely walk under the canopy of hundreds of trees in the cool September breeze sounded rather pleasant if she could get her stomach to settle.

After unsuccessfully trying to do anything that didn't upset her stomach for nearly an hour, she decided to attempt a walk.

The cool morning breeze was already diminishing to the hot sun, but it was still pleasant outside. Choosing a path that led toward the other end of the lake, she walked casually like there wasn't a thing in the world wrong. By the time she returned to the cottage she felt considerably better, almost like she could face the day; however, Adam and Domanick still hadn't come back.

She began fixing breakfast for them, trying to persuade herself that it was just a long walk, or perhaps Domanick got tired and it was taking them twice as long to get back to the cottage.

Ten o'clock rolled around and neither of them was back. They should all be at the hangar by now, but instead she was here wondering where the other two might be. At last, she figured she should head up to the hangar, make sure everything was ok there and check to see if Adam had left any clues as to his and Domanick's whereabouts.

Climbing into the pilot's seat, she started the Jet Ranger and slid the headset on. By the time she was passing over the lake she was beginning to wonder if this was really such a good idea. Only determination to find her missing husband and son kept her from landing back on the jetty and radioing in sick—really sick.

After two hours that seemed like eight, she reached the Brad's Air Service hangar. Landing professionally, mostly to avoid further upsetting her already upset stomach, she gingerly slipped out and walked inside.

'Kib, you're here!' Mr. Brad exclaimed suddenly, accidentally slamming down the telephone receiver in the middle of his conversation with a prospective customer. 'Me and Chezia have been busy all morning and none of you bothered showing up. Where've you been?'

'The cottage,' she replied tersely. Where did he think she'd been?

Chezia interrupted Mr. Brad's excited greeting. 'Kub, you shouldn't be here. At the cottage maybe, or better yet the doctor, but not here.'

'Not now, Chez,' Kiba shot off.

'You looked tired before, now you look positively awful.'

'And I feel that way too,' Kiba announced bitterly, 'you don't think I don't know that? But Adam–'

'No, no buts. You get in the 4x4 now and I'm taking you to a doctor,' Chezia told her in an authoritative tone that gave no room for and's, but's, or if's.

'Adam and Dom are missing,' she ignored her sister's warnings.

'Fine.' Chezia allowed, not in a mood for compromise. 'I'll take you to the doctor, then Mr. B and I will look for Adam and Domanick.'

Kiba didn't waste any more time with further arguments, knowing she wouldn't talk her sister into anything; instead climbed back into the helicopter she'd come in and took off.

'That went well,' Mr. Brad idly commented.

'Yeah, I know. I guess something more subtle would've helped. It's just . . . She makes me so mad when she does that. I don't blame her for not liking hospitals and doctors, she's had plenty of bad experiences with them; personally, I don't either, but when you can hardly keep yourself from collapsing, that isn't a good time to go flying and decide to be too stubborn to see a doctor.'

Mr. Brad agreed. 'Well, we better get started. Now we have to find Kib, get her to a doctor, and find Adam and Domanick.'

★   ★   ★

Chezia headed for the other Jet Ranger. 'Mr. B, call Jason or something and start looking for Adam and Domanick. I'll be back.'

'Where you going?'

'To the canopy. If I know Kub, that's where she's headed and I have to stop her before she hurts Shadow-Wolf or herself.'

Mr. Brad dialled the number to Rhino-Gate.

'What do you mean he's not there?!' he exclaimed. 'I need to speak with him now.'

'Sorry Mr. Brad,' the new assistant apologized, 'but he's currently in London.'

'Alex, is Alex there?'

'He's with Jason,' the assistant replied.

'Jamie?' he asked hopefully. 'Anyone I've ever dealt with?'

'He's on holiday, sir.'

Everyone was out of town, somebody had to be running Rhino-Gate. He could imagine the entire building empty except a single desk with a lad, hardly eighteen, sitting there and telling any callers that everybody was out of town.

One last person he could think of, what was his name? Adam had said it way back . . . 'Donavan, Jacob Donavan, is he there?'

'Yes he's here. Would you like to speak with him?'

What'd he think? Jason had a way with picking intelligent lads; this one must not have been one of his picks. 'Yes.'

A brief pause, then Jacob Donavan picked up in his office.

'It's Michael Brad. I believe you helped a friend of mine with a case involving a helicopter, jeep explosion.'

'Yes, I remember that. How could I ever forget? How can I help you Mr. Brad?'

'I need some help locating a missing person, actually missing people.'

'Who? How long have they been missing and where is their last known location?'

'Adam Davids and Domanick Graham White. They were last seen up at Kib's cottage last night. When everyone went to bed everything was ok, but she woke up this morning and they were gone.'

'But White is still around, right?' Jacob checked.

'Well. Sort of. She's been sick, but she didn't like the idea of going to the doctor while her husband and son were missing so she took off about five minutes ago in my Jet Ranger.'

'I'll begin a search immediately, but I certainly wouldn't mind a little help. Finding her should be your first priority; I'll work on the others.'

★   ★   ★

Chezia grabbed a hold of the outside of Shadow-Wolf before Kiba could get off the ground. It was a risky move on her part, but Kiba couldn't hurt her own sister and it was the only way to stop her.

'Get off,' Kiba's voice sounded over the loudspeaker as she hovered near the ground.

Chezia refused to move.

'One button and I'll be doing mach one in four seconds.'

Chezia still didn't move, hoping she was right about Kiba not being able to hurt her. When she was set to do something, Kiba could be pretty irrational, but she wouldn't go that far hopefully. From her position, Chezia could tell Kiba's thumb was located dangerously close to the button used to engage the jet engines. If she did it though neither one of them would make it, surely she knew that. The force would be too strong for Chezia, and Kiba was simply too weak to be flying at that speed.

'Get off now.' She sounded as if she was actually thinking about it 'Damn it Chez. You know I can't hurt you, but I can't go with you either.'

Chezia could feel her fingers slipping. The fall wouldn't hurt her, being only about ten feet from the ground, but she would lose all chances at stopping her sister. 'Make this easy for me and land,' Chezia pleaded uselessly. The cockpit was sound proof, so Kiba wouldn't hear a word she said, but it came naturally. Just when her left hand slipped loose Kiba started to descend.

As soon as Chezia's feet hit the ground Shadow-Wolf started back into the sky, but Chezia already had the door open and was struggling to pull herself in.

'Come on, Kub. Even Shadow-Wolf isn't going to help you if you don't know where to start and you're not in any condition to fly anyway.'

'I have to try,' she retorted. 'I have to help Adam and Domanick they're my family.'

'I know. They're my family too, but don't forget you're part of my family. I want to help you.'

'Not letting me look isn't helping anyone.'

'It's not that I don't want you to look for them, Kub. I do, and I understand what it means to you, but I want what's best for you too, and you should see a doctor.'

'If you understood, you wouldn't make me stop.'

Sighing in frustration, Chezia tried once again to reason with her sister. 'I wouldn't if I thought you were up to it, but you said yourself that you don't feel very well and you sure don't look any better.'

'How about a deal? For old time sake,' Kiba tried.

'A deal?'

'Y'know, when we were kids you and I would make a deal. You would do something or give me something so that I would keep out of your hair for the afternoon, something like that.'

'Ok.'

'Here's the deal, you let me look for Adam and Domanick Graham without saying anything else about needing to go to the doctor for the next forty eight hours or until we find them, whichever comes first. In return, I will go to the doctor when time runs out without complaint.'

'And listen to what they say?'

'And pay some attention to what they say unless they're crazy and think I need to be laid up in the hospital for weeks on end.'

'Alright,' Chezia agreed. 'It's a deal.'

★   ★   ★

Mr. Brad waited expectantly outside the hangar. It had been nearly two hours, and Chezia hadn't returned or even radioed. Finally he heard the wolf's howl belonging only to Shadow-Wolf. Judging by the distinctive way it landed, it had to be Kiba flying. Great, she left before Chezia could talk some sense into her, Mr. Brad thought. He was highly surprise when Chezia climbed out of the co-pilot's side.

'Come on Mr. B!' Chezia called above the noisy rotor wash. 'We've got forty eight hours to find them,' she said sending a sly grin to her sister.

'Kib! What are you doing here?' he barked, staring at Chezia. 'Weren't you supposed to drop her off at the-'

'Shh. Don't say that word. We can't say anything about that until we can find Adam and Domanick, or at least forty eight hours from now.'

★ ★ ★

Shadow-Wolf screamed over the tree tops and came to a mid-air hover above the cottage. 'Here's the last place I saw them.'

'Let's look around here in case they did go for that walk like you suggested,' Mr. Brad said, 'maybe something happened that delayed them from getting back.'

Every scanner running, Shadow-Wolf passed just above the tree line. Nothing appeared at first, but they persevered.

Kiba focused intently on the instruments in front of her as they started to blur together. She knew she shouldn't be flying, but she had to try to help Adam and Domanick; she couldn't let them end up like so many others she loved.

'Chez,' she murmured wearily, 'go ahead and take the controls.' She couldn't bear to think of what might happen if she passed out while flying so close to the treetops. Whatever happened it wouldn't be pretty.

'You ok?' Chezia checked. Kiba sure as hell didn't look any better as she rubbed her eyes tiredly. She promised she wouldn't take her to the doctor for another forty five hours, but she should go. She'll be alright for a while longer, Chezia told herself.

Darkness tried to overcome her. Flying hadn't been too great an idea, and mach one had been a huge mistake. She mumbled something almost inaudibly.

'What did you say?'

She admitted defeat. 'Go ahead and take me to the doctor, but drop me off. Look for them.'

If Kiba was volunteering to go to the doctor early she couldn't be feeling well. 'Jet engines,' Chezia called.

'No,' Kiba interrupted woozily. 'Please no jet engines.'

Even behind the green hair Chezia could see the ashen shade Kiba's face had paled into instead of the normal healthy colour.

'Alright,' she obliged. It probably wasn't a very good idea.

Nearly an hour later, they arrived at the doctor's office. Chezia followed her sister's lead, climbing out and walked towards the brick building.

'Look for them,' Kiba instructed.

'We will,' Chezia assured her. 'Don't worry, Kub, we'll find them, but I'm not leaving until you're safely inside.'

'You're acting like I'm four,' Kiba grumbled.

'Maybe, but I'd hate to have you pass out in the car park and have to stay there until we come back.'

'I look that bad?' Kiba asked, smiling sheepishly. It wouldn't surprise her much; she certainly felt that bad.

'Just gotta look out for my twin sis.'

Kiba welcomed the grin that threatened to spread across her face. Lately she needed somebody to look out for her.

★　★　★

'That should do it,' the doctor finished. It wasn't anything major, for once. Just a bad case of the flu and some added stress from the recent events. Anything else would be easy to catch with her immune systems still weak, so he had given Kiba a prescription to ward off any other complications while her immune system wasn't at its best, but other than that the usual get some rest and drink plenty of fluids. 'I noticed that you had someone drop you off, Do you have someone waiting?'

'No, but it's ok,' Kiba replied as willingly as she could.

'No problem.' The doctor proceeded with his next patient.

Kiba walked outside and pulled out her mobile phone to call the hangar, but then realized they'd all be out looking for Adam and Domanick. Feeling guilty for not looking for them, she could almost hear Adam scolding her and telling her to get some rest that it would all turn out ok. She hoped that little voice in the back of her head was right. Putting the phone back into her denim jacket, she didn't relish the idea of walking to Chezia's flat, but she didn't seem to have any other options, so started down the street in the late September afternoon heat.

Inside, she settled for a simple bottle of water. After her drink, Kiba lounged on the settee in the living room until she finally dozed off.

★ ★ ★

Someone at the door woke her. The key was inserted into the lock, turned, then jiggled a little because it stuck, then Chezia walked in.

'Kub!' she said in surprise.

'Yeah, I hope you don't mind the invasion. I wasn't quite up to flying again even if I had made it all the way down to the hangar and your place was closest.'

'No, you're welcome anytime. What did the doctor say?'

'To get some rest, drink plenty of fluids, and he gave me a prescription to fight off any infections or bacteria.'

'So it isn't anything serious?'

'Nah, just the flu and exhaustion,' she replied. 'Did you find them yet?'

Chezia shook her head. 'Sorry, I picked Dan up from school and was going to drop him off here while Mr. B calls Donavan to see if they've come up with anything yet.'

Her hopeful gaze disappeared as quickly as it had come. 'Oh, alright. If he doesn't mind, can I have Dan fly me up the cottage? I think I can make it ok as a passenger, but maybe piloting wouldn't be the most brilliant idea.'

'Sure. I'll get him, and he can even stay there in case you need something,' Chezia offered.

'Thanks.'

'Don't thank me, I'm volunteering Dante for all the work,' she grinned wryly.

'Then tell him I said thanks too, I still want to thank you for looking; I really wish I could be of some help.'

'Just rest up so you'll be useful next time, and we'll be good. Besides, we have to have room in Shadow-Wolf when we find them.'

'Yeah,' Kiba stated simply. Somehow that didn't make her feel any better.

★   ★   ★

Kiba slipped out of the Jet Ranger. 'Thanks Dan, but if you want to go home I'll be alright, probably just going to take a nap anyway.'

Dante shut off the helicopter and scrambled out of the other side. 'I'll stay, Kibby. It's always nice to stay at your cottage.'

Kiba nodded appreciably and started towards the door. About to step inside, she noticed a package that had carelessly been thrown onto the porch. She stooped over to pick it up and carried it inside.

'What is it, Kibby?' Dante queried.

'I don't know.' She fumbled around for a moment looking for a knife to cut it open. Taking the one from her boot, she sliced the outside edges and pulled out a CD case. A ransom disk, she thought grimly. She immediately reached for the radio. 'Shadow-Wolf come in.'

'We read you,' Chezia answered.

'I need you to come by the cottage now.'

'Kib,' Mr. Brad started in from the back.

'I don't need arguments; I need a pickup. Now!'

Chezia reached over to the communications panel to end the transmissions before heading for the cottage.

'You aren't actually going are you?' Mr. Brad demanded. 'She's just been dropped off because she's sick. What good will it do if we go right back and pick her up?'

'It's not the same,' Chezia argued. 'She figured something out.'

'She never said that.'

'She meant it, in her voice. It was different, more urgent,' Chezia explained.

'Whatever. Let her do as she pleases,' He told himself throwing his hands up in the air. Kiba and Chezia White—understanding and practically inseparable to the end.

As Shadow-Wolf came to a hover directly above the jetty, Wolf climbed to all fours and padded up the front porch steps, and Chezia landed in the place he had vacated.

'How'd you do that?' Mr. Brad grumbled. 'Darn dog won't ever move for me. I was beginning to think he wanted me to land on him, but doesn't think twice about getting out of your way.'

'Guess I'm just special,' Chezia quipped from the front, 'or just lucky this time.'

Descending into the darkness of the night, Shadow-Wolf growled as he crouched down, in anxious await of the hunt that was sure to come.

Kiba pushed the CD into the DVD player and pressed play.

Adam came into view on the TV screen. 'I'm alright,' he said nervously, 'but if you want me to stay that way you have to deliver Shadow-Wolf to Malibu in California, Sunday night at four PM. No games, an even trade—me for Shadow-Wolf. Come alone and no tricks; otherwise I'll be killed.' For the first time he looked up and tears spilled down his cheeks. Then the CD ended and the screen went blank.

Visions of those scared, tearful, emotion filled brown eyes were too much. Somehow, no matter what it took, she would get Adam back safely. 'Didn't give me much to go by,' Kiba grumbled. 'Malibu at four that's it. Didn't even say a thing about Dom!' She didn't bother with the usual impassive mask; there wasn't much point. They all knew what she was feeling. Some happy endings are just too good to be true, her musing dark and depressing.

'What do you mean didn't give you much to go by?' Mr. Brad asked. 'We're going to be with you when you rescue them.'

'No. I can't risk losing you too, and I don't even know if there is a them to rescue,' she replied tersely, 'but there better be, or I'll blow them all straight to hell.'

'Kib,' Mr. Brad started, but she didn't go any further; Kiba wasn't going to listen to any reasoning.

She placed the determined impenetrable mask, rolled up her sleeves and left the room without another word. Mr. Brad, Chezia and Dante followed before she could protest.

★   ★   ★

Shadow-Wolf shot off through the sky. Minutes later they hovered down the clearance and landed in the darkness below. As soon as the rotors had stopped, Kiba began unloading the armament, starting with the heat seekers.

'What are you doing?'

'Unloading,' she answered shortly. 'If, by some chance, I lose Shadow-Wolf I don't want to arm the enemy.'

'Shouldn't we at least let Jason and Alex know what we're doing?' Chezia asked.

'Jason probably wouldn't approve and they don't need to know what I'm doing. This is personal.'

'They're in London anyway,' Mr. Brad supplied.

'It doesn't matter. I'm going and I'm going alone,' Kiba stated defiantly.

Now changed into her Shadow-Wolf uniform, Kiba climbed in and started him up. The wolf growled as he woke from his slumber. All systems green. Ready for take off

Alright, Shadow. Let's go save our family.

★   ★   ★

Mr. Brad gaped at the empty space Shadow-Wolf had recently vacated. 'She actually did it. She went off and left us' well now we've got a shelter filled with various types of missiles. What do you think about that?' Shaking his head, he started up the jeep to drive back. The only thing left to do was hope and pray Kiba could do it alone.

★　★　★

Kiba sat in the pilot's seat high above Nottingham. Scowling, she said, 'Chez.'

Chezia climbed up from her hiding spot behind the cell console. 'How'd you know? I didn't make a single noise.'

'Knew from the moment I got in; call it sister's intuition or whatever you want, but I knew you would try to come along somehow.'

'Not trying about it. I'm in and I'm staying in.'

'Like hell you are. If you climbed out with me we'll both be shot, Adam will be killed, Dom will too if he's not dead already, and they'll get Shadow-Wolf, but they're professional enough to know to check the back for stowaways.'

'Ok, ok. I don't want to cause any problems, but you are still sick and needing help is a possibility.'

'Yeah,' she returned spitefully, 'It'd be helpful, but not necessarily possible. Look, I intend to rescue Adam and Domanick if they're still alive, no matter in what condition, and everything else will have to come second.'

'Fine,' Chezia said, 'but you can't let them get a hold of Shadow either. Even though he's disarmed now, armament can be replaced; it'll just stall them.'

'That's the point, to stall them.'

★　★　★

Adam shivered mercilessly in the chilly wet prison cell. He could remember his days as a Police officer; he'd seen plenty of these types of places, but from this point of view it was totally different. He remembered meeting Kiba White for the first time. What a name! he'd thought, How he missed her . . . Things had gone well with the two of them and now Domanick too. What had happened to him? Thinking back, he tried to figure out what his fate might have been, or would be.

★ ★ ★

Early Thursday morning

Adam had slipped out of bed quietly to avoid waking his sleeping wife. Silently tiptoeing across the landing, he reached Domanick's bedroom. 'Shh, daddy's got you,' he hushed him. Taking the fussy child with him, he descended the stairs. He was just beginning to doze when he heard something outside. He grabbed one of Kiba's guns from above the bookcase and stealthily slipped out. Before he could get any farther, a dark figure behind him hit him over the head with a blunt object and everything went black . . .

★ ★ ★

After he woke up he'd only seen Domanick once. He hoped he was alright, not that it would matter much in a few hours. Four o'clock would soon be here, and when Kiba failed to drop Shadow-Wolf off . . . He didn't even want to think of the consequences.

What he'd give to have his family safely together, but it didn't appear that would be, he thought with a frustrated sob. Kiba loved him and he knew it, enough to give Shadow-Wolf up, but it wasn't that simple. She couldn't hand him over, she couldn't just give him to the enemy, and Shadow-Wolf in the wrong hands spelt danger.

The annoying ticking from the bold black clock kept ticking away, counting down the minutes until his certain death, until it was interrupted by a burly man barging in. 'Mr. Davids, it's time to go for a little trip,' he laughed menacingly. He bound him up deftly then shoved him towards the single door that allowed entrance and exit from the shabby old building. 'Better hope your wife is there and waiting,' he chuckled, 'or you won't even get to see her before you die. don't worry though, I'll send her a tape so she can see even if she misses the show.'

He seemed to be getting a lot of humour out of this, he thought bitterly. Leaving him in a freezing cold prison cell; he had a feeling he wasn't completely in charge though. He seemed to be somewhat frustrated with the limitations but still accepted them.

After their arrival, he rechecked the chains that bound him and turned to look for the treasure that he, like so many others, wanted.

Shadow-Wolf was nowhere in sight. He sighed heavily. This was it. 'Goodbye Kiba, Goodbye Domanick' he whispered.

'Aren't you going to tell me goodbye?' Chezia whispered in question from the open side of the custom helicopter.

He barely suppressed the urge to scream in delight.

'Where's the keys?' she asked more seriously.

Of course, his shackles. 'Uh, around baldy's neck,' he said dismally.

'Alright.' Spying a toolbox in the back, she rifled through it for something useful. 'Hopefully Kiba can keep him busy.' All she found was a hacksaw. 'I wonder what this was for,' she mused. 'Oh-well. I guess I won't complain too much.'

'Hurry,' Adam urged as he watched out the window to the temporary location of Shadow-Wolf and the two people standing directly in front of him.

'I told her we should switch jobs; she's not exactly the talking type.' She continued sawing at the chain that refused to cut through. 'It's pretty lightweight, but it will still take a while to cut through.'

He nodded in understanding, still watching out the window. 'Did you see any sign of Domanick?' he asked hopefully.

'He's not with you?' she sounded surprised and disappointed. She could only imagine what Kiba would be like if it turned out that Domanick was dead. There could be other kids, but it would be a blow that she would never get over.

Persistently she sawed away at the chain, but it already felt like the mission was at least partially failed.

★   ★   ★

Kiba led the bald man back to Shadow-Wolf. 'I'll show you the controls if you want,' she offered.

'I don't think that is necessary,' he declined.

Suddenly Kiba realized who it was. No it couldn't be! But it was.

'Alright, if you'll show me my husband and son then, I'll give you the flight suit and you can take Shadow-Wolf.'

'The flight suit isn't needed, you can keep it, as a souvenir, and I never said anything about returning or not returning your son.'

'If you hurt my son, I will personally tear you apart!' She argued as she took a swing at him, he hit the floor hard as the other man took hold of her 'Back off!' she shouted as she pushed the man backwards.

'It's alright Charlie' the man said as he stood up, 'I'll show you to your husband, White Wolf, and maybe we can work together again sometime soon.'

Kiba sent him a deathly glare. 'I don't have any wish to do business with you again and you can write this down; if Domanick is still alive, I'll find him.'

'They're coming,' Adam hissed.

'Almost got it . . .'

'Go. Get out of here.'

'But I've-'

'Go!'

Chezia disappeared into the underbrush as quickly as she'd come. Adam looked longingly after her. So close to freedom.

'Here he is,' he took the key from the chain around his neck and unlocked him, but didn't stop there. Kiba reached forward to help her husband out, and the other pilot pushed her in on top of him before slamming the door shut and climbing back into his own seat.

By the time Adam and Kiba had disentangled themselves from each other and the chain they were high in the air. 'My friend will enjoy that beautiful bird immensely, thanks for your contribution.'

'What makes you think he can fly Shadow?' Adam demanded.

Kiba already knew.

'He can, maybe not quite as well as White Wolf, but you two aren't going to be flying Shadow-Wolf again so why not take a close runner up? He worked under the same one White did for a while. She might even remember him. Do you remember Shamus O'Brian?'

'Dad's co-pilot, so what are you planning to do with us?'

'Making sure you don't come back this time. Your brother died in a bridge accident, drown actually right? The same one that would have killed you if your sister hadn't been there to fish you out?'

She didn't answer.

'I figure you can get the real experience of drowning and include a helicopter since they played such a big part in your life. Am I a genius or what?' By now they were ten miles from shore over a choppy Pacific Ocean. 'Adios.'

★   ★   ★

Chezia found a man pouring over Shadow-Wolf's beauty. 'It's been a while,' he said, 'almost ten years.' He donned his own Shadow-Wolf uniform although slightly different from the one Chezia was wearing. Where did the flight suit come from? The question plagued her mind continuously, but that didn't matter right now. She just had to figure out how to get Shadow-Wolf back and find the others.

Reaching for her gun, she drew it and crept closer to Shadow-Wolf. Shamus opened the pilot's door and climbed inside, a gloved hand pushed the start up button since the purple cell rod was still in the cell reactor. The rotors began to lull lazily around, slowly gaining speed.

Chezia aimed the gun at the intruder before he could lift off. 'Where are the others?' she demanded.

The man stared down at the slightly different Shadow-Wolf flight-suit in wonder and a puzzled look crossed his face. 'Who are you?'

'Chezia White,' she glowered. 'Where are the others?'

Shamus shrugged nonchalantly. 'I have no idea. Ken said he wanted to spend a little quality time with White' He didn't recognize the woman. She looked the same age as Kiba with dark brown hair now slightly streaked with blonde. 'Say, are you two related?'

What's with this guy? He had a gun in his face, and he was set on making conversation.

'Before she left, due to Graham's death, she said something about having a sister, but she is MIA.'

'Was MIA, now stop distracting me and tell me where the others are.'

'Ken wanted his own Shadow-Wolf; I think he was a bit jealous of White to be honest with you. He wanted those good piloting skills, to be chief pilot, but he was better at the computers and only was second best at flying. When White dropped out we thought we'd seen the last of her, but when we got word of her possession of Shadow-Wolf he was determined to get it.'

Chezia just couldn't believed this guy. A simple question with a one word answer was turning into a long and detailed story.

'Ken decided to build his own custom chopper, it's pretty nice too, and it's a lot more roomy than Shadow-Wolf is, but it doesn't have the same speed. It at least equals Shadow-Wolf in firepower though. He was going to challenge White to an air battle, but when he came up with the idea of getting Shadow-Wolf too . . . Well, you can figure out the rest. Personally, I'd love to have a machine like this, but where would I hide it? Especially with all those other government agencies after it. I told him I'd help him get Shadow-Wolf if the money was right and I could borrow it once in a while.'

'Mercenary.'

'Sadly enough, that's pretty much the truth,' Shamus admitted. 'You know how it is. Anything can be done if the money is right . . . Sorry about your sister and her husband. I honestly don't know where they're headed. All I heard was something about a bridge accident. With the bills he has amassed to for that custom chopper of his. He'd have to sell that thing for a tidy sum to even think about keeping Shadow-Wolf for himself.'

Chezia didn't know what to do with this guy. He wasn't actually hurting anything or anyone, but he was in the way, and what was with that flight suit?

'So, I noticed the flight suit. Is that some new version or something? I still got the original one I started with, but I haven't been involved with the Shadow-Wolf project for about twelve years now. After White let loose on Wayne—Graham's engineer over in Yorkshire Dales, I decided to stay away.'

That explained the flight suit; so he was on her dad's side, but obviously not a die-hard supporter. In all, he seemed like a pretty reasonable guy.

'Just dropped them off,' Ken's voice sounded over the radio, smug and kind of evil, before giving his coordinates. 'I'll be back in thirty minutes, and I did decide to give their son back in case you were wondering. They deserved at least one last goodbye.'

One last goodbye? Did that mean Domanick Graham was dead? Kub would never get over it and Adam wouldn't take it well either. 'What did he do to them?' Chezia demanded concernly.

Shamus checked the coordinates. 'That's ten miles over the ocean!' he exclaimed. 'He wasn't supposed to kill White, we just wanted Shadow-Wolf.'

'Ten miles from shore? They'll never make it.' Chezia quickly started to devise a plan to pick them up, but first she had to get Shamus out of the way.

'He wasn't supposed to do that!' Shamus slammed the hatch door shut as Shadow-Wolf rose up.

Chezia didn't dare hang onto the outside of Shadow-Wolf like she had with Kiba because this wasn't Kiba. What could she do to stop Shadow-Wolf before it was too late? It already was too late, she thought miserably. She hadn't thought on her feet fast enough, and now Kiba and Adam would have to pay for her mistake—with their lives.

★   ★   ★

Domanick fussed, unhappy with the sudden splash of salt water when they were thrown out of the helicopter and into the Pacific Ocean.

'Shh,' Adam soothed, trying to keep them both afloat while he uneasily scanned the surface for any sign of his wife. She had still been struggling with Ken when he and Domanick had been thrown in. Since then he thought he'd heard a rather loud flat splash but still no sign of her. He desperately wanted to tell Domanick that everything would turn out all right, he wanted to tell himself that, but it sure wasn't looking like that would be the case.

Domanick struggled in his grip, trying to escape the salty, cold water.

'Stop that,' Adam coughed from the mouthful of water he got from his flailing. 'Kiba where are you?' She had to be around here somewhere. His attention returned to the upset child still fighting him. 'Domanick Graham!' he said firmly, 'Stop that now or neither one of us is going to last long.'

Violent coughing and gasping for breath had him turning around once again. 'Kiba,' he said in relief.

'H-here,' she said weakly between gasps of air. 'I managed to get at least one life vest.'

He took it gratefully and fastened in onto Domanick. 'Thanks. At least now he won't drown me just because it's too cold and salty.'

'Yeah.'

'You ok?' he asked, already beginning to tire from treading water.

'Never been better.'

What a stupid question. 'How far do you think shore is?'

'Eight or nine miles at least.'

'Oh,' he replied dejectedly.

'Let's go. Maybe at least part of us can make it,' she tried to encourage, already fully knowing she would sacrifice her own life to get them to shore. What would her life matter anyway if she didn't? Without Adam and Domanick she didn't see much point.

Adam started swimming toward shore hauling Domanick along behind him; on the bright side, he was starting to get over his fear of salt water.

'Let me,' Kiba said taking a hold of Domanick's life vest.

'You're too tired.' He reached for him back, doubting he would be able to make it all the way to shore anyway. Maybe Kiba could, and if the weather started cooperating and with the aid of the life jacket, he might have a slim chance to get back and Domanick too.

'I'll take him; I'm better trained for long distance swims anyway.'
She started again, powerful strokes pushing aside the water. Adam
right behind her.

★   ★   ★

Shadow-Wolf reduced to a hover then glided back the few feet
he'd already traveled. 'You coming?' Shamus asked, 'or do I have to
find White myself?'
Chezia looked up in surprise.
'Well?'
She clambered into the back. What did she have to lose? This way
she had a better chance of retrieving Shadow-Wolf and rescuing the
others, but she did find it rather odd that she was voluntarily riding
with her enemy.

★   ★   ★

Mr. Brad sat next to the radio, hoping to hear from Kiba. It looked
like Chezia had successfully made it along for the ride, assuming Kiba
hadn't dropped her off somewhere. But how were things going? It
had been hours since he had last heard from any of them, and the
wondering was killing him.
He picked up the receiver to the radio and tried Shadow-Wolf,
hoping he wouldn't interrupt anything, but it had been so long and
not knowing was simply unbearable.
'Brad to Shadow-Wolf, do you copy?'
'Shadow-Wolf, we read you,' the unfamiliar voice answered.
Who was that? Mr. Brad wondered. It sure didn't sound like
Adam and it defiantly wasn't either White.
'Mr. B, this is Shadow-Wolf. Come on back,' Chezia said.
'Yeah,' Mr. Brad replied. Maybe it had just been a bad connection
or something because that was definitely Chezia. 'How is everything
going?'
'I wish I could say everything was going well, but you taught us
not to lie. Kub and Adam have been dumped ten miles off shore and

Dom is with them. I'm not sure if he's alright or not, and the whole controlling Shadow-Wolf situation is, well, kind of strange.'

'Off shore as in the ocean?'

'Yep. We're on our way now.'

'Just hurry, kid. Kib was still tired and Adam wouldn't be able to swim ten miles either, so Shadow-Wolf getting there is probably their only hope'.

'We should be about there,' Shamus said.

Chezia traded the engineer's seat for the co-pilots and began to run the scans over the area, hoping to find her sister, Adam and Domanick

★   ★   ★

The waves had calmed down some at least, but Kiba wasn't sure how much longer she could keep this up. How far had they come?

Adam had finally passed out from exhaustion, but she couldn't let him drown so she pulled him along now as well. Her progress was extremely slow, but her brother drowning had been more than enough. She couldn't bear to lose him too. If she lost anyone else she wasn't sure she could ever be able to be pieced back together, there had already been too much loss. She would get him and Domanick back to shore no matter what the cost she would.

Another cold wave splashed over her head and Domanick resumed his fussing. Tired, too tired to continue. She pulled the other two along again; she couldn't give up yet. A ten mile swim at her best would have been tiring if she made it, but already weakened and having to pull two others along was impossible. She tugged them farther. She could make it she told herself. She hadn't given up yet, and she wasn't about to.

★   ★   ★

Shadow-Wolf hovered above the blue water, still hunting for the missing trio. 'Do you think they drowned?' Chezia asked, they had already been over the area countless times and still there was no signs of them yet.

'You think they tried to swim for shore?' Shamus offered.

'Ten miles is too far.'

'Maybe, but from the little bit of time I knew her, White's determined to do practically impossible things just to prove they're possible. What could it hurt to try swimming for it if you thought you were going to drown anyway?'

'We aren't finding them here so I guess it can't hurt to try.'

Shadow-Wolf glided over the water, hunting his pilot and family before it was too late.

'Incoming message.'

Chezia reached over to connect it.

'Where is my helicopter!' Ken demanded impatiently. 'Bring it back now or I swear I'll kill you.'

'There's been a change in plans. Taking Shadow-Wolf was pushing it, but you know how to work the weaknesses. Honestly I was only doing it for the money and getting to actually see it again. Killing people was not in the plan, and I'm not intending to make any changes to that, oh and just to inform you . . . This will always be White's chopper!' Shamus answered furiously and ended the transmission.

★   ★   ★

Kiba finally had the life vest attached so that it would float both Adam and Domanick. All three was too much for one vest; but at least they had a vague possibility of being washed onto shore, and now the tide had turned in their favour.

'Sorry I couldn't get you all the way,' she told them. 'Remember I always loved you.'

Domanick stared down at his mother with glassy blue eyes. 'Mummy.'

'Mummy can't,' Kiba told him, now struggling to tread water. Every second was a battle to keep her head above water.

'Mummy please stay.'

'Wish I could, buddy,' she gasped in exhaustion.

Another wave washed over her head as she went under and the others floated on the surface above.

★   ★   ★

A bright red spot contrasting against the blue water made them take a second look.

'That's them!' Chezia said excitedly.

Shamus reduced the speed to a stationary hover. Chezia climbed into the back and slid the left door open and threw down the rope ladder, but, to her horror, no one climbed up. She started down the ladder, earnestly hoping Shamus could be as trusted as he seemed to be.

She hauled Adam inside. Breathing hard by now, she went back to retrieve the child. At least Domanick was smaller and lighter.

Domanick had no qualms about leaving the water and readily allowed his auntie to remove his life vest and carry him up the swinging rope ladder.

The two year old stared down at the blue water. 'Mummy,' he cried.

Horrified, Chezia knew what that meant. She dove from Shadow-Wolf into the water; the salt stung her eyes, but she wouldn't come back until she had looked, she just had to know for sure. There was a sandbank beneath them and she could see her sister's lifeless body drifting toward the bottom. She came up for a quick gulp of air then dove back down. Just now reaching the bottom, Kiba's body came into full contact with the sandy underground bottom twenty feet below. Chezia wrapped her arm around her sister's chest and push herself off the bottom to the surface. She breathed in a grateful breath of air, and then struggled up the ladder dragging her sister along behind. With a great deal of effort, she pulled Kiba up and hoisted her inside.

Dropping heavily into the engineer's seat, Chezia, exhausted, slid the door shut then settled Domanick into the jump seat then checked on his parents.

'How are they?' Shamus asked, already directing them toward the nearest hospital.

Adam coughed and opened exhausted brown eyes taking in his surroundings. 'Chezia,' he immediately realized it was her who had rescued them and hugged her appreciatively. 'I'm so glad to be out of that salty, cold ocean.'

'Really? Looked to me like you were having a nice nap and you sure didn't help any when it was time to get out,' Chezia said trying to lighten the atmosphere.

'Sorry. I can't even say it was a very restful nap. Do you have a towel or blanket or something?' He asked shivering, 'or even something other than salt water to drink?'

Chezia handed over the flask. 'We don't have any blankets now, but we'll get you one and a change of clothes soon.'

'Thanks,' he thanked appreciatively. Realization hit him fast and hard though. If he had passed out, then Kiba must have had to drag him along too 'Is Kiba alright?' Adam questioned worriedly from his new position at the front.

'I hope so,' Chezia replied gravely as she tried to revive her sister.

Suddenly Kiba began hacking violently, heaving seawater between each cough, trying to draw in a breath of air to her oxygen starved body. After nearly a minute of continuous coughing, she finally drew in a full breath.

'I wish I had blankets,' Chezia murmured to herself.

'It's alright,' Adam replied.

Chezia looked down at Kiba's cloudy blue eyes, staring forward but not really seeing, too lost in her own little world, and hoped she would be alright.

'Approaching the hospital,' Shamus announced. 'Do you want me to get the doctor or stay with them?'

'Doctor please,' Chezia requested.

'No problem,' Shamus answered, landing smoothly on the hospital roof. 'I'll be right back.'

Shamus returned momentarily with a doctor and group of nurses.

'Your friend here told me everything seemed to be ok, but you want to get them checked over?'

'That's right doc,' Chezia answered.
'Alright. Let's bring them in.'

★   ★   ★

Adam walked out of the examination room with one of the nurses. 'He needs plenty of rest and to keep warm, but he'll be fine and the child too.'

Domanick giggled happily, obviously none the worse after their incident.

'What about Kiba White?' Chezia asked.

'She appears to be alright,' the nurse told her. 'For what happened, they are all very lucky.'

Chezia nodded her appreciation and they all went back up to the roof. Chezia had been expecting Kiba to be her typical stubborn self and take her normal position in the pilot's seat, but she silently climbed into the back without the slightest protest.

Planning to drop Kiba, Adam and Domanick off at home first, they stopped briefly at the cottage, then Chezia dropped Shamus off in town and went to take Shadow-Wolf back to the canopy.

★   ★   ★

As Adam put the simple dinner on the table and watched Domanick play in his food, he could see Kiba outside the window sitting by the lake.

Quietly slipping outside, he joined Kiba where she had been since they'd been dropped off. She stared off in space somewhere beyond the horizon.

'You alright, Kiba?' he asked concern.

She didn't answer.

'Kiba?'

Still no reply.

'Come on inside and eat something, you've got to be hungry after not eating all day.' He took her by the arm and guided her inside.

She silently came in, but didn't even touch her food.

He tried starting conversation, but she still offered no reply. Concern mounted up inside him. Why was she so quiet and unresponsive?

After dinner, Adam had put Domanick into bed and Kiba headed in that direction when the radio crackled to life.

He went to answer it. 'Go ahead I'm here.'

'I just heard about this afternoon; is everybody alright?' he asked, hoping that he would get an honest answer that everything was fine and they could all get on with their lives instead of the worries that continuously plagued him.

'I hope so.'

'What do you mean hope so? You all did get checked over by a doctor didn't you? Even that stubborn wife of yours?'

'Yeah, and they seemed to think everything was ok, but . . .'

'But what?' Mr. Brad interrogated.

'Kiba—she hasn't said a word and it worries me. Physically she's fine, but it's like she's not really here, so unresponsive, far away and silent . . . I'm worried she went into some kind of shock or something'

'Oh.'

He quickly noticed the sudden concerned drop in his voice. 'What is it? Should I take her back to the doctor?'

'No, if they do get her talking again it'll be just to curse at them and make a big scene then it gets worse, been there done that. If she's not better by tomorrow you might try Chezia.'

'Chezia?' he questioned.

'After the bridge accident that killed Vergil and nearly killed her, she was like that. The doctors said it is some kind of post-traumatic stress disorder. She was like that after her brother's death, for a while after Chezia was listed MIA and after Graham had been killed. No one could get through to her, even the doctors; they said they'd done everything they could. She didn't say a word for weeks, in the case of the bridge accident, it was Chezia that finally got though to her.'

That information didn't make him feel any better, only worry more. 'Thanks, Mr.B. I'll see if that works. Goodnight'

'Night.'

★   ★   ★

Adam peered at the old fashioned clock on the mantel. Kiba couldn't still be sleeping; it wasn't in her nature. Kiba White didn't sleep in past eight.

He climbed back up the stairs to see what she was up to. 'Kiba, you up?'

She seemed a little more with it today, or was it just his imagination. She still wasn't speaking with him, or anyone.

'Domanick seems to want to go visit Dante and Derek, you want to come?'

When he motivated her to join, she obeyed, still obeyed, still acting as if she had no will, just lost and alone.

And I complain she's too stubborn, this is ridiculous. She'll do anything you ask her to but speak. Adam thought to himself.

He loaded Domanick into the back, giving Kiba the pilot's seat, but she instead absently slid into the co-pilot's seat.

★   ★   ★

Chezia flipped the pancakes one last time and added it to the plateful. After the previous day's incident she figured Kiba and Adam would want some time alone so she decided to spend the day with James. Carrying the plate to the table, she called the others. Dante, James and Derek gathered around her little table.

'Hope everyone like's pancakes.'

'That's fine,' James smiled.

'My fav-rit!' Derek joined gleefully.

The doorbell rang and Chezia went to get it. 'Go ahead and eat. I'll be right back.'

She pulled the door opened, revealing Adam and the squirming toddler he held. 'You want breakfast too?'

'No thanks,' Adam declined, 'but I do have a favour to ask you.'

'Ask away.'

'Would you talk to Kiba, or better yet, get her to talk to you?'

'Sure why?'

Adam explained what Mr. Brad had said about the unusual silences, even from Kiba, and unresponsiveness. 'Mr. B said that maybe you'd be able to get though to her.'

'I'll try,' Chezia agreed, 'but I can't promise anything. Last time it took me three weeks, and even then her only words were go away Chez, I want to be alone.'

'Just please try.'

'I can do that much. Go ahead and come in and make yourselves at home. This could take a while.'

★   ★   ★

Jason turned in surprise to see Shamus, the last of the original Shadow-Wolf team, standing at his desk.

'Black,' he addressed.

'O'Brian.'

'Have you heard anything about White and her family? I just wanted to make sure they were all doing ok.'

'Actually, I haven't heard from any of them,' Jason answered, expertly hiding his curiosity and surprise at seeing Shamus again. 'Why do you ask?' He hadn't seen Shamus since Graham's death, twelve years ago, and to his knowledge neither had Kiba, and they'd never been friends per say, so why would he be asking after all this time?

'Rescuing her husband and son turned out to be more complicated than it was supposed to be, and she nearly drown herself to save them, so I figured the least I could do was to apologize and see how she was.'

Jason still wondered about Shamus's mysterious appearance and what was he apologizing for. He also wondered about this rescue attempt surely he would have known if one of the Whites, Adam or Mr. Brad had gone missing, he always did.

'I'm not sure I remember the way to the cottage even if I did have a helicopter to fly, but obviously she is working for Rhino-Gate again to have control of Shadow-Wolf so I thought maybe I could find something out here,' Shamus explained.

'She's freelance.'

'Oh. Well, next time you see her, tell her I hope she's doing ok.'

'I can do that,' Jason promised.

As Shamus left his office, Jason picked up the radio receiver and radioed the cottage and hangar but even after several tries didn't get an answer in either place. Still wondering what the real story was, he went back to work. They were probably on some job and he could get back to them later.

★   ★   ★

Chezia jogged across the road where the Jet Ranger had been parked in the car park, pulling the door open she climbed in next to Kiba. Her usually clear light blue eyes were cloudy and filled with more emotion that seemed possible, but her body language was devoid of all emotion and pretty much anything that might allow any insight to her thoughts.

'You ok, Kub?'

Her sister didn't answer, unblinking eyes steadily forward but not registering.

'We're worried about you; at least tell me to shut up again. Anything would be nice; you're simply too quiet, even for my crazy brooding sister.'

Was that a semblance of an almost smirk or was that just her wanting it to be?

'Come on, talk to me or I'll have to bring Simon in to talk to you.' That didn't help.

'You want something to eat or drink? I'll fix vegetarian just for you. Hell, I'd go vegetarian to keep you from being like this.'

Still nothing.

'Want to come inside?'

Kiba didn't reply.

Why was she like this? 'Just talk. I'll do anything you want if you'll just say something.' Somehow, she had to figure out what was wrong and get her to open up about it, but that was going to be a very difficult job.

Chezia looked lovingly across the cockpit at her sister. Much to her surprise, when she reached over to give Kiba a quick hug before trying to haul her inside Kiba didn't let go. She hung onto her twin sister tightly, refusing to even loosen her deathly grip. Quietly sobbing, tears poured off her face and onto the shoulder of Chezia's lavender shirt. She let out all the fear and worry she'd had, all the tragedy. For at least a good fifteen minutes she let go of it all, only content to share her heavy burdens with her sister. Chezia caught a few words between heart wrenching cries. She didn't care who saw or what happened; Kiba hadn't let go of it all since the awful day of the bridge accident in which their brother had drowned and she nearly had. She was grateful for Chezia fishing her out that day, but this had been too close, too similar.

At last she loosened her grip, even then not fully letting go. Chezia made no move to remove her twin sister's arms that clung around her neck. Nineteen years ago, on that terrible day, she had promised that she would be there if Kiba ever needed her. A lot had happened since then, but she still planned to keep that promise to the very best of her ability. She would do whatever Kiba needed her to do even if she had to sit out here all day.

Gradually the sobs subsided and Kiba looked at her twin sister desperately. For a moment all Chezia could see was that distraught ten year old girl that didn't look like she could face the loss of her brother and everything she had ever known.

When Kiba finally let go, Chezia pushed the door open to let in some air into the stuffy cockpit.

'Don't leave,' the weary trembling voice pleaded, 'please don't go.' After that she mumbled something about their brother, dad, Matthew, and all the others.

'I'm not going anywhere,' Chezia assured her, overjoyed to hear her talking again at least, but she couldn't bear to look into those hazy pain filled blue eyes.

'Thanks.' The single word of gratitude meant more than Kiba would ever be able to know or understand. 'And thanks for fishing me out, again,' she murmured.

'Glad to. I intend to keep you around for a long while.'

Kiba smiled faintly in return, the last of the tear glistening in her eyes.

★   ★   ★

Adam finished his conversation with James while the kids played in Dante's bedroom. They shared various stories, discussed the latest news, and made small talk while the girls were outside.

'Is Kie ok?' James asked seriously. 'They've been out there forever and I don't know her to be much of a talker.'

'Especially lately,' Adam put in. 'Since yesterday's incident she hasn't said a single word; it really worries me. Mr. B said she was like that for weeks after their brother's death but finally Chezia was able to get through to her, so I'm hoping.' Adam got up and went to the door.

'What is it?' James queried.

'I thought I heard someone coming through here,' Adam answered as he opened the door.

Just outside, the three kids sat playing.

'Wow, I never heard them,' James commented. 'You must have really good hearing.'

'It's nothing,' Adam shrugged, 'especially compared to Kiba's. I guess it's important living at the cottage though.' He definitely wouldn't want Domanick to sneak outside and fall into the lake; one near drowning experience was enough for him and Domanick; Kiba had already been through that before, and look how badly she was handling this, not that he could blame her. She had been willing to sacrifice her own life to see that they had a chance. Shoving the images out of his head, Adam took a seat outside to watch the kids play. They were all safe now, that's what mattered, he told himself, but Kiba talking would definitely be nice.

★   ★   ★

'You gonna be ok?'

'Yeah, but don't leave just yet.'

Chezia stayed put; 'I'll stay as long as you need me to.' They had been close as kids and she wanted to remain close. Sure, there were times when it was just too much and she needed to get away, but nine years of hoping she would get to see her sister at least one last time had paid to most of that. Even so, this was more than just wanting to be in each other's good graces.

'Maybe Simon was right; we do tend to be around each other just enough to bail each other out.'

'I want to be around more than that,' Chezia decided. 'I guess we'll have to get together for something a little more pleasant in the future.'

'Sounds good to me.'

'Hey, I know this guy and there's this really good archery spot with a beautiful waterfall view, think you might have an interest?'

'Only if you come along to fish me out.' Kiba smiled wryly, 'Although maybe I'll skip the almost drowning part this time. I should be good on that one for a while.'

'It's settled then, We'll leave first thing in the morning for a weekend of relaxation and shooting, but no drowning.'

CHAPTER NINE

Fallen Angel

Adam put Domanick to bed then resumed reading his book by the hearth, anxiously awaiting Kiba's return from a weekend archery trip with her sister. Thankfully, things were returning to normal, but he couldn't rid himself of the awful memories. He was already very grateful for Chezia being able to get her talking.

Hopefully that would never happen again. That silent, shocked, lost expression was just unbearable. Domanick had quickly drifted off, exhausted after the day's play, but Adam couldn't have fallen asleep if he'd tried. He would stay up until his wife returned this evening; although it was beginning to worry him that she wasn't back yet. They had said they would be back Sunday night, but he had assumed a little earlier than this. Lost in his own memories, the minutes passed without letting Adam know. The clock sitting upon the mantle now read eleven o'clock. Happening to glance up, he saw how late it was getting.

Please let them be alright and just running late. Torturously long minutes ticked by second by second. Noticing he had now gone through three more cups of coffee since he last checked the clock, he looked up once more, hoping it wasn't as bad as it seemed. Now eleven forty five, he was growing very concerned. They should have been back hours ago. A noise in the distance tickled his hearing. He hurried outside to see if it was the Jet Ranger with his wife.

He strained his tired brown eyes to see through the darkness. Whatever it was, was still too far away. At last the dark form could be seen well enough to see the distinctive red nose and white stripe belonging to the Brad's Air Service helicopter, and Adam let out a long relieved sigh. She was finally back.

He ran to greet her with a hug, grateful that she was finally safely back home.

'Miss me?'

'Lots. I was getting worried.'

She slipped a tired, colourful tattooed arm around him as they walked together back to the cottage. 'You worry too much. I said I'd be back Sunday night.'

'It'll technically be Monday in about two minutes,' he reminded.

'Ok, so I cut it a little close, but we were trying to catch up on good times and time kind of got away from us, then I had to drop Chez off at the hangar so she could take the jeep back to her flat. In my defence, I did make it back before Monday, so I'm still on time.'

'Alright, alright. Did you at least have fun?'

'Yeah we enjoyed it'

'At least you got to spend some time with just you and your sister.'

'Yeah, how were you and Dom here?'

'You know, the normal stuff, nothing exciting.'

'I know? I'm not so sure I know what normal is anymore.'

'Then it was just nothing super exciting. I can't say we did anything amazing, but we had a good time and it did give me and Domanick some quality time together.'

'Sounds good. Maybe you and I need to spend a little time together ourselves now that we've be spending time with everyone else,' Kiba suggested.

'Maybe you have a really good idea.'

★ ★ ★

Mr. Brad hustled everyone to their reassigned jobs. 'Come on. We have to hurry or the director is going to be up in arms before we even get there.'

'Up in arms you say? Maybe we should take the Devil instead of the Jet Ranger then.'

'Hilarious,' Mr. Brad remarked sarcastically. 'Kib, it's nice you're in such a good mood today, but now is not the time for that.'

'She's just jealous,' Chezia joined in, 'she didn't get to fly him the last time because she was busy drinking half the ocean.'

'Not drinking, drowning.'

'Better watch it twin sis, or Shamus will get his position after all.'

'Not a chance. I like my seat and plan to keep my seat for a good long time.'

Mr. Brad argued 'You better hope you do because we're going to loose this job if you two don't stop clowning around and get over there.'

'Ok, ok,' they replied together, still laughing as they climbed into the black, white and red Jet Ranger and lifted off. Exactly thirty seconds later the same chopper landed on the tarmac outside again, and Chezia slid out.

'Sorry about that. We need the other one,' Chezia explained as if it were the funniest thing on earth. Seconds later, the other Jet Ranger lifted off and headed in the direction of the filming site.

'I just hope they bring them choppers back in one piece.' Adam nodded his agreement. 'I don't know what was so hilarious, but they're going to have to get themselves under control. I hear Pollard is a pretty serious guy and doesn't put up with much joking around.'

'Yeah. Let's hope they don't loose the job either; we need the business.'

'Mr. B, you make it sound like Brad's Air Service is about to go under. I've done some of the booking lately; we've been a little slow, but it's not that bad.'

'I hope you're right.' Maybe it hadn't been that bad, but it sure didn't seem like they had been doing anything lately.

★   ★   ★

Brad's Air Service was silent other than the occasional flip of pages and the rare phone call. Mr. Brad looked through the photo album Adam had put his messy box of random pictures into. It really brought back memories, some good, and some not so well.

'Is that Kiba when she was younger?' Adam queried as he peered down over his shoulder. An old picture showed the cottage before its remodel with an twelve year old boy and two six year old girls, archery bows, and sloppy grins on their faces.

'Yeah. That was before the bridge tragedy struck.' Silently they continued flipping through the thick pages.

Adam recognized a younger version of Kiba in her army camouflage. Only a few pages later, He saw the other White in a similar uniform, Soon afterward didn't seen any more pictures of Chezia, only Mr. Brad and Kiba.

Must have been when she went off to Burma, He reasoned, then a picture of two young women and a young man, obviously taken in Burma. The two girls he recognized as Kiba and Chezia, but the man he didn't. The following pages were filled with pictures from Burma, archery competitions and from around the Brad's Air Service hangar, Mr. Brad himself, and Kiba, looking several years older. She still looked considerably younger than when he had met her though.

A wide variety of pictures, probably spanning many years, of the same kind continued. Finally one appeared different. In it, Kiba didn't necessarily look extremely excited, but she did look proud of herself, like she'd made a great discovery.

Adam looked out the window to see if the others were returning yet, but there was no sign of them. By the time he looked down again he saw Mr. Brad and Kiba looking positively smug. One picture he easily recognized as Kiba with only had her left arm tattooed colourfully at the time, and was wondering when that had been taken. The following page was full of pictures of Graham, Vergil and the twins. Eventually he identified a more recent picture of the whole family directly following a simple shot of Kiba and Chezia. In it, Kiba had bandages covering a good portion of her arms and obviously was very severely injured, but the joy in her smile as she leaned against her sister proved she wasn't feeling any of that pain, only glad to have Chezia back.

'Didn't she have any boyfriends or some friends to hang out with?' He found himself asking, although not realizing he'd asked out loud. Surely there had been someone other than the one he knew about—Matthew. Why weren't any of Kiba's friends included? A few of Mr. Brad's had been so why not Kiba's?

'Not really,' Mr. Brad's voice broke through the silence, causing Adam to realize he'd actually spoken.

'Nobody?'

'There was that one lad Franky; Kib met him when she worked for Rhino-Gate with Graham, they had been sent undercover as a band . . . Then the people they were looking for started a riot and someone stabbed him, died there and then, he was only sixteen'

'That's terrible!'

'The worst part is Kib was standing right next to him, and she walked away with hardly a scratch.' The landing of the Jet Ranger outside interrupted his further questions, but Mr. Brad had one more thing to say. 'You're good for her, Adam. I haven't seen her as happy as she is with you and Dom in a long time.'

Obviously the job with Pollard hadn't gone well, a definite step in the wrong direction as far as moods went. Before leaving, they'd been joking and laughing hysterically, but neither seemed to be in a very pleasant mood now.

'Here's the money,' Kiba said flinging a white envelope with a check inside onto the desk.

'Not go well?'

'That's an understatement,' Chezia remarked dryly.

'We got the job done, but he's got to be the most demanding person on this planet.' The green haired pilot simply slumped down into a nearby chair.

'We aren't doing anything right now; why don't you all go home, and I'll close up,' Mr. Brad suggested. Chezia readily agreed, and Kiba felt no need to stay any longer either, so everyone else filed out of the hangar and started to their separate homes

★   ★   ★

The following night at the cottage,

'So,' Adam said hoping to start conversation between Kiba, Chezia, Dante and Mr. Brad. At the hangar that morning neither had been in a better mood, and he was hoping to fix that problem. 'How was the stunt shoot today? I heard it was better than yesterday'

Kiba rolled her eyes and gave Chezia a chance to state her opinion because she sure as hell didn't have anything good to say about it. 'There's not much to say.'

Kiba, disinterested in the conversation, picked up her black and red Gibson SG guitar and walked out the door with Wolf at her heels.

'Looks like we aren't very good company tonight,' Adam idly commented.

Domanick walked across the room, 'Mummy!' he wailed. Seconds later the door opened then it closed again.

Ok, I guess I'm not very good company tonight, he amended silently.

'I guess you're right;' Chezia started 'I just don't understand why some of those directors have to be like that. Today, I just about had to bodily haul Kub out, but I'm not sure I actually would have had it come down to that because personally I would like to slug him one.'

Adam could sympathize, but that wasn't any way to handle business, and Brad's Air Service had worked hard to keep a valuable reputation. Hopefully whatever the future jobs were would prove to be less stressful.

★   ★   ★

'I don't want to help around the hangar,' Dante complained. 'Why can't I go to Shawn's party? You know I've been wanting to all week.'

'We could use the help and you haven't kept up with your chores lately.'

'I don't want to put all those tools back in the storage room; it'll take all day. I'm not going to pick up everyone else's mess and you can't make me!'

Adam turned his attention to the other side of the hangar where Mr. Brad and Kiba were griping at each other over something or another. Lately every one seemed to be at odds with each other, and he was tired of playing referee. Maybe he should just let them have it at each other, fight it out and be done with this mess.

"Fine. You go home then! You can spend the afternoon at your picture perfect cottage and shoot arrows all day or play your guitars while the rest of us work!' Mr. Brad erupted.

'That's not what I'm saying,' Kiba argued, surprisingly calmer than he would have expected but she was obviously losing it.

'Seems to me like that would solve all our problems.'

'Y'know, I think I will go!' Kiba threw down the keys to the 4x4 and stomped out of the hangar slamming the door behind her and taking off in the Jet Ranger.

Maybe they did need a referee, but Adam wasn't so sure he wanted to be the person for the job; he might get his head ripped off in the process. If the sudden mood change with Kiba and Chezia the other day had been a step in the wrong direction, this had to be at least two or three, maybe more.

A crashing noise from the office had Adam whirring around to see what it was. With Chezia and Dante arguing in the backroom and Mr. Brad fuming about his disagreement with Kiba across the room, he figured it had to be Domanick. He would be quiet all day, but you couldn't take your eyes off that mischievous kid for even a moment.

Trekking off in the direction of the office, Adam went to see what damage Domanick had caused. Shoving the door open, Adam wondered how in the world one kid, not quite three years old, could demolish the reasonably clean orderliness in so little time. The chair was capsized in the floor, contents of drawers scattered about, and papers littered everywhere, but the desk where they belonged. In the midst was a blue eyed mess giggling happily as he smeared sticky hand prints across the desk he was standing on.

★   ★   ★

Dante found himself screaming and yelling a good enough reason to excuse himself from Chezia's care. He found Domanick being forced to pick up the papers he had thrown on the floor while Adam searched the office for the phone. It started ringing and he soon found it in the bottom drawer of the filing cabinet.

'Brad's Air Service,' he answered wearily. For how long Domanick had spent destroying it, the office was taking an awfully long time to clean up.

'It's Alex,' the pleasant voice on the other end stated. 'Jason asks that the Shadow-Wolf crew come in to see him. He needs to speak with them about something urgent.'

'I'll see if I can stop them from killing each other long enough to round them up and bring them in, although I might have to tie and gag them for that to be possible.' Alex made no comment on Adam's statement, merely requesting they get there as soon as possible.

Adam promised to do so and hung up the phone, then put it back on top of the desk where it belonged.

'Dan, will you go get Chezia and Mr. B for me, please?' He obeyed, but only stayed within Chezia's sight long enough to say that Adam needed her before disappearing to find Mr. Brad. The last thing he needed right now was another long argument or lecture. Chezia and Mr. Brad both walked into the office, astonished to see such a mess.

'Alex called. Jason needs you, and since Kiba just left, I guess she misses out.' Honestly, it might be a good thing for her to sit this one out. Maybe it would give her and Mr. Brad a little time apart to cool down, and to give Dante and Chezia some time away from each other.

'Alright, I guess we better go see what the boss wants.'

★　★　★

Jason opened to doors to his office cordially after Alex had informed him that the Shadow-Wolf crew were here. 'Michael, Chezia,' he greeted politely. They came in and took seats across from

Jason's desk. Again seated in his chair, Jason pulled a file from the growing stack on the corner and handed it over.

'Dr. Victor Sokolov needs to be extracted from a Russian Laboratory immediately. He serves as an undercover agent for Group-Rhino and has recently gotten his hands on a lethal drug the Russians are experimenting with.'

'So you need us to fish him out before the Russians catch him playing with their new toy?' Mr. Brad reasoned.

'Where's Wolf?' Jason queried, realizing she wasn't anywhere to be seen or heard from, not that she said much to be heard from, but nonetheless.

'At the cottage,' Mr. Brad answered grumpily.

'Is everything alright?' Kiba wasn't known to skip out on her job, even if she was sick or injured she would typically haul herself up there, unless she wasn't in good enough condition to do so. Then she had someone else haul her up there.

'We had a bit of a disagreement. What does it matter though? We can do a quick rescue without her.'

'If only it were that simple. If that were the case we could send Dr. Sokolov out on a normal flight. Unfortunately, the Russians have already caught word of him having their new toy as you put it. We have to pick him up as quickly as possible without any fuss before the Russians know we're there. That's why Shadow-Wolf is ideal. Victor has some suspicions though that our Red friends are right on his tail so you won't know the exact location for pickup until you're there. The pickup could be an easy one or it could be, straining.'

'So, I might not be in good enough physical condition for this one,' Mr. Brad said bluntly.

'I don't know. It could be difficult for anyone of you or it might be easy. It would be wisest to have a full crew of the best possible people though.'

'And you don't think I can do it.'

'I know how well you and Wolf work together. Honestly, you're the best pair in my opinion, but I don't know what obstacles will be in the way and whoever is best rounded will prove to be the most valuable.'

Mr. Brad left the office in a kind of huff. Jason had tried to be diplomatic and polite, but he obviously didn't think they should go on this one alone. Previous experiences in Russia hadn't been all that pleasant and he wouldn't mind sitting this one out, but maybe the time away would do him some good.

'You think your friend Simon might have some interest in this one?' Mr. Brad asked as they walked back to the jeep.

'Maybe. Why though? The hangar doesn't have much of any scheduled business for the next week at least so Kub could go.'

'I love her like a daughter; you know I do, just like I do you, that's why it hurts me to have us fighting like this. Maybe a little time away wouldn't be such a bad thing.'

'Oh. I don't know, but I guess I can ask him,' Chezia offered. 'Don't you think Kub will get mad about us leaving her though? Shadow-Wolf is more hers than any of ours you know.'

'She said if I ever needed Shadow-Wolf I knew where to find him.'

'Yeah, but I don't think this is quite what she had in mind.'

'Then count it as for the good of our friendship. She'll get over it; in the end this is better.'

★ ★ ★

'Where's Mr. B?' Kiba asked for about the millionth time after coming back to the hanger, 'and Chez?' Adam, Domanick and Dante were still here, but neither sister nor surrogate father were to be found. 'Adam?' She asked demandingly. He knew something. She could sense it.

'I don't know,' he answered truthfully.

'Then what do you know?'

'Alex called, that's all. They never said anything about a mission or even the possibility of one.'

She picked up the phone and dialled the now well-known number to Rhino-Gate Headquarters. Jason might be underhanded enough to send them without letting her know it. He had promised to at least inform Kiba even if she wasn't able to go on that particular mission, but when they weren't in Rhino-Gate's favour the rules had a tendency to change. She demanded to speak with Jason immediately and the assistant didn't argue.

'Wolf? What are you doing?' Jason asked incredulously. 'You should have left two hours ago!'

'I'm unaware of that minor detail,' Kiba answered calmly. 'I was beginning to wonder when you were going to tell me where you sent Mr. B and Chez off to though.'

'You don't know?'

'How am I supposed to know, Jason? You didn't tell me.'

Cursing under his breath, Jason replied. 'Russia, and you're supposed to be with them. I asked why you weren't here for the briefing, but Michael said you were at the cottage and he would take care of letting you know everything. They were not only supposed to let you know, but also take you with them.'

'He sent me home and didn't say a damn thing about a mission,' Kiba replied, anger beginning to boil up.

'I specifically told those two not to go in alone because there are a lot of uncertainties in this mission.'

'Obviously they didn't listen too well.'

'It's too late for them to turn around now, I just hope Victor was able to come up with an easy rescue.'

★   ★   ★

Mr. Brad checked the monitors in front of him yet again to make sure they were on track, wishing that Kiba was here instead of Chezia and Simon, like the old days. He liked their company, but at least Kiba left you to wonder in silence with yourself, where as these two continuously talked about the forthcoming events, getting you all worked up.

'We'll be entering Soviet airspace in twenty minutes,' Mr. Brad reported.

Chezia made a quick thank you, and then returned to her pointless conversation with the marine. At last the conversation was broken with a radio transmission. It was Victor.

'The Russian's have got half their air force after me,' Victor panted. 'I try to meet in this park in an hour,' he promised in an heavy English accent before giving a more exact location and ending the call.

'That guy is British?' Simon questioned. 'Sounded Russian to me.'

'Jason did say he'd been over here awhile.'

'I hope that's it, and we aren't flying into a bigger trap then I know we already are.'

★   ★   ★

Adam listened in anticipation as his wife explained the information as to whereabouts the others were.

'Russia?'

He nodded gravely. 'And they didn't tell you?'

'If they'd told me I wouldn't have had to call Jason.'

'So I guess we just have to wait for them to come back.'

Kiba let out a long breath. 'Yeah, I guess that's all.' And hope they all come back in one piece.

★   ★   ★

Chezia brought Shadow-Wolf in close to the ground and hovered mere feet off the ground awaiting Victor to join them. Time passed slowly as the minutes wore by.

An hour later Chezia decided he wasn't going to show up and started off to find a safe place to hide until receiving further orders. Jason's picture appeared on the monitor in front of Simon.

'How'd it go?'

'No show,' Chezia replied succinctly.

'He never showed.' Jason cursed. 'I was afraid this would happen. I'll see what I can find out and get back to you. For now just lay low'

★   ★   ★

Victor crouched down low in the dark cave, trying to avoid the Russian police that came from every direction after him. In his haste, he'd lost his watch, but he was sure he had missed the pickup by a long shot. They'd probably gone back home, but maybe, maybe if he could get a hold of them they could try to reattempt the pickup.

Slipping back into the darkness of the night, he left the cave in search of a way to communicate with his rescuers

'Shadow-Wolf, this is Victor.'

The sudden noise broke through the silence in the cockpit, and Simon answered it. 'We're here.'

'Would you try again? I couldn't make it in time,' he apologized. 'There were too many and progress is slow.'

'Same place?' Simon asked.

'About. Try about a mile and a half east of that.'

Simon typed in the location and the computer pulled up the directions to Bor. Bor? That's the heart of Russia! Why couldn't something be easy just for once?

Victor Sokolov sank into the dark under bush hoping his rescuers would get here soon. He guessed they still had about ten minutes or so until they should arrive, but the dogs in the distance were starting to worry him. Times like this were when you wonder why you didn't get a typical summer job as a teen instead of committing to years of spy work. The dogs were getting closer, he needed to move on, but somehow he was going to get out of here.

He risked a glance upwards and saw a blue flash across the sky. What was that? It came by again; this time he recognized it as the blue body of the sleek navy blue helicopter, but it didn't sound like any helicopter. It growled as it rested on the ground, almost as if it was a real wolf.

Ridiculous, he thought, flinging himself toward it. This just had to be his rescue. The Russian police obviously saw him, the silent night was soon riddled with gunfire; round after round ringing out clearly against Shadow-Wolf's metallic armoured skin. Simon opened the left door and started out to retrieve the undercover agent, assuming it wasn't already too late.

The gunfire ceased. Finding a pulse, Simon threw the agent over his shoulder and helped him into Shadow-Wolf. He was hit, but it didn't look too bad and he could be more thoroughly examined once they were out of here. Almost there, gunfire sprayed across Shadow-Wolf's nose and the duo stumbled, almost falling, but continued on and made it to Shadow-Wolf. He shoved the other man up, and with Mr. Brad's help they got him inside; then Simon joined Chezia up front.

'You ok?'

'Yeah. Actually surprised I didn't get myself killed out there,' Simon replied.

'Thank you, but you must be crazy,' the agent commented. 'You could've gotten killed.'

'Part of the job. If you didn't make it, we as Brits, could be in much more trouble with the Russians than we already are.'

'Thank you nonetheless.'

Chezia dropped Victor Sokolov, at a Rhino-Gate clinic not far away, promising to return in the morning to take him home. After a good night's rest and some medical attention he should be better. In the morning they could make the long trip back home, and get on with their lives.

★ ★ ★

Kiba lifted her head from her work. Something was wrong. She didn't know exactly what, but something definitely was. She reached for the phone and dialled Rhino-Gate to see what the latest news was.

'Yes, Wolf. As usual, that eerie sixth sense of yours is correct,' Jason replied, 'but it's not anything too bad. Evidently the tail rotor got just a little bent from some of the crossfire,' he explained. 'It'd probably be alright to get all the way back out to the canopy, but Michael and Chezia both agreed it is best to fix it there and not run the risk of something going wrong.'

Made good enough sense, but she'd feel so much better if they were all safely home. She couldn't get over how nobody had even told her they were going though. Family-you have no choice but to love them that is if you can live with them without strangling them.

★ ★ ★

Chezia looked over the recently repaired rotor skeptically. 'Well, it should be alright, but as soon as we get back it should be replaced.'

Simon agreed. 'I'll help if you need me to.'

'Nah, it shouldn't be a big deal.'

Mr. Brad came back with Victor. 'You guys ready to get up there? I want to go home.' Victor watched the horizon uneasily, as if expecting something to jump out and get him. Mig 29's are what it sounded like, but no one else seemed to notice. Maybe he was just imagining it. Spending ten years in a different country, always on your guard would give any normal human being reason to be paranoid. The Mig's were closing in on them. If they didn't get out soon they wouldn't be able to make a move and the Russians would obliterate them all. The Shadow-Wolf crew continued talking, oblivious to the approaching onslaught.

'We have to get out of here!' Victor warned frantically. 'The Russians. They're coming.' The three looked skeptically at each other. Nothing was in sight or to be heard in the distance. 'You've got to believe me! They're coming!' he pleaded. 'Come on; get this bird off the ground and into the air.'

Mr. Brad slid into the co-pilot's seat and checked the radar. Reporting back, he said, 'The only thing coming is a little rain ten miles out, otherwise the scope is clear.' The escapee Rhino-Gate agent looked up again. Something was out there. He just knew it.

After finishing up the repairs, Chezia piloted Shadow-Wolf up into the sky again, leaving Russia behind. 'How are we looking, Simon?'

'Radar suppression is at ninety seven percent and we should be too low to catch the radar anyway.' They continued completely undetected by the Russians. Victor grew even more restless; every few minutes insisting the whole Russian air force was on their six. Once, he had even grabbed for the stick, trying to evade a non-existent missile despite not having any combat experience, much less any combat flying.

After Simon salvaged them from ploughing into the hillside and Chezia finally got him pinned down, they unanimously decided to sedate him until they got back to the UK. 'Almost out of Russian airspace,' Simon remarked, 'And there's actually something on the radar.'

'Got an ID?' Chezia asked.

'Four Mig 29's. We're already at maximum radar suppression and they're closing on us.'

Shadow-Wolf ducked out of sight further into the canyons, disappearing from sight. The Russians followed. 'They're gaining on us.' Chezia almost called out for jet engines, but soon thought better of the idea. With the tail rotor iffy at best, extra strain caused by that speed wouldn't be good at all, and she wasn't sure it would hold up; they'd have to do without. 'Russian interceptors ETA three minutes.'

Shadow-Wolf darted across the land, just skimming the ground. The Mig's followed. The first Mig let off a missile, which easily missed Shadow-Wolf, but the second came a lot closer. Having obviously been spotted, Chezia directed Shadow-Wolf out of the canyons and into the sky where there was more room for maneuvers if it came down to that. A Mig followed them up. 'We picked up a tail—semi-active radar seeking air to air missile.' Chezia tried to evade it, but it stuck to them like superglue, gradually growing closer and closer.

'Mr. B, give me jet engines on my count.'

'We can't—the tail rotor'

'Six . . .'

'Chezia! It could rip the rotor right off!' Mr. Brad warned.

Chezia realized, "if we don't, we're done for anyway.' Mr. Brad and Simon both grew silent in realization, but still wanting to avoid the risk, not that they had any choice. 'Now.' Reluctantly, Mr. Brad pushed the green cell rod and gave Chezia usage of the jet engines, hoping it wouldn't be the death of them. With a sudden burst of speed and power Shadow-Wolf shot up and turned on itself.

'Give me a heat-seeker.'

'Heat-seeker,' he confirmed slotting in the red cell rod. Two missiles impacted each other and exploded together into a single fireball. The relief didn't last long though. The chatter of gunfire slamming against the armoured navy blue skin soon filled the air. The 50mm gunfire denting the metallic body as it loomed dangerously close to the main rotors.

'Watch the-'

'I know,' Chezia interrupted, wanting full concentration. Suddenly Shadow-Wolf swung around one hundred and eighty degrees. She fired a Heat-seeker at the first Mig 29 and a second at the other Russian aircraft. Two down, two to go.

'Missile!' Mr. Brad warned too late. Chezia yanked back on the cyclic in a vain effort to avoid the missile. It did miss Shadow-Wolf, hardly, but the force from the explosion into the mountainside shook them thoroughly.

'He's coming back.' Simon said even as Mr. Brad loaded a Heat-seeker and Chezia sent it hurdling toward the AA-10. Then it exploded in a bright, flaming cloud. The last pilot was just as brave, but went down with a single missile.

Shadow-Wolf shuttered ominously. They were low on fuel and he was worse for wear, definitely in need of some love and attention, but first they had to make the lengthy trip home and hope he didn't give out before then.

'I'll radio in and see about getting them fuel rods a little early,' Mr. Brad said, already in a way dreading their return. Kiba wouldn't be the least bit happy and neither would Jason.

★   ★   ★

Kiba pulled into the canopy, parking her motorbike out of the way in the shadows. She'd found out from Jason that Chezia and Mr. Brad had taken Simon Kenty with them; she wasn't sure if she was happy about that or not. At least they didn't go gallivanting off without thinking, but that meant they had purposefully left her out of the loop. She would find out the real story when they got back hopefully not long from now. It was strange seeing the canopy so empty, much like it had been before her boy had made his home here.

Late afternoon sunlight shone through the branches, but the beauty that usually basked in its warmth was gone. He would be back soon though. The cold from the night was just beginning to set in when Kiba heard Shadow-Wolf in the distance. That was Shadow-Wolf wasn't it? It didn't sound exactly like him, but it was similar and who else would be flying that low over the forest at night?

As she walked out from under the canopy she saw her helicopter. Descending ever so slowly and carefully down into the clearance, Shadow-Wolf finally came to rest on the grassy floor. Her eyes opened wide in surprise.

'What did they do to you Shadow?' Kiba spoke out,

Two tired men and a woman disembarked, oblivious to Kiba's presence, and went to change out of their flight suits. When they returned each was met with an icy glare.

'What the hell did you do to him?' If she was perfectly honest with herself there was a time or two Shadow-Wolf hadn't come back in remarkable shape, but right now he looked downright pitiful.

'There really is a good explanation.'

'There had better be, and I want to hear ever bit of it. Right now.' Kiba listened as Simon, Chezia and Mr. Brad all gave accounts on the mission and the sedated man in the jump seat.

'Look Kib, I'm sorry,' Mr. Brad apologized. 'I just though you and I might do better after not being in each other's faces for a couple days. We'll get your boy all fixed up in no time flat and I won't let it happen again.'

★   ★   ★

'What parts are you going to need?' Jason asked. He wasn't exactly excited about having to replace numerous expensive custom parts, but if he was going to continue to get use of Shadow-Wolf, he had to keep up his end of the deal.

'Don't know yet, but it's probably not as bad as it looks.'

'Well, thanks for picking up Victor. In case you were wondering, he is doing better now. Once you come up with a list of parts send it over and I'll get it filled in as soon as I can.'

Kiba appeared out of nowhere with her hands behind her back. 'It is as bad as it looks, worse actually.'

Mr. Brad noted the sudden change of expression from the previous day's anger. She was angry before and had every right to be, but today she seemed more regretful for her sudden outburst.

'What're you doing here anyway? Chezia and Simon should be around soon, but I already told you that you don't need to help; it's our mess and we'll clean it up. You really don't need to—it most likely isn't that bad.'

Kiba ignored Mr. Brad's insistence. She had already taken a closer look for herself, and she knew what she saw. 'I realize I've made a pretty big mess of things before and you helped me. I also took a closer look at the tail rotor.' She showed Mr. Brad the pieces she held in her hands. 'It was barely hanging on; I touched it and it fell off,' she stated sadly. 'I was that close to losing you all forever.'

Mr. Brad saw the honesty on her face and the sincerity in her eyes. She wasn't trying to make him feel any better about the damage they caused, she was stating simple facts. All their lives had depended on a bent, damaged and worn out light blue strip of metal that had been moments away from giving out.

They turned together and looked at the sleek sides dented with riddling of 50mm cannon fire, he'd definitely didn't come through this one unscathed, and they had been lucky to. Things could have some easily turned out so much worse. How had that strip stayed on so long? Under the circumstances they should be dead.

'I guess there's only one explanation—God sent us a Fallen Angel.' Mr. Brad smiled.

CHAPTER TEN

Missing

Wounded and now fuelled by anger and fury, she flew across the grassy land in hunt of her prey. He wouldn't escape, not this time. Facing each other menacingly, they each waited in silence for the other to make a move. He would give in; he, of all people, knew what this wolf would do to protect his new pack, and he didn't have a fighting chance. Something was wrong though. He aimed carefully then pulled the trigger of the assault rifle. That bullet wouldn't hurt this wolf though; it darted across the air, slicing through it with precise deadliness. Kiba White, his new master, aimed the sniper rifle, knowing that one cold hard bullet would take care of their prey, the one that had caused her so much pain and grief. But nothing happened. Then, before any move could be made to prevent it, the single bullet went through the fuel cell rod and Shadow-Wolf crumpled to the ground in a massive, flaming fireball.

★   ★   ★

Kiba woke up covered in enough sweat to make her wonder if she had been standing too close to the explosion that had supposedly just killed her seconds before. She was glad that wasn't how things actually turned out. Wayne didn't deserve to get away with something like that, but it would have saved her a lot of heartache if Wayne had killed her. She never would have met Adam though, nor Domanick; who knows whether Chezia would have ever been found and rescued, probably not. Amazed she hadn't woken her husband; she slipped out of the bedroom and downstairs. Outside, she could hear the steady drizzle of rain pitter-pattering against the cottage walls and roof. Nevertheless, she crept outside and leaned on the railings. Cold rain splashed her and soon became frigid, pelting streams pouring out of the dark grey sky at an ever-increasing rate. Gusts of wind blew the cold water onto her, but she didn't mind. Right now she found it refreshing and calming, a reassurance that she was still actually alive. The weather grew increasingly worse, but not enough to make her go back inside. She was alive and now had a family—that was something to be thankful for—so was the rain that watered the trees that provided shade and lumber. Going inside now would spoil the moment. Most people nowadays thought this kind of weather was a nuisance and nothing more, but there was so much beauty in it, the swaying trees, the roaring waves, streaks of lightning flashing across the sky. If it kept up like this, flying wouldn't be good, but the hangar was closed today anyway so that wouldn't be too big of a deal, just no way of getting out to work on the Devil. Oh well, the parts wouldn't be in yet anyway. Her, Adam and Domanick would just have to stay in today and enjoy it. Gradually the dark sky gave way to the light breaking over the horizon, a warm orange ball of sunlight shining over the tree tops and causing it to glitter majestically. It was always even more beautiful after a storm; she could just get lost in the beauty.

Next thing she knew, Domanick had climbed up into her lap. Domanick wasn't the early morning riser that his mum was, but he seemed to share the love of the beauty of it. He sat on his mother's lap and dropped his head against her chest, looking out at the surrounding area; his wide crystal blue eyes full of wonder. Kiba sighed contentedly. Things couldn't get much better

★   ★   ★

Adam joined Kiba in the Jet Ranger after securing Domanick into his seat. The sky was still grey and cloudy, threatening of more storms to come, but as of yet not bad enough to cancel the film shoot this morning. They could make decisions about the rest of the day after that.

For this particular scene Kiba would be in the Spitfire up against a German BF-109. Adam would work with ground control and Mr. Brad, where he was needed most, but hoped that next time he could be up in the air. There he felt more useful, and it was a lot more exciting. The spitfire swooped down behind the BF-109 and let loose a barrage of gunfire, The other plane stalled and smoke poured out of the starboard engine ominously, but the pilot was too stubborn to give in. He would win, or die trying. With most of his weapons taken out, the BF-109 abruptly turned around into a head on kamikaze run. Kiba's plane ducked down on que, but the other pilot had anticipated it and also dropped down.

'Anthony, you're cutting it a little too close. We'll fix it up in editing. Just do what the script says,' the director warned. Anthony was definitely not the first name Adam would have guessed for the thirty two year old German pilot, but there was no doubt about his flying skills being as good as he claimed they were. He evidently, like to push the envelope though. The smoking and sputtering BF-109 inched closer toward the Spitfire. Kiba pushed it a little harder, realizing just how close the other plane actually was. 'Get off my damn tail!' she radioed to the other pilot, She reluctantly finished the scene, afraid that if she slowed down too early the other guy would just run into her and in her opinion the spitfire was too beautiful to ruin. She brought the old plane in for a quick landing. The BF-109 stopped just behind her, and Anthony had barely climbed out when both Kiba and the director lit into him.

'Ok, ok. I get it,' Anthony answered non-apologetically. 'I wanted it to look realistic though and you have to admit I did a good job at that. What's wrong with having a laugh up there?'

'Messing around up there is dangerous,' Kiba ground out.

'Whatever. I think little Yorkie here, was just a little bit scared,' Anthony taunted.

'Listen here Jerry, If I ever work with you again, I'm using live ammo' Kiba fired back, Adam and Mr. Brad stepped in between the two, at least putting off the fight that was sure to come

★   ★   ★

Chezia left the Brad's Air Service office obviously not in the best of moods.

'What's eating you? I'm the one that was about to get my tail toasted' Kiba asked,

'That was Mr. Rogers from Dan's school. One of the teachers saw Dante hit this other kid, bruised him pretty bad.'

'So you're going over there?'

'Yeah. Mr. Rogers would like to see me right away.'

'Right away, huh? Sounds more like you're the one in trouble, to me,' Kiba remarked dryly.

'I guess it does, doesn't it?'Chezia replied with a half-hearted grin. 'Do you want to come? I don't think Mr. B needs either of us for an hour or so'

★   ★   ★

Mr. Rogers waited in the once spacious office, now cluttered with framed awards, trophies, and bits of work still waiting to be done, behind a bulky brown desk across from the non-repentant looking boy. He greeted the White sisters as they came in politely, but seemed surprised to see them both.

'Miss White, I wanted to bring to your attention what your brother here has been up to. One of our teachers here reported him fighting with some of the older boys near the computer rooms, and in the past two days there have been a considerable number more visits to see the nurse, most of which are somehow related to Dante.'

'I didn't-' Dante's protest was met with a stern warning stare from Mr. Rogers, but he didn't give in. 'I didn't start those fights.'

'Whether you did or didn't remains to be seen, but that is not the problem here. He has been in a minimum of three fights in the past couple of days and, although not severely, injured some of his fellow students. I'm just trying to do my job of informing you and doing my best to keep all the students safe.'

'What exactly are these fights about?' Kiba directed the question towards her brother rather than the head master.

'First these guys-'

'I have limited time here and what these little scraps were about, is not the point of this meeting. What is important is the safety of my students here.'

'I believe I asked Dan,' Kiba met his glare with a darker one.

'The other guys just started the first one for no good reason, I think they were just trying to get me in trouble, and the other time they were picking on Ruby and I told them to leave her alone. They kept messing with her, and when I tried to stop them, they started on me too.'

'I understand things happen and everyone has those moments when they act before thinking, but this type of behaviour isn't acceptable. I'll let it go this time, but don't ever let it happen again.'

'I'm not promising it won't ever happen again because I would do it once more if I had to,' Dante retorted hotly. 'I don't want those guys picking on me or anyone else just because they're older, bigger, and know when the teachers aren't looking.'

★   ★   ★

Mr. Brad paused, looking for Kiba and Chezia but only seeing Adam.

'Dante's school called and they went up there,' Adam explained. 'They should be back soon though.' With that said, the Brad's Air Service jeep pulled in just in front of the hangar. 'What's the news?'' Adam queried.

'I don't like Rogers much,' Kiba replied matter-of-factly. 'It's like he's after Dan for something that's not really his fault. In his place I would've done the same thing, and in my opinion he did the right thing.' Kiba said.

★ ★ ★

Chezia rang the doorbell at James's house, and he answered it almost immediately. 'Chezia it's good to see you again. Dinner is almost ready so come on in and make yourself at home.'

Chezia settled into a chair just outside the kitchen. 'You need any help with that?' she offered.

'No, I'm almost done. Say, where's Dante?'

'He's gotten into a few fights at school and the headmaster isn't too impressed. Kub went along for the meeting, but didn't even listen to his point of view, but immediately leapt to Dan's defence.'

'What about you?'

'Me? I don't know yet. If it was his fault I don't want to let him get away with it, but on the flip side, I don't want to punish him for something that isn't really his fault. Kub said that in Dante's place she would have done the same thing, so it's like he thinks it's suddenly ok. Let's just get on with the evening; I'll worry about it later.'

Derek came running down the stairs, shouting something about cookies.

James smiled knowingly. 'After dinner I told him we would have some cookies,' he explained. 'If you can stand my chocolate chip cookies we would love to have you join us.'

'Sound good enough to me; I love chocolate chip cookies.'

After a most satisfying feast, movie, and cookies, Chezia said a lingering goodbye then started the jeep and began the journey back.

When she arrived she opened the door and walked up the stairs when she noticed the dirty footprints tracked across out of Dante's bedroom. Peering into the darkness, Chezia looked at the messy room and the few pairs of clothes that littered the floor.

The curtains were pulled wide opened, revealing a full moon that shone brightly through. It cast a frosty glow on to the bed, Dante was gone

★   ★   ★

The Cottage, 9PM

Adam couldn't sleep that night, something stopped him, silently he climbed out of his bed, and walked down the stairs to get a drink. The radio came to life, quickly he walked towards it careful not to wake his wife who was probably asleep by now, 'Go ahead Mr. B'

'Adam it's White, Dante's gone, the window was wide open,'

'We'll be right over.'

★   ★   ★

Adam looked through the room again. 'I just don't know where he could've gone.' Kiba had figured he ran away much like the time when he first stopped over at his friend's house, but they had already looked all of the places they could think of that he might have gone, and still no Dante. The police officer, Renolds, re-entered the room, reporting they still hadn't found anything out. Kiba quickly noticed the strange resemblance this man had to Mr. Rogers and found it extremely hard not to take an immediate dislike to him as well.

'Might any of you have an idea where he is?' Renolds asked accusingly. 'We've already searched every place we can think of.' The first day without Dante was already drawing to a close, and none of them were any closer to finding him.

Renolds promised to continue the search, 'You should all go home and get a good night's sleep. Something should turn up soon.'

★   ★   ★

Adam watched as his wife paced between the settee and the counter, muttering about how it had to be her fault that Dante was gone. 'Didn't you hear what the cop said about getting some rest?'

'You actually think I'd be able to sleep?' She paced back and forth yet again. 'Maybe with the Devil I could find him' she slowed the pacing down dejectedly as she remembered the condition the Devil was currently in. He wouldn't be doing much of anything until he'd had some major repairs. 'Major—Do you think he went to Simon's house? It's not too far from Chez's, and they do get along pretty well.'

'Already tried. Simon's out on some course for the marines. Survival course or something like that.' Shaking her head, Kiba went back to pacing again. 'You can't blame yourself for him running away, you know.'

'Who said I was?' she returned defensively.

'You did actually,' he replied gently. 'Besides, I know you and you know you are. You always do.'

'Doesn't it have to be? If I stayed out of the whole mess there wouldn't have been that big argument, and Dan probably wouldn't have left.'

'You don't know that,' Adam pointed out.

'Maybe it is though.'

'Just because something bad happens doesn't automatically mean it's your fault.'

'Maybe not everything, but an awful lot of things that happen do link back to me one way or another.'

'You're going to wear a hole through the floor if you keep that up.'

'I'll be back, I think I'm going to go for a little run to clear my head.'

'It's getting dark out. You don't want to fall and-' run was right; She was gone.

Choosing a path around the lake, Kiba started at a slow pace to warm up and gradually increased her speed, but her thoughts raced. Where was her brother? When would they find him or when will he come back? Why exactly had he left? What was the whole story? Was there any strange link between Rogers and Renolds or was it all in her head? She tripped unexpectedly after running into a fallen log in front of her. Maybe Adam was right; running as it got dark wasn't the most brilliant idea. As she rolled onto her back she saw the land around her illuminated only by the moon and a scattering of stars. She got to her feet and started back the way she'd come, still lost in her own puzzling thoughts. Somehow, they were going to find Dante and get him home safely. She wasn't sure how, but they had to. At last the stone cottage came back into view, smoke streaming up from the chimney. The cottage had always been home, but with Adam and Domanick it was truly complete. Maybe she wasn't as cursed as she thought . . . Forget that. Dante was gone and it was all her fault.

★　　★　　★

Early the next morning,

The Jet Ranger landed suddenly on the tarmac just outside the hangar. 'Anything?' Chezia asked hopefully.

'Nothing. Mr. B should be back in a few minutes; maybe he would have found him.'

'Yeah,' Chezia sighed heavily, 'maybe.' This wouldn't be the first time Dante had run away, but this time he was really gone. Officer Renolds had promised to let all the local transportation agencies know about his disappearance and to be on the lookout, but what was left to search? Mr. Brad arrived, but with no better news. Amongst the four of them it seemed they had searched every inch of South Yorkshire by foot, car, and air, but still no sign of Dante White.

'We'll find him,' Adam encouraged. Somehow they would find him; he only hoped it would be soon

★　　★　　★

At the end of another long, tiresome, useless search, Mr. Brad returned to his own house while Kiba pulled into the hangar for the last time that day. She would pick up Adam and Domanick then head back up to the cottage for a couple hours of sleep before searching again at daybreak. Exhausted from the day's work Kiba shuffled into the hangar. The phone rang incessantly. Who would be calling the hangar this late? Ignoring it, she went to find her husband. The phone began ringing again. She answered it irritably.

'Miss White, don't ask questions. Leave the search alone and answers will come soon enough.'

'What have you done with my brother!' Kiba demanded.

'No questions. Let it be, or this game will be a most unpleasant one for you, Miss White,' his menacing voice warned then the line went dead

'Who was that?' Adam queried upon reentry. 'Kiba?'

She threw the phone towards the wall, 'Whoever has Dan says to call off the search or things could get unpleasant.' She explained unlocking the desk drawer and forcing it open.

'How unpleasant?'

'He didn't say, but I know one thing for sure.' she grabbed the two .45s 'I sure as hell am not about to give up now.'

★   ★   ★

Renolds strolled into the Brad's Air Service office where Chezia was awaiting his latest report. He obviously wasn't in any hurry, Kiba noted, and Rogers had seemed barely sympathetic at best, both of them blaming her for Dante's disappearance. Maybe it was her fault, but couldn't they at least show a little compassion?

'Dante White,' the officer drawled, 'still missing, still no signs of him.' He pinned Chezia, Kiba and Mr. Brad down with an accusatory stare. 'You sure you don't have anything else you would like to add? If this kid seemed reasonably happy before this mess happened, and he had as little money as you claim'

'No, there's nothing else.' Mr. Brad said

Kiba looked up from the ground where she set her eyes ever since Renolds came 'Don't you think we want him found? If we didn't then we wouldn't have called you, not that it has done us one bit of good!' she argued

Renolds leaned back on his heels lazily. 'I'm just saying, we're doing all we can to find him, but if he's anywhere in Yorkshire he is one darn good hider.'

Dante had been missing for three days now and chances of finding him were growing slimmer and slimmer. Where would a thirteen year boy with very little money go? Maybe he had more money than they thought. Maybe he had gotten out of town somehow. Maybe . . .

'It couldn't hurt to widen our search a little' Chezia inputted as soon as officer Renolds had left, 'after all we can't seem to find him here anyway.'

'Brad's Air Service, cottage,' the radio came to life, but the voice didn't sound like Adam's. Who else besides Domanick would be there? 'Come to the cottage; come quickly.'

'What is it?' Kiba demanded from the unfamiliar voice, alarm growing by the second.

'No questions. Find out for yourself.'

Try as she might to get a response, the man was gone, whoever he was, and he had been at the cottage. She had to get back there and make sure everything was alright.

'Chez, will you cover for me while I go up to the cottage for a little while? I think something could be wrong.'

'Yeah, sure. Hey, you need any help?'

'I think I'll be alright, I hope.'

Climbing into the Brad's Air Service helicopter, her fingers flew over the familiar instruments deftly to start up the Jet Ranger. Lifting off, Kiba started for the cottage.

Gradually, the suburban scene disappeared, turning into secluded woods that encircled the lake. She must have made record time for the Jet Ranger, but it seemed the opposite way around—maybe record for slowest time.

Everything seemed in order. Calm waves scattered through the tranquil lake, a cool late autumn breeze blowing through the trees, and Wolf napping on the end of the jetty. Avoiding having to wait on him to move, Kiba landed the helicopter in the clearing next to the cottage.

Obviously, something had been wrong when whoever it was radioed in, so Kiba slipped in noiselessly, guns in hands. She scanned the living room carefully before going up to the bedrooms, then thoroughly searched there as well. Nothing seemed out of place, but something wasn't quite right either; now if only she could place what. Lastly, she went to check the kitchen. Before she got there Domanick appeared and grabbed her leg, pulling on it as hard as he could.

'Something wrong with Daddy!'

Kiba kept the guns in hands, but followed the youngster into the only remaining room to be investigated.

It was dark and messy, not usual at all, a few broken dish fragments were scattered about the counter tops, sink, and on the floor, as well as silverware and other various utensils.

Finally convinced that whatever had caused this mess was no longer a threat, she tucked the .45s back into her holsters and continued to examine the kitchen further.

In the last corner to be checked of course, a bruised and bloody man, Adam started to regain consciousness.

'Kiba?' he mumbled, still trying to make sense of the mess of events muddled in his brain.

'I'm here,' she whispered has she sat leaning against the bottom cupboards.

'A guy—he didn't say who he was—came here. Said he guessed you'd have to learn the hard way. Something about an unpleasant game,' he explained. 'Said to leave the search alone or next time it will be worse.'

'You're sure you're ok?'

'Yeah,' Adam answered, 'just a headache, some bruises, and a big mess in the kitchen to clean up.'

He watched as she observed him suspiciously as if still trying to determine whether or not he was well enough to go to the hangar, but she didn't want him at the cottage alone either, since obviously Dante's disappearance was more complicated than him simply running away.

'If I have to put up with your I'm fines when you're more than half-dead, you can put up with mine.' he told her.

'Alright, but please, no flying for today, just to make sure you really are ok.'

'We'll see how it goes.'

The three of them piled into the Jet Ranger to head up to the hangar and discussed the next plan of action.

They arrived just as Chezia and Mr. Brad were pulling up.

'We need a new plan,' Kiba broke the awkward silence as they others noticed the bruises that covered Adam.

'I'll say.'

'I don't think Dan's disappearance was just as simple as running away. With yesterday's incident and the simple fact that even when he has run away before he's always come back before now. It only seems reasonable to think that there is more than we first assumed.'

'So what do we do?'

'I don't know. We can't stop looking for Dan, but he could be anywhere, and we wouldn't even know where to start, but this guy, whoever he is, is dangerous, specifically to you all.'

'How all of us?' Chezia asked. 'What makes you in so little danger?'

'It's not that I'm not, it's just different. He said this could turn into an unpleasant game for me and he's already proven how he plan's to hurt me—though you.'

'Letter for White' the young boy announced.

Chezia took the envelope and opened it carefully. Inside was a note pieced together from mismatched newspaper and magazine clippings.

'Oh how creative' Kiba stated as she placed her hands in her pockets.

'It says Dante, Shadow-Wolf, or one of the others?

'What others?' Mr. Brad asked as he took the note and read it aloud as did Adam; none of them had any clue what the others were, or how they could even work this one out. How would they even reply if they had a decision?

An elderly man shuffled slowly into the hangar. 'White,' his voice crackled, 'Give to Wolf.' He handed over a piece of paper with a message scrawled almost illegible across it.

By the time Kiba had received the note and deciphered it, the old man was long gone and so were Chezia and Mr. Brad.

'The others,' she read aloud, 'The ones that disappeared right beneath my nose.'

★   ★   ★

Adam listened anxiously as the news reported by his wife just grew worse and worse. Mr. Brad, Chezia and Dante were all missing now, and if everything went according to plan for this mysterious kidnapper, Kiba could keep one of them or Shadow-Wolf, her choice.

'I'm to meet one of his men in a park just outside Doncaster if I want Dante, or up in Leeds for Mr. B, but if I want Chez, she's being held all the way over in the lake district.' In Shadow-Wolf, she could easily make the journey before the deadline, but that whole thing was very meticulously planned. She would meet in Shadow-Wolf at her choice of location at midnight tomorrow or each one of them would be killed. Chezia, presumably the one she would be most likely to choose and if, by some stroke of luck, she managed to get away with Shadow-Wolf the others would be too far away to get to in time to save them all.

'What are we going to do?'

She sighed dejectedly. 'I don't know what I'm going to do.'

'You can't do it all by yourself and you know it,' Adam protested boldly. 'I will help somehow. When I proposed this marriage I knew I'd have to put up with your stubbornness and now you're just going to have to put up with mine.'

'I don't remember that being in the marriage vows, and no you're not going. You've already been hurt once and that was once too many. Don't worry, I'll give him a piece of my mind, but you aren't getting involved in this anymore.'

'Kiba, you have to let me help. You don't have any real choice if you want to get the others back in one piece.'

'I don't need anyone,' she retorted defiantly.

He looked away, surprised, shocked, and hurt. If she wanted to go off by herself and get herself killed, fine, let her! If she didn't need him why should he need her?

★   ★   ★

The canopy, the following afternoon

Drenched in sweat and more exhausted than she thought physically possible, Kiba left the newly repaired Shadow-Wolf to change into her blue flight suit and get ready for the eventful night to come. He wasn't anywhere near one hundred percent, but good enough for tonight, hopefully.

Domanick crawled out from beneath Shadow-Wolf and came over to investigate his mother's latest change in apparel. She didn't need anyone, she'd said, that was before she thought about having to watch Domanick when Adam disappeared to wherever he had gone.

For some reason, she hadn't been able to get a hold of Jason or Alex and Simon was still out of town. It seemed like everyone had deserted her but Domanick; she'd have to be able to do it on her own because no one else was around and she knew what it was like to be orphaned and didn't want Domanick to have to go through that. Her and Chezia had been lucky to have Mr. Brad.

Sliding opened the back door, she called, 'Come on buddy, we've got a family to save, and you're my only backup.'

★　★　★

Chezia tried to drag herself up off the cold cement floor, but found it to be an almost impossible task. The fuzzy images inside the small enclosed room whirled before her eyes as she tried to push away the overwhelming pain and force herself into a more upright position. Whatever they'd hit her over the head with sure hadn't been the slightest bit forgiving. It was a small room and difficult to escape from, about ten by ten, cement floor, and concrete block walls, with her only source of light and air flow being the small window far above reach. That and the solid single door looked to be the only possibilities for escape, and that was only if she could gather herself with enough energy to attempt escaping. She didn't have any idea what her captor's plans were for her and hoped to not stick around long enough to find out. If her escape failed the consequences would be great, but she couldn't expect anyone to come after her, and she wasn't about to just sit here and wait for them to kill her.

Chezia sent an appraising glance around the room once her vision started to clear, but there wasn't too much to appraise. A metal framed bed in one corner with a tattered and torn blanket thrown carelessly onto it, that was it.

If she was going to get out of here alive, she'd have to think through things logically, but it was so hard to think through the heat radiating through the room making her want to collapse back onto the cold floor. It was October! Shouldn't the heat at least be starting to decrease?

Thinking grew harder and she didn't think it was all because of the heat, although that probably had a large role in it. Hungry—she was hungry. When was the last time she'd had a decent meal anyway? It was probably her second day here and she hadn't eaten yet nor the day before.

'Better get yourself together, Chez,' she said to herself, 'while you still have enough energy to put up a little fight.'

★   ★   ★

Shadow-Wolf soared with the clouds above the varying landscapes. First it had been feilds and trees, and now they were crossing above a rocky road and a small village.

'Doesn't look like we have any high security centres,' she mused aloud. Indeed, it was only a small village with very little—well, very little anything. Maybe this wouldn't be so hard after all.

Setting up a scan for Chezia White, Kiba began searching the area for her missing sister. Hopefully, she could rescue Chezia, take out her captors, and still be back in time to pick up Mr. Brad and Dante. It was spreading herself thin, but what choice did she have? She couldn't have let Adam go and possibly get hurt; she already hadn't done enough to protect him as it was. Kind of strange that she was taking Domanick though, she smiled slightly at the irony. Definitely wouldn't have been her first choice, but she couldn't exactly leave him alone either. Everything would just have to work. It had to, and not because of her. If everything didn't go according to plan she would probably be dead and Domanick alone. He needed a family to grow up with and to love him, he deserved one.

★   ★   ★

Chezia shoved herself up to her feet, only then fully realizing just how weak she actually was. Only sheer will and determination would be able to get her out because she sure wasn't going to be able to do it on pure energy. Now, what was the escape plan? First off, see if there was any possibility of getting through that window.

She went back to her worn bed and pulled it in front of the window. Propping it against the wall, she carefully climbed to the top of it. Perched dangerously on the ledge of one upturned end, she reached for the ledge of the small, glassless window. Reaching out into the moist evening air, Chezia tried to grasp something to aid in pulling herself through the small opening, but all she caught was a handful of grass. Toppling over, the bed crashed into the floor and with it went Chezia.

Outside the door, she could hear someone, probably whoever was supposed to be guarding her, rustling around and picking up something. His footsteps quickly coming nearer the room Chezia was being held in. One quick look and the guard would know exactly what she was up to. What else was there to do in here though? Maybe, she could surprise the guard and take him out and escape, but she didn't know what kind of reinforcements were outside that door. Was it worth the risk?

After fumbling with a ring full of keys, the guard inserted one bulky, old fashioned key into the rusty lock and fought with it to get the door opened.

Last seconds were fast ticking away. In a hopeful attempt, Chezia threw the worn bed back up against the wall and mounted the thin rail on the upward facing end once more trying to escape before she was caught.

The dilapidated rail framed bed wavered unsteadily and the distinctive screech of metal on metal scraping against each other as the left side bent slightly.

'Havn't fell yet,' Chezia remarked in surprise, praying it would continue to hold. Once again she reached out of the window trying to grab a hold onto something firm and get out, but what was out there to grab onto?

The metallic, nail scraping sound of metal against metal scraping together could be heard as the bed began to fold and bend under the added strain.

Desperately reaching for anything within arm's length, Chezia tried to avoid the inevitable crash back into the cement below. Just as the bed collapsed, her hand was grabbed firmly and it started to pull her out of the square cutaway that served as a window.

Chezia shoved herself though the small square window, scraping her shoulders against the medal frame as she fought her way free. Reaching down, a black clad pilot grabbed her other forearm, throwing all their weight and muscle into hauling Chezia through the tight opening. Panting with exertion, they dragged her into the dusky twilight shadows next to the building where they had been standing,

Chezia looked at this mysterious person; they were currently looking round the corner to see if anyone was there. Whoever it was they were dressed from head to toe in black and looked more like a threat then a saviour. Taking her chances as soon as the black clad turned around Chezia punched them in the nose,

'Damn' They cried out.

That one word made Chezia realize who it was 'Jesus Christ Kub! What the hell are you doing dressing up like some ninja!' she argued.

Kiba stood up and pulled down her hood 'What am I doing? Clearly rescuing you' she took her bandana off and wiped her bloody nose with it 'I didn't want to be seen so I put some black clothes over the flight suit . . . Come on let's just get back to Shadow-Wolf. Domanick is probably getting impatient.'

'Domanick? We are thinking about different Domanicks aren't we?'

'Not if you are thinking about my two year old son,' she replied and began running toward Shadow-Wolf.

She's outta her damn mind Chezia thought before running up beside her sister quickly. 'You brought Dom? No, you wouldn't. Why would you?'

'Yes I did,' she answered as they returned. 'I wanted backup.'

'Backup? You wouldn't have brought him along and I know it.'

'Then think again. He's sitting in your seat.'

Chezia pulled open the door, thinking how stupid Kiba had to be to think she would actually fall for that one, but sure enough, Domanick was actually sitting there just like Kiba had said. 'Why?'

'What else was I supposed to do? You, Mr. B and Dan were gone; I couldn't get a hold of Jason and Alex, and who knows where Adam is.'

'Adam is missing too?' Chezia queried, worried about how serious things were getting.

'Yeah,' she replied succinctly, 'but I don't think he got kidnapped. He's mad at me and I haven't seen him since yesterday afternoon.'

'What'd you do to run him off?'

'I told him he couldn't go. This one is just getting too dangerous and I can't risk losing him too.'

'Looks to me like you already did,' Chezia pointed out.

'I know, and I hate it, but I would rather lose his love and even as a friend that watch him die in front of me or because of me.'

'Kub, he's not-'

'Matthew' she finished with a heavy sigh. 'I know, but would it really matter who he was if he died because of me?'

Chezia paused, trying to come up with something to say that her sister wouldn't completely shut out because she knew just how fragile this ground was, but she hesitated too long.

'Come on. We still have to rescue Mr. B and Dante.'

Chezia took the back seat, still amazed she had been pushed out by a two year old, even if he was Kiba's son.

'What were you doing leaving him in Shadow-Wolf anyway'

'Shadow was babysitting for me. What was I supposed to do? Bring him with me to get punched in the nose?'

'No, but . . . never mind.'

'Chez, get a hold of Rhino-Gate and see about getting us a cell rod pickup will ya?'

'What, your co-pilot can't do that for you?'

'Do you want me to find out?'

'No, I'm working on it. You probably would though.'

'Never too early to start learning right?'

'Yeah, sure.'

★   ★   ★

11:45PM, Leeds, West Yorkshire.

Shadow-Wolf growled as he slipped out of the heights of the dark sky and down towards the well lit streets of Leeds. Setting down in the darkest possible corner, Kiba made sure Chezia understood her part in the plan and the timing. They didn't really have time for this pickup, and getting back to Doncaster in time to get Dante would be pushing it even at mach one, but they'd have to try their best and pray that that was enough because right now there wasn't any way to do things differently.

'Remember, if Mr. B and I aren't back in five minutes leave, and get Dante and keep Domanick safe.' Kiba explained.

'I can't just leave you, Kub,' Chezia protested.

'Hopefully you won't have to, but if you don't leave here in five minutes they'll kill Dante too. I don't have any more time to debate—that's the way it is . . . Love you both.' Taking the clean bandana out of her back pocket, she tied it behind her head, pulled it up and ran off towards the designated building, disappearing into the night.

'Five minutes,' Chezia shook her head. 'Who could pull off a rescue in five minutes?' Kiba better be able to.

★   ★   ★

11:49PM, Shadow-Wolf's cockpit

'Kub, where are you?' Chezia demanded in worry and exasperation. Blow the building and save Dante—that was her job as of now, but could she really do it? As much as she hated it, it had to be done.

She had promised to take care of Domanick if everything didn't work out and Kiba was killed or not physically able of taking care of him, but Domanick's likeness to his mother would be so hard to live with knowing she was the cause of her own sister's death.

Nonetheless, Kiba was right; it had to be done.

Rising off the ground, Shadow-Wolf aligned in front of the building and Chezia went to shoot the first missile.

Error. Crew safety at risk—Kiba White, Michael Brad. Orders?'

'Damn you, don't you think I know that?' Chezia cried out. It was like he was trying to rub it in that she was about to kill her sister and surrogate father. If she didn't though, they'd still be dead and so would Dante.

'Override error and fire the missile.'

Nothing happened. Permission by chief pilot Kiba White needed first.

Now what?

Suddenly, the rocket pods slid out and the missiles slammed into the building, followed by another and another. That was it; it was done. Streams of tears threatened to flow down Chezia's face, but she tried to blink them back. There would be time for tears later, now she had to go save her brother.

Just as she started to pilot Shadow-Wolf away from the scene and clearing smoke, two people staggered out of the darkness of chaos, flames, smoke, and debris.

Mr. Brad came around the left as Kiba moved stiffly around to the right. Chezia slid over into the co-pilot's seat after relocating Domanick to the jump seat in the back.

Mr. Brad slid the left door open and moved to his usual seat in the back just as Kiba pulled the right door open. 'Chezia, get that lass to a hospital, she's hit.'

'I'll live,' Kiba protested.

'That's debatable,' Mr. Brad returned.

Carefully removing the black jacket, Kiba looked down at the flight suit finding it to already be ruined; she wiped her bloody hand on it and grasped the collective and cyclic.

Momentarily, Shadow-Wolf shot off towards Doncaster.

★   ★   ★

Kiba waited impatiently in Shadow-Wolf while Chezia and Mr. Brad went in to rescue Dante. She understood she wasn't in any condition to be going in with them, and watching Domanick, even though he was asleep, was plenty for her to worry about.

She reached into the first aid kit for yet another piece of gauze and held it in place over the other pieces. At least the bleeding was starting to slow, or was it just taking that long to seep through layer after layer of gauze?

Domanick slept fitfully in the jump seat, random twitches or jerking and rolling back and forth not uncommon. He couldn't be getting much rest. Kiba would have woken him, but getting back there would be difficult being too weak.

Suddenly awake, Domanick scrambled up, and climbed into the seat next to his mum.

'Hey, buddy,' Kiba whispered.

Domanick looked up at Kiba even in his young eyes understanding and concern was evident. 'Mummy?'

'Don't worry, I'll be ok,' she assured even as a blissful darkness threatened to overcome her. No, she told herself, be strong, have to be for Dom.

★   ★   ★

Dante tried once again to loosen the tight bonds that held him. Other than being taken off for the occasional meal, he'd been tied up like this for at least a few days, he thought, but time was beginning to swim together into one massive, chaotic sum lump.

The door flew open and two guards threw in two more bound prisoners, then slammed the door shut again. These prisoners he knew though—Chezia and Mr. Brad. Rescue wasn't looking so hopeful any more.

'That didn't go well. Kub told me climbing through windows wasn't my thing though. I guess I should have listened better.'

Mr. Brad looked up at her questioningly, but received no answer.

'How long do you think until Kub comes after us?' Chezia asked.

'Depends if she's passed out yet or not. We need to get her to a hospital though.'

'I think she's coming now,' Dante broke in.

Sure enough, outside the door, shouts, breaking of glass, and crashing as bodies hit the floor could be heard as Kiba put up all the fight that was left, but more guards appeared from beyond the corner and shoved her onto the hard ground, tied her hands, then unceremoniously hoisted her into the room with the others.

'Go see what she did with that helicopter,' one yelled. 'What the heck is that kid doing here? Where'd he come from?'

Looking more than a little confused the two men shrugged.

'Never mind,' the man snarled. 'Just get him out of here. And while you're at it, make sure all of them are tied up good and lock the door. They're no more use to us.'

'Yes, sir,' both men answered.

★   ★   ★

'Kub, you alright?' Chezia asked, knowing full well that she wasn't alright and that she was beginning to show the first symptoms of shock.

'C-cold,' she mumbled.

Dante, Chezia and Mr. Brad were already huddled up around her, trying to share any body heat they could, but she'd already lost a lot of blood and there wasn't anything they could do more than that now.

Dante got up and looked out the barred window. 'Hey guys, I think we can get out of here.'

'How?' Mr. Brad asked as Chezia grabbed the knife from Kiba's right boot and started cutting through her ropes, Kiba long since having given way to unconsciousness.

'There's a helicopter out there—Shadow-Wolf but not Shadow-Wolf. It doesn't sound like him. While they are distracted, if one of us could get out of here and get the keys, we could unlock the door.'

Walking back over to Domanick, he whispered something in his ear.

'Uh-uh,' Domanick refused.

'Please,' Dante pleaded, 'For your mummy and so you can see your daddy again.'

He seemed to at least be thinking about it now.

'Let's play a game. The first one to get the keys on the other side of those bars and bring them back to Uncle B wins.'

Domanick climbed up and tried to squeeze through the close metal bars.

'I'm going to win,' Dante taunted.

'No I win!'

Finally slipping through, he grabbed the ring of keys and wedged through the rails again, handing the keys to Mr. Brad, proudly announcing his victory.

Mr. Brad inserted the key and turned the handle, allowing them their freedom, then took charge of Dante and Domanick while Chezia carried Kiba, who was fading in and out of consciousness.

★   ★   ★

'Shadow-Wolf at last,' the pilot captor said in awe, 'he really is beautiful.'

'Thank you Smith.'

'All in a day's work, it really wasn't that big of a deal.' he shrugged offhandedly as he walked away.

★   ★   ★

Reaching Shadow-Wolf at last, Mr. Brad got in first then helped Chezia get Kiba loaded in. Finally Dante and Domanick scrunched in and they started off.

'Four heat sources down there,' Mr. Brad reported, 'and they sure are active. Wait, only one now; the other three are dead.'

'Saves us some work.'

Soon the Shadow-Wolf mimic was right on their tails. 'Mr. B, load me up something to take that out of the sky.'

Summoning all her strength, Kiba uttered a weak don't, but the missile lit up the early morning sky in the distance as they sped off towards the hospital, and she succumbed to the painless blackness once again.

'Are we about there yet?' Mr. Brad asked. 'She's looking kind of blue and her breathing ain't so great.'

Even over the hum of the computers, Chezia could hear the quick ragged gasps from her sister in the back, and the blood, there was blood everywhere up here, the sticky substance covering the outside of the first aid kit, collective, cyclic, and the seat.

Mr. Brad monitored the temperatures from the back. He was getting hotter that he should, but they couldn't afford to waste any more time. Kiba needed immediate medical attention half an hour ago. Now hopefully emergency medical attention would be sufficient. The Devil would make it, he had to, but it really was amazing that Kiba had even been able to get him running in such short order, but there was no question about not being in the best possible condition.

'Damn. The second engine's flaming out again. We got to set down; he can't handle this anymore.'

'We're almost there, and I'm not sure Kub can hang on much longer.'

The hospital roof finally came into view, but the quick, shallow breathing had grown even shallower and the bleeding had started again.

Mr. Brad knew the truth in Chezia's words, but he wasn't sure the Devil would hang on that long either. 'Alright. Just don't kill us in the process.'

'Where's Dom?' Dante questioned suddenly. 'He was right here–I thought he was sleeping, but'

Taking his eyes of the rods and monitor in front of him for a brief moment, Mr. Brad scanned the cockpit for any sign of Domanick, Finally his gaze came to rest on the two year old. He had curled up on his mother and rested his head on the one clean spot left on the blue uniform, his hand tightly clenched around Kiba's, indicating his refusal to be moved.

The resemble was uncanny in the two, he was like a miniature Kiba, opposite gender, blonder, but he had the same crystal blue eyes, that were also currently shut.

'I found him, and he's alright where he is.'

'Approaching the hospital,' Chezia announced.

Kiba briefly regained consciousness as they landed and the medical team started to unload her, unbearable pain filled her body, sharp claws of it ripping into her flesh, but when she managed to open her eyes, all she could focus on were the two, scared, blue eyes looking longingly after her.

'Wait,' she pleaded in a harsh whisper.

Everyone froze in astonishment that she was awake and coherent, even for a moment.

Everything went fuzzy and she could feel herself starting to drift off again, but was able to manage a clear view of the family she had left.

Domanick unashamedly crept up and threw his arms around his mother, who in turn brought shaking arms around him and pulled him close. 'I'll be ok,' she whispered. 'I promise.'

★   ★   ★

'They aren't giving up all hope, but . . . things aren't looking very good,' the nurse informed them.

'How bad is it really?' Mr. Brad asked.

The nurse shook her head gravely, obviously not enjoying having to be the bearer of bad news. 'She has gone into a progressive, stage of shock. We've already given her a blood transfusion and have her on oxygen and antibiotics and fluids, but she's beginning to show the early symptoms of septic shock. They're doing all they can for her, but at this stage we can't promise anything.'

'Cut to the chase,' Chezia bit out. 'What are her chances?'

'With just the septic shock the survival rate is only about fifty percent, but things are a little different for Kiba White. Typically, septic shock affects children, individuals with weak or no immune systems, and the elderly, it seems she usually has a very good immune system, so the odds would be slightly in her favour if it weren't for the other injuries.'

They'd been waiting for at least a good four hours, desperately wanting to see her, but her getting proper medical attention was more important right now, so they would continue to wait.

★   ★   ★

A week later,

What were they giving her? Trying to shake off the tired, foggy feeling, she searched the room for the familiar faces she was expecting to see, but nobody was there. Her only companions in the lonely hospital room were a get well card and a drawing that looked like it was from Domanick. The methodical mechanical beeping and chirping from the various machines were more annoying than reassuring, a sense of numbed pain ached throughout her whole body, especially her midsection where she'd been shot. She pushed away the covers and revealed a bandage on her right forearm and the IV needle in the left. Where was everybody? She looked for a clock; it could be the middle of the night—that would explain no one being here.

She did pick up the card from the table next to her. It was a cheerful shade of yellow with a bright design on the front, but that was about all she could tell. Flipping it open, she struggled to read all of the signature, but they blurred together into a fuzzy mess. She closed her eyes and tried to clear her head, then read them again. With much concentration she recognized Mr. B, Chez, Dan, and a scribble that had to be Domanick. It was just as she'd feared—no Adam, and now she had a monstrous headache on top of it all. What was wrong with her head?

Kiba began to sit up, only receiving a light-headed dizzy feeling and a stabbing pain in her stomach. Sinking back into the pillows, she allowed herself to drift off again. Maybe when she woke up everything would be ok.

★   ★   ★

Hours later, she woke again, pain more evident but not yet unbearable. After blinking several times, she squinted at the bright light. She tried to sit up but soon realized she couldn't. Panic. What really was wrong with her? This wasn't any better than that previous awakening, it was worse. Something heavy pressed against her chest.

Looking down, she saw it was Domanick. This time he looked much better than last time she remembered seeing him. Before, he looked scared, afraid, lost, worried, now a peaceful, reassured smile tugged at his lips even as he slept, like he knew everything would turn out ok in the end.

She was actually kind of surprised they had let Domanick up on the bed with her, but so glad they did. It was just about the best thing there was to wake up to.

Coming out of the ensuite bathroom, Mr. Brad happened to cast a cursory glance at his surrogate daughter and his grandson who now laid on her, and then a surprised but pleased look became evident on his face.

'You're awake.'

Trying to form words but failing, she simply nodded.

Domanick stirred for a moment, sliding farther over onto his mother.

'Here, let me get him off of you,' Mr. Brad offered, reaching for him, but he was met with a silent protesting shake of the head.

'You sure? It must be awfully hard to breath and they only took you off the oxygen late last night.'

'I'm sure,' she replied in a harsh whisper.

'Ok then, if you think you two will be okay for a minute I'll go round up Chezia and Dante,' Mr. Brad offered. 'They went to get dinner,' he explained.

Kiba nodded in understanding, 'Ok,'

'I'll tell the doctor you're up and have him come by while I round up the others.'

★   ★   ★

'You've sure made an amazing recovery, White,' the doctor commented. 'It's like your body went into hibernation for a week, but when you came out of it, you were well beyond the worse parts.'

He saw the tired blue eyes searching him, imploring him to skip the extra dialogue and get straight to the news she wanted to hear.

'You are recovering remarkably well considering the condition you were in when you got here. On a good number of painkillers, but that is to be expected and you're already being worked off part of those. We can very gradually start working you off the other medicines and get closer to being back to normal.'

'What about the fuzziness?' Kiba questioned hoarsely.

'Probably just a side effect from the drugs. We'll get the rest of the test results in this evening to make sure, but it wouldn't be an uncommon side effect.'

'When can I get out of here?'

'Slow down, there lass. You're just coming out of a very serious injury and can't expect to go home immediately.'

'How, long?' she repeated.

'It depends on a lot right now. If all your tests come back clean and you can hold down your food, you should be able to go as soon as we make sure all the infection is gone, but at the very minimum it'll probably be a week, maybe more.'

★ ★ ★

Two weeks later,

The Brad's Air Service Jet Ranger came around the tree tops and landed on the jetty. Home sweet home.

'You sure you don't want me to watch Dom for you? The doctor did say you should take it easy for a while.'

'I can do it.'

'I know you can, but I don't want you to run yourself into the ground doing it.'

Occasionally Kiba would still get spells of light-headedness and fuzziness and it worried Chezia enough to be leaving Kiba here, much less Domanick with her, especially with Adam . . . well, wherever he was.

'Tell you what . . . get settled back in here, and I'll drop Dom off with you in a day or two.'

'I want Domanick here,' she requested, almost a plea. If she couldn't have Adam and Domanick, she at least wanted Domanick.

'If you're sure . . .' Chezia began doubtfully.

'I'm sure. You can come by tomorrow for dinner and if I feel differently, or like I can't handle it yet, then you can take him with you.'

'Just remember, I wouldn't find it a burden, and I did promise to take care of him if you ever needed me to.'

'I'll remember and be eternally grateful, and you have done a great job at it the last few weeks, but I think I'm up to it now.'

Chezia nodded understandingly. She would have felt the same way. 'Alright then.'

'See you for dinner. Just remember, if you want meat, you bring your own'

'Is there anything else you want me to fetch?'

'Mr. B brought enough food to keep us feasting for three months.' she smiled, 'three days for you though' she added relenting when she saw the continued worry on her sister's face.

★   ★   ★

Waking up early the next morning, Kiba started the hot cup of tea and stepped outside to admire the sunrise. It was stunning, much more beautiful from the ones she'd seen lately from her hospital bed. An idea suddenly occurring to her, she went back inside, returning a moment later with Domanick in her arms.

She settled on the steps of the front porch with her son on her lap, enjoying the most beautiful sunrise she'd seen in a long time.

'Pretty,' Domanick commented.

'Yeah, pretty.'

Pretty sunrise, pretty nice life. Everything was pretty good, probably the closest to perfect she would ever get.

Adam seemed to be gone from her life, but he could very possibly be gone a different way if she had allowed him to come along. She still couldn't quite believe he'd left both her and Domanick though. Especially Domanick. Pain bubbled up in her chest at the thought, even as she shoved it back down ruthlessly. Life wasn't perfect and she would have to learn to live with whatever it threw at her. At least she knew he wouldn't be hurt, or even killed, because of her. Fate didn't have a good previous record for letting those she loved live, but somehow she still had Mr. Brad and had finally found Chezia after all those years. Domanick was, in so many ways, like her, in looks, in personality, and in that he had already experienced more than his fair share of problems, but he also seemed to have that eerie, unnatural ability to survive. Kiba could only hope, he wouldn't have the same problems she had had, because she had plenty of close calls and even she knew eventually her luck would run out. For now though, she tried to be thankful for what she did have, even as she looked out on the still lake and thought longingly of Adam.

CHAPTER ELEVEN

Single Parent

Pink and orange rays peaked over the tree tops, dawning another beautiful day. Kiba, having been up for only a few minutes, enjoyed her cup of tea and the sunrise with Domanick and Wolf as companions. Before long they would have to head up to the hangar, but for now they would watch the sun rising into the sky and warm the chilly November air.

Soon, the two of them were in the Jet Ranger heading for Brad's Air Service. It was good to be back in the air, something she'd missed dearly since her injury while rescuing Chezia, Mr. Brad and Dante. Finally she had gotten the all clear and found herself back in the air as soon as possible. Today would be her first day back at work and she was looking forward to it.

★　★　★

By the time Kiba landed the helicopter outside the hangar, Chezia was already leaving with the second Jet Ranger, and Mr. Brad was barking at some stunt coordinator about how ridiculous a certain stunt would be for such little money. She settled Domanick in the back and checked to see what jobs they would have and if she was scheduled to do any of them today. No doubt Mr. Brad would try to keep her grounded as much as possible until she was absolutely positive there were no long lasting effects from her injuries, but she needed to be in the air, it was a good portion of her life and she had no qualms about that. Getting paid for what you love evidently was actually possible, and nothing could keep her down today.

Finally she saw Mr. Brad slamming down the phone receiver, only to have it start ringing impatiently again.

'Brad's Air Service,' he answered gruffly.

Only minutes later, he marched himself into the office and stood by the desk Kiba was sitting at. Grabbing for the large black, white and red book that resided there, he skimmed the notes scribbled in it. He read it again, hoping to find some way to avoid putting Kiba up for the stunt across town, for more than one reason. Everyone else would be in and out, but not have enough time to do the stunt themselves. Adam could do it—if he were here. Where was he anyway? He'd never officially quit, nor had he even made the slightest hint that Kiba was pushing him too close to the edge, that he was even thinking about leaving her and Domanick. Something had obviously put him over the edge, but what? He sure wasn't getting yelled at by Kiba, who obviously figured it was all her fault and missed him, but somehow figured that in the end it was better this way. Just what she needed, Mr. Brad thought, to go through the whole love thing again. Probably had something to do with her thinking she was jinxed or cursed thing again. Well, time was running out and he'd have to face the conversation sooner or later.

'Hey Kib, you ok?'

'Yeah, why? If I weren't up to flying I wouldn't have shown up for work today.'

'What about Adam?'

'That's between him and me. Yeah I miss him a hell of a lot and I wish . . . I wish he were here, but maybe it is better this way.'

'What'd you mean better? He is good for you and you know it.'

'Was good for me. I can't force him to stay at home all the time after we got him into the whole mess, but I don't want to risk losing him too. And before you get started with you're not jinxed or cursed; and he's not Matthew or any of that, don't bother because I'm not interested.'

Her prediction of Mr. Brad's intentions were true, of course. They'd gone round and round on this one, but when would she learn? She had been doing so well at handling old fear like this lately, but then she pushed him away. Now she was a single parent with a two year old to watch over, a slightly more risky than normal job flying movie stunts, and more than plenty of enemies and risks due to Shadow-Wolf and all those related missions. How could one normal human deal with all of that?

'Did you have some job for me or not?' Kiba asked, interrupting Mr. Brad's musings.

'Oh yeah, if you're up to it I'd like you to do a stunt across town . . .'

'And?' she asked impatiently. There was something Mr. Brad hadn't bothered telling her, something he didn't want to say.

'And nothing. The director tells you what to do and you do it—that's all.'

'Alright. I'll be over there by two.'

'It's at—hey, how did you know?'

'I overheard,' she replied wryly. 'You were kind of hard not to overhear though, probably even Phil in main airport knows about your stunt at two.'

'Well, I otta get going then.'

'Yeah, me too before long.'

★   ★   ★

Chezia came into the hangar and made herself a cup of warm tea while she took a quick break. Next, she would refuel the Jet Ranger and wait until Mr. Brad got back who would watch Domanick until Kiba finished the stunt on the other side of town, then she would go pick up Dante from school who would do his homework and she dropped off the film. The business was good, but the work was exhausting, would have been nice to have another person.

'Chezia,' Mr. Brad called. 'Chezia!'

'Huh, what?'

'Need to get going.'

'Oh yeah,' she answered, having evidently dozed off during her short break.

★ ★ ★

That night, 8:00PM

As the sun was sinking into the wispy clouds and the shadows cast by the trees the Brad's Air Service Jet Ranger came to rest heavily on the jetty; Kiba, with a sleeping toddler cradled in her arms, climbed out of the Jet Ranger and made for the cottage.

Tonight just a simple dinner would suffice. Her, for one, was too exhausted to do much else and Domanick looked like he was planning to sleep through dinner anyway.

Mr. Brad had made a wise choice in not giving her all the details for the stunt because if she'd known she was going to have to work for Pollard again she wouldn't have gone at all, or better yet, she would have gone just to knock him out then come back. Maybe next time instead of bringing in the helicopter a little too close for comfort she'd just land on the guy.

Now she was in no mood for being reasoned with or doing anything useful. Going to bed sounded good. Tomorrow would be better, maybe.

★ ★ ★

2003

In the steamy Southeast Asian jungles of Burma, she waited. Silently estimating and calculating how hard it would be to get the children out of this village, so she could begin her hunt for Chezia again. She'd already been missing for the better part of a year, but somehow she knew that her sister had to still be alive. She had already lost her brother on a bridge accident and Franky in a bar fight in town, and recently just lost her father due to a house fire. She couldn't bare to lose her sister too, her only family left.

She watched as the Coyote unit rendezvous with her from their scouting and ready to return with their reports. Again they marched through the all too familiar dense green jungles. Taking up the rear, she followed; at least until a shabby prison camp caught her eye and pieces of torn army fatigues. After reaching down to pick them up, she wiped off the sticky mud, revealing letters that read 'UB' and one tattered piece before it that could have been an 'C.' Could it be Wolf Cub's? She was almost sure of it, and there were a few prisoners in that little cage . . . No one appeared to be around; what could it hurt to take a look?

Cautiously approaching, she saw why there were no Burmese guards here—there were no living prisoners to guard. None of them appeared to be the sister she knew and loved though. Guiltily feeling thankful, she ran to catch up with the rest of the group.

All was as well as war can be the next day until one of her commanding officers brought her aside to lead another scouting mission for another village. She agreed, not knowing what awful thing she would find.

It was late and dark, an oppressive heat still hanging in the air, but everything she felt, had gathered, collected, calculated, was all gone, washed away and pushed aside and allowing her only to be able to focus herself on the dead body in front of her, of Chezia.

'No!' It was so wrong, so unreal. Chezia couldn't be dead, just couldn't be. Unheeded tears flowed generously down her dirty cheeks as a shaking hand reached for her sister. 'Wolf-Cub! No Chez, you can't be dead!'

★   ★   ★

Startled back into consciousness by her own cries for her sister, Kiba pushed aside the covers and slid out of bed, willing herself to get the awful compilation of feelings, memories, and fears out of her head. Chezia was alive and safe so why couldn't these terrible dreams stop haunting her?

In the other room it didn't sound like Domanick was sleeping any better, begging to be let out. She obliged, carrying him out of the bedroom 'You're too young to be getting nightmares,' she scolded teasingly.

Domanick simply slung both arms around her neck and hung on as they descended the stairs.

'You want some hot coco?'

Domanick nodded his approval of the idea.

Soon the two of them were enjoying cups of hot chocolate by the warm fire, the soft crackling and aroma of burning wood an almost silent comfort against the cold night and their rather unpleasant dreams.

It was kind of strange, the things that brought the two of them closer, Kiba mused silently. Her and Domanick made an interesting team, her only regrets being that they had so little time together and that she had run Adam off because of her fear of being cursed.

'Music?' Domanick asked as he climbed off the settee and walked toward the guitars.

'Sure.' There wasn't any reason why not. There wasn't anyone to disturb and neither one of them would be getting any sleep anyway.

Domanick reached for the black acoustic, and brought it to his mum who took it kindly and placed it on her knee, picking out the union jack guitar plectrum from the small bowl on the coffee table she ran it across the strings and began to play.

★　　★　　★

When Mr. Brad arrived at the hangar the following morning, he was greeted by the aroma of tea and the sound of giggles and laughter from the office. Glad to see Kiba was in a good mood; he'd been afraid of that now being the case after he set her up to work with Pollard again, but he hadn't had much choice, and Kiba hadn't been totally agreeable to anything since Adam left, so this was a very good improvement. Figures, it would be the two year old to get through a problem he'd been battling since Kiba was in her early teens. At least somebody was, that mattered more than who got through to her, and Domanick did share more than his fair share of resemblances to Kiba, almost like a miniature version.

'I'm still taking the charter to Great Yarmouth at three, right?' Kiba checked.

'Yeah, I guess so.'

'If I'm not back when you close up then would you mind watching Dom until I get back? He'd probably prefer not to have to go on the ride with nothing to do, wait, then come all the way back.'

'No, I don't mind, didn't have any plans for tonight anyway.'

'You're sure?'

'I'm sure. Now get back to having some fun with that kid. We don't have anything to do right now and they grow up so fast.'

Mr. Brad was right. It was hard to believe Domanick had become a part of her and Adam's life two years ago, and not long after they had officially become a true family, even if the marriage did only last nine months. It ripped him apart every time he thought about it too. At least now Adam, wherever he was, could find someone more deserving, and someone that wouldn't get him killed in some foreign Shadow-Wolf mission abroad. What bothered him the most though, was that he didn't take Domanick or ever said anything about him at all. Domanick would always have a place in his heart and life, and honestly he wanted to keep him, but why didn't Adam even seem to care anymore?

★   ★   ★

Chezia was watching Domanick while Kiba went to get dinner then she would take a lesson out later in the afternoon; other than that, it was quiet around the hanger.

Mr. Brad, having finished catching up on the paperwork, left the office and offered to help carry dinner in as Kiba arrived with the 4x4 and a brown paper bag and a pizza box, shaking her head in disgust.

'If you actually eat all this I'm not sure you're going to be able to get the chopper off the ground,' she remarked.

'You can put it away too, Kub,' Chezia retorted.

'Ugg, not like you two. With all that food Mr. B left at the cottage, Dom and I planned on feasting for a good while; with you it'd be dinner for one day.'

She watched as her twin sister and surrogate father munched down the entire bag of burgers, chips and pizza.

'You sure you don't want some?' Mr. Brad offered. 'Even Dom is enjoying it.'

'Let him, and he can enjoy mine too. That stuff looks positively terrible.'

On the other end of the room, the phone started ringing.

'Since you aren't enjoying our feast, will ya get the phone?'

She got up and started for the phone, the phone rang again, impatiently beaconing her to hurry up. 'I'm coming, I'm coming,' she grumbled. 'Brad's Air Service,' she answered, upon reaching the phone.

'White, it's Alex. Jason has a mission for you and Michael and would like to see you in an hour. He's in a meeting now, but as soon as it's over he needs you here.'

'Me and Mr. B specifically?'

'That's what he said. There's nothing wrong with bringing your sister or Adam if they're available, but you and Michael specifically.'

'Alright. I'll tell him and we'll plan to be there in half an hour.'

Hardly even having hung up the receiver, Mr. Brad was already asking about the call.

'It was Alex. Jason wants to see you.'

'Me?'

'Yeah, you.'

'Since when did—oh wait . . . Does he want the £1.10 back for coffee?' Mr. Brad asked sarcastically.

'I don't know;' Kiba smiled, 'I guess you'll just have to pay him back went we get there.'

★   ★   ★

Jason dropped back into his chair after a rather unpleasant meeting with the rest of Group-Rhino, expecting to see Kiba and Mr. Brad in his office, but instead he was greeted by more than just the two, but it without the extras he'd come to expect. He eyed them inquisitively.

'Chezia's on a charter,' Mr. Brad supplied, 'Dan's still in school, and somebody had to watch Domanick.'

'Adam?'

'He won't be flying any more Shadow-Wolf missions and I wouldn't be expecting to be seeing him around much.'

'Why?'

'He left,' Kiba answered bluntly. 'Gone. I finally pushed him too far.'

'Gone?' Jason repeated, feeling vaguely stunned. If he felt this way, how must Kiba feel? Somehow he couldn't quite believe it.

'He left me, Jason,' Kiba replied irritably. 'I told him he couldn't go with me to rescue Mr. B, Dan and Chez because it was too dangerous. He said he could and that I needed his help. I told him I didn't need anyone's help. It's as simple as that.'

It couldn't be. Adam seemed to be dealing with Kiba's stubbornness pretty well all things considered, and he wouldn't just leave, not if he knew him at all. And what about Domanick? Didn't he care what happened to him? He knew Kiba wouldn't have any problems financially supporting him, and she was physically capable. The only real problem would be the Shadow-Wolf missions, and she obviously wasn't planning on taking any unnecessary risks on her family. She could definitely be a good mother, evidently just not the wife he had wanted.

'Did you call us here for some reason other than picking apart my failing personal life?' Kiba interrupted his thoughts abruptly.

'Alright, back to business.' Kiba's personal life, going well or not, wasn't his business. 'I was hoping to use Shadow-Wolf's highly sensitive scanners for a search and rescue party very similar to one the two of you have done before. There is a-'

'Jason,' Alex entered the room with a single sheet print out in his hand. 'They found him—he's dead.'

A brief moment of sorrow and grief flickered across the spy's face before he pushed it aside ruthlessly. It was his job not to get attached; he already did that too much. 'I'm sorry to waste your time, but it seems there is no longer a mission unless you can make the dead living again.'

'Only the man in charge up in heaven can do that,' Mr. Brad answered.

'Then no, it's too late.'

★   ★   ★

The calm breeze howled through the leaves of the trees as Kiba and Domanick walked on. Finally the sun began to set and Kiba took off her sunglasses and directed them back towards the cottage. It had been a pleasant walk and she enjoyed the time with Domanick, but she'd hoped to sort through things like both Chezia and Mr. Brad had suggested. Everything had its consequences and it seemed there was no right choice; something was wrong with all of them. What she needed was some rest, relaxation, and a good long time to think everything through.

★   ★   ★

A full moon shone through the trees and onto several form targets. Maybe a quiet evening in the forest was just what they needed. A cool breeze whistled by and the trees danced in return.

They let the peacefulness wash a sense of serenity over them.

Now it was late and dark and neither of them could see the targets anymore, so they both began to walk back to the cottage. Once they had reached it, she unclipped her quiver and helped Domanick with his then put the bows near the window. They should get to bed for now and worry about life's problems later.

★   ★   ★

Jason, dawning the usual grey shirt and jeans although a bit rumpled, dropped into his grey leather chair, exhausted.

He had been up most of the night looking for more information on this possible drug smuggling. He was determined not to let this one end up badly if he could prevent it, but the knowledge they had still was sparse and not near enough to going after them. If he could just get something more to insure their chances of success, especially without injury, he'd feel a lot better, but whoever it was had done a remarkable job at covering their tracks.

'Sir,' one of his assistants, Donald, addressed.

'Yes?'

'White is here to see you.'

'Thank you.' He turned to lead the Shadow-Wolf pilot in, but Jason stopped him briefly. 'Is it just Wolf or . . .'

'No sir, she brought her son too.'

'Thank you. That's all.'

Kiba carrying an archery bag walking in with her son. It had only been a few days, maybe a week, since he had seen mother and son in here together, yet it amazed him how every time the young child seemed to grow more and more like his mother, not that he'd had many other influences especially lately, but the resemblances were truly astounding. Just what he needed—another Wolf—he thought with an incongruous grin.

'What brings you here today?' Jason asked, although he figured he knew why—the drug smuggling, of course. Maybe somehow they had picked up some useful clue. It wasn't the most likely, but miracles did happen, even in this business. 'Some new development on the mission perhaps? For such major smugglers, it was remarkable something hasn't been heard about them before.'

'Actually,' Kiba said quietly. 'I think it's time to call it quits and start a quiet life, just Dom and me.'

Jason Black stared in disbelief. He should have seen it coming, but not now, definitely not now.

'It would give him a chance to live a more normal life, and it wouldn't be fair to put his life at risk for something I'm involved in, and with Adam gone, I have to be around and able to take care of him. I can't afford to be in the hospital just barely clinging to life or even get shot and not be at a hundred percent for a while, and as much as I hate to admit it, I don't heal as fast as I used to.'

'You're sure?' Jason asked, still trying to process his words. Of everything he'd expected, this most certainly wasn't even in the cards. Kiba had almost given up like this once before, but when her sister went missing she jumped right back in. That had been because of not believing she was physically able though, this one did have a little more merit.

'I'm sure.' Kiba said grimly. She didn't give herself a chance to change her mind and threw the bag on Jason's desk 'I can't fly Shadow-Wolf, take care of Domanick, and keep it all from affecting his life too much on my own. Sometimes it's just better to face the truth and that's it, whether I like it or not.' Opening the bag Jason saw all eighteen pistols Kiba had in her possession, including the two shotguns and her sniper rifle. Looking up he saw the sadness in her eyes 'I'm sorry Jason, it is what it is'

★　　★　　★

Saturday Afternoon.

It was a cloudy grey afternoon, overcast and windy, but amazing for relaxing. The weather right before it rained was genuinely pleasant although a bit chilly. Being a good way out though and the seeing the ominous grey clouds looming closer, she finally gave in and started rowing back towards the shore.

Domanick peered over the side, watching a silver-green fish streak by with fascination.

'Buddy, why don't you come sit over here by me?' Kiba suggested. The waves were getting larger and rougher, and she didn't relish the idea of having to fish her son out of the cold water, but Domanick didn't join her at his side. 'Domanick Graham,' she addressed with a firm parental authority. Domanick still made no move. Sending an annoyed glance back after another rolling wave, she realized Domanick was no longer behind her in the little boat.

Alarm instantly took over, adrenaline coursing hotly through her veins. She scanned the surface of the waters for any sign of her missing son, only catching passing glimpses that she wasn't sure of.

She prepared to dive in after her son when another swell capsized the boat.

Tumbling waters turned her around and around, disorienting her briefly, but she managed to poke her head above the choppy waters and draw in a ragged gasping breath. The cold water threatened to pull her under again, as it ebbed away all her strength but she didn't even notice. Right now she had one goal—find Domanick—and that was all that mattered. Catching another glimpse of what might be the treasure she sought, she took powerful strokes towards it.

At last, coughing, sputtering, and obviously not happy, but alive, she saw Domanick before another blue wave blocked her view again. Thank goodness for life jackets. Oblivious to how tired and cold she should have been, Kiba persevered. Finally she reached her son. Pulling him along towards the shoreline, she fought the wind and waves continuously, the adrenalin starting to give way to the normal human physical limitations and the shore slipping further off into the distance.

A fleeting glance upward revealed the true majesty and beauty of the storm's fury, too bad it was set on killing her. Fighting with all the strength she had left, they gradually began to make some movement, bringing the shore into a more attainable range.

Dropping heavily onto the muddy shoreline, Kiba panted, only able to draw in short ragged breaths. Raindrops began pelting down in thick sheets, further drenching the two on the shore. Wearily shoving up to her feet and gathering her son in her arms, Kiba staggered back in the direction of the cottage.

By the time she made it back she was practically crawling through the dirt and mud, too tired to go any farther.

What would Adam think of her now? She thought bitterly. She had said she didn't need any help from anyone, but that was before she found out how hard it really was. She had been so determined, persistent, strong; what was she now? Tired, muddy, and pathetic— that's all she looked like, so what more could there be? She held onto Domanick so tightly he was her only son, all she had left of Adam, and it was her responsibility, but more than that—she loved Domanick, and Domanick unconditionally loved her back, either oblivious or accepting of the dangers that crowded even everyday life; Domanick was a lot more than she deserved, she thought blackly.

She had lost nearly everyone she loved, almost having lost even her son who was only two; what made her think that this time would be any different? As much as she didn't want to admit it, hated even thinking about it, it would have been better if Adam had taken Domanick with him when he left. Then he too could have had a safe and normal life—something obviously not meant for a Kiba White. She had pulled away from the dangers—missions, espionage, even Shadow-Wolf—mostly for the sake of her son and to simply get a taste of how normal people live, but now even that seemed impossible. If Adam were to come back right now, he'd probably pick Domanick up and walk right back out; why did she try anymore? She thought in desperation. Why bother? No matter what she did, fate wasn't on her side and ending up with a truly happy life was a mere dream.

With the meagre amount of energy she could summon up, Kiba cleaned up the two of them and put Domanick to bed. Wearily shuffling to her own bedroom, she mechanically went through the motions, more on auto pilot than actually registering her own actions, until she went to set her bracelet onto the nightstand by the bed but dropped it onto the floor. Reaching down for it, her fingertips brushed something soft. She pulled it up to see what it was—Adam's slipper. She threw it across the room in anger and frustration.

'He's not coming back,' she told herself angrily, raking frustrated fingers through her damp green hair. 'If he was he'd have already done it.' Adam had just left; he hadn't taken anything with him except her heart. But if that was the case, why did everything suddenly feel so empty?

Adam obviously didn't have the same feelings, or at least not strong enough for them to overcome this obstacle; and she was going to have to learn to live with it. Being left, although usually because of death, was no new fact of life to her. Definitely, it was something she should've learned to deal with by now, she thought with a depressed sigh. Collapsing on the bed, she wondered how she was supposed to put it all aside and try to move past yet another damaged piece in the crazy jigsaw puzzle that made up her life.